"[Rae Meadows's] gemlike novel . . . rests—panting, gasping, breathing—in the span between Anya's tiny but powerful shoulders. With every cracking bone and snapped ligament, we long for Anya's success even as it imperils her. We long for her rescue even as we both know that success means buying only a little more time before the end."

—**Megan Abbott**, *The New York Times*

"Quoting aptly from the poems of Marina Tsvetaeva and liberally slinging Russian vulgarities along with gymnastics lingo, Meadows . . . captures the risks so recently headlined by Simone Biles and other champions in her fifth novel. . . . Spanning the final decades of the 1900s, [*Winterland*] is a genre-bender that fluently integrates sports with accents from political and psychological thrillers."

—*Library Journal*

"Chillingly good . . . The author's sensitive exploration of her story's historical context makes *Winterland* a sports story like none other."

—*Duluth News Tribune*

"The brutal landscape and the gracefully rendered, even more brutal lives of Anya, Vera, and others make *Winterland* a perfect winter read."

—*City Book Review*

"A story of an era shaped by glory and loss and about forging a life when you no longer are what you were." —**Historical Novel Society**

"*Winterland* is a rich and powerful novel in which Rae Meadows displays her talents and her subtilty as she captures the essence of sport, the power of ambition, and the menacing hand of totalitarianism whether wielded by the state, society, or individuals."

—*New York Journal of Books*

"Rae Meadows' captivating 1970s Soviet-era tale echoes the stark landscape of its Siberian setting. A ballerina goes missing; her husband pieces his life together, as their young daughter is ushered into the grueling sport of Olympic gymnastics. Meadows testifies to the invincible human spirit."

—*The Christian Science Monitor*

"Meadows paints a poignant portrait of life behind the Iron Curtain, palpably conveying her vividly rendered characters' deprivation, longing, and self-sacrifice. Fans of Megan Abbott's *You Will Know Me* should take note."
—*Publishers Weekly*

"Meadows' absorbing fifth novel follows a promising young Soviet gymnast as she enters a ruthless sports system that emphasizes winning at all costs.... Writing with a confidence based on excellent research, Meadows vividly depicts the Soviet training system—and its abuses.... An enlightening portrait of a now-vanished world."
—*Kirkus Reviews*

"Meadows skillfully articulates the risks and rewards of high-level competition, the divine feeling of being chosen to represent one's country and the fragility of the human body.... *Winterland* is a historic look back at a generation of Soviet talent, ambition, and sacrifice, inside and outside the gym."
—*Booklist* (starred review)

"With meticulous precision and smart, poetic prose, Meadows vaults us into the chilling and eerily relevant world of Soviet-era gymnastics. Get ready to fall in love with eight-year-old Anya, who offers us a heart-wrenching view of what it means to live, love, and compete in a sport where one wrong move or the whisper of dissent can ruin you. This book is full of heart."
—Georgia Hunter, *New York Times* bestselling author of *We Were the Lucky Ones*

"*Winterland* gripped me from the first page. I loved this story of strong women fighting to keep their humanity in the face of terrible forces: Siberian winters, demanding gymnastics coaches, lost mothers, and Gulag camps. Rae Meadows is a gifted writer, and I was thrilled to find myself in a landscape I knew nothing about, rooting for a young gymnast named Anya."
—Ann Napolitano, *New York Times* bestselling author of *Hello Beautiful*

"In the best of cases, books are more than just entertainment. Sometimes, they play a vital role in connecting us during divided times, across generations and cultures, reminding us that as human beings, we all have the common ground of love and want and pain. *Winterland* is one such book—an intimate look at the Soviet Union in the 1970s, a lost mother, and a daughter's journey to become a star Olympic gymnast, forced to choose between what's right for her and what's asked of her by a state that demands the impossible. Steeped in rich cultural detail and written with the confidence of someone who has spent much time in the trenches of gyms just like the ones Anya inhabits, *Winterland* will immerse you in rich period detail, the joy and anguish of first love, and the heartache of unimaginable loss and sacrifice. Both a searingly immersive tale and an important book for our times, *Winterland* is a must-read, for it will remind you that while we may live in a world divided, we are, as individuals, all similarly fragile, hopeful, and ultimately human at our core. Impeccably researched and beautifully written."

—**Kristin Harmel,** *New York Times* **bestselling author of**
The Book of Lost Names **and** *The Forest of Vanishing Stars*

"*Winterland* is a story as gripping as it is a powerful rendering of the true cost of perfection. In beautifully written, thrilling prose, Rae Meadows takes us deep into the world of the USSR's gymnastics program. As we see eight-year-old Anya rise to the top of this ultracompetitive and punishing sport, the mystery of the disappearance of her mother begins to unfold. Combining a page-turning plot with fully formed characters, Meadows has written a novel that reflects the current moment. I was left breathless."

—**Lara Prescott,** *New York Times* **bestselling author of**
The Secrets We Kept

"Rae Meadows brings the grueling world of Olympic dreams to vivid life in *Winterland*, a searing tale of a young girl finding her path in Soviet-era gymnastics. Anya's childhood is centered around the mysterious disappearance of her mother, an event that anchors the book in a spiral of questions. Heartbreaking and thought-provoking, imbued with the beautiful fragility and terror of athletic excellence, this is a story of unfolding friendship and adversity that will linger with readers for long afterwards."

—**Yangsze Choo,** *New York Times* **bestselling author of** *The Night Tiger*

"Rae Meadows always writes with absolute clarity and power, and it is a pleasure to soar through the air with her in *Winterland*, weightless, strong, and capable of anything."

—**Emma Straub,** *New York Times* **bestselling author of** *All Adults Here*

WINTERLAND

A NOVEL

RAE MEADOWS

A HOLT PAPERBACK

HENRY HOLT AND COMPANY

NEW YORK

Holt Paperbacks
Henry Holt and Company
Publishers since 1866
120 Broadway
New York, New York 10271
www.henryholt.com

Grateful acknowledgment is made for permission to reprint the following
selections by Marina Tsvetaeva: "A kiss on the forehead," "Where does such
tenderness come from?," and excerpts from "From Poems to Czechoslovakia"
and "From Poems for Blok" from *Dark Elderberry Branch: Poems of Marina Tsvetaeva.
A Reading by Ilya Kaminsky and Jean Valentine.* Copyright © 2012 by Ilya Kaminsky
and Jean Valentine. Reprinted with the permission of The Permissions
Company, LLC on behalf of Alice James Books, alicejamesbooks.org.

The Library of Congress has cataloged the hardcover edition as follows:

Names: Meadows, Rae, author.
Title: Winterland : a novel / Rae Meadows.
Description: First edition. | New York : Henry Holt and Company, 2022.
Identifiers: LCCN 2022035961 (print) | LCCN 2022035962 (ebook) |
    ISBN 9781250834522 (hardcover) | ISBN 9781250834539 (ebook)
Subjects: LCSH: Women gymnasts—Soviet Union—Fiction. |
Gymnastics—Fiction. | LCGFT: Thrillers (Fiction) | Psychological fiction. |
    Novels. | Sports fiction.
Classification: LCC PS3613.E15 W56 2022 (print) | LCC PS3613.E15
    (ebook) | DDC 892.8—dc23/eng/20220729
LC record available at https://lccn.loc.gov/2022035961
LC ebook record available at https://lccn.loc.gov/2022035962

ISBN 9781250834515 (trade paperback)

Our books may be purchased in bulk for promotional, educational, or business
use. Please contact your local bookseller or the Macmillan Corporate
and Premium Sales Department at (800) 221-7945, extension 5442, or
by e-mail at MacmillanSpecialMarkets@macmillan.com.

Originally published in hardcover in 2022 by Henry Holt and Company

First Holt Paperbacks Edition 2023

Designed by Meryl Sussman Levavi

Printed in the United States of America

1 3 5 7 9 10 8 6 4 2

For my mother, Jane Elizabeth Meadows (1931–2021)

WINTERLAND

Katerina smoothed back her hair, tucking in a dark strand that had come loose from her bun. The tips of her fingers were cold and leached of color. This had happened when she was pregnant with Anya, and now here it was, returned, as if her blood had retreated to the center of her body.

She had let her Ballet III girls out a few minutes early, and she was alone in the studio, the steady tic tic of dripping icicles in the sun outside the window. She rested her right hand lightly on the barre and rounded her left arm above her head into fourth, her body still, back straight. She pushed into the earth with her standing leg and, hips square, brushed the toes of her working leg against the floor, extending, lifting her leg high, up into a grand battement. She lowered her leg in a controlled sweep, cleanly through tendu into fifth.

What was she doing? She was stalling, she was late. She held her fingertips in her fists for a moment to try to warm them before she pulled a skirt and sweater over her leotard and tights. She cinched the belt of her old red Moscow coat, its fox-fur collar soft against her face.

In the dance institute office, Galina crunched on sushki, a messy pile of bread rings right on her desk.

"I have an appointment," Katerina said.

Galina flicked her eyes up and sniffed.

She has probably talked to them already, Katerina thought. Galina would volunteer information; she would not have to be prodded. Katerina had asked Vera how the camps could have happened, and here was her answer: lumpy, pale, petty, ordinary Galina.

"You have a lesson with Inna," Galina said, brushing crumbs from her lap, her brown skirt in strained folds over her hips. "In an hour."

"I will be back," Katerina said. But would she?

Gather yourself together, she told herself. She thought of her Anya, that dark and blazing little creature. "Your whole body breathes when you dance," she'd told her. "You expand and then come back to the center." Anya was only five, but she understood, nodding with seriousness.

Spin me, Mama.

It was spring, but still freezing. Sun shot through the heavy, polluted sky. Dirty snowdrifts three meters high edged the street. At least the snow disguised the rubbish and rubble underneath. Katerina walked with her chin tucked in, the piercing cries of gulls circling overhead. A man walked behind her, the flaps of his ushanka tied up above his ears. Large square glasses, vodka blooms across his cheeks. She pulled her coat tighter and tried to coax blood into her fingers, her hands shoved in her pockets as she walked. A mud-crusted Moskvitch sputtered past, a plume of exhaust in her face. She crossed the street. The man followed.

The District Office was an immense pale-green building repainted every summer. The longer daylight showed its cracked façade, the gray snow line, patches of mildew like continents on a strange map. Yuri attended Committee meetings here; she had never been inside. But she had been summoned.

What would they say? *We have heard things. You have complaints, comrade?*

She couldn't feel her fingers, but she could feel her fear in her tight inhales. She stood in front of the massive wooden door, her heart knocking against her ribs. The man leaned against a lamppost, took off his gloves, and lit a cigarette.

She could run. But what then? Even if she got away from the man, they would not let her go.

Katerina looked up from the valley to the hills on the edge of the city. There was so much beauty out on the steppe, she could lose herself in the boundless tundra. Thousands of unforgiving kilometers. A place that existed long before humans, wild and brutal and empty. They wouldn't find her there. To spin and spin in all that nothingness.

The man was waiting to see that she went in. She looked back at the door and then turned and kept walking.

PART I

NORILSK, 1973

CHAPTER 1

"Wake up, *Dochka.*"

Anya's father brushed the hair from her face. His breath was warm on her ear, and she smelled the faint bitter herbs from his morning tea. She rolled over under the weight of a thousand blankets, or so it felt, quilt upon quilt to keep out the relentless chill. It was night dark. The sun would not rise today. Her father pulled the chain of the small brass lamp next to her narrow bed.

"You don't want to be late."

Anya sat up with a start, remembering what day it was, immune, suddenly, to the cold.

"Breakfast is on the table," he said.

She cartwheeled across the small bedroom they shared, her heart leaping ahead of her, and flung open the door to the amber light of the kitchen. Her skin was as pale as milk, a thin shroud over the blue lattice of her veins. Her hair, as dark and sleek as mink, hung halfway down her back. Like her mother's. They will make you cut it, he had told her.

The table was set with tea and bread and cheese, and in the middle of her plate, one perfect orange.

"Papa!"

She held the orange to her face and breathed it in. The rarest of indulgences in Norilsk. She closed her eyes and let the extravagant smell transport her, for the briefest moment, to somewhere warm and bright.

"A special occasion," her father said. He crossed one arm over his chest and rubbed his fiery beard with his free hand. His eyes glinted green in the lamplight. "We'll celebrate tonight."

She didn't ask, What if I am not chosen? It was what they had worked for.

"Irina's made *vatrushki*," he said.

Irina lived on the first floor of their building. She came over sometimes and sat at the kitchen table and drank vodka with Anya's father, and they would sing Komsomol songs and hug each other.

Anya peeled the orange with ritualistic concentration, pulling off the white membrane string by string. She held the soft puckered orb in all ten fingertips and then laid the little half-moons in a ring on her plate like petals.

Norilsk was north of the Arctic Circle, three thousand kilometers from Moscow. A Siberian town reachable only by plane or ship ramming through cracks in the frozen Arctic Sea. The home of some of the largest deposits of nickel and copper on earth. Anya was born here and had never been anywhere else. The rain burned her skin, the fog made her throat itch, and the air made her cough. The snow blew gray and sharp like tiny nails. The Daldykan ran red from the sludge of copper smelting. During the polar winter, the sun didn't rise for two months. But Norilsk Nickel employees each received a Yunost' black-and-white TV, and the state store shelves were stocked with sweetened milk, while everyone else scrabbled for a block of margarine. The wages were almost twice what workers made on the mainland, the rest of the Soviet territory that wasn't their inaccessible outpost.

Anya lived for summer to arrive, that brief chapel of light, from late May to late July, when the sun never set, and a manic joy infused even the drunk old men who left their chess games and traipsed along the tundra hills. Herds of deer emerged from the taiga and came north, galloping right through town. The melted snow revealed a glittering landscape of scrap metal and unfinished train tracks warped from the cold. She and her father would shiver into Dolgoye Lake near where the town's heating pipes passed through. Afterwards they would sun themselves on the rocks like seals. They would fill baskets with bittersweet golden cloudberries under a vast, translucent sky, the heat like balm.

There were the bones, of course, that rose up and washed ashore each June, reminders of the camp closed fifteen years before. No one spoke of the labor camp, Norillag. The kerchiefed *babushki* collected the femurs and ulnas and skulls and buried them next to the gardens they tended like children, lovingly caring for every plant that dared to grow in that brief reprieve.

"Sometimes you need cruelty to appreciate beauty," her father told her after he and Irina had started in on the vodka.

Anya glanced out the dark window at a row of streetlights that would stay lit all day. It was a long time until spring. Her father packed cold sausages in his lunch pail to take to the copper plant. At least he didn't go in the mines, she thought, down into the depths of the earth in blackness so complete it could rob your mind. It frightened her to imagine him there. Her classmate Viktor told her he'd gotten to ride the elevator down the mineshaft once with his father. When the door had opened back at the top, a voice over the speaker said, "We bid you farewell. May your life be filled with much good news."

Anya placed the last section of orange on her tongue and held it there before crushing it with her teeth.

* * *

They had to have a plan before they went outside. No dawdling. The air felt like shards of glass in Anya's lungs. Her father wrapped her in wool scarves and her fur-flap hat until all that was exposed was her nose. She was barely able to see through slits where the edges of the scarves met. The school had declared *aktirovka* two days last week, but the wind had died down enough to reopen, despite the snow and temperatures that dipped to forty degrees below zero.

"Go to Vera's after school," Yuri said. "I will fetch you there."

Their neighbor was older than the *domovoi*, but she had a bowl of little chocolates wrapped in silver foil. She had looked after Anya since she was five, when her mother went missing.

They paused at the door. Their building was painted soft pink so it could be found in the blinding monochrome winter, grouped with three other buildings around an enclosed courtyard to save them, for a few moments, from the wind.

"When will he come?" Anya asked.

Her father pulled her scarf down so he could hear her.

"I don't know. The director just said today. Do your best, *Dochka*."

She always did. She was a serious child. Not prone to laughing or playing around like others her age. "You carry around your own storm cloud," her friend Sveta teased. You can't change yourself, Anya knew. You are who you are.

Her scarf made her neck itch.

"Did you hear about the naturalist?" she asked.

"Who, Ledorsky?"

The eccentric professor lived on the fourth floor and subsisted on kasha and fermented milk, which he claimed protected him against the toxic air.

"He took in a polar bear cub. An orphan. In his apartment."

"Sometimes I forget you're only eight," her father said.

"I'll ask Vera about it today."

He laughed. "Let me know what you find out."

When they saw the headlights of the bus, they pushed into the darkness and steeled themselves against the biting air. You couldn't wait at the bus stop or you might die from exposure. You couldn't smile or the saliva would freeze in your mouth, and the pain in your teeth would make your eyes water, and then they would freeze shut. Anya couldn't see the looming smokestacks in the dark, but even the cold couldn't take away the smell of sulfur. They hurried down Leninskiy Prospekt as the bus stopped in front of the stone Lenin, a foot of snow on top of his head.

They fell into seats on the warm bus.

"*Vsegda gotova*," she said. Always ready.

"*Vsegda gotova*," he said.

He had taught her the Young Pioneers motto when she was two.

* * *

The class sang "May There Always Be Sunshine" to start the day. Anya never sang the third stanza, "*May there always be Mama*," but came back strong for "*May there always be me*."

"It's today," Sveta whispered. Her pale hair was pulled tight in a bun. "He's coming today."

"I know," Anya said.

"Svetlana Nikolaevna Alexandrova!" the teacher snapped.

When the bell rang, the children stripped down to their underpants and laid their clothes on their chairs, sliding their slippers underneath. Boots were lined up outside the door; they never bothered with shoes. Viktor passed out the dark goggles. They filed into the small windowless room and made a circle around the quartz lamp for their daily UV light bath. Sveta bounced on her toes, up in *relevé*, down, up, down. Anya pointed one toe out in front of her, then the other.

"There's a man in our building who has a polar bear cub," Anya said.

Sveta's eyes flashed wide, and she grabbed Anya's wrist.

"What's its name?"

"Aika."

"Have you seen it?"

"Not yet."

"I tried on my mother's lipstick last night," Sveta said, dropping her voice. "Pink. But she caught me, and I got in trouble."

To Anya, lipstick was more exotic than a polar bear cub. Makeup was a way to stand out when you were supposed to look like everyone else. It was irresistible, of course.

"How did it look?"

"Gorgeous."

Anya had a memory of her mother, a flash of an image, skin powdered and lips red, her hair piled high on her head. What had she been doing? Where had she been going? She'd looked ghostly, unreachable, like a character in a fable, the pretty one being watched by a wolf. Or maybe it wasn't her mother at all. Maybe just a picture she had seen.

After the light session, the children put on their physical culture uniforms. But before they could line up for the gym, their instructor walked in followed by a barrel-chested man in an ill-fitting suit, his shirttail hanging down below his jacket in the back. The man tapped out a Laika and lit it, holding it in the corner of his mouth. He looked them over with an imposing, heavy brow, his eyes squinting through the smoke.

Sveta shot her eyes to Anya. But she already knew.

CHAPTER 2

Yuri had met Katerina on the Arbat in 1954. In those heady days in Moscow after Stalin was dead, people started smiling again, and the wide pedestrian street hummed like a beehive in the sun. At seventeen Yuri believed he was living through history, a part of something great. All of them Young Pioneers and now Komsomol, all of them believers. Their fathers had defeated the Germans in the Great Patriotic War. They would build a just and modern nation. But it wasn't the Motherland on Yuri's mind that May afternoon, the smell of balsam poplar buds in the air, when it was warm enough to hold his jacket over his shoulder, taking in the market stalls, the mushrooms and cabbages and goat milk, the sketch artists who would pencil your likeness for a few kopeks, the old blind accordion player. The only thing on his mind was sex. He blamed the springtime. And his virginity.

Yuri found himself walking behind a trio of teenage girls with tight buns and turned-out feet. The little one in the middle with the darkest hair. Her ears were velvety pink, and he wanted to roll them in his fingers. She turned around and narrowed her eyes at him.

"Buy a ticket," she said.

Yuri laughed, blushed. "You are a dancer."

"You're smart."

The other two girls giggled and pulled away as Katerina moved in step with him. She was as small as a child—her head didn't reach his shoulder. Her eyes were almost black, with a cavernous depth. She stirred something in him, and not just because he wanted to kiss those rose-petal lips.

"You walk like a duck," he said.

"Quack," she said.

Yuri felt like he had lived a century since then. He sat in the windowless cement room outside the Hades-like potroom of the smelter and drank cold tea from his thermos. He had been a pyrometallurgist at Norilsk Nickel for fifteen years. A red-and-yellow poster was pasted to the wall opposite: COPPER IS THE BACKBONE OF OUR ELECTRICAL AGE! He knew the gritty and fearless workers were the true builders of Communism. Work was work, but he liked the predictability of it; he liked doing his part.

Copper-rich ore was clawed out of the depths below Norilsk, smashed to powder in giant drums, which were then flooded with water, the copper sulfate floating to the top. This was where Yuri came in. He lowered canvas filters into the huge bins to skim the blue salts from the water. The roaster burned off the sulfur, and massive furnaces refined what remained into molten copper. Chunks of shiny black slag were hauled out and dumped in massive heaps along the edge of the city.

On his way out of the plant each day, Yuri liked to pass by the gleaming 225-kilogram ingots of copper. He still felt it, the call of duty to build a great Soviet Union, from each according to his ability, to each according to his work. If not that, then what? He had once held a position on the City Party Executive Committee but was dismissed without explanation, a typed note on yellow paper. Because of Katerina? He would never know; you didn't get to ask why. He still had his Party membership, but he had lost favor.

Anya looked so much like her mother it was as if he'd had nothing to do with her making. Her single-mindedness should not have come as a surprise. He would not hold her back even though he knew it meant he might lose her. He would not make that mistake again.

The whistle blew. It was time for plant workers to do their midmorning calisthenics.

* * *

Anya felt her heart scamper and then catch up with a thud as the man from the sports school looked them over. He took the cigarette from his mouth and blew smoke to the ceiling.

"Who wants to be a gymnast?" he gruffed. "Girls only."

Anya and five other girls raised their hands.

"Stand up."

He shook his head at Sasha, the tallest girl in the class, and she sat down. He pinched the fat on Maria's arm and frowned, but he didn't dismiss her. He eyed the rest of them.

"Follow me," he said.

They went to the school gymnasium. Instead of the balls and hoops and nets that usually littered the floor, the gym had been cleared out and outfitted with a thick rope to the ceiling, a freestanding metal bar, and some thin rubber mats. Anya and Sveta held hands, their bare feet white and bony against the floorboards.

"Gymnastics is not for little birds," the man said. "It's for little Marina Chechnevas."

Chechneva was born in the north, a war pilot, a Soviet hero.

To Anya, gymnastics was the glittering key that would unlock a world that most people could never know. What it felt like to fly. Gymnastics would turn her into herself.

"It's fun, too," Sveta whispered. "Maybe he doesn't know that."

Sveta was the tiniest and best among them. She'd been flipping off chairs and bending her back in a full circle since she was four. But last year Sveta's father, a mineworker, had gotten in trouble. He'd told a joke to a friend while sitting in the sauna at the *banya*: "A portrait of Stalin hangs on the wall behind a speaker who reads a report on Stalin, the choir sings a song about Stalin, a poet reads a poem about Stalin. What's the occasion? A night commemorating the anniversary of Pushkin's death." Someone informed on him. He was interrogated at the district militia's office for eighteen hours. Stalin had been dead for twenty years, Solzhenitsyn had been excerpted in *Novy Mir*, Stalingrad had been renamed Volgograd—and yet Stalin had won the War, and a neo-Stalinist headed the Party Committee in the north. Making jokes about Stalin, and really, a joke about the Soviet Union, was suspect. And hadn't Sveta's father been heard criticizing Brezhnev, himself a neo-Stalinist? The Thaw ushered in by Khrushchev had been long over. Sveta's father emerged with a black eye—"I fell, I fell," he said—and worse, he was stripped of his Party membership. A Russian expelled from the Party was a man in exile in his own country.

"He was lucky," Yuri had told Anya. He'd landed his palms flat on the table as punctuation, and then turned up the radio in the kitchen in case someone was listening. "There was a time he would've been sent away to Vorkuta to dig coal for ten years."

Sveta's father was a small, wiry man with twinkling eyes and a quick laugh. Anya couldn't imagine how he could be dangerous to anybody.

Sveta squeezed Anya's hand for luck. The stout man led the girls around the gym, through drills and exercises. He didn't want to see what they knew how to do. He wanted to see who was strong, flexible, tough.

"Climb the rope. Faster. No feet! Legs out!" he barked.

He held a stopwatch and marked things on the side of an envelope.

"Little chubby one," he said to Maria. "You are too slow."

He didn't say anything to Anya, but she did not let up.

* * *

Yuri had trained as a promising gymnast at Dynamo in Moscow until age eleven when he was sidelined by a torn rotator cuff, and Katerina had been a prominent dancer for the Bolshoi. When Anya was three years old, they had received a visit from a sports and culture administrator, a stocky woman in a navy-blue skirt and jacket who sat on the edge of the sofa, her knees pressed together.

"Will it be ballet or gymnastics for the girl?" she asked. She tapped her pen on a stack of papers she held in her lap.

Yuri was flattered. Katerina was wary; she knew what would be ahead for her daughter.

"You don't have to decide now," the woman said with a shrug. But it was clear a decision, if not made *by* them, would be made *for* them.

Later when Anya was asleep, Katerina spoke softly near his ear.

"She will never be full, Yurka. Her body will never not hurt. Always clay for men's fingers," she said.

"Don't you want to see her dance?"

"Not yet. Please. Let's give her time to be a child."

So they waited.

And now, despite Yuri having lost his prominent status with the Executive Committee, Anya had already been deemed an asset to the Soviet Union. Two years ago, Yuri had enrolled her at the ballet school. Surely Katerina would have wanted this for Anya? Their girl was different! She was destined! But Anya chafed under the cold eye of Marina Korolya, herself having once danced for the Bolshoi. "Again, Anya. Extend, Anya. Lighter, Anya. Why aren't you more like your mother, Anya?" Sveta, who had only ever wanted to be a gymnast, taught Anya how to cartwheel, how to stand on her hands. Anya found a joy she had never felt in ballet.

And then Anya and Yuri had watched the Olympic Games in Munich on the television. Everyone knew the Soviet gymnasts were the best in the world. Ludmilla Tourischeva had won everything for years—the USSR, European, and World Championships. She was pretty, like a film actress, her dark hair styled in a smooth sweep, her tall, curvy body graceful and dramatic. But it was the newcomer Olga Korbut who transfixed Anya. As she watched, something physical happened in her body; she felt her hands tingle, her hair stand up. Korbut was seventeen but looked ten, small and flat chested, with a lopsided smile and messy pigtails adorned with loopy yarn bows. Tourischeva was of the earth; Korbut defied it, whipping her body through the air, flitting with audacity.

The Soviets dominated, as always, winning the team gold. Korbut won gold on the floor and silver on the bars. But Tourischeva won the most coveted all-round gold.

"People don't like too much change at once," her father said. "Korbut will have her day."

In the end the medals didn't much matter to Anya. Anya recognized something in Korbut, and she wanted it. She knew that by not choosing ballet she was turning away from her mother. But Katerina was gone. Anya felt a new kind of want, a current turned on in her body.

"Papa," she said.

He looked at her for a long time and then turned away.

"I know that look," he said.

Yuri exhaled a big breath through puffed cheeks. The state system was unparalleled. It was an honor. It was brutal. But she would be taken care of, a job for which he felt ill equipped on his own. They had gotten by for three years, just the two of them, but life had felt perilous and unsettled. Sometimes when he looked at Anya, he was scared by all the things he felt, a bone-jarring love, but fear, too, that she depended only on him, and a reminder, always, of the wife he had lost.

"They pick later this year," he said.

"Sveta told me."

"If you make it—" He stopped.

She knew, even at her young age, that if she made it, if she kept going, she would have to leave him. She saw the sadness in him, but she saw something else too. Pride. A spark of excitement.

"I will help you," he said.

He trained her in their apartment. Frog jumps and push-ups, back bends and hollow holds. He pressed on her back as she sat in a straddle until her body pancaked against the floor. He pushed her to stay on her hands against the wall for thirty seconds, a minute, two. She sweated and ached and cried and got up again. He fashioned a bar from a thick dowel across the bedroom doorway for pull-ups and leg lifts.

Anya's focus never wavered, even when her legs noodled from exhaustion. It was more than a goal. It was a vision. A bright burning spot that eclipsed, for the time being, that ever-shifting feeling of unease she carried in her core.

"We'll make your body and mind strong, *Dochka*," Yuri said.

* * *

The bristly rope was like stinging nettles on the ripped skin of her palms. Her stomach muscles quivered from leg lifts from the bar. Her inner thighs were sore from center oversplits, one foot held above the floor on a folded mat. Sveta, still full of energy, executed flawless back walkovers while waiting for her turn, a 180-degree split leap when they moved stations. The man with the cigarette did not seem to take notice.

"I can do a front walkover," Sveta said. "Would you like to see?"

"You were not asked," he said. He folded his arms across his broad chest and looked away. "Get back in line."

Anya tried to focus only on the tasks at hand. She knew enough to know she could only look out for herself.

The five girls hung in a row from a bar.

"Pull yourselves up and stay there."

They struggled up and held their chins over the bar, their bodies swinging slightly. It was quiet. One by one the other girls slipped down and fell in heaps until it was only Anya and Sveta, arms taut and shaking.

I will win, Anya told herself. She closed her eyes and forgot about her friend, settled into the pain, and imagined she was hanging over a chasm of ice. Falling would mean death first by broken bones, then by cold. She heard nothing but the coo of the wind.

"Anya Yurievna Petrova."

She opened her eyes, and she was alone on the bar.

"Enough," he said.

Anya hopped down from the bar. One classmate was in tears, and Maria sat hugging her knees against the wall. A third stood with her head down, shoulders hunched. Sveta, seemingly even smaller than she'd been before, flashed Anya a rueful smile. Anya mouthed, *"Prosti."* But she wasn't sorry.

* * *

There was nothing left for Anya to do but wait. She felt old and calm, like a towering oak tree she had only ever seen in books. Her hands, raw and smarting, smelled like metal with the faintest perfume of orange.

"Do you think we made it, Anya?" Sveta asked.

They ate cold *pelmeni* and hot soup from the lunch cart amidst the bleach-and-rag smell of the cafeteria.

"We did what we could," Anya said. She wished that hoping for something counted for anything, but she'd learned long ago that it didn't.

"Poor Maria," Sveta said. They looked over at the girl who sat alone, not eating her lunch. "She's just a little soft, like a baby."

"Come over tomorrow. We'll meet the polar bear," Anya said.

Sveta leaned over and kissed her on both cheeks.

After school, when Anya got off the bus in the dark, she was met with the wall of cold, but above, curtains of colored light billowed in the sky. Pink, green, yellow, blue, violet. The northern lights. The extreme cold brought more colors. She was used to them but could never really be used to them. They stopped her, held her. Yuri had explained to her the phenomenon. As the sun boiled and bubbled, it discharged solar particles, which hurtled into space. As the particles passed through earth's magnetic shield, drawn to the North Pole, they mingled with oxygen and nitrogen and transformed into the dance of lights. But knowing this didn't erase what Anya felt, that there was more than what you could see. There was sound, too, a kind of music in the silence.

She never told her father, but she believed that in some magical way those mystical lights held something of her mother. That she revealed herself to Anya, a brightness. I am here.

But Anya could never fully rid herself of the feeling beneath it all, a shape-shifting lack. Her mother was gone, and Anya was left without her. Rage and tenderness swirled and then settled within her into something as heavy as ore.

She had stopped for too long; her nose was numb and the air stung her lungs. She ran through the dark along the snowdrift that bordered the road, the lights moving above her, a shifting wave now mostly green and blue, moving higher and higher. She wanted to jump and grab the aurora, to pull it to her, to keep it from fading away. But soon there was nothing. And she was alone with all that dark, dark sky.

CHAPTER 3

Vera Vasilievna Kuznetsova was born in 1897, in Novgorod, a city on the Volkhov River, founded in the ninth century, when the streets were paved with wooden logs. She had lived in Anya's building on Leningradskaya Ulitsa for longer than anyone, even the naturalist Ledorsky, who Anya guessed was a hundred. Her mother had spent many late afternoons visiting with Vera, Anya in tow. "I came looking for a sitter," Katerina had said of their introduction, "and I stayed for three hours."

Anya took the stairs two at a time, then launched into a round-off down the hall, clumsy in her heavy layers.

"Anya Yurievna," Vera said, opening the door. "I thought you were an elephant." She hugged Anya and kissed the top of her head. "Come in, *dorogaya*."

Anya unwrapped her scarves and coat and shed her boots by the door. Vera's apartment was large for one person. It smelled of incense and must. Her sofa was shabby, but she draped it with a shawl of purple velvet. A red scarf over the lampshade cast an otherworldly glow. Vera held out a glass bowl of foiled chocolates.

"As many as you want," she said.

Anya took one. Vera shook the bowl, and she took another.

"Tell me about your day."

Vera's skin was brown and creased in soft folds. She wore her silver hair in a braid wrapped round and round in a circle at the nape of her neck. She sat and took up again with her abacus, stacking black wooden beads, restacking. Click, click, click. Anya wondered if she counted all day long in these rooms.

"Irina says you count the rubles you have stashed around your apartment," Anya said.

Vera smiled. "That would be nice, wouldn't it? But I just count. Something to occupy my hands."

Anya knew it was not true, knew there was more to it. But you didn't press people, especially old people, her father told her, unless you were prepared to hear terrible things. Vera had spent ten years in Norillag, she knew that.

Anya unwrapped the candies and put them both in her mouth at the same time.

"Hungry?"

"I tried out for the sports school today. In gymnastics."

"To bring glory to the empire," Vera said.

"I want to flip like Korbut."

"Ah. Be careful with your wants."

"You have to want something," Anya said. "Unless you're a toad on a log."

Vera laughed. "Let me get the tea. Come, come."

Anya glanced at the antique clock on the wall; Vera's things were all from long ago.

"This looks very old," Anya said. "And it still works?"

"It was my grandmother's," Vera said. "I had it in my own house in Novgorod. My son used to watch the pendulum swing back and forth when he was a baby."

It was jarring to remember that Vera had been younger once, that she had had a whole life before Norilsk, a life even before the Revolution.

"Before my mother died, she sent me a crate of things she had saved for me during the years I was away. It took two years to arrive. Most of it was ruined. But the clock still worked."

Anya followed her to the kitchen. She had never met her own grandparents. Her father had told her that leaving their families was part of the sacrifice of coming north for their country. They could not afford to fly to Moscow, let alone arrange steamship passage. Mail service to and from Norilsk was spotty. It was just the three of them, and then the two of them. At least there was Irina now. And Vera, like the *babushka* she had never had.

Vera set an ornate silver tray on the scuffed table. "You can keep your soft white bread. There's nothing better than salted black bread and sweet tea on a winter day."

Anya closed her eyes and saw a letter. Black type. Folded into thirds. An official Party stamp. When would it come? She imagined it flying to her in the beak of a tern.

"Show me something," Vera said. "A turn, a jump. Show me a trick."

Anya stood in a straddle and pressed up into a handstand on the kitchen floor, then pirouetted in a circle on her hands before stepping down.

"I am amazed! That makes me happy," Vera said.

"My friend Sveta is better," Anya said.

Vera clucked. "There will always be someone who will be better. Comparisons bring misery. That was marvelous."

Vera poured tea into glass cups held in *podstakanniki*. In Norilsk, tea glass holders were nickel-plated, of course. But Vera's were slightly tarnished silver, decorated with ornate filigree and a delicate rose pattern looped along the bottom edge. Anya traced it with her fingertip, the metal already turning hot. She sipped the tea, and it burned the roof of her mouth. She quickly took a bite of bread.

"Now I want to show *you* something," Vera said, disappearing into her bedroom.

She came back holding a small board.

"The Mother of God of the Sign is one of the most revered icons."

Anya stared at the muted colors, the gold, the scene of a mother and child. It was strange, the baby looked eerily like an adult.

"The pregnancy of the Virgin. See her hands raised for praying, and that's the holy infant in the circle," Vera said.

Soviets were atheists. Religion was folklore, superstition. From before the people knew better, Anya had been taught. But there were the old women who refused to let go.

"In Novgorod there is a church. The Cathedral of Saint Sofia. Built in the eleventh century. It's made of stone. With five gilded domes. As a girl I would go and stare at this icon and feel the holy wisdom. Or so I thought."

"Do you believe in God, Vera Vasilievna?" Anya asked quietly. She had never met a Christian. She felt nervous about the secret but pleased too. She couldn't wait to tell Sveta.

Vera continued without answering. "The icon is said to be miraculous. It saved the city when it was besieged by the army of four Russian kingdoms in 1170."

"Why do you have it?"

Vera laughed. "It's just a copy. The Germans destroyed almost every stone building. But the cathedral made it through. So maybe the icon saved that too."

Churches in the Soviet Union were used for schools or warehouses or administrative offices—everything except places of worship. Anya pictured herself running through the empty cathedral, her feet echoing in that dark and cold space.

"What do they do with it now?" she asked.

"It's a museum of history. But I remember it as a church, a holy place."

Vera crossed herself, two fingers and thumb, forehead to belly, right shoulder to left, as Anya had seen the old Orthodox women do in their black kerchiefs, standing at the edge of the lake under the midnight sun.

"Aren't you worried they'll find out?" Anya couldn't say who she was worried would hear, but there was always someone listening, someone waiting to tell. That was life. The walls had ears, the clouds, even.

"No one cares so much about an old woman," Vera said. "You can't spend your life worrying about what might happen. Besides, there's nothing left for them to take away. Not really. Not even the sun." She smiled, her teeth big and gray, some toppled over like old gravestones.

Anya looked at the ever-dark window. Pick me, she willed, pick me. Her palms burned from the rope climbs. She did not want to know more sadness from Vera just now. She saw herself standing on the top of the uneven bars like Olga Korbut, for just that moment, above everything, the pause before flipping backwards into nothing.

"People want to forget," Vera said. "I will tell you sometime. But not today, *dorogaya*. Don't worry. Don't make that puss face. You look like your mother when you make that face. But I'm sure you know that."

* * *

When Anya had gone, Vera returned the icon to her bedroom and propped it up on the wooden chest her grandfather had made from the birch trees that had surrounded their house. As children, she and her sisters had pulled off pieces of the white bark for scrolls, using a paring knife to carve messages, and left them under each other's pillows. She went back into the living room and sat heavily into the sofa, the abacus beside her, and moved a bead down its wire with her old fingers, knotty like twigs.

They'd taken the *troika*, just the three girls in silk dresses and sable-lined coats, warm under a horsehair blanket, over the snow, the horses snuff-huffing in the winter air, the brass bells jangling on the reins, because their mother and father weren't yet ready and they didn't want to miss a minute. Beyond, the golden domes of the cathedral flashed in the light of a big moon. A fox hopped off the path into the woods. Their *nyanya* had packed them bread and pâté of venison in wax-paper packages she'd tied with blue string. Olga, Vera's oldest sister, tossed the whole thing into the snow.

A Christmas party. 1910? 1911? Long before it all. Inside the grand house it was warm and close, furs peeled off and tossed to maids. Napoleon III furniture and eighteenth-century paintings in heavily gilded frames. Crystal bowls of caviar, black and briny. The dark rich meats of pheasant and quail, jellied sturgeon. The sharp-cheekboned Mongol servers dressed in black with white gloves. The tinkling of forks against china, girls' laughter, glass flutes knocking together. A whole table of iced vodka. Needles of ice in the champagne. The sweet scent of *papirosa* smoked with long cardboard mouthpieces.

She stood with her sisters on the edge of a large room where the furniture had been moved out. A quartet played.

"Dance with him, Vera," Olga said. "Don't be a turnip."

Oh, how she had loved Alexei Egorovich Zubov from afar, a new officer in the Imperial Army, on leave for the holiday. His hair shorn close to his head, his mustache waxed and slightly curled up at its ends. He wore a dark green tunic with gold epaulettes, and in his leather cross-belt an épée instead of a saber for civilian company.

"I can't ask *him*," Vera said.

"Smile," Olga said. "Put your shoulders back." Olga was the oldest and had always been bossy.

Tatiana, the middle sister, sulked. The boy she liked had yet to show.

Alexei smiled at Vera and bowed in greeting. But he danced with the daughter of a Saint Petersburg banker, her bosom like two over-risen *pirozhki*, her corset so tight she moved like her middle was carved of wood.

Vera sighed heavily at the memory, trying to get her jumpy heart back to a regular rhythm. Condensation filled the corners of the dirty window from which she could see nothing but the darkness and the auras around the streetlights. She was getting cold and pulled a blanket around her legs. Everyone she'd ever loved, ever known, was dead. A cough caught her, her lungs wet, worse this winter than they had ever been. When she could breathe again, she inched herself up from the sofa. She should eat something. She would like some hot buckwheat and bacon—peasant food, her mother would have said—but that was too much effort. Cabbage soup would be fine.

* * *

Irina arrived at the apartment door with pastry in one hand, vodka in the other.

"The party may commence," she said.

Yuri had known Irina since their student days in Moscow. They had all come up together, the group of them, the poet Vitka, the engineer Paul, the philosopher Ivan, the woman with the crooked nose, also from the philosophy department—what was her name—Zoya who painted those messy flowers, and he and Katerina, of course. Irina, working on a novel, was Vitka's *lyubovnitsa*—she didn't want to be called his girlfriend, liberated as she was.

Her hair was still blond though darker than it had been then, a mess of curls that seemed always in the process of coming loose from whichever way she had tied it back. She was almost as tall as Yuri and big-boned, and often wore large sweaters to obscure her ample breasts. She taught Russian literature at the Norilsk State Industrial Institute. She had very few students—the focus of the college was mining and transport systems.

Yuri and Irina were the only two left in Norilsk, and there was a kind of love there, a loyalty certainly. They had slept together three times in the past couple years, though one of those times he'd woken up in her bed, naked, smelling his own vodka sweat, and couldn't remember what had happened. She was good to Anya. She knew his history. He sometimes wondered if that could be enough.

He cleared away the bowls of char and salted sauerkraut from dinner. Irina fell into a chair at the kitchen table and pushed a curly tendril from her forehead. Her eyes were deep blue, bloodshot, tired.

"Anya, tell us," she said.

"I hurt all over," Anya said.

"You were ready though," Yuri said.

Anya eyed the *vatrushka* on the table and saw that Irina had added raisins especially for her. Irina was kind that way. Anya had always thought of her as an aunt, if not by blood then by familiarity. But these days she realized Irina wanted to be married to Yuri, and Anya didn't know how she felt about that. Irina had come upstairs in her socks, big gray woolen ones that looked like wolf paws. Irina poised a knife over the pastry with a questioning look at Anya.

"Shouldn't we wait?" Anya asked. But she didn't want to wait to taste the smooth, creamy, sweet cheese and yeasty dough.

"We don't celebrate victory. We celebrate your bravery," Yuri said.

Her father and Irina clinked their glasses.

Irina cut large pieces of the tart and passed them around.

"You have all you want, Anya," Irina said.

Anya ate greedily, the raisins sticking in her teeth. "Did you see the lights?"

"I used to think I could hear them," Irina said. "Do you know what I mean? It's almost too intense for just your eyes. I'm sorry I missed them. I came home early today. No one showed up for my class."

"They probably heard you were teaching Bulgakov," Yuri said.

"I don't even have to hide it. His books are officially unexpurgated."

Anya tuned them out. She was so tired she feared she would fall asleep mid-blink. She wished Sveta were here. She took the knife and cut a triangle piece of the dessert to wrap up for her for tomorrow.

"Remember this one?" Irina asked.

She started singing and then Yuri joined in: "*We are the new blood of the city's veins. The body of the fields, the thread woven of ideas. Lenin lived, Lenin lives, Lenin will live!*"

Yuri put his arm around Irina and kissed her with a smack on the cheek. They looped arms and drank more.

"Do you believe in God?" Anya asked.

Irina snorted. "God is for weak souls. A bourgeois invention."

"Vera does. She keeps an icon in her bedroom. And crosses herself like the old ladies do."

"Ah, well," Irina said. "What she's been through."

"Do you know what God is, *Dochka?*" Yuri's eyes smiled, but he tried to keep his mouth serious.

God was flying, her mother, an orange, the sun. But she couldn't explain it. It was a feeling she had. Something she knew. It was not the religion of Vera, but it was not nothing. She shook her head.

"More important," he said, clearing his throat, "did you ask Vera about the polar bear?"

"Ah!" Anya smacked her forehead.

"We must go now!" He clapped his hands three times.

"It's past ten, Papa. He'll be sleeping." She should be asleep too. She wished her father knew how tired she was. She sometimes had mean thoughts—her mother would have known.

"Who?" Irina asked.

"Ledorsky."

"I'm pretty sure Ledorsky doesn't sleep," she said.

And then there was a quiet swish, an envelope slid underneath the door. They turned, stuck for a moment, unable to move, before Anya jumped up, knocking her chair over. She ripped the envelope open with her teeth.

Official notification, Executive Committee of the Communist Party of the USSR. Norilsk Administration. December 1973. Anya Yurievna

Petrova has been accepted to the Metallurgist School of Sport for artistic gymnastics.

Anya skimmed the page without getting it, stopped, and read again. Accepted? Her eyes blurred. Her old life was over. There was no turning back.

"*Dochka*," Yuri said. He placed his hand gently on her arm. "Tell me."

She looked up. She smiled.

"We did it," she said. "I did it."

CHAPTER 4

The gym smelled like cigarettes and mildew and feet. The walls were drab and unfinished, the ceiling cracked and snaked with yellow trails from leaks, the leather of the vault torn, the floor carpet worn, the wooden beam so much higher and thinner than Anya had imagined it. On the uneven bars, an older girl stood on the bottom bar and clapped a cloud of white magnesium chalk before catching the top bar again. She then jumped up and threw her legs back, landing with her hips against the lower bar, her legs wrapping around, and whipped back up to her feet. Anya was mesmerized. How could a body do that? She never wanted to leave.

The man who'd come to the school was Anatoly Popov, head coach. Here in the gym, he wore shorts, a maroon V-neck sweater, his dark chest hair curling over the top, and plastic slides on his feet, a cigarette in the corner of his mouth.

"When you are here you are mine," he said.

"Yes, *gospodin*," Anya said.

He coughed and laughed at the same time.

"I'm not the czar," he said.

"Okay. Sir."

He shook his head. "*O, Bozhe.*"

Anya stood with her hands behind her back. She didn't know what to do. Where was Sveta? There were twenty girls of varying ages in the gym. She was clearly the youngest and the only one new.

"Katya!" the coach barked to the skinny girl on the bars. "You arch again, fifty push-ups."

"You need a leotard," he said to Anya, with a derisive sweep of his eyes over her shorts and t-shirt. "Ask Marta. There's a box of old ones somewhere."

"Now?" she asked.

"You are such a timid duckling. Go!"

Anya walked along the edge of the floor mats in the general direction Anatoly had pointed and found a door. She pushed it into a dimly lit, cluttered room. On the wall was a poster of a smiling little boy in a red scarf on the lap of a muscled man: IF YOU WANT TO BE LIKE ME, JUST TRAIN! CCCP—A MIGHTY SPORTS POWER! An old woman slouched behind the desk. She looked over her glasses at Anya.

"A little thing," she said. She rummaged around at her feet. "Try this one."

She tossed a rumpled red zip-front leotard at her.

"Here?"

"Get on with it," she said. She went back to her ledger.

Anya didn't know if she was supposed to keep her underpants on—she'd never worn a leotard before—but decided it was best not to ask and went without. She backed out into the gym and dropped her clothes in a corner.

On the thinnest of mats a girl was working on standing back flips. One after another. She landed one on her knees and Anatoly scoffed from across the room. Anya felt a kernel of fear and was angry at herself for feeling it.

The previous night, Irina had eventually passed out on the couch, and Yuri had put Anya to bed.

"What about school, Papa?" she had asked. The letter had said to arrive at the sports school at nine a.m.

"You're finished with your old school. You'll have a teacher there at the gym. Part of the day set aside for studying. That's how it's done."

She felt tears rise, a hot lump in her throat. It was happening so fast.

There would be no good-byes to her classmates. It is what you wanted, she told herself. And Sveta surely would be there with her.

"I didn't know it would be this soon either." Her father crouched down next to her bed and pulled the blankets up to her chin. She turned her head from his vodka breath. "It's an honor to your country. Remember that always. When it gets hard. When you want to quit."

She wasn't worried about quitting.

"Your mother would have been better at times like this. She knew what it was like."

Anya thought of her mother's small hands and the smell of the lavender oil she daubed on her wrists. She thought of the delicate bracelet she always wore, small amber globes set in silver linked together. The way it clacked on the table when she picked up a glass.

Anya rubbed each smooth honey stone, warm under her finger.

"They say amber is tears of the sun," her mother said.

"They look like pieces of candy," Anya said, "and I want to eat them!"

Her mother laughed brightly and kissed her on the temple.

"Yes, Anushka. What flavor do you think?"

Anya pushed the memory away and rolled back toward her father and touched his hand.

"Tell me a story about Mama."

Her favorite thing to have him tell her was what it was like to watch her dance. Sometimes he indulged her when it was late like this, when he was softened by drinking. How he didn't recognize Katerina onstage at first. How she twirled so fast her skirt spun straight out, the muscles of her legs taut and defined under her tights, effortless on her toes, her feet with those exquisite arches. How he gasped when she leaped into the air, sure she would fly off the stage.

"You don't need stories, you need sleep," he said.

It was the wrong thing to say. She looked at him and willed him to read her eyes, to make her feel better somehow, but he didn't know how, and that frightened her. She had seen into the future then, how one day soon she would have to depend on only herself.

"Good night, Papa," she said. She patted his head.

* * *

Anya tugged at the leotard, too tight around her legs, and walked back over to Anatoly who stood with a young man coaching a group of older girls on vault.

"Faster. Just run past. Go!" the man yelled. His blond hair was razored close to his head, his arms smooth and muscled. Sergei was the junior coach. He had the loucheness of a soldier on leave, the curled lip, the slouch.

"You," Anatoly said finally. "To beam."

Anya had never been on a balance beam, didn't know how to get up there. She placed her hands on it and pushed herself up onto her palms, swinging her leg over. It was smooth wood, only ten centimeters across.

"Up," he said. He motioned with his hand for her to stand.

She slowly rose to her feet and wobbled before finding her balance.

"It's high," she said.

Anatoly blew smoke through his nose and tossed the butt into a bucket.

"Walk."

She walked, one careful foot in front of the other.

"Backwards."

She walked backwards, feeling for the beam behind her with her foot.

"Now close your eyes."

Anya froze. She closed her eyes then opened them.

"I'll fall."

"Then fall. Close your eyes."

She closed her eyes and took a step and another and another, and then her foot slid off and she landed first with her hip hard against the beam before she hit the floor with her feet and fell to her knees. Her hip burned, her knees ached. She bit her cheek not to cry.

"Again," he said.

Anya got back up.

"It's not a tightrope. It's not a wire over a pit of crocodiles. You're walking on a line. It's a field. Grass and flowers. Earth. Relax. Do it again."

Anya closed her eyes and tried to block out where she hurt. She imagined a meadow under her feet, or the green scrub of a tundra hill in summer. All the light of the sun. She put her arms out. And walked.

* * *

Sveta was waiting for her when she got home, sitting with her back to the door. Anya wanted to call out, "Where were you?" smarting, angry. But as she got closer, Sveta looked like a little mouse with her red nose and her hair sticking up from the folds of her old brown coat, and Anya knew she had not been chosen despite her talent. Because of her father. They were used to arbitrary rules, but Sveta being shut out was cruel and unfair. She willed the tears back.

"You brought your black cloud," Sveta said. She sprang to her feet.

Anya felt the tears rise up again. She felt rubbery and spent from the day at the gym, from all of it.

"It's okay. It's not your fault," Sveta said. "I wasn't good enough."

"You are good enough," Anya said. She unlocked the door.

Sveta followed her in and did a front walkover across the living room, her hood flipping onto her head.

They pulled off their gear and threw it in a heap on the sofa, then went straight to the kitchen. Anya had never been hungrier in her life. She started the water for tea and rummaged in the refrigerator. She pulled out the piece of *vatrushka* she'd saved and tossed it on the table in front of Sveta. Anya unwrapped a log of salami and bit right off the end.

"They only let us eat at midday. Puny portions."

"You don't have to make it sound bad for me," Sveta said. She took a big bite of the pastry, the white cheese filling somehow dotting her nose. "You're so lucky you don't have to go to school. Viktor barfed in physical culture today."

How far away it already seemed to Anya. At the gym, after they'd cleared their lunch plates, Marta had emerged from the office and gathered the girls, a motley group of varying ages, at two large wobbly tables and passed out Russian history textbooks, the pages wavy from moisture.

"Read for twenty minutes," she said.

Anya flipped through the pages. Was she to start on page one? There were a lot of difficult words. Byzantine and Slavic and Rus and Mongol.

The words floated right off the page. She nodded off once, her forehead landing in the open book. She looked at the other girls. None of them was very friendly. She was the youngest, so she was the enemy, she supposed. In her they saw their replacement. Once a girl reached a certain age, her hopes of a spot on the national team were over.

A half hour later, Marta returned, chewing on a roll, and passed around pencils and paper.

"Write something about what you read," she said. And then she was gone again.

Anya panicked. She'd read nothing. She looked around the table. One of the younger girls, Masha, her hair in a stubby ponytail, had looked over and smiled a little, showing a broken front tooth.

"She doesn't read them," she'd said. "She just throws them in the bin."

Sveta put her feet up on the kitchen table and crossed her ankles. "Come on. Tell me about it."

"The balance beam is really slippery."

"You went on it already?"

Anya pulled down her pants to show the nasty bruise.

"Ah, *Bozhe moy!* Ouch."

"That was the coach who came to school. He smells rotten. Like old onions."

"Did you go on the bars?"

"Just for pull-ups and pullovers."

"Are they good? The other girls?"

"A couple older girls were doing back tucks."

"How old?"

"They had *bufera*." Anya put her hands on her chest and shrugged.

The questions went on and on. Sveta tore off a hangnail with her teeth, the blood pooling. She sucked her finger.

"Was it heaven, Anya?"

Anya thought her friend's face would break in two.

"It's all I ever wanted," Sveta said. Her eyes darted about. "I will try again. I will keep working at it, and Papa said maybe next year I can try again."

"Yes. You must," Anya said. "I will teach you everything I learn. Oh, I have something." She ran back to the living room and fished out her dirty leotard from her bag. The woman at the gym had given her another worn leotard as she was leaving. The seam in the armpit was torn, but Anya would mend it tonight.

"For you," she said.

Sveta held it up and smiled, then hugged her friend close.

"It's like Tourischeva's," she said. "I will never take it off."

Sveta could try again, and they could be together at the gym, how it was supposed to be.

"Sveta," Anya said, "we almost forgot!"

"What?"

"The polar bear! Let's go!"

They ran out into the hall without their shoes, the tile floor cold and wet—the building's *babushka* had just mopped—and skipped the stairs two at a time to the fourth floor. At Ledorsky's door they stopped and looked at each other. Anya hoped Sveta would knock, which she did.

The naturalist opened the door and eyed the girls through his glasses. He was bald on top with white wispy hair in a ring around his head. He wore a black suit made for a much larger man, the shoulders of the jacket hanging off his own, its lapels wrinkled and stained with droplets of grease.

"Comrades," he said. He bowed slightly.

"*Gospodin,*" they said in unison.

"May I help you?"

"Is it true?" Sveta asked.

"That you have a polar bear cub?" Anya asked.

"Can we see him?" Sveta asked.

"Her," he said. "Yes, you may see Aika. Come in. She has just awoken from a nap."

The smell was immediate, like wet dog and mud, as they stepped into the overstuffed apartment. Newspapers and books stood in towers around the living room, plants lined the windowsills. In a large cage in the center of the room, a small white creature, her belly fur yellowed, licked her paws.

"Her mother is dead most likely. I came across her on a walk. She was thin and lethargic, mewling. She should have been in a den. She's only two or three months old."

"Will you let her go?" Sveta asked.

"She can't be let go. Once in captivity."

Aika wobbled to the edge of the cage and sniffed the air. Anya kneeled down close; the bear's breath smelled muggy of sour milk.

"You'll keep her then?" she asked.

"Goodness, no," Ledorsky said. "She'll grow to be 250 kilograms. I'm trying to arrange her transfer to a zoo. The one in Moscow doesn't want her. But perhaps the one in Perm."

"Can we play with her?" Sveta asked.

"I'll take her out, but she may bite."

Aika stepped uncertainly onto the ragged Persian rug. She barked a squeal. The girls got down on all fours next to her.

"Her skin looks black," Anya said.

"Keeps her warm. It helps soak up the rays of the sun," he said. "How is your friend Vera these days?"

"Vera from the third floor?"

"Yes. I knew her long ago."

Anya shrugged. "She's fine, I guess. Still counting on her abacus."

Ledorsky nodded. "That's good she is fine."

"I'm sure she would like a visit," Anya said. "She's always there."

"Maybe one day," he said.

Anya reached out to pet the bear's head between her button ears. The fur was thick and oily. Aika swiped her paw, leaving deep red scratches on Anya's arm.

"Yes, well. You never know how wild animals will react I'm afraid," Ledorsky said.

The old man lifted the bear cub up and set her back in the cage. He slowly straightened up.

Anya watched her skin as the scratches rose up in welts.

"Her claws have gotten me a few times too. She didn't mean to hurt you," Ledorsky said. "Animals aren't like people in that way."

Sveta hung her fingers on the wires of the cage.

"Good-bye, Aika," she said. "Have a pleasant journey to the zoo."

"I wish we could keep her," Anya said. "She's just a baby."

"I don't think the District Committee would be too happy about it," the naturalist said. "I wouldn't be able to procure enough meat for her anyway. As it is, she has to eat a lot of kasha."

"Can we visit her again?" Anya asked.

"She could do with some seal meat. Or if you bring herring that would be fine too."

* * *

Yuri peeled off his wet, black-crusted coveralls. His skimming shift was over, his hands stiff, his back sore. Today he'd received a check for fifty rubles. They called it a scholarship for Anya, and it would arrive monthly. It felt vaguely shameful to him, and yet, why should it? It was the *sistema*. He would buy her a chocolate bar, his Anya. She reminded him more and more of Katerina, the distinct bones of her face and her eyes like obsidian. It was troubling how their faces were beginning to blur into one in his mind. He had only one old wedding photo of Katerina, and his memories, which he chased and turned over and mined for new details, anything he might have missed before. Memories were fragile things, emotional guesses. He clung to the tail of hope that a memory, examined enough, would become real again.

Katerina had become extraordinary by her vanishing, he knew that. What if she had come back that evening and combed out the tangles in Anya's hair and they had sat down at the kitchen table for sardines and radishes? Would today they be growing tired of each other? Would the marital grievances have become entrenched? He'd seen it happen to others. The truth was she had begun to change without his really taking notice, and then, all of sudden, it seemed to him, she talked about God, she talked about the great sadness of Soviet life. She talked about regret.

A few weeks before she disappeared, he'd come home to find her slamming utensils around as she fixed dinner.

"I could have been a soloist," she said quietly. "I could have traveled. Seen Paris. Now I'll never get to go."

"I didn't make you come here."

"No," she said.

He was tired and irritated by this conversation, one they'd had before. "What brought this on?" he asked.

She whirled around. "They sent people away for nothing. Vera. They sent her away for nothing. This thing," she said waving her hands, her amber bracelet sliding up and down her wrist. "This thing we gave up everything for."

He sighed and poured himself a drink. He could hear Anya in the other room in singsong play with her doll.

"What did you give up, Katerina Vladimirovna?" It was a cruel thing to ask, but he wanted her to say it. The stage. The spotlight. The glory. He knew dance was more than that to her, but he wanted to take the moral high ground: I'm sorry you gave it all up for me and the betterment of your country.

She nodded and nodded, and turned to the potatoes on the stove.

"Mama, come play with me," Anya called.

"I'm sorry," he said. He came up behind her and held her small shoulders in his hands. She had softened to his touch but had not leaned back into him like he had hoped.

In the dank locker room, Yuri worked the stiffness from his hands and gathered his coat. He tried to replace the unease he felt with an image of Katerina at nineteen on a snow-covered Moscow sidewalk, showing off for him then, a spectacular firebird leap, quick and light into the air.

He shut his locker and waved to others leaving for the night. He would stop at the *traktir* for vodka before the bus ride home, the reward for a day of good labor. He knew he drank a lot, more than Katerina would have accepted, but he blamed her partly. Irina didn't mind; she was right there with him.

Irina had come to the north with all of them to build a great nation. Oh, how they had believed in it! Those late nights when they had gathered at Vitka's apartment on Lomonosovskiy Prospekt, right across from the Philosophy Department, enshrouded in cigarette smoke, warmed by vodka and idealism. They would go to the far north and civilize it, help tap the natural resources for their country. They did not need to be exiled. They would lead the way to Siberia, young and eager.

He knew Irina and her friend Zoya, with their sturdy shoulders and wide hips, had snickered about Katerina joining their group. "What is she going to do, *jeté* across the taiga?" Irina had drunkenly asked one night. Yuri had known, even back then, that Irina was jealous of Katerina, of her beauty, yes, but also because she was with him. Irina was with Vitka, but she didn't love him. He called himself a poet but hadn't written anything in months. Irina told Yuri years later that she'd had an abortion their third year at university and resented Vitka for it, and she knew they were doomed even as they set off for adventure together.

They were all twenty-one years old. They joined a student brigade to work on the Abakan-Taishet Railway, a Komsomol shock construction project. They left Moscow for Abakan, the capital city of Khakassia, 4,250 kilometers away. Everyone was young, singing songs and falling in love and feeling full of themselves and their value, even as they rode freight cars with wooden bunks, a bucket behind a sheet for a toilet. This was history! This was life!

Yuri slid kopeks across the wood-planked table and put up two fingers. The barman filled two cloudy glasses—he never washed them, just refilled the ones emptied by others—and Yuri downed both. The warmth in his belly, he told himself, would help brace him for going outside. He wondered if Irina was still in her office, surrounded by books and tea-stained papers and ringed coffee cups. She'd told him that in the spring she could see the glint of the Yenisei from the window behind her desk, the river that began in the mountains just south of Abakan, where they had begun, and flowed 725 kilometers north to the Arctic Sea.

In those early years they'd hauled railroad ties, felled timber, worked at a brick factory. They were dirty and cold all the time. Ivan lost two fingertips to frost bite. Zoya got scurvy. When her teeth started to loosen, she went home to Moscow and Ivan followed.

It was no surprise when Irina and Vitka fell apart. No one cared about his poems, and he drank away every kopek. The novel Irina had started—hardly more than a romantic trifle, Yuri had thought sadly—went dead.

But he and Katerina loved hard, believed still, worked with the passion of acolytes. She may have looked like a sparrow—he could encircle her waist with his hands—but somehow she was tougher than all of them. He and Katerina cried when they were given their Party membership cards. They married without a bourgeois ceremony. With their residency permits they were assigned their apartment. She was rewarded with a job at the ballet school. He was given his position at the copper plant.

Yuri wiped his mouth and began the big bundle-up to face his cold trip home.

And now there was Irina. She looked older than thirty-five but so did he, their skin thick and rough from perpetual winter. In Norilsk you aged double time. He knew she'd been in love with him for years. In her twenties she'd married Joseph, the ex–camp guard with his sinister widow's peak, who hit her when they fought. It lasted two years. Poor Irina. Yuri tried to tamp down the pity he sometimes felt for her. He liked her. And here they were, the two left. Could they have passion together? It seemed a destination he wanted to reach, but he didn't have a map. Katerina haunted every room, every street corner. But maybe there could be something. Irina was smart, and he wanted her warmth and company. He might even need her.

I love you, she had whispered to him in the predawn tangle of limbs on the sofa. He hadn't answered. What a coward he was. He'd pretended he hadn't heard, rolled over and coughed, and had run his hand down her head like he was petting a cat.

Yuri bought a chocolate bar at the *magazin* and watched for the bus headlights in the evening darkness. In one day, Anya had gone from being a schoolgirl to being a gymnast. What if she got hurt? What if she was not good enough? Of course she would be good enough. And maybe this is what he feared more than anything. She was only a child, but there was no stopping her, and she would become theirs—the sports school's, the coaches', the state's. What he had wanted and what Katerina had feared. A product of this grand political experiment. Greatness for the uplifting of all. Show the world what the Soviet Union could accomplish.

* * *

Yuri came home, bringing the cold with him. His red beard was frosted. His socks left damp footprints on the kitchen floor. He swept Anya up into his arms before setting her down.

"My little gymnast," he said. "Ah, what happened here?" He pointed to her arm.

"Polar bear scar."

He looked sidelong at her. He knew even Ledorsky wasn't batty enough to keep a polar bear in his apartment. But Yuri would let her have her imagination.

"I see. Well, best give polar bears a wide berth." He turned to Sveta. "Your highness, Svetlana Nikolaevna Alexandrova. At your service."

Yuri bowed deeply from the waist and Sveta giggled. He had known Sveta would not be chosen, but he didn't have the heart to tell Anya ahead of time. It would have been an acknowledgment of the unjustness of a system he had given his life to upholding. He was sorry for Sveta—it wasn't right—but there would always be sacrifices for the greater good. Yuri retrieved a bottle from the cupboard. He pulled the chocolate bar from his pocket and held it out to Anya.

"Papa!" She grabbed it and smelled it through the wrapper and held it out to Sveta to smell. "Don't tell Anatoly."

Yuri's face contracted some. The familiarity startled him. "The coach," he said. You see? he imagined Katerina digging at him.

He poured himself a tall glass of vodka. He felt something spin in his chest. Anya slipping just a little from him.

"They don't feed them there," Sveta said.

"I'll feed you," Yuri said.

"They don't teach anything either," Anya said.

Yuri raised his eyebrow at her.

"The school part."

"I wouldn't complain about that if I were you," Sveta said.

"Maybe we can have Vera tutor you," Yuri said.

Katerina had always regretted her lack of education once ballet had begun in earnest. "No one cares if you can write a sentence," she said. So she read everything she could, took all Yuri's books from school. He gave her Voznesensky and Akhmadulina and even Pasternak. Despite his allegiance to the Party, he gave her Marina Tsvetaeva, circulating via a worn and stained *samizdat* copy.

They had been together for a year, sleeping most nights in his dormitory room, sharing his narrow single bed, her head on his chest, her hair tickling his chin. Katerina was in the *corps de ballet* at the Bolshoi, favored by the choreographer Zakharov, that exacting little man who had just chosen her to be a soloist. She was rising fast, and with Zakharov behind her, her stardom seemed destined. And yet there was something about Katerina that clouded her ambition; her feelings could overtake her.

"Yurka." She called him by his diminutive only late at night. "Did you read them?"

"Read what, my love?"

"The Tsvetaeva poems."

"A lot of love and God, no?"

"Sure. But the beauty. I didn't know words could do that."

Fall was coming to Moscow. Rain tapped the window, and outside, the bare limbs of a chestnut tree squeaked as they rubbed together.

"It's like dancing."

"What is?"

"What she does with words. You can't pull them apart or see what's underneath. It enters with a feeling, and you try to grasp it but it eludes you. Like a web that you can see only with dew."

Yuri was bemused, tired. He knew ballet was essential to her, but he saw a day when she would move on from it, choose a life with him. Poetry had never been his thing.

"Read it to me." She turned on the lamp and pulled the *samizdat* from under the mattress. "This one."

He shouldn't have been surprised by her fervor—he had seen her onstage—and yet there was something that struck him, a sudden note in a minor key, something that made him uneasy, something off-kilter, which he would turn over and examine later.

"This one: 'Where does such tenderness come from?'" he asked.

She nodded, her eyes shining like black marbles.

He read:

Where does such tenderness come from?
These aren't the first curls
I've wound around my finger—
I've kissed lips darker than yours.

The sky is washed, dark
(where does such tenderness come from?).

Other eyes have eyed—
and stolen from my eyes.

He stopped mid-poem. It struck him as odd that the poet would be writing about love during the tumult of 1916, but he didn't say so to Katerina because when he looked up from the page, she was quietly weeping, not bothering to wipe the tears.

"Why?" he asked.

She flopped back on the pillow and covered her face with her hands.

"I don't know," she said. "I can't explain it. She just knows something. Don't you feel it? Like she's knocking on the door to your soul?"

Yuri read the rest to himself:

But I've never heard words like this
in the night
(where does such tenderness come from?)
with my head on your chest, rest.

Where does this tenderness come from?
And what will I do with it? Young
stranger, poet, in this city of strangers:
you and your eyelashes—longer than anyone's.

He knew he was not the lover in the poem, and never would be. He also feared he didn't have the same depth of feeling, the emotional intensity that Katerina had. He didn't even have it in him to go into the poem with her tonight. He had to rise in three hours to get to class, and he really just wanted to sleep. Had he known then that he would disappoint her?

"Come here," he said. He gathered her to him, her small frame he could carry like a child, and curved his body around hers. "I love you."

He had fallen asleep and didn't know whether she had responded or not. Maybe she had stayed awake staring at the window until the crack of new sun lit the world.

CHAPTER 5

As the weeks went by, Anya thought only of gymnastics. When she woke in the morning, she felt the ache in her muscles and ligaments, and she imagined working the pain out in that damp gray gym that was her world. When she closed her eyes, she saw herself executing long round-off back handsprings with legs together and pointed toes, kips on the bars with straight arms into high hollow-body casts, handstands on beam, her back leg a ninety-degree lever.

Irina was around more and more, so Anya would put herself to bed without saying good night to her father, not wanting to interrupt. She scrambled under the blankets to escape the cold and imagined herself flying into double twists and Arabians, shooting straight into a blue, cloud-streaked sky. When she was at the gym she didn't think of her father, of Irina, of Sveta, of the winter that would never end, or of the darkness, which sometimes felt alive to her, like it was watching, taunting even. She hurt all the time, her body stretched and pounded and worked more than she thought possible. But here she was, day after day, leaner, stronger, more flexible than the day before. She felt her mother with her when the fear came, when Anatoly made her do something new. He didn't believe in spotting. If you fell, you fell. It was all on you.

Once when she'd been scared of going to sleep in the dark, Katerina had told her to pretend that fear was a thing like a black nugget of coal. "Even if you can't get rid of it entirely, you can push it away. Sometimes

I would joke and try to hand off my fear to another dancer and she would scream and run away," she said. "We're all scared, Anushka. It's okay to be scared. But the trick is to know you are stronger than your fear." Anya tried to train herself to hold the fear in her fist and squeeze.

Tuesdays started with flexibility, standing splits against the ladder—What are you doing? Hold your chest up!—and now middle splits with each foot up on a chair. Next to her was Masha with the chipped-tooth smile. She was ten and had been at the sports school for two years. She was a good tumbler but had rough form, and she cheated on conditioning exercises whenever the coaches weren't looking. She scooted one of the chairs in so her knee rested on it.

"When I quit gymnastics, I'm going to stuff myself with ice cream," Masha said.

Quit? To Anya there was only going higher, getting better. There was no end point. Anatoly said it took ten years of training, eight hours a day to make a good gymnast. She told herself ten years was unacceptable.

"Why do you do it then?" Anya asked.

Masha rolled her eyes.

"My father drives a truck and my mother is a cashier and I have four brothers and sisters. We're poor. If you make the national team, they give your family three hundred rubles a month."

The coach Sergei stood behind the springboard and made the girls run right at him, having to clear his head to get their hands to reach the vault. Karolina, a quiet girl of seventeen, balked and crashed into him.

"Stupid," he said. He shoved her away.

"They're screwing," Masha said quietly to Anya.

Anya didn't know what that meant.

"It's how you make babies," Masha said.

Anya didn't know what that meant either. A naked man and woman that somehow went together.

Masha shook her head at Anya's naiveté.

Anatoly came over to them and stubbed out his cigarette on the bottom of his slide.

"You have the shape of a bulldozer," he said to Masha. "You like all that weight? What are you eating at night? Go look in the mirror."

Masha made a googly face at Anya as she dragged her feet to the office. She came back and stood belly out, knees bowing back.

"Well?" the coach asked.

Masha shrugged.

"You are an impudent little cabbage," he said. "One hundred sit-ups."

"Besides," she said to Anya, resuming the conversation after Anatoly walked away. She sat on the mat next to her, in no hurry to start. "Without gymnastics I'm a nobody."

Anya knew the truth in that. Everyone was equal, but everyone knew that was a lie.

Masha told her the last time Anatoly had sent someone to Round Lake to train with the national team was 1966. And the girl had done nothing, injuring herself before the European Championships and then going weak in the head from concussions. Seven years without success. However ingrained *tufta* was in other areas of Soviet life—"They pretend to pay us, and we pretend to work"—sports were exempt. There were consequences for failure.

"He's in trouble higher up," Masha said. Anatoly needed a win.

Gymnasts stayed at the sports school until they were eighteen, and when it was clear they had no future glory, they had to move on to state jobs. The lucky ones got to be coaches, though they had no choice where they were sent. A girl last year, a candidate for Master of Sport, failed to catch the national director's eye and was sent to a village at the base of the Urals by herself to lead gymnastics classes at the school. But Anya wasn't worried about what was so far off and incomprehensible. She planned on winning.

"Hit your shapes," Anatoly said. "Find space in your ribs. Arms next to your ears. Look between your hands. Head in. Point your toes."

She wanted to learn to flip, but he had her doing handstands.

"Every muscle should be tight in a handstand: arms, belly, bottom, legs, feet. A handstand should make you tired because you're working so hard to be still."

Anya's arms quivered, and she thought her head might explode from being upside down for so long.

"You girls think it's about learning tricks. It's not about tricks," he said. He swatted her leg. "Come down."

The ballet instructor, Madame Anastasia, came in and sat on a metal folding chair on the edge of the carpet. She looked down her long nose and frowned at the young girls lined up before her. Her hair was dyed black and pulled tightly into a ponytail, a stripe of gray around her face where her roots had grown in.

"Whose mother was the ballerina?"

Anya shrank into her too-big leotard, another castoff, heat rising from chest to neck to cheeks.

"Hmm?" She held a black pointing stick and tapped it on the edge of the chair.

Anya raised her hand meekly in front of her.

Madame looked her over.

"Leap. Go across the floor." She waved her pointer.

Anya somehow knew she could not succeed however well she performed. But she put her chin up. She blocked out her teammates and imagined she was her mother on a stage, rising up and up, leaping from corner to corner.

"Your hands are like this." Madame flopped her wrists back and forth. "Show through your hands, out through your fingertips."

Madame motioned to Eva, a gymnast who'd aged out but had yet to receive her job orders, to begin the accompaniment on the beat-up piano.

"Everyone, line up. Why are Soviet gymnasts the best? Because no one dances like the Russians. Do not embarrass your country."

The other girls knew a sequence of steps, a *grand jeté*, a full turn, a *tour jeté*, which they began with the piano. Again again again. Anya tried to get it, stumbled, and righted herself. On the fourth time she stayed with the group.

"Where are your expressive lines? Masha, you want to look like a little piggy? Straighten your legs!"

Madame whacked girls' hands, elbows, torsos, anything that gave her displeasure.

"You cannot disappear out there, even for a second," she called. "Karolina, you went like this and then like this." She exaggerated an ugly arm movement. "Follow the music. On your toes."

Finally, Madame called for the music to stop. She scowled and sighed.

"I expected better," she said to Anya.

Anya stood rigid and thought, Okay, then, I will do better.

"A light," her mother had told her once. "You have it here." She had pointed at the center of Anya's five-year-old chest. "It's there and it will always be there. You are more beautiful than a rose, than the stars, than the sun."

Anya laughed as her mother spun her around in the summer sun, her hair warm on top of her head. Her mother's eyes like the black oil that sometimes spilled from the pipeline.

"Again, Mama. Spin me again."

She did, her small hands lifting Anya up, her feet flying out behind her, before her mother set her down.

"I mean it, Anushka. They will try to tell you there's no such special thing. But they are wrong. It's there. It will always be there in you."

Her mother's hands were barely bigger than her own. Slender, pale fingers. Anya would see her sometimes moving her hands through the air with a grace that had made her want to cry without understanding why. Her mother became someone else when she moved her hands like that.

"You know this?" she asked, pointing to her bracelet. "I wear it always to remind me of who I am. All the way deep in the center. It reminds me that I am me. Do you understand?" Anya nodded, though she didn't really understand. "And no one can take that away. They will try to tell you that you are like everyone else. They are wrong. Here, try it on." She unclasped it and wrapped it around Anya's tiny wrist. The stones golden brown in the sun. It slipped right off, too big, of course. "I will hold on to it for you," Katerina said, "until you are ready to wear it. I will keep it for you and then it will be yours. To remind you of you, of what doesn't belong to anyone else. Okay? So for now it will be *ours*." She refastened the bracelet around her own wrist. "Besides, amber is good luck!"

"Did it bring you luck, Mama?"

"It brought me you, my love. It connects us forever!" Her mother lifted her up and spun her again, so fast the ground was a blur beneath her, and Anya felt like if she let go, she might fly off into the air.

After Katerina disappeared, Anya looked for the bracelet around the apartment, hoped it might appear under her pillow or be delivered in a package. She convinced herself that it would be a sign meant only for her, that maybe if she found the bracelet, her mother was alive and that she would come back. It was *theirs*. But Anya didn't find it. She couldn't ask Yuri about it either; the bracelet was a secret she shared with her mother. As the months went by, her father stopped telling her Katerina would come back. Still, some small part of Anya thought, Maybe she will.

"To bars," Anatoly barked to Anya. "Kips."

Anya took a deep breath and grabbed the bar and glided her feet out. She visualized herself, the timing, the groove of it, feet quick to the bar, body up. She didn't make it and hit her chin before falling.

"Again."

She chalked up and tried again. She felt a callus on her hand rip, a stinging red divot.

"Arms like steel rods. They should never bend," he said.

She tried again. She didn't make it up.

"Switch your hands to shift your weight."

Again.

"You're strong enough. It's timing. Get your feet to the bar faster."

Again.

He lit a cigarette and looked out over the gym.

Again.

When it was lunchtime and the other girls filed out, she looked sideways at Anatoly but did not ask.

"You eat when you get it," he said.

An hour later, her hands ripped, her feet bruised, her arms quivering, she felt she was getting worse. Her stomach gurgled.

"Do you want to know something?" he asked. "I didn't pick you to be a good foot soldier." He waved his hand around. "I have those. Do you know why I picked you?"

Anya swiped at her eyes, angry, exhausted. She shook her head.

"I picked you because I knew you wanted to be a general."

She couldn't be sure it was a compliment, but she felt something solid and heavy in her core. She felt stronger.

"There is a competition," he said. He smoked with one hand and scratched his stomach with the other. "In Surgut."

She ground the chalk into her torn palms and started again.

* * *

After forever, the light returned. Each day the sun now rose above the horizon, a bronze sphere giving out a thin, watery light, each day hanging in the sky a little longer than the day before. By the time Anya left the gym for Vera's, it was dark again, the air biting into her face as she ran for the bus, the snow like ash blowing over her feet. But spring was coming, and she had gotten her kip, and soon there would be her very first meet in a town far from Norilsk.

Vera pulled gherkins from fenneled brine and set them on a plate with poppy seed biscuits. Her knobby fingers were surprisingly nimble. Yuri had said once that Vera must have been a beauty in her day, though it was hard for Anya to see something different from the old lady who busied herself before her. They had fallen into a routine, and Anya had found herself looking forward to these late afternoons with Vera and her stories.

"I was thinking this morning about the pigeons," Vera said. She sat across the table and wrapped her shawl around her shoulders. She poured the tea.

"I've never seen a pigeon," Anya said.

"Ah, yes. No. Not in Norilsk. Back in Novgorod."

"Is that far away?"

"About two hundred kilometers from Saint Petersburg."

Anya furrowed her brow.

"Leningrad." Vera smiled. She pulled her abacus to her lap and ran her hand lightly over the beads.

Anya nodded. Leningrad she had heard of. The other side of the world.

"When I was a girl, about your age," Vera said, "my sisters and I would go with our father to Sofiyskaya Square on Sunday morning to the animal market. Dogs, cats, rabbits, chickens, canaries. Even live fish in buckets. The men would yell at each other bargaining, raising their voices over the barks and chirps and crows. We loved it. It was like a carnival. 'Please, Papa, can we get a dog? Can we get a cat?' We knew he would say no, but it was all part of the fun."

"Did he ever buy you a pet?"

"No. But there was one reward we did get. You could buy freedom for the pigeons. They cooed, and we girls would look sadly at them in their little wooden cages. My father struck a deal with the vendor who grumbled about the price but finally relented. Then with quick flicks of his hand, the man would fling open the little doors and the birds would fly out, right up into the sky, captives no longer."

Vera placed her hand on her chest.

"Such lightness," she said. "Such a rush of good feeling. True happiness as they flew up."

She slid beads on her *schyoty*. Anya waited.

"It was a trick," Vera said, smiling quickly. "One day we followed the pigeons through the square and over to a little park where they settled on the grass and tucked their wings. They were tame, you see. They waited there until a boy came to collect them. He took them right back to the bird seller."

"Maybe they felt safer there," Anya said.

"I think you are right, *dorogaya*. Freedom, when you are not used to it, can be a scary thing, no?"

Anya sipped her tea and ate a biscuit and tried not to think about the birds going back into their cages. The folding of wings.

"Why did you stay here?" Anya asked.

"Here in Norilsk?" Vera pulled her shawl tight.

"My father said you didn't have to stay."

"My husband and my son are buried here. I wanted to be close to them."

Anya felt a wave of love for the old woman. She had been left too.

"But you, Anya. You will leave someday. Your mother said you were born so fast it was like you already had somewhere to be."

Anya reached to set her tea down and winced. She had landed wrong on her ankle today, and her inner thighs were like cords that had been pulled too much and were now frayed and ill shaped.

"I get to go on an airplane," she said. "Up into the sky."

"I've never been on an airplane. How exciting. Where are you going?"

"Surgut."

"Surgut. South through the taiga."

"We have a competition. Third junior category. Anatoly says Larisa Latynina sends a scout to watch."

"It's a gift you have, you know. Like your mother had a gift. They will claim it as theirs. But it's yours too."

Anya didn't understand but she nodded. It was something her mother would have said. She knew when Vera talked this way, she was not to tell her father.

Vera held out the bowl of chocolates, and the girl took two. She didn't know the date, but given how the light had returned and lingered orange in the afternoon, she figured they were close to spring, the glorious season when the glaziers used to come to remove the double frames from the windows of her family's house, the gutters pattered with their incessant drips, sleighs were traded for carriages, and the Volkhov began to break up, white blocks of ice crashing against each other in the thawing river. With the return of the larks, Vera would help the cook make *zhavoronki*, putting the raisin eyes on the bird-shaped sweet buns.

"With spring coming, Easter is not far off," Vera said. "Are we painting eggs together?"

Anya clapped her hands and bounced on the sofa. Just a child, still.

"When I was young, we used vegetable powders mixed with boiling water and vinegar to make red, green, blue, yellow. Then we used a scrap of bacon fat to grease the eggs shiny."

"We'll tap eggs. See whose cracks first."

"I'll win, of course." Vera smiled. "I'll make *kulich*. Lots of icing."

Vera was seventeen, the last of their Easters. The floor smelled of beeswax. Their *nyanya* had taken the *kulich* wrapped in paper to the church to be blessed. Vera and her sisters were supposed to go to town and ring the bells of Saint Sofia; on Easter day, anyone was allowed. But, instead, they waited impatiently in the salon. The dressmaker was late, and her mother feared they would not get their new dresses in time. Vera's was of emerald silk, blouson sleeves and a sashed waist, and she couldn't wait to wear it. Alexei would surely come by later and take notice of her. Neighbors knocked with joyful "Christ is risen!" as greeting. The cook would bring out the suckling pig with its crackled skin and half-mast eyes, a blue egg in its mouth. Vera did not know about anything, not the peasant uprisings, the massive *stachki*—strikes across the country—or the massacre on Bloody Sunday when unarmed demonstrators in Saint Petersburg were fired upon by soldiers of the Imperial Guard. All she thought of was looking fetching for an officer. What a silly, silly girl she was.

There had been one harrowing glimpse, one moment that she'd never spoken of. She'd gone to town to fetch some ribbon from the shop near her father's mill. She wandered. It was a late spring day after a drenching rain, the sun restored and making everything sparkle. In her understanding of the world, there were rich people and workers and peasants, and that was the way things were. Being poor didn't mean you weren't happy. Vera came across the *kamorki* where the mill workers lived. She was curious; it was always fun to see what other people's lives were like. It was the middle of the day, and maybe no one was home. Just a peek.

The door wasn't latched, a heavy wooden slab like a barn door, and she could already smell smoke and something moldering like mushrooms as she got close. As she pried open the door, she felt swallowed by the stench—sweat and dirty bodies and mold and excrement and wood smoke—the same beastly smell she would experience years later when she arrived at the camp barracks and opened the door beneath a plywood rainbow that read: With just work I will pay my debt to the Motherland—and in the dark hovel she could see eyes shining like rodents' and heard a chorus of coughing and shouting and crying. Vera couldn't move, as much as she wanted to flee. As her eyes adjusted, she was met by the stare of a woman stirring her iron pot as she nursed a rag-swaddled baby. Washing hung from wall to wall, dripping on the mud floor. It was a world devoid of light and air and mirth, a trapdoor to misery. Vera had thought, How can they live this way?

And then, 1916. The chaos. The image of the *kamorki* would return to her. Her father sat on the velvet settee in the parlor, dressed in his suit and coat and hat and spectacles and leather gloves. "These are the hardest good-byes," he said, and to her, "Be good, my sweet Vera." White snow and birch trees splattered with blood. That's what she imagined. He was taken into the woods, and they never saw him again.

"Vera Vasilievna?" Anya patted her hand. "Are you awake?"

Vera blinked the room back into focus.

"Ah, Katerina," she said.

"Anya."

"Yes, Anya. She used to visit with me, your mother. She'd bring you when you were a baby. You would play with my *schyoty*. Slide the beads with your chubby little paws."

"What did you talk about?" Anya asked.

"I told her stories mostly." And you told her about God, Vera said to herself. You told her about the camps and your dead child and dead husband. And she told you things too. And then she disappeared.

Vera picked up the abacus and held it out to Anya. "I suppose we should get to our math lesson. Slide all the beads to the right."

* * *

Anya sat naked on the edge of the bathtub, the porcelain cold against her thighs, as it filled with water tinged yellowish green. She pulled the rubber band from her ponytail and felt her hair brush her lower back. Bruises dotted her legs. She unwrapped dirty tape from her fourth toe, purple and blue and puffed up too big. Broken, probably, but there was nothing to do about it. Her tendons snapped as she rolled her ankles. Anatoly told them that the first duty of athletes was to make their bodies listen to them. Hers had not listened well enough today. Round-off back handspring back tucks while holding a chunk of foam under her chin. Again and again, she lost the foam. "Should I bring you a bed? You came to work, so work," he had said. "Look what you are doing. Fix it." She felt the temperature of the water and twisted her back, happy to find it hurt a little less than it had in the morning. Her muscles made a grid across her belly.

Yuri knocked on the door.

"The woman from the sports school called," Yuri said.

"Marta?"

"She didn't say, but I suppose yes."

"What did she want?" Anya felt cold. Had she done something?

"The coach wants you to go in early tomorrow. She didn't say why. We'll have to leave by seven."

Anya tore off a callus from the base of her ring finger. She turned off the bath water.

"I would like to watch you, *Dochka*. See all your skills. Maybe I could come in with you."

"Anatoly says no one in the gym."

"Ah. Okay."

Anya could hear that she had wounded him, but what could she do? She saw her father for an hour or two a day; she saw Anatoly for eight. Anatoly decided her days, her weeks, her whole life.

"I'll show you some things. On Sunday maybe. The snow is melting on the hill," she offered.

"I'd like that," he said.

She slid into the too-hot water and pressed her lips together to take the pain until she eased into the heat and it took over the aching of her muscles, her skin blooming red. She slipped in further, the water covering her ears and framing her face. Her hair floated out around her shoulders. She closed her eyes and imagined herself a jellyfish, that fantastical boneless creature Sveta had shown her in a book about oceans. Pink and diaphanous and graceful, carried by its undulations and by the movement of the water. Her body disappeared and she was just herself, moving toward the sun she could see above the surface of a warm sea.

* * *

Anya still wore her fur hat but no longer needed a scarf around her face. The morning darkness was not absolute; there was softness to it, the sun waiting to peek through. They waited at the bus stop now, the fog of their breath visible in the streetlight, until the bus took them in and carried them across town.

"Do you want me to come in with you?" Yuri asked, hopeful.

"No, Papa."

He rubbed his beard and peered out the window at the sports school as the bus approached. His eyes were red rimmed and watery, his breath stale.

"I don't see any lights on," he said.

She put her mittened hand on his shoulder and kissed his cheek.

"He said for me to come."

Yuri watched her hop down from the bus and bound across the street. He was drifting, from Anya, from himself. He knew it yet couldn't seem to catch himself. Here he was, no longer in charge of his child. The state would take care of Anya. The state would make her into a great athlete. He knew that. But he felt a ribbon of rage at Katerina. Your fault, he said in his head, which he knew wasn't true. Where did you go? What did you do? We are still here, two instead of three. He would get to work early, time enough to stop for a drink at the *traktir* to keep his thoughts warmer, muddier, less accusatory.

When he sat up and straightened his coat, he could smell the ripeness coming from under his shirt and sweater. Tonight he would shower, make dinner, talk to Anya about what she was learning at the gym, what she was learning from Vera, get her to laugh, braid her hair, let her eat a whole handful of lemon candies.

It had been three years since Katerina had left the ballet school in the middle of an April day, to take a walk, or go to the market, or get something she'd left at home—depending on who you asked—and had never returned. The secretary Galina, smug in her insistence that Katerina had gone to some kind of appointment and said she would return. Had she gone to Moscow? Had her old mentor Zakharov, who had implored her to stay at the Bolshoi, helped her? Had she defected? She wouldn't have left Anya, she couldn't have. Was there someone else? Was she dead? No theory made sense, no evidence pointed to much. How did no one notice a small, beautiful woman in a red coat? A flurry of visits from *militsiya* officers, even from a KGB operative who questioned her Party loyalty. Anya would cry herself to sleep moaning "Mama" over and over again.

* * *

The front door of the school was locked. Anya walked around to the side door, which she found open. The janitor, his Kazakh eyes shining in the dim overhead bulb, swirled a mop across the dingy tile floor and nodded in greeting. Down the hall, she pulled open the door to the gym. It was dark, but the office light was on.

"Hello?" Nothing. "Hello? It's Anya."

Anatoly opened the office door, smoking.

"Come," he said.

"Should I get changed?"

He shook his head.

"Take off your coat. Have a seat."

His mood seemed okay, so she relaxed some. The office was smoky, the other chair stacked with binders. She pushed them over and sat on half of the chair.

"Coffee?" he asked.

She shook her head.

"No, thank you."

"I was just thinking about this film, *The Communist*. Urbansky is in it. Have you seen it?"

"No."

"Ah well. The story is, eh," he shrugged. "But Urbansky is a good hero. He died a few years ago. Only thirty-three."

"How did he die?"

"In a car accident. While filming a scene for a movie." He stubbed out his cigarette. "Immortalized though."

Anya was confused. Had he forgotten that he had summoned her here?

"Am I in trouble?" she asked.

He looked over his glasses at her and then took them off. He pursed his lips and shook his head.

"You are a strange child," he said.

Anatoly pulled out a big pair of old scissors from the top drawer and laid them on the desk. He came around next to her and hitched up his sweatpants.

"Turn." She inched to the side of the chair, teetering on the edge of it. She could feel him behind her. His gut grazed her back, and he put his hands on her shoulders.

"A coach and gymnast. The smallest team. If you don't believe in your coach, it's very hard to believe in gymnastics."

Anatoly took her hair in one hand and the scissors in the other. Her head pulled back with each snip of the scissors.

"It's a shame, really. Pretty hair." He held up the long dark ponytail that was no longer hers and dropped it in the trash can.

Anya reached her hand up to her hair, now blunt cut above her shoulders. She bit the insides of both cheeks, but quiet tears came anyway. She no longer had hair like her mother's. She felt exposed, something taken from her, her neck naked to the world.

"Come now. Do you want to be vain, or do you want to win?" he asked. He fell heavily into his chair and yawned. "Judges don't like long hair."

She knew that, knew she couldn't keep her hair long forever, but he had been so quick, so heartless. The scissors splayed open obscenely on the desk, hair caught between the blades. Her face felt clammy.

"Why do you look like a scared rabbit? As if I would throw you on a bed of rusty nails. Go. Suit up. Stretch out."

Anya stood and then sat down again.

"I don't feel well," she said.

"That's too bad. Get out of here. We're starting on vault."

CHAPTER 6

As the light came back, and the snow began to melt, the buildings of Norilsk emerged dirtier, more decrepit. Fog rose from the surface of the lake. The views, no longer blocked by darkness and snow, grew long over bare tundra, all the way to the hills on the edge of the steppe. Long-dead skeletal tree trunks stood like sentries. Chimneys plumed sulfur dioxide in white billows that merged with the low clouds. Green shrubs showed through gray ice in stubborn patches. And with the light came the sounds, no longer muted by wind and snow. The echoing clang of the coal train from Dudinka, the rumbles of the mining trucks, the almost imperceptible yawn and shake from gouging out the earth a kilometer below, and the sad, piercing cries of the seagulls.

It was Sunday, Anya's day off, and she and Sveta had set out to spend every minute of it outside in the sun. The clouds over the water kept the dirty air in, and the girls coughed into their hands, gloveless and pink. Once the temperature hit zero centigrade, it might as well be summer. Anya wore her new purple coat, afforded by the sports school scholarship, unzipped. Sveta wore her tatty old brown coat, the one she'd been wearing for years, the cuffs frayed, her bony wrists poking through.

They'd taken the bus to the edge of town and now walked over lumpy hills, the cemetery of unnamed graves from Norillag. They walked and kicked ice, stepping over remnants of metal debris. They found a patch of grass, and Sveta bent back and kicked her leg over.

"Show me a back handspring, Anya."

Anya jumped into a back handspring. She had moved so far past Sveta in skill, she found herself sad and sorry she'd shown off. But Sveta smiled wide and clapped.

"Again!"

Anya did it again. "I'll teach you," she said. "Stand here and pretend you're going to sit in a chair. Push back, not up."

Sveta jumped and arched her arms back, and Anya threw her legs over her head, and they collapsed in a heap on the wet ground, laughing. Sveta stood, and Anya kneeled next to her again, her knees stinging from the cold, wet ground.

"What do you think Vera did to get sent to the camp?" Anya asked.

Sveta tried again, hurled herself backwards, and Anya got her legs over. It was a mess, but it was a back handspring.

"My father says that people made stuff up about their neighbors to save themselves," Sveta said. "But my mother says he's soft in the head." She shrugged.

Anya tried to imagine Vera living in the tumbledown wooden barracks along the water, the cold air swirling in and gripping her like talons. The buildings were storage sheds now, but they remained intact, available, they seemed to suggest, if needed again.

"Viktor got chosen for the sports school. Fencing. *Malenkoye dermo.* The little shit," Sveta said. She scratched at a constellation of irritated bumps along her jaw, her fingernails dirty.

"Does he still pick his nose behind his hand?" Anya asked.

"Like we don't know what he's doing?"

The girls laughed and cartwheeled down the small hill, their hands muddy, their feet kicking up snow.

"I would like to go to Moscow," Sveta said. "Truthfully, I'd like to go to America."

"Sveta! They're capitalists. They worship money there."

"What does that mean really?"

"I don't know. They have no morals."

"I bet they're allowed to wear lipstick."

They walked along the edge of the lake, the water frothy and green.

"Do you think she's dead?"

"Who?"

"Your mother."

Sometimes Anya tried to imagine her mother was dancing in Paris, roses thrown onto the stage, even though she knew this wasn't true. It hurt the most to think she chose to leave. More often she saw her turn into swirls of white smoke that moved higher until they were gone. Death felt black and thick like tar, oozing down into the center of the earth.

"I don't know," Anya said. "After death there is nothing. You die and that's it. My father used to say she went away. But now he just says she's gone. I think she's gone but really gone, like up in the sky. Maybe someday it will feel like she is dead."

"When I go away to Moscow, when I'm a film actress," Sveta said, posing her hands under her chin, "I will look for her. I wouldn't have wanted to stay here either if I were her."

But I am here, Anya thought. Sveta's remark had knocked her in the stomach. She thought of the amber bracelet, which she had never found.

"There's a meet," Anya said. It was a jab back, and she knew it.

Sveta turned quickly. "A meet?"

"A tournament."

Her eyes crinkled at the edges and then dropped. "Oh, Anya," she said. "I wish I could come." She started singing softly the anthem, "*An unbreakable union of free republics.*"

"It's only to Surgut," Anya said. "Siberia still."

"You get to go somewhere."

"Yes."

"Your hair looks good. More like Korbut."

Anya touched her short ponytails, lopsided and coming loose.

"I liked it long," Anya said. "The coach is mean, Sveta."

"Does he beat you?"

"No."

"He can't be so bad then."

"I guess you're right."

The sun was dipping, the lake had disappeared behind mist and fog. Anya knew she was lucky.

"Another back handspring," Anya said. "You can show them next time. Arms by your ears. Let's go."

* * *

Anatoly stood with Sergei laughing, arms across their chests, as Anya came into the gym. Karolina stretched her splits in the corner. Masha and the other younger girls held handstands on the beam. Anya was going to join them when Anatoly called her over.

"Show Sergei the flip. He doesn't believe you can do it."

"Here?"

"Do the flip." He twitched a smirk and hiked up his shorts. Sergei smelled like he'd bathed in Chypre, the cheap cologne favored by soldiers.

"On the floor? There's no mat," she said.

"Do the flip."

Anya stood with her arms up, gnawing her lip, trying to stanch the fear.

"Go," Anatoly said. "Fear is a weed. If you let it grow, its roots are too tough."

Anya lowered her arms as if to jump but stopped. She wouldn't look at her coach. She didn't know what she feared more: falling or Anatoly.

"You'll never amount to anything," he said. "I'm wasting my time."

Her face grew hot, her skin prickly under her leotard. She was so angry, she did a back flip on the wooden floor.

Sergei laughed.

"Not bad," Anatoly said.

It was the closest she had ever come to a compliment from him. He might have handed her a golden trophy, that's how it felt. She stood taller, lifted her chin. How quickly the anger was replaced.

"Now five more times perfect. Mess up you start over."

Anya stood on the line. Spot the wall, she said to herself, jump up, high set, chin tucked, see your knees. Don't think about cracking your head open. Flip. Land.

The next one she landed short and hit the floor with her knees. She got back up, ignoring the throbbing ache. She was used to physical pain. As long as she could move, she would be fine.

"Again!" Anatoly shouted.

She flipped again, low, but landed.

From her periphery she watched Sergei saunter over to Karolina.

"Time for massage," he said. She followed him into what they called the trainer's room, though they had no trainer.

"Not good enough," Anatoly said. He stood close without offering to help. "Do it better. I have taught you what you need to know."

She did it better.

"The desire to be the best either emerges or it doesn't," he said. "I don't know yet with you."

She knew.

"You're doing it on beam next," he said. "Ultra-C element. We will show them in Surgut what we can do."

* * *

Irina came up for dinner, and as Yuri opened the door, he felt his chest open and something settle comfortably into place. Okay, he thought with relief. Gray hairs wired up from her curls, and her eyes were cartoonish behind her large glasses, but her face retained its handsomeness, strong bones and an easy smile.

"And how were your students today?"

"They don't care much for literature." She held a pot in her hands and handed it to Yuri. "They'll all get jobs at the plants or mines or transportation system."

"Ah, well. Freedom through labor." He smiled and kissed her on both cheeks.

Anya stood upside down in a handstand against the wall.

"How long, Papa?"

"Your face is purple, Anya," Irina said.

"I need to make five minutes."

"You don't spend enough time in the gymnasium?" Irina asked.

"You're at two minutes forty-five," he said, looking at his watch.

"You have great willpower," Irina said. "What do you imagine will happen if you come down too soon?"

"I will fall into a pit of vipers."

"I see. Good reason to stay up."

Yuri set the pot of dumplings that Irina had brought on the table and poured her a drink.

"Papa?"

"Four minutes."

Irina sat at the table and removed her glasses, rubbing the red marks on the sides of her nose.

"I got a strange letter today," she said.

"Yes?"

"From Vitka."

Yuri raised his eyebrows and felt a twinge of jealousy. Vitka who had been her paramour, who'd come with them to Norilsk.

"What did the old poet have to say for himself?"

She lowered her voice. "He's been in Perm."

Yuri exhaled. Perm was a town known for its prison camp at the western edge of the Urals, where dissidents were sent after the Gulag closed. In Stalin's era it had been roulette; anyone could be arrested for any reason: peasants, workers, Party bureaucrats. Now the KGB arrested people for *something*, but Yuri supposed political charges were still murky. Vitka had believed as they had believed. Had that changed?

"For what?" he asked.

"Article 72."

Article 72 was the political crimes mantle: Organizational activity of especially dangerous crimes against the State.

"Vitka?" Yuri asked.

"He wasn't licensed by the Writers' Union. They said his poetry promoted the cult of the individual."

It was hard to imagine Vitka, the loyal propagandist poet in their student days, writing anti-Soviet verse.

"You made it, Anya! Five minutes!" he called. "Maybe he was guilty, what do we know?"

Irina looked at him with scolding, wide eyes.

"His letter made it past the censors," he said.

"He says he was rehabilitated," she said. "He renounced his old poetry."

Anya stayed up for five more seconds and came down, collapsing onto the floor, panting.

"Where is he now?" he asked.

"He stayed in Perm. There's a zoo there. They have snow leopards and Amur tigers. He works cleaning cages."

"Who cleans cages?" Anya asked.

"Irina's old boyfriend."

"You had a boyfriend?"

Yuri chuckled and Irina made a face.

"Maybe he will meet Aika the polar bear," Anya said. "Ledorsky put him on a barge heading south."

Yuri smiled and rubbed her head. "Sure he did."

Anya took a dumpling with her fingers. "I never want a boyfriend," she said.

"That's good, *Dochka*. You have bigger things."

Irina spooned potatoes with fennel seeds, cabbage, and *pelmeni* onto plates.

"Have you ever seen the sea?" Anya asked.

"The Arctic," he said.

"That doesn't count," Irina said. "As a girl I went once to Riga with my family."

"Where's Riga?" Anya asked.

"Latvia. After the Great Patriotic War, my father was sent to establish Soviet standards at the university there. I don't remember much of the city except for some bombed-out buildings in the center. But I remember the sea. I went with my mother to Jurmala. To the beach. The sand was soft and white and very hot on my feet. I walked out into the cool water, maybe fifty meters out, and the water was still shallow. My mother looked so small on the shore, her old dress blowing in the wind. She looked like a painting."

"Can we go sometime?" Anya asked.

Yuri saw the three of them there on the beach. A new configuration of family.

"It would be nice," he said.

"I was so happy," Irina said. "I turned away from my mother and looked out to where the water met the sky, the sand squishing between my toes."

"Papa, what did Vera do to get sent to the camp?"

Yuri met Irina's eyes across the table.

"I don't know," he said.

"Is it true people were sent for nothing?"

"Who told you that?" Irina asked.

"Sveta."

"Be careful what you say outside of here," Yuri said. "What we say at the table is different from what we say out there."

How could he explain that he supported a way of life, a Party, that had given them the Gulag? He had dreamt of worldwide revolution, thought it was possible. He didn't like to think about the costs.

Irina refilled their glasses. "You know what I wrote on my Party application?" she said. "I'll always remember it. 'I accept the Party Program and regulations. I am prepared to devote all of my energy, and, if necessary, to give my life to my Motherland.'"

"A regular Marat Kazei," Yuri said.

"Who's that?" Anya asked.

"A Young Pioneer who joined the partisans at thirteen and blew himself up with a grenade in a standoff with Germans."

"Hero of the Soviet Union," Irina said.

"We are part of the grand scheme of things, Anya, still are," Yuri said. "There is discomfort for some, sacrifice for the greater good."

"'To the grief of all bourgeois, through the world, we'll spread the fire,'" Irina said. "The purpose of life is whatever makes you rise above."

"Who do you think mastered the north? The prisoners and us," he said, gaining zeal, buzzing. "Everyone has a big Motherland and a little homeland. This is our homeland. *V gostyah khorosho, a doma luchshe!*"

But did he believe it still? Did Irina? If he were being honest, he would say Katerina had stopped believing sometime after Anya was born, but he had not let her talk about it, had tried to convince her otherwise. It had no longer made sense to her.

"I would like to go to the sea," Anya said. She picked at the dumpling on her plate with a fork. "The blue-green water of the Black Sea. I remember Mama saying that."

Yuri laid his fork on the edge of his plate. Irina looked at her lap. He had felt buoyed but now he sank, heavy like platinum into his chair. The room had a vodka tilt.

"Sochi," he said. "She danced there when she was fourteen. In the company. A special performance. Stalin had a dacha there."

"She danced for Stalin?" Irina said.

Yuri nodded. She had been so proud of it when they had met, and then in those last years, the memory had curdled into shame.

"What he did, Yuri, to think of it," Katerina had said. "To think of how I sought his face in the audience, danced only for him."

Her small shoulders had collapsed, and she had curled into him, as if to hide from it all.

"Without him we would be ruled by Germans," he had said.

It had been a weak response, not what she needed, but he had feared her brazen questioning, the criticism she didn't try to hide.

"I'm sorry I never saw her onstage," Irina said.

"It was something," Yuri said. He reached for Irina's hand and squeezed her fingers.

"I'm sleepy," Anya said.

She took her plate to the sink, washed it, and kissed her father good night. She paused, and then hugged Irina, and Yuri felt warmth and gratitude for his good daughter. When Anya had gone to the bedroom, he scooted his chair next to Irina's and put his arm around her shoulders, the ceiling spinning above.

"We remain," he said. Irina was here. She was his.

* * *

After lunch, after the hour of afternoon schoolwork, Anatoly whistled loudly through two fingers and told them they were going on an excursion. They put coats on over their leotards and piled into an old van, its bottom rusted out. Anya sat on Masha's lap. The van coughed and lurched, Anatoly behind the wheel, Sergei in front.

Anya felt excited. She had never seen any of them outside the gym, and here they were setting off together to an unknown destination. The sky was pink, a rosy glow from the late sun, made more lovely by the veil of poisonous smoke in the air.

"Where are we going?" Masha called out.

"The river," Anatoly said.

They parked at the edge of the Yenisei and tumbled out of the van.

The spring melt had freed large chunks of ice on the river's surface, the water dark below.

"It will bring down inflammation in your muscles," Anatoly said.

"And purify your souls," Sergei laughed.

Anya didn't know what they meant. Two older girls started shaking their heads and backing away.

"You're going in," Anatoly said.

"*Ty chyo blyad*," Masha said.

"Watch your mouth," Sergei said.

"Strip down," Anatoly called.

Anya dropped her clothes in a pile on the still-icy ground, and stood, like the others, in her leotard and shoes. Her skin was goose-pimpled and waxy. The older girls crossed their arms over their chests.

"Look at all the cowering little bunnies," Anatoly said. "Shoes off too."

He lit a cigarette. Sergei pushed Karolina toward the edge. She shrieked, and he picked her up and dropped her into the freezing water.

"I'm coming for you next, Masha," he said. "You're so fat I might not be able to pick you up."

Masha ran away, but he caught her and tossed her in like a sack of coal.

Sergei caught Anya's eye and moved toward her. She did not want him touching her. She ran straight to the water. She jumped.

It felt like hitting cement, the sting and shock of the water. She could not make her body do what she wanted. She descended into the dark, a floe of ice above her, and she lost which way was up. No sound. Falling. Alone. She needed breath, her lungs punished and empty. She felt how easily she could die. If she surrendered, she could stop and sink all the way to the bottom. Would she see her mother again? Or would it be all this nothingness? But there it was, a flicker of light somewhere above her, and she furiously kicked her legs until she rose toward it and broke the surface.

She gasped and sputtered. Anatoly held out his hand to her, but she could not close her fingers. He pulled her out by the arm and handed her a rough towel. A sob caught in her throat.

"You're fine," he said.

"I almost drowned," she said. She blew river water from her nose and swiped at her face with her hand.

"You didn't, though," he said. "So? It's good for you. Without effort, you won't pull a fish out of a pond."

Anya shivered, her heart slowing from its panicked racing, the feeling of her limbs returning. The smallest team, he had called them, gymnast and coach. She couldn't say she hated him because she needed him too much. But didn't he need her too?

"The heat is on in the bus," Anatoly said, clapping her on the back. "Back to work."

CHAPTER 7

Vera walked close to the sooty ice ledge along Leninskiy Prospekt
hugging her bag of food parcels, more than she needed, but she
would never be comfortable without a stockpile. Plus, she liked having sweets for Anya, who could use some padding on her bones. Vera
dodged puddles, trying not to slip. She was amazed that she had made
it to seventy-seven, felt guilty about it some days, about how she had
survived and so many had not. The arbitrariness of it all she could never
reconcile.

State Store 42 was as far as she ventured these days, and she usually
walked—the bus frightened her, the door opening with a sinister beck-
oning. A car passed, spraying her ankles with dirty melt. She looked
around, always half expecting to be stopped by police. For thirty years
she'd had a recurring dream about her sentence having been extended.
"There's been an error," the *nadziratel* says. And then he laughs and he has
no teeth, just pink gums like a baby.

But here it was spring, overcast and muddy, but light, which felt
miraculous every year it arrived. She crossed herself with a subtle move
of her hand. After she'd been released, she used to see men and woman
in town who had been guards, and invariably they would wave and call
her *tovarishch*—which had been strictly prohibited inside the *zona*, politicals having lost the privilege of being called comrades. Interacting with

her former jailers would leave her feeling dislocated and strange, the difference of a day, one side of the barbed wire to another.

She was exhausted by the time she reached her apartment building, short of breath from the walk and the polluted haze. She stopped and leaned against the damp wall. She had stayed in Norilsk for reasons that twisted in on themselves—guilt, punishment, sadness, inertia, even fear. She couldn't bear the thought of seeing those people on the streets of Novgorod who had gone on like nothing had happened, because they had been lucky or had informed to save their own hides. The university professor, she knew now, who had turned her husband, Ilya, in. Did he know what it would mean for them? The police had come in the middle of the night, banging on the door with the butts of their guns. They were given ten minutes to get out of their pajamas before being shoved into a transport truck to Leningrad and the old czarist prison. In the first weeks after her arrest, isolated in a *boks*—an empty cell with a bench—between interrogations, Vera had been consumed by trying to figure out who had turned them in, as if by knowing who it was, the error could somehow be undone. She could not bear to think of her son, twelve years old, who'd also been arrested, or she feared she would go mad.

"Your husband has been sentenced," the officer said.

"There was no trial."

"Ah. In these dangerous times they sentence in absentia. Operational measures for the liquidation of clandestine groups of Trotskyites and Bukharinites as well as other counterrevolutionary groups. Your husband was charged under Article 58 of the criminal code for counterrevolutionary crimes. Fifteen years."

It was cruelly absurd. Her kind husband who was a botanist at the university, who shied away from political discussions, who wept with joy when their son was born, who brought her peonies in the spring. During the Great Terror, the special commissions bypassed even the sham of a trial. Vera pressed her tongue to the roof of her mouth and pinched the area between her thumb and forefinger as hard as she could, to hide her emotion from this man.

"And I? My son?"

"Members of the family of an enemy of the Revolution."

"We are innocent."

"I'm merely carrying out my duties. Why don't you tell me about your husband's involvement in a Trotskyist sabotage organization?"

"This is a mistake."

"We don't make mistakes. Did he doubt the rightness of the Party?"

The NVKD man leaned back. Vera knew there was no point in trying to appeal to his humanity. He was an extension of Stalin's leaden hand, which hovered over the vastness of the Soviet Union, pressing down, blocking out the light. Vera was so hungry her head seemed to float away from her body. She'd been kept awake for two days. She could not process that this was it, that she was not going home. Her child had been taken. Chestnut hair and big feet and loamy, little-boy smell. Ruddy cheeks in the cold. Nose in a book. Relentless about wanting a dog— why had she not gotten him a dog? Gentle, funny, curious. Playing chess with his father at the kitchen table. A good boy.

"Would you like some water?" The agent drew his chair around the table to sit next to her, thigh to thigh. "Do you like that prison soup made of rotten cabbage? Maybe you'd like some fresh bread?"

She hated herself for wanting the bread as much as she did. Her stomach was an empty, shriveled balloon. Her body tried to overtake her sense of right, a fight that would rage in her for years to come.

"It says here your father was an enemy of the Revolution."

"He owned a mill."

"You were the fat and sweet."

"I was just a girl."

"You could help your son, you know."

He let the words hang, waiting for her to bite.

"Give me information," he said. "Conspirators at the university."

"I won't."

He laughed, his front teeth angled together like a muskrat's.

"That's what everyone says at first. Nothing to be ashamed of. But we're all *stukachi*. We tell on each other. Root out the bad ones."

In the years that followed, after the choices she made, the sadist's words would come back to her.

"*Ushi vyanut*," she spat, her anger overtaking her fear.

"Ah, I see," he said under his breath, nodding his head. "What you say makes me sick to hear too. So where does that leave us?"

"I don't have any information," she said, wilting.

He sniffed and pushed up his glasses. He turned, and she thought he might punch her in the gut.

"Well, then, that's too bad!" he said, patting her leg instead, as if they were old friends. "Here's what I can do for you. I'll have the three of you sent to the corrective labor camp in Norilsk. You can join your husband. They have a boys' camp there too."

Norilsk. It was the first time she had heard of it. She assumed it was somewhere in Siberia, one of the exile towns forced into existence from the inhospitable wilderness.

"It's a little cold there, I hear," the officer said, his tone now jovial. "Fifty below in winter. No sun for months. But you're lucky, you know. You get to live. What's a little hard work? It'll do you good. Fresh air. Contribute to your country. Rehabilitate yourself."

She felt some relief then. She would get to see her son again. They would leave her alone, let her hunker in her cell until she was shipped out.

"You will receive your sentence in the next day or two."

He smiled and pinched her arm and twisted so hard she thought he would break through her skin, and then moved in close to her ear.

"You are filth," he said.

There were many details that were lost to her now. What shoes was she wearing? Did she hear other prisoners through the stone walls? Did they give her a blanket? But she would always know that man's voice in her ear. The terror of no longer having any control.

Vera righted herself and shifted her bag of groceries. It was warmer but not warm, and her hands were stiff in her gloves as she fumbled with the key to the outside door. Anya was coming today, and that was always good for her mood. She reminded her of Katerina, of course, who had knocked on Vera's door one winter afternoon with a dark-eyed baby on her hip, looking for a sitter and a moment later asking if she would like company. Imagine, Vera thought. That small, beautiful woman had been the only one Vera had told things to, the only one who didn't want to pretend that it was best to forget.

* * *

Anatoly and Sergei stood with their arms crossed on the side of the floor as Anya and Masha did rope climbs. The 1974 World Championships were taking place in Varna, Bulgaria, and it was all they could talk about.

"She's past her prime, Tourischeva. Getting old," Anatoly said.

"She did a Tsukahara on the horse. She still wins," Sergei said.

"Well." Anatoly flashed his eyes upward. "Whatever that means."

"Gold is gold. Besides. Look at her." Sergei raised his eyebrows in quick succession.

"Girls are going to do double backs," Anatoly said. "Soon enough."

Sergei blew a puff of air in disbelief.

"Sure they will," he said. "When the lobster whistles on the mountain."

"I think I hear whistling. Dance won't matter. Skills will."

"You're crazy."

"You watch."

"They don't like Korbut. They make her get silver."

"That's the Party bureaucrats. The kids love Korbut. Anya Yurievna, who do you want to be like?"

"Korbut," she said. She reached to touch the top line of the rope, and lowered herself hand under hand. She felt good and strong today, kip casting to full handstand on the bars again and again. Her routine for Surgut was close.

"See? I'm making my bet." To Anya, Anatoly said, "Hop down. We're going to vault."

She skipped behind him.

"Korbut did a full pirouette entry onto the horse at Worlds," he said.

"A full twist before her hands touched?"

"It's all punch and angle. Getting a good block. We're going to work on it."

Anya twisted her body, trying to imagine which direction she would be facing when she landed. She could do a front handspring vault, but she'd only just gotten to where she could land it decently.

"I'll never be able to do that," she said with a laugh.

She saw immediately that her comment had been careless.

"What did you say?" Anatoly's face grew stony, his nostrils flared. She felt her head grow light, darkness in the corners of her eyes. She had made an egregious misjudgment.

"Don't ever question me," he said. He spoke so quietly she could barely make out his words. "You are nothing. Remember that. A gymnast is nothing but raw material in a coach's hands."

Anya stood at attention with her hands behind her back. Fear made her go cold. Her fingertips tingled. She thought she might start shivering and never stop. He looked like a giant viper, ready to strike.

"Go," he said.

She stood still.

"Get out."

Anya stumbled to the edge of the gym, her tears making everything blur. She put on her coat over her leotard, not bothering with pants, and pulled on her boots without socks. She did not look back.

"Anya Yurievna, where are you going?" Masha called.

Anya's boots squeaked on the floor of the empty hallway. She had to use her whole body to get the door open. The fog was wretched today, and her eyes smarted. The air was damp on her legs. She didn't know what to do. The sun sat high in the sky, a gauzy yellow orb behind the haze, the clouds purple and charcoal. Dirty Skodas and Lada cabs rattled by. It was as if she'd emerged into a world she did not know. A seagull pecked at the black bags of garbage piled high near the curb. It smelled of fish and acrid smoke, and the rotten-egg stench of sulfur pumped into the air from tall chimneys like guard towers in every direction.

A woman with a squished face and a hitch in her gait passed by in galoshes, a wet-bellied German shepherd tugging her along.

"Why aren't you in school?" the woman shouted. She looked angry, as if Anya were some type of hooligan.

Anya slunk back behind the building into the shadows of the fenced-in cement lot, the chill stronger back here. A roll of barbed wire rusted orange leaned up against a dented filing cabinet missing a drawer. Was Anatoly kicking her out forever? Without gymnastics what would become of her? The shame moved through her, slick like hot oil. She could not tell her father; he was counting on her to make it.

Would Anatoly come looking for her? She knew nothing of her coach outside the gym. How old was he? Did he prefer *kvas* or tea? Did he dream about leaving Norilsk? She tried to imagine him in the suit he'd worn to her school, waiting in line at the butcher, riding the bus. He wants what I want. I will do better, she thought.

Anya jammed her fists deep into her pockets. Her legs were marred with red scrapes and the yellow shadow of bruises, two pallid sticks from the bottom of her coat. She pressed her tongue against the roof of her mouth, a way to stop from crying that Vera had taught her.

She would not be so easily defeated; she knew she could not just wait for what came next. It was her move. Anya took two big breaths, put her head down, and walked around to the side door of the building. She took off her coat while she walked down the hall and stepped out of her boots at the door to the gym.

Anatoly was on the other side of the gym near bars. She did not look at him for fear she would wither in his gaze. She squatted a few times to get the blood moving in her legs, and punch-jumped again and again, her eyes on the floor. An older girl, chicken pox scarred on her forehead, elbowed Anya as she walked by. What it meant Anya didn't know, but it was a reminder that there would always be those who wanted her to fail.

Anatoly did not say anything, but she knew he was watching, the smoke from his cigarettes curling in her periphery.

She walked to the end of the vault runway and wiped her sweaty palms on her leotard. She ran hard toward the horse, hurtling onto the springboard and flying over in a front handspring. When she landed, she didn't look up; an electric tension spanned the gym. She jogged back. This time she tried to rotate her body after taking off, but her hands got only a quarter of the way around the vault and she punched over sideways, missing her feet and slamming into the floor mat, knocking her head. She got up slowly, her vision pricked with stars. I am not a soldier, she thought. I am a general. She walked with her head up back to the start of the runway.

"Think of a round-off," Anatoly called to her, as if nothing had transpired. "Keep your hollow body. One hand and then the other. Strong block."

She ran hard and imagined pushing off the horse and flying off into the sky. Her hands made it around almost far enough. She landed on her feet before falling.

"Better," he said.

She looked up then, for the first time, but he didn't come closer. He stood across the floor and smoked. Something had been restored. She would be allowed to stay another day.

For an hour she ran at the vault and rotated her body in the air until her hands hit right and she landed squarely facing it on the other side. It was only the beginning—she was far from Korbut—but in that half twist her body felt how it would work, how she might one day get there. Her shins burned and her head hurt.

Day had turned to evening, and the other girls had gone home. Anatoly stacked mats.

"I'm sorry," she said.

But he would not acknowledge her as a girl. Only as a gymnast.

"You're still piking after your block," he said. "You're going to do a half on, half off in Surgut."

She told herself she would do whatever she had to, sleep at the gym if necessary. How she felt didn't matter. She settled into the simplicity of it: get better at gymnastics. She didn't think about what was missing. The world had shrunk to the size of the gym.

* * *

Anya pounded on Vera's door, out of breath.

"I was worried! You're so late," Vera said.

"I learned something new today," Anya said. "On the horse."

"The horse?"

"The thing you vault over."

"The thing *you* vault over. I'm afraid my vaulting days are behind me." She could see a bump on the girl's temple, raised and faintly purple. "That's new too."

"It doesn't hurt unless I press it. It smells good in here."

"I have a surprise for you," Vera said, ushering Anya toward the kitchen. "I made *zhavoronki*."

"Ah!" Anya picked up one of the bird-shaped buns and pretended it was flying. "It's still warm. Can I eat it?"

Vera smiled. "They are for you."

Anya picked out the raisin eye and ate it.

"My son would do the same thing. I made these each spring. He liked to cut the diagonal through the dough to make the wings."

"What was his name, your son?"

"Come sit at the table. Here's a glass of sweet milk. His name was Pyotr."

"How did he die?" Anya didn't know if she should ask this, but she felt like she could ask Vera anything.

"Pellagra. It's a disease of malnutrition. He died when he was twelve. A little older than you."

"He didn't have enough to eat?" Anya asked, astonished.

"He was in the boys' camp."

"They put children in the camps?"

Vera nodded and nodded. "They did many things."

Anya looked out the window, the sun catching her with the last of the orange light.

"Did you see the sky yesterday?" she asked.

Vera had seen it. A rare blue. No haze or clouds or snow or rain. Just the blue of happy stories and light hearts and hope. But it was impossible for her not to feel the other force, the pain underneath the beauty. Katerina had said the distance between happiness and melancholy was as thin as a scythe's edge. With that clear sky Vera thought of seeing Pyotr across the *zona* when his brigade would head to the brick factory in the morning. He would wave wildly to her and smile, the one moment they had together each day, even as he was shrinking, his head so big on those little bones under parchment skin, his eyes too large and sinking; and her heart would fill, and she would squeeze the place between her thumb and forefinger until the tears held. Ilya had died in the first weeks at Norilsk, succumbing to dysentery and crushing sadness. But they had made it through that first winter, she and Pyotr, and it was turning warm, and there was a tiny root of hope in her that they would survive, and maybe her boy would be released early and he would go live with her mother in Novgorod under the golden domes of Saint Sofia. But then one day she saw him, sores along his jaw, and he didn't smile, and the day after he didn't wave to her, and the next day he turned away with the burning eyes of a *fitil*, a candlewick, the flame already blown out. And then he wasn't there at all.

"Wasn't it beautiful?" Anya asked. "The sky?"

"It was beautiful," Vera said.

She would have moments now when she would feel herself warm in bed, full after a supper she had cooked from ingredients she had chosen, and she would feel utter amazement. To be deprived of everything and then to have it, never fully sure it all wouldn't be taken away again. It was a feeling all of them who had lived through it shared, she knew. How could it be otherwise? Pyotr. Please let him not have died scared and alone. Please, God, comfort him.

"I pray for you at night. That you won't get hurt doing your crazy gymnastics," Vera said.

"What does it mean to pray?"

"I ask God to keep you safe."

"Sounds like worrying," Anya said.

Vera laughed. "A subtle distinction between the two."

"Do you look at your icon when you pray?"

"Sometimes," she said. "But it's usually silent in my head."

Anya scrunched her face.

"How can God hear you?"

"He hears everything, whether you say it out loud or not."

"I'm sorry about your son. About Pyotr. You must miss him."

"I miss him all the time. But enough sad talk. You are alive, *dorogaya*."

"You are alive too, Vera Vasilievna."

Anya worried a tear of skin on her hand. Her palms were tough now, the skin thick and hard at the base of her fingers, but they still ripped from the bars, no matter how much of the fine white chalk she rubbed into them. Sometimes she talked to her mother in her head. She couldn't be sure if her mother heard her or not, but she guessed Vera couldn't be sure about God either.

It was horrifying to think of Vera's son starving to death. Anya couldn't really comprehend it. She thought about being hungry. How could people think a boy like that was a danger? Or Vera? Vera was so kind to her. It made her scared. There weren't camps anymore, were there? She would ask her father about it.

"I wrote out some math problems for you to compute," Vera said. "You remember how the beads go?"

Anya followed her to the living room and picked up the abacus.

"This wire is the thousands?" she asked.

Vera nodded. Anya flexed her wrist, sore when she bent it back.

"Does your hand hurt?"

"Everything hurts!" She laughed. Being a gymnast hurt. If it didn't, you weren't doing it right.

"Anya Yurievna?" Vera asked.

"Yes?"

"What is your coach like?"

"He's. I don't know." Anya stopped. How could she describe someone who determined everything about her life, from the way she stood to whether she would fall and crack her head? She rubbed her rough, calloused palms together. She had to believe in Anatoly. "He wants me to be better," she said. "To be good."

"Does he make you do things that scare you? That you don't want to do?"

Of course he does, she thought. But he has to do that. She shook her head, but she knew Vera knew she was lying.

"What's good for the Motherland isn't necessarily good for you."

It was something no one said. Anya felt a chasm opening beneath her, her feet dangling over air.

"He wants what's best for me," Anya said. But she didn't know if that was true or not. "I want to do well for him."

Vera hung her head a bit, a white tendril from her plaited hair coming loose around her face.

"What does your father think?"

"He wants me to be a champion. It's my way to serve my country."

Vera smiled and patted Anya's hand, her skin dry like paper.

"Show me some gymnastics."

Anya wanted to do something to make Vera see, to show her what gymnastics meant, how strong she was, how she could fly. Something big. She would do the back flip. Right here on the tile floor of the living room.

"Be careful," Vera said. She tucked her feet to the side of the sofa, out of the way, her mottled hands flat against each other as in prayer. "How about you walk on your hands across the room."

Anya shook her head no and pushed the table toward the window. She tried to summon her mother's face but couldn't. A meadow, she thought, I'm in a meadow on the soft grassy earth so nothing can happen. Believe in your body, Anatoly always said. She closed her eyes and opened them. Raised her arms up next to her ears. Don't look back. Go.

But Anya had forgotten she was wearing socks. Her left foot slipped forward when she jumped up, so she took off crookedly, and as her legs came around, watching her knees like she was supposed to, no problem, she thought, her toe clipped a chair, which then knocked over a lamp, and she landed with all her weight on the edge of one foot, which buckled under, and her body collapsed to the floor.

"Anya!" Vera cried.

Anya at first felt only shock that she had fallen. She'd made it around, and she'd been far enough away from anything, hadn't she? Then the pain came, and it felt like a cobra had sunk its fangs into her ankle. She gingerly got to her knees and rolled over. She felt bile claw up into her throat.

Her foot was twisted at a ghastly angle. Blood dyed her sock as she watched. A piece of glass from the broken lightbulb stuck out from her heel. What had she done? She couldn't yet cry. She saw Anatoly's face in front of her, red and huge and distorted, the vein along his temple like a pulsing worm.

Vera kissed her head and hurried to the telephone.

This is how it ends, Anya thought.

CHAPTER 8

Yuri ground out the end of his shift, lowering the last round of canvases into the water to skim the copper sulfate. After a day of breathing steam and sweating, the thought of cold vodka made him twitchy with desire. He coughed, spitting up metal dust from his lungs.

It was almost Anya's birthday, nine years since he had sat in that pea-green-tiled waiting room in the clinic—there was no hospital in Norilsk—Katerina screaming from the other room, sounding more captured animal than human, and he was not allowed to be with her. "Take a walk, *tovarishch*," the midwife said. "There's nothing you can do." Yuri felt like he was failing Katerina, like she would die and it would be his fault. But then. A dark little creature with a full head of hair wrapped in white. Quiet. As if she were about to say something.

"We'll call her Anya," Katerina said.

"You mean Anna?" he asked. Anya was a diminutive, a nickname. No one was given the name Anya.

"Anya," she said, not to be deterred, convention be damned.

A girl. He felt suddenly fragile and full of fear. She would die someday, and that was too much to bear. But he had looked at Katerina then, and she did not look scared at all. She looked like she could lift a building, this small woman, her cheeks red and hairline damp, her eyes like smoldering coal. She looked like she could see into a glorious future.

"This girl," she said. "Our girl. She is going to soar. Maybe all the way to the moon."

The three of them crackling with life. How he missed her.

"'Your name is a—bird in my hand,'" she said, quoting Tsvetaeva, always quoting the banned poet. He looked around to make sure the words didn't register with the nurse. It shamed him now, this worry, but she was already getting careless by then, already chafing against the constraints of the state. Reckless even.

The whistle blew. Yuri pulled off his gloves, soaked, his hands shriveled and white like the hands of a corpse pulled from the sea. They tremored, he was horrified to see, from too long between drinks. It was not the first time he had noticed it. Like his father's had when he'd raised a bottle to his lips, still in his wool coat, just inside the doorway, after waiting for hours in line for his ration. Yuri wiped his hands on his gritty jumpsuit then shook them to get them still. He hadn't even been a soldier, hadn't seen men's hands blown off or had to eat grass from hunger or had to kill a German boy—so small a boy, his father had said, his coat was hanging past his hands—with a knife to his neck.

What had Yuri given to his country? He had come to Norilsk, never to see his parents or Moscow again, but now, here he was, old, his life as it would always be. What would Katerina think of him now?

He could never shake the feeling that he had let her down in some essential way, and maybe that was why she had vanished. Was she dead? Did she take her own life? His mind poked at the thought he rarely allowed himself. He saw bones in the dirt, as small as a bird's. It had been almost four years now. He followed his fellow workers to the locker room, unzipping his uniform on the way. Toward the end she didn't really tell him anything anymore. Her questions, her disappointments. She saved it all for Vera. And yet he could never bring himself to ask the old woman what she might have told her.

"*Tovarishch,*" a young man said, his hand on Yuri's arm. "A telephone call came for you."

Yuri's first thought was that it was Katerina, and for just an instant, warmth ballooned in his chest. But it was a fool's hope.

"Who?" he asked.

"It's not for me to know. See the director."

No one got telephone calls at the plant. Certainly no good news came that way. He ran to the office. The director, his double chin loose over his shirt collar, sat with his hands tented on his desk.

"It's your daughter. You are needed at the clinic."

* * *

Irina was waiting for them when they returned home, Yuri carrying Anya, her foot bandaged so heavily they had to cut the leg of her pants to fit over it.

"Come, come," Irina said. She'd laid a pillow and blankets on the sofa.

Anya felt groggy from the medicine they'd given her. Her ankle throbbed, a giant white appendage at the end of her leg. She had screamed through gritted teeth when the doctor yanked her foot to snap it back into place. When he tweezered out the glass, piece by piece, she'd fainted.

Irina's hair was a mess of curls, like she'd emerged from sleeping two whole days, and Anya, in her fog, thought she looked like some kind of forest creature. Irina sat next to her on the sofa and fed her *borshch* and bread, as if she had lost the use of her hands as well. But Anya liked it. It made her feel like a young child, back in the days when she would scramble onto her mother's lap during dinner. She felt warmly toward Irina, her head still swimmy from painkillers, and she reached out and took her hand.

"Papa. What will happen?"

"You'll be fine, *Dochka*. It'll heal up no problem."

Yuri scratched his beard, his eyes looking everywhere but at her.

"At the gym. What will happen at the gym?"

She tried to picture Anatoly when he saw what she had done. She saw him a coiled snake, ready to wrap around her and squeeze until she could no longer breathe.

"Anya. Don't worry about that," Irina said. "You are a little girl, and you are hurt. Soon we will get you to bed." She pressed Anya's hand between her own.

But Anya could see that her father's face was cloudy, uncertain. It was terrible to see his worry. His features slid together, and when she blinked, he looked like an altered version of himself, his eyes a little closer together, his nose off-center.

"You'll take her tomorrow to the gym," Irina said quietly. "To talk to the coach." Yuri took a moment before he nodded, and Anya felt his reluctance like a cold wind on her neck.

"I'm scared of the snake," she said.

"The snake?" Yuri asked.

But Anya was so tired she couldn't say more.

Irina patted her hand and fed her another spoonful of soup.

"I'll borrow crutches from Ledorsky," Irina said. "Remember he hobbled around last year?"

"Take me to see the polar bear," Anya said, but then she remembered Aika had already been sent to the zoo. "Oh. She's gone."

"Okay. I think it's time for bed," Yuri said.

Anya put her arms around his neck as he picked her up, and she wished he would carry her like this forever.

"It's almost your birthday, *Dochka*," he murmured. "Nine years old. How could you be nine? I remember when you fit in the palms of my hands." He laid her gently onto her bed, and she winced, holding her leg in the air. He stacked two pillows, and she set her foot down.

"I'm sorry," he said. "I'm so sorry."

She shook her head. She didn't have the energy to say it was not his fault.

Her mind drifted to walking on the steppe in spring with her mother, the earth spongy and wet, the grasses yellow. Her mother wore a white dress blown by the wind, and she let go of Anya's hand and leaped in that magical way of hers that made her look like a wood sprite, a *lesnaya nimfa* come to life, toes pointed even in boots, and Anya tried it too, clumsily, but with so much joy it didn't matter.

"This is where the last of the mammoths roamed," her mother said. "Many thousands of years ago. We are part of the ancient world out here."

They found a patch of baby's breath and lupine and gathered big bunches of the flowers.

"You will live forever, Anushka," she said. "Look at all this beauty."

She held the amethyst and white flowers in both hands like a wedding bouquet; but the flowers would wilt before they could make it home.

Anya's eyes fluttered as her father pulled the covers to her chin.

* * *

Anya and Yuri stood outside the gray, water-stained sports school in the clear morning light of spring, the sticky tires of cars on wet asphalt behind them. She wedged the too-tall pair of crutches at an angle under her armpits, her hurt foot held off the ground. Once the stitches healed, she could start putting weight on her foot, but it was unclear how long that would take.

Practice had not yet begun; they hoped to catch the coach early. But neither of them was eager to go inside yet. Anya saw in her father's fidgety hesitation that he might be scared of Anatoly too.

Ledorsky's crutches were on the lowest setting but still ridiculously tall. When she moved forward, she was lifted off the ground in an arc.

"Maybe I should just carry you," her father said.

Her toes were fat and purple where they squeezed through the bandages, her ankle having swelled around the tight taping done at the clinic.

The lights were on in the empty gym.

"So this is the place," Yuri said.

They looked around at the dilapidated room, and it felt strange to Anya to see it like this, from a remove, the equipment off-limits to her. Her father set her down on a stack of mats. The tears came fast and hard. She bit her sleeve to try to stanch them. She felt her muscles ache to move, to feel the pound of a round-off back handspring or the worn leather of the horse under her palms.

"Hello?" Yuri called. He cleared his throat and then said it again louder.

Anatoly emerged from the office, squinting over his glasses, his large middle straining against his sweater.

"What is this?" he asked.

Yuri ran his hand through his hair. His shoulders hunched as if to make himself smaller.

"I'm Anya's father," he said finally.

The men did not shake hands. They stood far apart as if squaring off, Anatoly's hands on his hips, Yuri's head lowered some. And it was only then that the coach looked over and saw Anya sitting, her foot up, and his expression changed from annoyance to confusion to anger. She knew that look and tried to keep breathing. Her father was here, her father was here.

"Anya," Anatoly barked. He held her gaze, his eyes black, until she broke it and looked at her lap.

"A dislocation," Yuri said. "Tearing in the ligaments. Stitches where pieces of glass were removed. It was an unfortunate accident."

Yuri looked from Anya to Anatoly.

"The doctor said she can come back in four weeks, see how it goes. She'll be as good as new. Eventually."

"Good as new?" Anatoly said. He rubbed his face with both hands and turned back to Anya as if Yuri were not even there. "Have you forgotten we have a competition? How did this happen? Were you showing off for one of your little friends?"

"I don't think this is the time—"

Anatoly cut him off.

"You will be here tomorrow. We will work everything possible."

Anya looked at her father. He lowered his bloodshot eyes and nodded his head a little, agreeing to whatever Anatoly said. She felt betrayed, but it was confirmation of what she already suspected. Her father had relinquished her. She was no longer his daughter who was a gymnast. She was a gymnast first, and she belonged to Anatoly. She willed herself as rigid and cold as stone.

Anatoly went into his office and came back with a wrinkled scrap of paper. He held it out to Yuri.

"The clinic doesn't know anything. Go see Doctor Bazhanov."

Anatoly slithered up to Anya and leaned down. He came in so close she thought he might kiss her.

"*Idiotka*," he hissed.

* * *

Dr. Bazhanov was young, his black hair buzzed short and bristly. Instead of a white coat, he wore brown slacks and a thin button-front shirt, his dark chest hair visible through the fabric. His office had faded putty-colored carpeting and a wooden desk, a makeshift examining table in the middle of the room. Anya sat in a chair next to her father. The doctor picked her right up under her arms without warning, even though she could have hopped over and gotten up on the table herself. His hands were cold and doughy. His breath smelled of fennel.

"You lose muscle the very first day," he said. He spoke to Yuri as if Anya were not there. "The key is to get her moving as soon as possible."

He took a long pair of shears and slid them between the tape and her skin. Anya closed her eyes, sure he was going to slice her open.

"Ugly," he said. "But no break, that's good."

"The doctor at the clinic said four weeks at least," Yuri said.

Bazhanov waved his hand.

"We have different priorities. Come back in two weeks for an injection."

"The coach wants her back in the gym tomorrow. That's too soon, no?" Yuri asked.

"Anatoly Popov will make her a champion for the Russian people," Bazhanov said. "It's never too soon. How old is she?"

"Almost nine."

"I have something to stop the—" He made a vague hand gesture over his chest to indicate breasts. "In a couple years. It's a new era. They want to keep them little girls as long as possible."

Yuri looked stricken. Anya wanted to be away from this man, this room, where the walls were a sickly shade of yellow. Her foot was marbled purple and blue, her ankle lost somewhere in the swollen skin. Black tracks of stitches ran up her heel. The doctor prodded the whole mess with his finger, like it was a grotesque cut of meat he didn't want to touch.

"There will be a state representative at the competition?" the doctor asked. He looked at Yuri, eyebrows raised. "It's what I hear. A chance at the national team someday. What do you think, little one? Represent the USSR at the Olympics?"

She nodded.

"No greater honor. It works out well for the families too," the doctor said. "If you stick with the program." He rewrapped her ankle, the tape painfully tight, and covered it with a brace he laced up like a corset.

"Here," he said, filling a dropper from a small vial. "For the pain. Lift your tongue."

The cold tincture filled her mouth with a chemical bitterness.

"The Romanians are getting quite strong," he said.

"No one's better than the Russians," Yuri said.

The doctor shrugged. "Let's hope."

"Papa," Anya said.

"I will give the coach an update," the doctor said. "It's my opinion she should report to the gym as requested."

"I'm so tired, Papa," she said.

"Pretty girl," the doctor said. "You can rest when you're too old to be good at gymnastics."

I will never be too old, she thought. I will twist and flip forever and never have to feel anything again.

* * *

The next day, Yuri had to go to work. Anya stayed home. For a while she read the book Marta had assigned them, Ostrovsky's *How the Steel Was Tempered.*

"Social realism is the best teacher," she'd said. "The struggle to free humanity!"

But Anya thought Marta was more interested in the romance between Tonia and the heroic Bolshevik Pavel than with his growing socialist consciousness. Masha claimed to be at the juicy part, but it was slow going for Anya:

> Pavel had a glimpse of the bottommost depths of life, the very sump
> of its ugly pit, and from it a musty, moldy stench, the smell of swamp
> rot, was wafted up to him who so eagerly reached out for everything new
> and unexplored.

She tossed the book aside. Without stretching and moving she felt jumpy in her skin. The sun was out, streams of light cutting through the sulfurous clouds. She hopped to the window and tried to wrench it open; it wouldn't budge. Outside, Norilsk was a different place. People didn't zip their coats. As the ice melted, the entryways to buildings got higher and higher from the ground. Gray lines marked where the snow had been for the past eight months.

Anya cartwheeled and landed on her good foot.

If her father and Irina were in love, did that mean they would get married and she would move in? There was only the one bedroom that Anya shared with her father. But Irina was okay to have around, she thought. When Irina was there, she made it feel warm in the apartment, made the evening into something more, and though she felt mean thinking it, Anya was glad that it wasn't always just her and her father. She couldn't remember what her parents had been like together. She had felt that her mother was hers alone, that hot fire gaze only for Anya. Her memories were of the two of them.

In the kitchen there was little to discover. Some stale crackers, sauerkraut, onions. She wiped the greasy dust from the tin of cooking oil. A half-empty bottle of vodka in the cabinet. She unscrewed the cap and smelled it, familiar, intimate almost, this close. More and more it was what her father smelled like all the time. She took the neck of the bottle in her hand and brought it to her mouth and drank. She coughed, eyes watering, shocked somehow that it tasted like it smelled.

She missed the gym. Outside of it she floated about like a bubble on the wind without a place to land. Even at home she no longer felt entirely comfortable. She couldn't sit still. She tried to move her hurt foot in its tape and brace until she felt a twinge of pain. If she closed her eyes, she was sure she could feel her muscles shrinking, growing weak. She slid down into middle splits, despite the strain of ligaments in her ankle. She would will her body right. She pushed herself up again and went to the window.

A migrant wheatear landed on the other side of the glass. She knew she should chase it away—it was a bad omen to have a bird land on your windowsill—but she could see the feathers up close, and the rarity of this creature made her wait. The white breast and black wings. She'd only seen one once before, from afar, out on the steppe, never in town. Ledorsky had told her that in autumn, the northern wheatears flew all the way to Africa, where their ancestors had wintered.

"Extraordinary," he had said. "They keep coming back."

The bird opened its beak, releasing a crackly, whistling song, muted through the glass. But it saw Anya then and flew on.

Below, a woman pushed a stroller over the rough, potholed asphalt that had been hidden all winter under snow. Her hair was black under a white kerchief, her eyebrows heavy and dark. She pushed the stroller into the weeds and snow so it wouldn't roll and fished a cigarette and matches from her pocket. Wisps of hair escaped and flew about her face in the wind, and she batted them away before lighting her cigarette and turning her back to the stroller. Anya wondered if the baby was crying. The woman, young, little more than a schoolgirl, took a few steps away and put her head back and blew smoke up into the sky. She took a few more steps, looking around to see if anyone was watching, the stroller behind her lodged crookedly into the scrub beside the road.

Don't leave, Anya thought.

The woman turned then, her head cocked as if she'd heard something. A car slowed before passing. She tossed her cigarette into the old snow. She hung her head with her hands on her hips for a moment longer, before dragging her feet back to the baby.

Anya hobbled away from the window to the bedroom. She knew there were things of her mother's her father kept somewhere. She checked his dresser, but the contents were all familiar. There was a small chest though, she knew, under his pair of winter boots, where he kept his Komsomol memorabilia, his Party acceptance letter, his residency papers, his marriage certificate. She dragged it out of the back corner of the closet into the room, the dust making her sneeze. Her father had brought the trunk, which had been his father's, up to Norilsk from Moscow when they had first traveled north.

The papers were yellowed and cracked, a stack tied with string. She lifted the bundle out and found below it some photographs: a black-and-white of her father and other Norilsk pioneers; his father—her grandfather whom she'd never met—in his army uniform before he left for the front, hearty, even cherubic, a confident smile on his face; her parents on their wedding day. She had seen this photo a hundred times, but she studied it again, mining for clues. Did her mother's eyes give something away? Did her parents stand a little farther apart than they should have? Did she look happy? But there was nothing new. Anya knew every centimeter of the image, how her mother's feet were turned out, her hair pulled tight, her fingers of one hand slightly blurry as if she had been reaching for her new husband. Yuri puffed his chest out, his eyes sparkling, a slight smile that seemed to proclaim victory, rightness, optimism. Anya sighed and set the pictures aside. Underneath lay her father's Young Pioneer red scarf, mold dusting one of its corners.

She pulled out a moth-eaten tutu, white tulle gone ratty in spots, from a paper bag, and at the bottom her mother's worn pink satin *pointe* shoes, the tightly packed paper in the toe boxes eroded to dust. Anya imagined her mother, after everyone was asleep, doing *pirouettes* around the apartment, dreaming of Moscow and the stage. She slipped her foot into one of the *pointe* shoes. It was too big, but she tied the ribbon around her ankle and held her leg out to admire the long line.

She had hoped her mother's bracelet might be in the box, those amber stones that always felt warm, but it was a familiar feeling not to find it. She ran her hand from corner to corner just to be sure. There were some old medals scattered on the bottom, a small, tarnished silver tray, some paper rolled up. Anya unrolled the typed sheets and held them flat with both hands. Poetry. She'd never seen *samizdat* but recognized it immediately, writing not allowed in the Soviet Union but passed hand to hand. It made her feel nervous that her father had this saved. She thought of Sveta's father and how he was punished for telling a joke. Or Vera sentenced to a forced labor camp. The slightest misstep could get you in trouble.

The poet was Marina Tsvetaeva, whom Anya had never heard of. At the top was typed: "Poems to Czechoslovakia." She read slowly, out loud, struggling to contain the images, to understand the words.

I refuse to——be. In
the madhouse of the inhumans
I refuse to——live. To swim

on the current of human spines.
I don't need holes in my ears,

no need for seeing eyes.
I refuse to swim on the current of human spines.

To your mad world—one answer: I refuse.

Anya felt a sickness rise in her stomach. She couldn't fully grasp the poem's meaning, but she knew it was dangerous somehow. The word "refuse" made her scalp prickle. She was nervous to read any more of the poems. But on the back of one of them there was writing. Her mother's loopy hand, followed by her father's tight scrawl; they were having a conversation by sliding the paper back and forth.

The preservation of the state requires individual sacrifice.
A state without art has no soul.
There is art! Soviet art!
Art should be free from the imposition of authority.
What if it stokes chaos? What if it incites the cult of the individual?
What if it evokes beauty? What if it stirs happiness?
You are impossible, *solnyshko.*

(Here her mother had drawn a smiling stick figure ballet dancer in a leap.)

It scares me how you have changed.
Norilsk is built on bones.

Anya closed her eyes to try to contain the fear and uncertainty springing loose. Part of her wanted to burn the whole thing. She took the *samizdat* and hid it under her mattress.

CHAPTER 9

It was June. The sun was up and it did not come down; they had
reached the days of the midnight sun. Coats were stuffed into closets.
Traktiry served vodka all night. Women hiked up their skirts, showing
legs as white as icebergs. The permafrost never melted, but the layer of
earth above it grew green. Yuri splurged on wilted cucumbers and shriveled tomatoes, shipped up the Yenisei River from the mainland. The
mosquitos moved in buzzing clouds. The people of Norilsk who could
fall asleep in the light did so in netting over their beds with the windows wide open as the temperatures settled into balmy. Others stayed
up all night singing, dancing, drinking, and loving until they passed out
in the bright dawn. The wedding season had begun, one ceremony after
another. Couples posed outside the Department of Public Services after
the *rospis v zagse*, the official civil ceremony, releasing white doves into the
sky.

Anya wondered what happened to the doves when winter came. They
had one brief, magnificent season. She imagined their wings freezing, the
doves dying midflight and crashing down somewhere over the taiga. She
used to fear the polar nights, to worry that the sun might never return,
but when the summer came, it seemed the sun would never go away. She
ran her finger along the scars on her heel. The stitches had been removed,
leaving raised red lines in a starburst pattern. She spent half the day at
the gym doing conditioning and stretching, working bars with her brace

and a weight around her good ankle. Anatoly barely spoke to her other than to yell at her to work harder.

Marta shocked them all by bringing in paints and paper for their study time. It seemed summer mania had no limits. Anya painted rose bells, those showy deep pink pasque flowers that lit up the tundra. She filled whole pages with the yellow-centered blooms. Masha painted a dour black tree. Karolina slinked out of the room when Sergei stuck his head in and said it was massage time.

After practice Anya met up with Sveta at the battered playground near school. They slid headfirst down the rusty slide and stood on swings, pumping so high their feet caught air at the top. Anya tested the limits of her ankle. The girls walked on their hands over wet dirt.

"Do you think he'll marry Irina?" Sveta asked. She wore scuffed plastic boots with shorts.

"I don't know," Anya said. "Probably."

"Would you call her Mama?"

Anya threw a pebble at her.

"Maybe she'll have a baby. I bet she wants one," Sveta said.

"Isn't she too old?" Anya asked. It had never occurred to her that this was a possibility. Irina was around her father's age, thirty-five.

"Viktor's mother had a baby last year, and she's forty-six."

"I don't want to think about it," Anya said.

Sveta ran and did an aerial, easily making the cartwheel without touching her hands. It was as if time slowed when she was in the air. Anya felt awe and sadness converge in her.

"That was perfect," Anya said.

"I taught myself at school when we were supposed to be running laps."

"I can't do an aerial without putting my hands down. Do it again."

Sveta stood and threw another aerial. It was light and high and pure. A body in flight. That was what Anya loved about being a gymnast; she was not rooted to the ground like everyone else. It was a secret power she knew she had gotten from her mother. If only Anatoly could see Sveta, he would have to change his mind. Anya stopped herself from saying it out loud. There were rules, even if they didn't make sense.

"They're teaching us a song in school. To perform for the District

Director." Sveta started singing in a mock-serious voice: *"In our Norilsk there is frost with snowstorms, in our Norilsk, there are blizzardy weeks, but everyone is in love with their city, and friendship is our sacred law!"* She marched around the playground.

Anya collapsed laughing on the ground. "In love with Norilsk?"

"You laughed! Where'd your storm cloud go? Let me teach it to you."

They linked arms and sang the beginning together.

"You should come sing with us!"

Anya stopped and felt a well open up in her chest.

"I don't think so," Anya said. "But it will be fun. You're lucky."

"My mother says you are the lucky one." Sveta swiped at her nose. She was ragged, her shirt dirty, her shorts too small. *"There is no heart more luminous and hot, and no smile more warm and bright, than of northern people, than of Norilskites,"* she sang.

"I think the coach Sergei and one of the old gymnasts are screwing," Anya said. She still didn't know exactly what that meant, but she wanted to say it.

Sveta whipped her head around, her eyebrows raised high. Her hair rose up in the breeze, almost silver in the sunlight.

"Are they in love?" she asked.

"It doesn't seem like it. He takes her to the training room and locks the door."

"Do you think your father and Irina do it?"

Anya frowned. That's why they slept on the couch together. "Ew," she said. "I don't ever want to do that."

"Me either," Sveta said. "Unless I fall in love with someone handsome who wants to take me to America."

Anya flicked her eyes to two women on the bench smoking and watching their toddlers.

"Careful," Anya said, her voice low.

"My father sits at the kitchen table all day long and stares out the window. My mother has to trade sewing for milk." Sveta bounded up the ladder of the slide. "I want to live bigger," she said, holding her hands wide. "You get to. I want to too."

* * *

Vera had awakened from a dream that left her worried about Anya. She hadn't seen the girl much since the accident. How stupid she had been to ask Anya to show off. Now she was afraid Yuri had deemed her unsafe. First Katerina, now Anya.

When the sun stayed up, and summer wrested the Arctic away from itself, Vera's body remembered the summer forty years before without her even thinking about it. Her heart lurched erratically, dread and fear like gravel through her veins. Why couldn't it be the sunlit memories of the three of them that would come to her when the weather grew warm, chess across the bright kitchen table, picnics on the banks of the Volkhov, Ilya coming up behind her with his hands on her waist, Pytor catching frogs. The ordinary, wonderful things.

They had been shuttled from the Leningrad prison where they had been held, and loaded up in a cattle car heading east, bodies pressed together wearing layers of clothes, all they had, despite the sticky heat. The smell like a hog barn. They were pigs, snuffling and stinking and shitting in the pen. A hole was cut in the floor for a toilet. An old man held up his black wool coat as a curtain. They got one mug of water per day. Sixty grams of bread in the morning. The bargaining that would mark the next ten years of her life set in. Should she eat, ravenous as she was, all at once, or try to save some for later? Should she give her bread to Pyotr, her sensitive boy, but risk dying and leaving him alone? Ilya sucked on a few crumbs until they dissolved in his mouth. Prison had rendered him near mute. His hands shook. He stooped like he was seventy, not forty. He gave the rest of his bread to Vera and Pyotr. But her hunger was stronger than her compassion. She took the bread and placed it in her mouth with trembling fingers. They had no illusions about survival. Some would make it, some would not. "Through work you must earn the forgiveness of the Soviet people," she had been told in the prison.

The train stopped, and a soldier slid open the boxcar door.

"Any dead?" he asked.

No one spoke. They had traveled hundreds of kilometers; outside was nothing but land and sky, barren of human markings. The Soviet Union was more than twenty-two million square kilometers. Vera felt they could have been anywhere, lost in the expanse of territory.

"Mama," Pyotr whispered. He had grown so much the past year they were nearly eye to eye. He pointed to a man facedown in the corner.

"*Tovarishch?*" Vera said. She nudged the man with her toe.

Ilya shook his head for her to be quiet.

"Only us, *lyubimaya moya.* We can only think of us," he said. You didn't want to call attention to yourself.

The soldier pulled the dead man down by his arms and slammed closed the cattle car door. Families murmured but kept to themselves. They were all condemned politics, but most were *kulaki* from the country, prosperous peasants who owned land, and thus enemies of the collective state. They still had mud on their boots. One of the older women cried when they were locked back in, her view of the world taken away.

"I'm sorry you never saw the painting. The Ryabushkin," Ilya said suddenly.

He loved Ryabushkin's *Novgorod Church*, a small oil painting depicting a spare village church on a grassy hill, in a muted palette of green, white, and gray. He'd seen it as a boy. He was to have taken Vera to Leningrad to see it.

"I will see it one day," Vera said. "You will show it to me."

She held his hand to calm its shaking. He was beginning to say goodbye, but she would not accept it. His lips were peeling. The train lurched forward.

"We will see the painting. We will go home again," she whispered, and she believed it.

They rumbled along, east and east and east—thinner, sicker, more despondent. Three more died. But all the way, Vera thought, This is a mistake. We are Soviets, we are Communists. We will forgive them all this and go back to how it was. Someone will intervene. But when the train made its final stop, and she saw the Yenisei River, the port, the rusty cargo steamer groaning against the pier, she felt her hope leak out in one long hiss. Transport. She could see the terror in her son's eyes. In her husband she saw defeat. They were being shipped north, and Vera felt the black fear of falling off into nothing.

The prisoners were moved on board at night and confined in the hold, crude wooden slabs for bunks. Guards threw potato scraps into the darkness, and people pushed and grabbed and fought for them.

Water was lowered in a bucket from the deck. The politicals were in with the criminals, the *urki* and the *vory*, the thieves, rapists, and murderers who took possession of the plank platforms, leaving the others to squeeze onto the dirty floor and the narrow space below the bunks. Pyotr did not complain. Ilya was silent, shrinking, fading. Vera could only think of air and when she might breathe it again. The ship rolled. Some prisoners moaned, some vomited from seasickness, some cried out in anguish. They sailed straight north up the river. Vera could not fathom what awaited them, could not think about this hideous fate for her child. Ilya held her hand in the wretched darkness.

They arrived at Dudinka in northeast Siberia. The prisoners too ill to walk were taken to a makeshift hospital. Ilya leaned heavily on Vera. He would not leave them, despite being wracked with fever, his skin cracking, the hunger gnawing at his sanity.

The convoy guards led the prisoners, politicals and criminals alike, to the small railroad that would deliver them to the industrial complex of Norilsk, newly launched by the Soviet Council of People's Commissars. It was September and already achingly cold this far north, the blue polar gloom settling early.

"Labor in the USSR is a matter of honesty, glory, and valor!" a soldier shouted at them.

Norilsk was pale and wide, lunar. They had reached the top of the earth. At the camp, a series of squat buildings along the lake, they were told they had reached their final destination. A banner was draped over the main gate: WITH AN IRON FIST, WE WILL LEAD HUMANITY TO HAPPINESS! Vera could not comprehend it. Prisoners. Ten years. Doing what? Digging out nickel from the frozen earth? She thought of her father, shot in the woods twenty years earlier.

The men, women, and children were separated into *lagpunkty* in different parts of the *zona*. Vera thought it was just how they would sleep, that they would then be reunited. Her hand on Ilya's cheek—it was the last time she would touch her husband. Her son. Maybe it was better that she didn't know she would never speak to them again.

They were counted and recounted, then taken to the *banya* where Vera and the other women had to take off all their clothes under the gaze of male soldiers. They were washed and their bodies shaved, in order to delouse, to humiliate. Long underwear, a black tunic, quilted outer jacket, a felt hat with earflaps, rubber-soled boots, and fleece-lined mittens. Drab, torn, ill fitting. They became shapeless, colorless figures. Vera's transformation into a *zechka* was complete.

Vera first started telling Katerina about her time in the camp slowly, in bits, until she felt she had to tell her, a compulsion. At the beginning Katerina had put her childlike hand on Vera's arm and said, "The socialist system is the most progressive in the world. How could this be?"

"I don't have an answer," Vera said.

But she knew it wasn't just Stalin, wasn't singular evil run amok. The Gulag was everyone. Those who feared, and those who had power, those who informed and those who stayed quiet, those who thought on some level the prisoners deserved it, even when they knew better, those who laughed and ate and worked with willful ignorance. It was random and calculated, an interlocked puzzle you couldn't solve.

"I don't know how you survived it," Katerina said. She cried openly in those afternoons, Anya bouncing on chubby legs while holding on to a chair, not yet walking.

Vera thought she'd known grief when her father was killed, but after Ilya and Pyotr, she felt she would never climb out of the tar pit of sorrow. She sometimes thought God had turned her heart tough then, encased it with a thick rind, enough to withstand another day. Or that her mere survival was her own form of resistance. Or that people have to suffer to recognize grace when it comes. But Vera also knew what everyone in camp knew. The worm of shame would crawl around but never leave. Because if you survived, you had in some way compromised your very being.

A knock at the door startled her, and Vera sat up straight, her heart beating lumpy and quick, caught as she was in her memory, unsure of where she was in time. Her fingers, old and crooked, resting on the abacus, brought her back. She took a rattled breath. I'm still here, she thought.

It was Anya. Vera felt relief full and heavy.

"*Dorogaya*," she said, opening the door. She hugged the girl so hard and long Anya coughed and laughed. Protect this child, Vera thought, at once overwhelmed by how no one is safe in the stark and brutal world.

"I have missed you, Vera Vasilievna!"

She limped in with surprising agility on her wrapped ankle, her hair wind whipped, cheeks flushed, and Vera saw a trace of Katerina there.

Anya did a full turn on her good foot.

"No more demonstrations," Vera said.

"They took the stitches out," Anya said.

They went to the kitchen. Anya poured milk into a small glass as Vera filled the teapot.

"You are going back to practice soon?"

"To the gym? I never left it."

Vera turned to Anya. It was incomprehensible that this wounded child was allowed no rest, but it wasn't.

"They didn't let you recuperate?"

Anya shrugged. "There is no time for that."

Vera felt her worry for the girl return; a tightness gripped her shoulders. If only Katerina were still here. Vera knew it hadn't been suicide; Katerina had been too full of curiosity and feelings and love. "Anya is like one of my organs growing outside my body," she had said. And yet she had wanted more, hadn't she? She had yearned for a different life.

One of the last times Vera saw her, Katerina had sighed and sat on the sofa in that graceful way of hers, folding herself up small. She sipped her tea and laughed a little.

"What is it?" Vera asked. "What's funny?"

"I saw a radish today at the market," she said.

"That is funny," Vera teased.

"It was so lovely, Vera Vasilievna. Crimson, cerise? How can something be that color? I cried." She smiled and scrunched her face, embarrassed by her showy emotion. "Imagine, crying at a root."

"There is still beauty," Vera said. "Even here."

"I danced yesterday. In the apartment. I put my hair up in a high French rolled bun the way Zakharov liked, powdered my face, put on red lipstick. I don't have any of my old costumes, but I have a tutu. I tied the ribbons of my last pair of *pointe* shoes across my ankles. I wanted to dance in a different way than I ever can at the ballet school, to feel that again. You can't imagine the exquisite pain of my feet when I went *en pointe*. And my *fouetté* turns were just horrid. As the black swan I used to transform into a spinning top! But my *pirouettes* were not terrible. I could have done *pirouettes* for hours without coming down from my toe."

Katerina set down her tea and held her arms out in front of her in first position, rounded so her fingertips almost touched.

"It's like being a marionette," she said. "Imagine invisible strings holding everything up while you turn on one foot, holding that center line. You have to believe you are weightless."

"I would love to see you dance," Vera said.

Katerina smiled and shook her head.

"It was silly. I put everything back in a box in the closet. I could never tell Yuri. It would worry him. But I miss it so. I know I'm too old for the stage. But to be around it, the spectacle and excitement. Creating something beautiful like that. I get letters from him from time to time."

It was such a strange turn, and Vera felt something new and heavy in the atmosphere between them.

"Letters from whom?" Vera asked.

"Zakharov. The choreographer. I was his muse, you know. He's still at the Bolshoi. He knows people all over the world."

"Do you write him back?"

"Yes. From the ballet school. It's where I get his letters. So it looks official."

"What are you saying, Katerina Vladimirovna?" Vera had asked.

"I don't know," she had answered.

Now here was Anya in front of her without a mother. The girl bounced in her seat, unable to sit still. She tried to point the toes of her taped foot. She tapped her finger against the window and drew a small heart in the condensation.

"I was afraid you wouldn't come back. To see me," Vera said.

"I like coming to see you."

"I know, but your father?"

Anya shrugged. "He doesn't blame you."

In the year following Katerina's disappearance, Vera expected Yuri to appear at her door, looking for answers, accusing even, wanting to know what they had talked about all those afternoons. What would she tell him, what would she withhold? But he never came, instead arranging care for Anya without mentioning Katerina at all. He had been such a red-faced enthusiast, resettling in Norilsk voluntarily, so perhaps he didn't want to know how far his wife had wandered away from believing.

"I almost forgot." Vera rose from her chair and reached for a tin up in the cupboard. She opened the lid and shook the candies wrapped to look like strawberries. "For you. But first, 352 times 8."

There were moments Vera forgot herself when Anya was around. A fleeting lightness, what it felt like not to be lonesome.

"Can I use the *schyoty*?"

Vera shook her head and tapped her temple.

Anya worked for a while, biting her top lip.

Vera pretended to nod off and snore, which made Anya giggle.

"Okay, okay," she said. "2,816?"

"Are you asking me?"

"2,816."

"Good girl." She held out the candies.

During the camp years, loneliness had been an indulgence. Bodies pressed close in the barracks shared bedbugs and foul exhalations. They exposed their tired flesh in the *banya* and were given a cup of water and a sliver of mean-smelling soap. Vera could still recall the shapes of sharp hips and sagging breasts, and the fishy smell of their filth. (The *klikusha*, that bewitched old woman who shrieked in hysteria, was dragged out and never seen again.) They labored shoulder to exhausted shoulder clearing snow in work brigades, collapsing into haunted sleep pressed next to those same bodies. Forced proximity was its own form of intimacy.

But now loneliness was a leaden presence, a shapeless form that sat on the opposite chair: memories, grief, desire, contentment—they were all in there somewhere. Decades of living alone had winnowed human interactions to a minimum.

"It's so good," Anya said, a candy knocking against her teeth. "Anatoly would not be happy to see me eating sweets."

"I am happy to see you eating sweets."

At the beginning, in the early days after Vera had been released, Ledorsky once came and sat on her sofa and drank tea, and they tried to talk—he had been let out soon after she had. She asked him, in stilted formality, about his work as a naturalist—"Are you a taxonomist, then?" "Well, yes, I suppose in some ways, but I'm primarily a biologist." "Ah,

I see."—and he would ask her about Novgorod. "I believe the Germans destroyed many of the old buildings. I hope they spared the cathedral," he said. "Yes, yes, it made it through," she answered. But conversation was halting and painful and strange. It was impossible not to talk about the camp; that was what they shared. Each knew what the other had done to make it through, holding up a mirror to each other's shame by merely being present.

Anya unwrapped another strawberry candy.

"Did Ledorsky really have a polar bear in his apartment?" Vera asked.

"Yes. It was a baby. He kept it alive," Anya said. "Sveta and I petted it even. It went to a zoo. In Perm."

Even though they lived in the same building, Vera hadn't seen Ledorsky in many years. After the long-ago visit, she avoided him. He had tried to talk with her a handful of times. Once at the market, he waited for her to finish her transaction with that expectant look he had, but she had waved and quickly walked the other way. Another time he left her a loaf of fresh bread with a note inviting her to tea. She never responded. She just couldn't bear it. Sometimes, though, she imagined interrogating him.

"Who did you tell on?"

"I did what I had to do."

"You were one of the *pridurki*."

"I agreed to tell the operative commander if I heard about plots. I never told on anyone."

"Of course not."

"I was a collaborator. I admit it. And what about you, Vera Vasilievna. Shall we talk about what you did to survive?"

CHAPTER 10

Anya was doing push-away kips on the bars the following week when Dr. Bazhanov appeared at the gym. He wore a tracksuit and carried a black bag. She recoiled at the sight of him but followed him to the training room, unhappy that Anatoly wasn't coming with them. Bazhanov closed the door and lifted Anya up onto the massage table, his hands lingering too long, moving down her torso. She stopped breathing until he took his hands away.

"Lie down," he said.

Anya kept her eyes on the door. She could hear the pounding of the springboard as the girls vaulted, yet she felt far removed, imprisoned. He untied her brace and unwrapped her ankle, his hands, all of a sudden, quick and efficient.

"It's okay almost. We'll keep it taped."

It did not look okay, still bruised and swollen. Her foot felt floppy, unsecured. He didn't ask how it felt; she knew it didn't matter.

He pulled a large syringe from his bag and filled it with clear liquid from a vial.

"This will hurt for only a moment."

He jammed it into her ankle. Anya bit into her cheek, tears running into her hair.

"You don't want to take it easy for too long, you know. You're already starting to get soft," he said, prodding her thigh with his finger.

Bazhanov smiled, and then he ran his hands down her front, insistent in their searching, without hurry. He kneaded her hips. She thought about the doves and their frozen wings.

"Everything's in place, good working order," he said.

Anya pressed her lips together, her body a plank of wood.

"You come see me each week. Yes? Do you know I've known Larisa Latynina for many years?"

Whether he knew the coach of the national team or not, Anya felt the cold clench of a threat.

"You don't want to disappoint your coach. I'll help you get better, maybe even put a word in with Latynina. And you can help me in return. Be good and quiet. *Usluga za uslugu.*"

Anya sat up and swung her legs off the table. Her ankle throbbed, but she could now roll it without pain.

"Stop scowling," he said. "You mess up your pretty face." He chuckled. "You're a feisty one. No wonder he likes you."

She emerged into the gym without looking back. She locked her arms across her chest and limped out with her head down. She felt like her body was streaked with dirt.

"Anya," Anatoly called.

She didn't answer, and she would not look at him. He crossed over to her and stood, waiting. He flicked his eyes to the door.

"What?" he asked, his voice uncharacteristically quiet.

She cleared her throat, rubbed her nose.

"The doctor said you are ready?"

"He said, '*Usluga za uslugu.*'" She met her coach's eyes and looked down at her feet. A favor for a favor. It's all she could say of it to him.

He looked hard at her face, and she saw a flicker of understanding in the squint of his eyes, a softening.

"I don't want to see him again," she said.

He lit a cigarette and blew smoke to the ceiling in a fierce exhale.

"Okay," he said.

Anya stepped gingerly on her foot; she couldn't feel her ankle at all. She jumped up and landed, tried again.

"We start slow today," he said.

She shook her head.

"No. I'm ready."

* * *

There was never decent meat in Norilsk, and like everywhere else in the Soviet Union, there was never enough. The butcher on Leninskiy Prospekt was rich even though he was rarely open—he sold meat on the black market to bureaucrats—and when he was open there was often little more than soup bones to be had. There were times when Yuri turned to *tushonka*, the stewed canned meat for soldiers, but that was almost worse than no meat at all. He waited behind fourteen women and pensioners, including Vera, close to the front. Her face was a terrain of deep creases and prominent bones, her body shrunken but upright, her chin straight and steady. She did not talk to anyone. He had been wary about how much time Katerina spent with her, as if Vera were some sort of *Baba Yaga* in her turning, chicken-legged hut. He sent Anya to her partly to prove that he didn't harbor any ill will toward the old woman. But that didn't mean he didn't fear her in some small way, for what she might know about his wife.

Soviets were used to being hungry. The famine in 1932 had killed millions. His father had insisted it was because the *kulaki* burned their crops and killed their livestock instead of supporting the country with collectivization. Then came the cursed war years when there was nothing to eat, nothing even to ration. Bread lines formed before dawn. Every weed in Moscow was harvested; every mushroom, seed, and berry foraged. Yuri's mother told him she'd traded a clock for a squirrel carcass, baby ferns she'd found near the train station for a cup of moth-infested flour. His father was on the front; everyone was on the front. Mothers fought for potato peels, herring bones, bruised cabbage leaves. Yuri, only an infant, did not remember, of course, but deprivation was the legacy they all bore from that time.

But being used to little didn't stop Yuri from wondering why there was so little now. He tried not to tie this lack to a failure of the political system, but you couldn't blame it on *kulaki* anymore. He knew his full-hearted belief in a better world through socialism had slipped some.

More and more he had to convince himself through cerebral arguments of the things he used to know without doubt. But maybe it had started even before, with Katerina. The brightness that she refused to mute in their dark part of the earth, her steadfastness in picking away at Soviet absolute truths. It was dangerous for someone to want like she did, to have rising expectations.

She said once that Americans seemed happy.

"Americans are weak in spirit," he said. Russians never considered the pursuit of happiness. Pleasure, maybe, but there was no illusion that these were the same thing.

"Maybe because they don't spend their lives waiting in line," she said. "Maybe it's as simple as that. You can't be happy waiting in line. Waiting breeds melancholy. Despair even. Contempt for the people ahead of you. Especially when you know by the time you get to the front there will be nothing there."

Had she always been this way and he hadn't seen it? No, she had walked away from a career as a soloist at the Bolshoi to make a greater sacrifice and become an *udarnik*, a worker of exemplary productivity, like him. She had changed in the last years, and he had tried to ignore it, tried to steer her back on course with a refusal to engage in her troublesome lines of inquiry. Maybe it was no longer being able to dance that had changed her, or the poetry, or getting older, or becoming a mother, or maybe it was simply all the darkness of Norilsk.

* * *

After an hour Vera reached the front of the line. She had to hold on to the counter, the bones in her feet aching from standing so long. She bought a *kolbasa* and 250 grams of rib steak, blowing her allotment of rubles for the month. She wanted to make a decadent stroganoff with fried potatoes, even if she didn't have much of an appetite anymore. The *kolbasa*, paired with butter and bread, would last for weeks. She wished Anya would come cook with her, but she knew the girl trained all the time. How could her father have given her up, she sometimes thought, even while knowing the reasons were not simple, that he believed he was doing the right thing. And maybe he was. Anya was different, she knew that, like her mother. Her duty was to use her athletic gifts for the glory of them all. Or so they were supposed to believe.

Pyotr would have been fifty years old. "Don't cry, Mama," he had said, as he lay smashed against her on the squalid floor of the transport ship. "It's a mistake. We'll be home before my birthday."

She took her brown paper bundle and glimpsed Yuri farther back in the line. His face looked puffy and ashen, his red beard flecked with gray. He had been a glittering-eyed young man when she'd first met him all those years ago, robust, vigorous in his idealism. Now he looked as worn as everyone else.

"Did you believe in God when you were in the camp?" Katerina had asked her.

"I did."

"But he didn't help you."

"God does not work that way, I learned."

"When your husband died? When your son?"

"Of course I doubted," Vera said.

"I could never believe if something happened to Anya."

Vera knew Katerina didn't talk to Yuri about such things. Katerina would come to Vera's apartment, a conspiratorial hand on Vera's arm, ready, always ready, to have some sort of hushed discussion.

"Did you ever think of trying to escape?" she asked.

"There was nowhere to go," Vera said. "You couldn't go to town; you'd be turned in immediately. They didn't even need the barbed wire. There was the camp, and the mining pits, and the empty wilderness."

"Did you ever think it might be better to say good-bye, even if you were to die?"

"I thought it many times. But I always came back to Ilya and Pyotr and feeling like I owed them to make it through."

Vera used to weigh which was better: To remember or forget? To dig up or let lie? She decided that not to tell anyone about the camp would be a form of forgetting, or a form of forgiveness she was not willing to bestow. Old dark things should be remembered, had to be acknowledged. She was not ashamed of having been a prisoner, and she trusted Katerina more than anyone else. But even to Katerina she could not tell everything.

Vera stopped next to Yuri.

"You're almost to the front," she said.

"Vera Vasilievna," he said. "You were successful?"

She held up her parcel of meat.

"I have been thinking about stroganoff," she said. "We used to have it when I was a girl. '*Povar, povar, ya khochu stroganov!*' we would chant while tugging on the cook's skirt." Vera smiled. "Sometimes she would oblige us. She was from the Crimea. She used a lot of bay leaves."

"A different time." Yuri gave her a tight smile, and she knew it made him uncomfortable, even now, her wanton talk of her upper-class, halcyon childhood.

"I miss your Anya," she said.

"Yes," Yuri said. "I do too. She is training all hours now. For the competition."

"She has such a talent," Vera said. "Her mother would have loved it, don't you think? To see her flying through the air."

He looked at her and then away, eyes unable to settle. Vera wondered if he would ever ask, or if the fear of what he might find out outweighed the ache of not knowing. He was next in line.

"I miss your Katerina too," she said. But if he heard her, he pretended that he hadn't and shuffled forward toward the glass case with what remained of the gristly meat.

Vera's thoughts returned to Katerina. "I could never say good-bye to Anya," she had said. "But sometimes I want to say good-bye to all the rest of it." She had flicked her wrist, with that familiar jingle of her bracelet, looking graceful even in her disdain.

"Is this about the choreographer?" Vera asked.

"He talks about the old days. And the Bolshoi now. Life in Moscow."

"You miss that life."

Katerina smiled quick and bright.

"He has invited me to Moscow. He can arrange it. A state-approved visit for the Bolshoi anniversary celebration."

"Have you told Yuri?"

"No," she said flatly. "I could never tell him. Even if it were just a visit. He wouldn't understand."

"Katerina Vladimirovna." Vera dropped her voice. "And if it were not just a visit?"

"Zakharov can't come out and say it, of course," Katerina said. "But to go somewhere else. To run away. Balanchine is Russian after all. There are ways."

It frightened Vera to hear her talk this way. She knew too well the consequences if Katerina were to be found out.

"It is tempting. To be someone again. I know I shouldn't think that way. I know it's selfish. Individualistic." Katerina spun her bracelet around her wrist, her eyes focused inward. "But I mattered then, Vera Vasilievna."

"You matter now." Vera reached over and placed her hand on Katerina's. "You have Anya."

* * *

Summer was long behind them. Anatoly and Anya worked from seven in the morning until six at night. They were inseparable. There was no denying that Anatoly only cared about Anya in the gym. The other girls gave her withering looks. Even Masha stuck out her tongue at her. Madame came in every day to correct Anya's form, her lightness, her presentation.

"Stretch your legs, higher, finalize on both feet, bigger extension, tense your *yagoditsy*, straighten your feet, don't rush. Show every move. Present, present, present." She whacked her pointing stick against the wall as punctuation. Eva, the accompanist, cleared her throat and started again.

Anatoly spent a lot of time huddled with Sergei or on the phone in the office.

The competition would be compulsory routines, not high in difficulty but needing to be technically perfect; everyone in her age group would be performing the same elements, with no room for error.

"The representative will be there, I have been assured," he said.

"Who is it?" Sergei asked.

"I don't know him. He's a coach, reports to Latynina. But he is looking at the juniors."

"Ozero Krugloye?" Round Lake was the national training center outside Moscow.

"Eventually. Junior team. He's looking to select future candidates for Master of Sport of the USSR. This competition would qualify her."

"And you, Anatoly Grigorovich?"

"Yes. It gets me there too," he said.

Anya could do all the necessary skills. On beam: connected back walkovers, cartwheel, press handstand, full turn, cartwheel back tuck dismount. On bars: kip cast handstand, front hip circle, back hip circle, bar beat, flyaway dismount. On floor: round-off back handspring back tuck, aerial, front handspring front tuck. On vault: front handspring. The more difficult tricks they'd been working on she would have to keep in her pocket for later.

Anya felt attuned to her body in a new, precise way. Slight variations in angles, rotation, distance, she could sense immediately. She relished the feeling of control, of getting better. Her ankle swelled in practice, but she ignored it, taped it tighter. Anatoly kept his word; Dr. Bazhanov had not returned. A nurse from the clinic gave her a weekly shot so the pain felt far away.

"Your switch leap is low," Anatoly barked at her.

"It's not," Anya said. She knew herself, knew she was right.

"Excuse me?"

"I can see it in the mirror. I'm hitting 180 degrees."

"I don't care what you see. It's what I see that matters. Who is in charge?"

And before she could check herself she said, "I am."

Sergei chuckled. The other girls in the gym went silent.

"Leave the gym now or I will throw you against the wall," Anatoly said.

Anya looked at him to gauge his seriousness, and then lowered her eyes.

"I'm sorry," she said.

"Go," he said.

She walked to the edge of the floor toward the door, but then she saw Marta, who motioned her into the office.

"Sit," she said. "Close the door."

Marta wore her gray hair parted down the middle and pulled tight in a small ponytail. She took a drag off a cigarette and tapped the ashes into a mug. Anya fidgeted with a thread on her old leotard, waiting to be spoken to. Bulging water-logged ledgers, the paper inside thickened and wavy, were stacked against the wall under a pipe filmed with condensation.

"Anya Yurievna," Marta said, looking over her glasses. "You're having difficulty?"

Anya wanted to answer no, she wasn't having difficulty; it was Anatoly who was wrong. She looked at her lap.

"Did you know I was a gymnast?" Marta asked.

Anya looked up, eyes opened wide. It was hard to imagine Marta had ever been young enough. A piece of ash landed on her shelflike bosom.

"In the late forties," she said. "We didn't flip like you do now. It was classical." She pointed her hand out with dramatic, balletic fingers. "Lyricism, expressiveness, femininity. We took it very seriously. Embodying what it meant to be Soviet. Do you know what they used to tell us? 'The Soviet woman is confident but modest, ambitious yet self-sacrificial, heroic yet vulnerable, strong yet weak.' And we were supposed to show that in our routines." She laughed, coughing smoke.

"Did you compete in the Olympics?" Anya asked.

She shook her head. "That didn't start until 1952, Latynina's time."

"The coach," Anya said.

"She's not just a coach. She's the highest officer of the national team. She favors the classical style, Tourischeva over Korbut. You know what they say about those two? Tourischeva lives to win; Korbut lives to amaze. What do you think the state values more?"

Anya held her arms across her chest. Korbut was daring, exciting. A natural flipper, like she was. "Korbut is the better gymnast."

Marta shrugged. "Things are changing, Anya Yurievna, but this is the Soviet Union after all. Change is a glacier. Larisa Latynina is not shy in her opposition to the more athletic gymnasts."

"Is that what I am?"

"You are part of the new school. It's a wave coming. Anatoly knows it. But it is a dance, no? You have to bend some to the way things are." She stubbed out her cigarette and exhaled the last of the smoke before she began again. "Your father used to be on the City Party Executive Committee."

Anya was confused by Marta's sudden change of subject, but she knew there was danger in it. She felt the hair on her neck rise.

"Your mother was independent in her thinking."

Anya knew her father had been dismissed without explanation from the Committee, had heard him lamenting with Irina. But she'd never imagined it had something to do with her mother. She thought of Sveta, whom she hadn't seen in weeks, derailed by her father's actions. There would be no sports school for her now or ever. No amount of skill or practice would give her a chance.

"There are half a million gymnasts in the Soviet Union to take your place, Anya Yurievna. Work on your switch leaps."

* * *

Yuri pulled the lever to raise the canvas from the water. The copper sulfate, copper salt, was crystalline bright indigo, beautiful, toxic, corrosive. He wished it weren't so dark in the boiler room so he could see that color emerge from the dirty water. It was time for exercise. He had been Anya's age when he started gymnastics at Dynamo, quick and strong and with too much energy for his mother to deal with. Now he could barely touch his toes, his lungs hurt, he felt used up. He had fifteen years before he was fifty and could retire and wait in the vodka line with his pension.

A woman's voice came over the loudspeaker. "Your Motherland calls for you to be ready for work and defense!"

The health and vigor program meant daily exercise at the plant. Prime condition equaled greater productivity. Be strong, be fast, be educated, be intelligent, be proud, and be free. Yuri held out his hand to see if there was still a shake. He pinched the bridge of his nose, the pain dull and throbbing as though a stone were lodged there just behind the bone. He had told Irina that when the summer was over, he would try to drink less. It was an easy promise when the sun was high and summer held them in its bacchanalian grip, when it wiped out their memory of the rest of the year, and they gorged on jewel-red lingonberries the *babushki* had missed on the steppe, so tart they made his eyes water. Summer had barreled in with its show of heat and light and life, but by August, the northern plants turned scarlet, russet, and gold almost overnight.

There was no denying the first hard frost of autumn, winter at its heels.

"*Beryozka!*" called the voice. "Hold for one minute!"

Yuri grabbed his square of carpet and rose into a candlestick position, on his back with his legs straight up in the air.

"*Bochka!*"

He rolled down and held his knees in a barrel roll. Five, four, three, two, one.

"*Koshka!*"

He turned over to his hands and knees and arched his back like a cat. The other workers around him all did the same movements. No one dared otherwise. It was assumed you were always being watched in some way, by the boss, by the state, or by a worker envious of some commendation bestowed on you for productivity. Besides, it was duty. Yuri hollowed his back. Arch hollow. Arch hollow. It felt good, he had to admit, to move his body. To stretch.

"*Nasos!*"

He stood and bent his torso to the left and to the right, like the pump of an old fire engine. In the years Katerina had been gone, he had been stuck, inert, getting old, watching life, drinking to dull everything. Irina told him it was time for a change, and she was right.

Before the first frost, he and Irina had gone looking for carnivorous butterwort growing in the moist tundra, searching the ground for those flowers like violets atop straight, bare stalks. They hiked up, the air thin. Irina led the way. She reached her hand back for his to pull him along. They stopped to catch their breath. Irina broke off a branch from the carcass of a spindly tree.

"Do you think she's dead?" she asked.

He wished it didn't always come back to this, but how could it not? Of course he thought Katerina was dead. To imagine her alive would require something magical, some narrative that curved up and out into a universe of possibility. Irrational hope. A daydream. Was it an accident of some kind? Suicide? Murder, even? He couldn't play it out, couldn't discern which seemed more likely, or less horrible. Each scenario offered a bad death, too soon, before, the old *babushki* believed, the time God had assigned. Each brought its own unique sadness. If he started committing to one—surely it was an accident and she slipped and fell into the sea—he would start to think, But, wait, what about how she dwelled on bad things and refused to accept the way things were? What if she did something to herself? And then he would switch to another story, and then another.

"Yes," he said at last. "I do."

"There," Irina said, pointing to three purple flowers.

When he looked at her now, he saw the young Irina disguised as the older Irina, her eyes still big and blue behind her glasses, her face glowing from exertion and fresh air. She crouched down next to the plant. She had come to collect the leaves, which she would use to curdle milk into fermented *varanets*. As they watched, a mosquito landed, its legs quickly stuck to the gooey surface of the leaf.

Butterwort caught insects on its leaves and then digested them. The mosquito thrashed about and triggered the secretion of enzymes. The leaf, now smelling like a foul fungus, curled in closer toward its trapped prey.

"It's hard with Anya," Yuri said. "When is a good time to say I think your mother is dead?"

Irina took her glasses off and set them in the curls on top of her head to get a closer look at the butterwort and the insect body being broken down for its nitrogen.

"My mother came down with diphtheria when I was thirteen," she said. "It was a sore throat at first. She was tired. Her voice got so hoarse I had to lean in close, but the smell of her breath made me gag. I felt awful about that. I would come home from school and tend to her. My father stayed at the university later and later. A rumor started in the building that my mother had died. I went around and knocked on every door to tell them that she wasn't dead. One day I came home and she was not in her bed. My father said she'd gone away. He wouldn't say she died. So even though I knew she was dead, since he wouldn't put words to it, there was a little sliver of my brain that thought: maybe, just maybe."

The mosquito was a lifeless bit of wing and husk. The butterwort leaf began to flatten out again.

"It might be good for her," she said. "Not to wonder."

Practical Irina. Yuri knew she was talking about him anyway. You could not destroy your past or what it does to you, he knew. It's never really over. But you could name it and put it off to the side.

"Irina Igorevna," he said. "I love you." It was the first time he had said it, and although he felt the reach in his words, he did, just then, believe it.

* * *

It was dark when Anya emerged from the gym. She walked across the street to the bus stop and stood beneath its battered overhang. She held her coat closed with her hand, the zipper broken, her feet in boots without socks. There was no denying fall. The sun was weak, the days rapidly growing short, the air arriving in biting gusts. A rusted car putt-putted by, spewing exhaust in her face. Her ankle throbbed in its tape cast, her lower back was sore, her arms were quivery, a tendon in her thigh was pulled taut, and her neck was stuck so she couldn't turn her head very well to the right. She leaned against one of the metal supports, cold through the fabric of her coat. Exhaustion was just how it was. It was necessary. Gymnastics, doing well, was her job, her way to serve her country. But she didn't need encouragement. This was who she was now and what she wanted. Higher, faster, stronger.

Down the block there was a loud clang, like a rock hurled against metal, then laughter, shoes scuffling against the pavement. *Bezprizorniki* most likely, the rough street kids who got by however they could. Stealing, robbing, or begging. Imprisoned parents or drunk parents or violent parents or no parents. There was one *detskiy dom* in Norilsk, but everyone knew the institution was full of horror and the children housed there were dead-eyed or crazy. She had seen street kids sleeping in the stairwell of the school once, piled together for warmth. They looked like a nest of shivering mice.

Anya straightened up, the voices coming closer. From the low light a group of them emerged, boys older than she was, their hair buzzed unevenly, pants torn, coats filthy. They shouted and shoved each other, sniffing rags soaked in turpentine.

"Meow, *kotik*," one yelled at her.

Anya shoved her hands into her pockets. She couldn't tell how many of them there were.

"Out here alone, huh?" one asked.

"I got something for you," another said.

But then from the back of the group there was a girl's laugh, high, silvery.

Anya saw her hair first, that blond so light it almost glowed in the evening darkness. Sveta wore her same pair of shorts, tight with a threadbare hole the size of a kopek, and a big olive-green jacket with sleeves hanging down past her hands. She had grown taller over the summer. She looked older.

"Ah, Anya!" She hugged her and then punched one of the boys hard in the arm. "Leave her be."

Up close Anya could see the edge of Sveta's nose was pink and inflamed. She smelled like paint thinner, her hair a tangled thicket. She had crossed a border to somewhere Anya didn't belong, didn't feel welcome. Anya felt a lonely wave of guilt; she had done the same to Sveta with gymnastics.

"Are you taking the bus?" Anya asked. She knew the answer but thought maybe she could will Sveta away from these boys. She wanted to go back to when they were little, cartwheeling together just for fun.

"This is the famous gymnast," Sveta said. But the boys had already moved on, walking in the middle of the street, honked at by an oncoming car. "Wait," she yelled, "*zasranets!*" It was a crude curse Anya had only ever heard men say. "Bye-bye, Anya. I miss you." Sveta kissed Anya on the cheek with her parched lips and then flitted off, her bare legs skinny and white.

"Sveta Nikolaevna!" Anya called. One of the boys mimicked her from far away. She could see the headlights of the bus.

Her father liked to say Russians were strong, clever, and resourceful. But what if you were all those things and it was not enough? There was always *byt*, the circumstances of their lives: waiting in lines, not having enough money, being cold, saying the wrong thing, being listened in on, informed on, fighting neighbors, small apartments, unpredictably stocked store shelves, ugly shoes, vodka, darkness—all *byt*. Some were hit harder than others. She and Sveta had been the same, and now they had bent off the trajectory in opposite directions.

Anya wondered, Who gets to be lucky?

CHAPTER 11

Surgut was more than 1,100 kilometers from Norilsk through the impassable taiga, so Anya and Anatoly would be flown on a transport plane out of the Alykel airstrip west of town. There was no room for Yuri, not that he would have been allowed anyway.

"A state mission," Yuri said. "It's an honor."

"I know, Papa. But I want you to be there." She didn't ask why he couldn't come; it was the way things were.

"Are you nervous?"

"No," she said. "Yes. A little. Have you ever been in an airplane?"

"No, not me. But your mother flew to Prague once with the Bolshoi. She said her favorite part was being with the sun above the clouds."

Anya opened up the small, floppy-buckled vinyl suitcase, light brown, borrowed from Irina. It smelled like mildew and plastic. She had never packed before, never had reason to.

"What do I take with me?" Anya wanted to ask a million things, but this was all she could manage. Now that the day had finally arrived it seemed she was leaving everything familiar forever.

"Your leotard. Some clothes. I don't know. Who will do your hair for the competition?"

"I can do it okay. Marta showed me how."

"I wish I had a sweat suit for you."

"One of those blue ones with 'CCCP' on the front?"

Yuri smiled. "Soon enough, *Dochka.*"

She pulled underpants and socks from her drawer.

"*Raz, dva, tri, chetyre, pyat,*" he sang. The beginning of a nursery rhyme her mother would sing and act out with her hands.

"*Vyshel zaichik pogulyat,*" she added, curving her fingers like bunny ears.

Anya felt her mother rush through her like a hot wind, and then she was gone, her absence hanging heavily in the room. It was cold in the apartment, yellow cones of light around the lamps.

"It's only for a few days," Yuri said. His voice got fuzzy, and she was afraid he might cry. He finished the vodka in his glass and rose to fill it again in the kitchen. "How is your ankle?" he called back.

Anya looked at it. It hurt most of the time, made a crunching sound sometimes when she landed on it, but now it was numb. The woman from the clinic had given her a shot that morning.

"Fine," she said.

Yuri came back in with his glass in one hand and a billowy white ribbon in the other.

"Irina picked it out. For your hair."

Anya saw herself from afar with the big white ribbon fanned out at the nape of her neck. It seemed she was seeing another girl. For a moment she had a hard time catching her breath.

"You don't have to wear it," he said.

"No, I love it. It will make me look like a real gymnast. Thank her for me."

Yuri smiled and smoothed her face with his hand.

"You are already a real gymnast," he said. "*Vsegda gotov.*"

"Always ready," she said.

* * *

It was past ten but Vera wasn't tired. She sat on her bed holding the icon and brushed her hand across the Virgin's face. How long would she live? she wondered. One year? Five? She was not frightened by it; she would see Ilya and Pyotr again.

"Do you think poetry can drive one mad, Vera Vasilievna?" Katerina had asked.

"Life can drive one mad," Vera had said.

"I read Tsvetaeva, and I feel all twisted up. It's like some kind of code. The answer to something. But it's dangerous too. I know it is. It upsets Yuri when I try to talk to him about it."

She closed her eyes and recited:

> *Your name is a——bird in my hand,*
> *a piece of ice on my tongue.*
> *The lips' quick opening.*
> *Your name——four letters.*
> *A ball caught in flight,*
> *a silver bell in my mouth.*

Katerina held her elbows in her hands. Vera felt coldness in her center, worry for this creature. Someone would notice Katerina's difference, overhear her saying something. The dreaded knock on the door.

"She killed herself," Katerina said. "Tsvetaeva."

"I know," Vera said. "I met her daughter in the transport camp. Ariadna. Dark hair and heavy eyes. Not unlike your Anya."

Katerina sunk back into the couch and exhaled. Anya played with her doll in a patch of sunlight near the window.

"Her mother had put her and her sister in a state orphanage during the famine, hoping that would save them. She removed Ariadna when she got sick. But her sister later died there of starvation."

"What punishment for a mother," Katerina said. "Not that I need to tell you that."

Vera nodded. She hadn't thought about Ariadna in many years. They had spent two days together waiting to be assigned, and then they were sent to different *lagpunkti*. She never saw her again.

"Why was she there?" Katerina asked.

"Her fiancé turned NVKD informer. She was arrested with her father for espionage. He was executed. She got fifteen years."

Katerina murmured:

> *A stone thrown into a silent lake*
> *is——the sound of your name.*

The light click of hooves at night
—your name.
Your name at my temple
—sharp click of a cocked gun.

Katerina had always been a tiny woman, but it was as if she was becoming smaller, her wrist so thin and delicate as she drank her tea, her bracelet almost rolled right off her hand. Her eyes were drawn, her cheeks hollow. Anya started crying then, having bumped her head on the windowsill, and Katerina snapped out of her fog and leaped up to tend to her.

She carried Anya back to the sofa and kissed her head, breathing in the child's smell.

"What if I was wrong about it all?" she asked. "What if we were wrong? I hate it here."

Vera leaned the icon against the wall, her back catching as she leaned over. She felt the vague grainy feeling of guilt for something she could not pinpoint. Had she encouraged Katerina's loss of faith? Should she not have been honest? She had not told her everything, of course. No one tells the shiny blackness in their soul for fear it will ooze out and never stop until they drown.

A knock on the door lurched her heart even now. You are old, Vera; they have not come for you. She rose from the bed and undid the chain on the door, and there was the raven-haired girl, all sinew and muscle, as if she had been summoned from Vera's rumination. Anya stood there barefoot in her nightgown, hopping from foot to foot.

"Did I wake you?"

"Come, come. I was just fixing some tea. I've missed you. I have no one to teach math to."

"I'm going on an airplane tomorrow."

"*O, Bozhe moy!*" she said. "In the sky?"

Anya laughed. "Yes, Vera Vasilievna. I'll be back to see you in a few days."

She followed Vera to the kitchen.

"How are you feeling about the competition?" Vera asked.

"I want to win. It's important that I win."

"Is it?"

Anya looked at her with those bottomless eyes. It was unheard of to question the seriousness of winning for the Motherland.

"What happens if you don't?" Vera asked.

"I don't know. I don't like to think about it. It scares me."

"You are worried what will happen to you?"

"It's not that. If I think about failing, I feel like I'm going down into the mine. It's dark and cold, and I don't feel like I have a body anymore."

Vera touched Anya's hand with her own. A child. A child! She held out the bowl of chocolates to her.

"Fill your pockets. For the airplane."

"Anatoly won't like it."

"Pfft. Just don't offer him one."

Anya grabbed two handfuls.

"That's better," Vera said. "You are unbreakable, Anya."

The girl shrugged.

"It's deep down, deeper than Soviet."

"I don't know."

But Vera guessed that she did know, that at her center was an iron strength she was born with, forged by the loss of her mother.

"It's not just today. It's yesterday and tomorrow. It's what runs through. What's in there." Vera pointed at her chest. "Remember that. Also don't trust anyone, *dorogaya.*"

"Vera Vasilievna!"

"Not fully. You can only trust yourself." Because human beings are selfish creatures, Vera thought. You have only you.

"I heard the naturalist has taken in two seagulls with broken wings," Anya said.

"Ledorsky and his wounded creatures."

"I will see what he is up to when I come home."

"When you come home, we will celebrate and make marshmallows together."

"If I win."

"Anya, I would love you the same if you never did another handstand."

* * *

When Anya had gone, the night hers alone, Vera got in bed in all of her clothes. She worried about Anya being at the mercy of her coach, of men, and of a system that didn't care about her, and in that worrying Vera knew the memories would come.

It was a night at the end of her first year in camp. She walked across the *zona*, late, as she knew she shouldn't, but there had been no water earlier, and she felt that trying to clean herself at least a little kept her human. It was cold but not yet full winter, and she heard the fast footfalls on the gravel and knew it was coming before she could turn. There were his arms around her from the back, and he threw her down. There was no use screaming, but she did let out one, short, throaty cry. It wasn't a guard. It was a fellow prisoner, one of the *urki* by the obscenities he muttered in her ear, part of the professional criminal network that held all the power in the camp. It was expected that female prisoners would be raped; they all knew it. They were spots to be rubbed out. The young ones got it worse. The pretty ones, worst of all. And no one came to help because, because. The rules were intricate, immutable.

Vera did not fight. She tried to remove her mind to somewhere else and wait for it to be over. She tried to take herself back to Novgorod, tried to imagine birch trees and summer rain, as the frozen ground scraped her back raw. I am the cold, hard dirt, she thought. His breath, his stink, his dead eyes. His hands mapped with the blue-black blur of thieves' tattoos. She couldn't even hate him because what was the use; he'd lost his humanity long ago. She closed her eyes and lay limp like a dead fish. She imagined the lice from her mixing with the lice from him. The pain was a thing, an object in the distance. He smacked her across the cheek with the back of his hand, but it was not with much force, an act almost, what he thought he was supposed to do.

He spit into her mouth.

At least Ilya is no longer alive, she thought; at least there's that. The man was rough but quick, and then he pushed himself off her, pulled up his quilted pants, the same as hers, and was gone. When she was alone, sounds came back to her, shouting, clanging, singing from different corners of the camp. Life moving on. Minute by minute. Her horror frozen.

She didn't remember how she got back to the barracks, how she felt, if she cried. She remembered blackness. The *rezhim* started all over again the next morning, a waking siren at four a.m., the count, a small bread ration, another count, her brigade being marched off to work. But that particular morning there was a *zek* playing the accordion, cheerful tunes as they trudged off to break shale. How could there be this music? she thought. How could all of it coexist? "March strong! March happy!" the *nadziratel* shouted.

Vera felt something leak down her leg; blood or semen, she didn't know which.

In that moment she thought her mind might take flight. She raised her knees high, a histrionic caricature of a march. I will be shot, she thought, or my mind will break open and my sanity will float into the ether.

But as they passed through the gate the music stopped. The *zek* laid down his instrument and ran to join his brigade as they headed toward the mine. Vera returned to herself. The low, oppressive clouds, the wind off the lake, the blocks of prisoners in their ugly clothes, the hollow cheeks and sad shoulders, and all the days and months and years ahead of her. But she decided: yes. Survival was its own victory. "I don't need your work; I need your suffering," she had been told by camp commanders. She would not give them that. She was no longer scared of anything.

* * *

Yuri and Anya took a taxi to the crumbling airstrip outside the city. Anatoly was there in the warming hut, standing side by side with a plump woman in a fur hat. Was this his wife? Anya blushed, never having imagined he was married, or maybe it was his girlfriend, and that was somehow worse. Under his coat he wore the same suit he'd worn to her school. He looked uncomfortable outside the gym. He said something to the woman, cleared his throat, and embraced her quickly with stiff, bent-elbowed arms, before walking away, leaving her to dab at her nose with a handkerchief. Yuri shook Anatoly's hand and then stood there in awkward silence, holding Anya's suitcase. She felt like she was being handed over like a parcel.

It was loud on the airplane, the jump seat uncomfortable, and she had nothing to say. Anatoly looked out the window. She wanted to please him, but without gymnastics she did not know how. They could not find purchase with each other.

"If you do well tomorrow, I will get you ice cream," he said.

"Strawberry," she said.

"Yes, sir," he said.

As the plane rose into the air, she watched Norilsk recede until it disappeared and all there was below was the empty, wide-open steppe where the mammoths had roamed. She was leaving home. It was only for a few days, but it seemed she was flying into the future. She closed her eyes and saw herself on bars, her body whipping around the bottom bar like a propeller, perfect eagle catch of the top bar behind her, hop to low bar kip. A never-ending loop until she fell asleep.

And then they reached the swampy lowlands of western Siberia, descended through clouds thick and low, like cutting though wool, revealing Surgut all at once, edged by scrubby stone cliffs that lined the slate-blue water of the Ob River. Oil had been discovered ten years ago and Surgut was booming. It was one big construction site, with raised gravel roads leading to nowhere, and oil wells bobbing up and down in every direction.

A taxi took them into town to the new state-run Intourist hotel, a concrete hulk of a building with a portico that curved up like a ski jump. It was the tallest building Anya had ever seen. Inside, the lobby was high ceilinged and spacious, with carved wooden panels and red leather chairs. Even Anatoly seemed cowed by the sleekness of it.

"Go see the *dezhurnaya* at the end of the hall if you need toilet paper or soap," he mumbled. "I will see you in a while."

They had rooms next door to each other. Anya had never been in a hotel, wasn't sure where she was allowed to sit. A room to herself? It was so quiet. She put her suitcase on the bed and then sat down next to it. She went to the bathroom and then went back to the bed and sat down again, opening the drawer—empty—of the nightstand. She still hadn't taken off her coat. She pulled a chocolate from her pocket. She missed a mother she was forgetting with each passing year. She flopped back on the bed, the chocolate melting on her tongue. The luxury of being alone in a hotel left her feeling small, adrift.

Get to work, Anya. Visualize, she told herself. Hold your body tight on beam, square your hips, stay centered. Stretch your body in your hand-stand. Taller, open your shoulders. Stay on. Grab the beam with your toes. If you fall off, you fall into a pit of quicksand. On vault: elbows in on the run. Don't ride the horse; touch it like it's a sizzling griddle. Land a body length away or you will have to do a thousand sit-ups. Straight body cast to handstand on bars. Head down. Hollow out, stomach in, straight line. You feel empty. You feel like there's nothing inside you.

"Anya Yurievna?" Anatoly knocked softly.

She opened the door. He had changed out of his suit into warm-ups and plastic slides, and it made her relax to see him this way.

"They have a restaurant downstairs."

"I'm hungry," she said.

In the lobby there were other gymnasts, little girls and grown-up coaches and no one in between. The girls sized each other up with fur-tive glances. Anya was sure they all knew things she didn't. Fear crept down her arms and settled into her fingertips. Hold it in your fist and push it away, her mother had told her. She was not special here. She was just one of many who wanted what she wanted.

The restaurant had white tablecloths and burgundy napkins. Anatoly drank vodka, and she drank sweetened goat's milk. Around them oilmen smoked foreign cigarettes and spoke German, English, Farsi. The menu was a bounty of fish from the Ob prepared every which way. They were served *stroganina* to start—frozen fish eaten with salt and pepper before it melted. Also huge steamed *pelmeni* stuffed with beef and cedar berries, a heaping plate of mushrooms in varieties she had never seen, and a bowl of ruby-red lingonberries. It felt magical, as if the *leshiy* had come in from the taiga and laid out this bountiful table. She wished Sveta were here with her, to gorge on the food, to jump on the beds and do flips. To share it with someone. But Sveta seemed lost to her now.

"It doesn't matter about the judges," Anatoly said.

"What do you mean?"

"You have to perform flawlessly, of course. I'm not worried about the judges. What's more important is Latynina's representative."

Anya thought about her back somersault on beam. Could she do it during the warm-up? She knew it was risky. You followed the regimen. Showing off could get her disqualified.

"How do you feel about beam?"

"I fell in the routine three times yesterday. I don't feel all the way ready."

"I decide when you are ready."

She smashed the lingonberries with her fork, the red jelly squishing through the tines.

"Remember on beam. Soft grass. Trust your body."

Anya closed her eyes for a minute and tried to picture it. She would practice in her room tonight.

"Do you have any children?" she asked.

"What? No," he shook his head, befuddled, embarrassed.

"Were you a gymnast?"

He nodded. "Any more questions?"

"If I make it to Round Lake, do you come too?"

"That is how it works," he said. "I would keep being your coach."

"Good," she said.

Anatoly laughed. "You and me," he said. "We will do great things together. Don't disappoint me tomorrow."

* * *

The Friendship Sports Complex was brand-new, still ringed in dirt. It smelled of cement and fresh paint. When Anya walked into the gym she stopped. It was magnificent—the airiness and white walls and new equipment.

She had done her own ponytail, but once they were inside, she handed the ribbon from Irina to Anatoly.

"What do I do with this?" he asked, holding the ribbon in front of him with two fingers as if it were a soiled diaper. He looked around but saw no woman to come to his aid. "Okay, turn around." He tied it around her hair in a tight, lopsided bow, with a grunt of dissatisfaction.

Anya could see right away that the other girls were good—tight bodied, streamlined, with impeccable form, like paper cutouts. No toe unpointed, no arched handstands, no clumsy fingers. Anya closed her eyes and imagined herself alone on the ridge outside of Norilsk, the wind blustering and too cold to breathe. Only you, she said to herself. You and your body that knows what to do.

Anatoly paced the sidelines, unsure who the national scout was. There were a few men hanging around the gym watching intently.

"I don't know," he said. "He could be any of them."

He was so agitated she walked away to be alone.

* * *

Anya knew competing would be different from doing routines in the gym, but the strangeness of it knocked her off-kilter. All of a sudden, the gym was too bright, too chalky, too loud, too big. Calm, she told herself, breathe, compulsories are easy. She barely heard the accompanist on floor. The bars wobbled. Bile rose in her throat as her scores were flipped and held high. But at the end of the second rotation, she was second on floor and fourth on bars. Not good enough, she knew, to get herself noticed without looking like she was trying to. There was no room for deductions. As she waited until it was time to move over to beam, she sat next to Anatoly, who glowered and smoked. He did not know who the man from Moscow was. Other girls were smaller, lighter, cuter, more charming, more graceful. What kind of gymnast are you, Anya? she thought.

And then Anatoly seemed to light up, and he jumped, sitting straight in his seat.

"It's him," he said under his breath. Anya looked sideways at a man who stood with his hands behind his back, chin up, an imperious gaze. He'd entered the gym from the side entrance.

"How do you know?"

"I know," he said. "It's all on beam for you. Show him."

Show him. Anya thought it might be a message from Anatoly, who could never come out and tell her to veer from the program.

The man flicked his eyes to her as she waited for the judge to signal. He is watching, she thought. There is one shot. Her ears hummed, her body buzzed, electric. And then the judge's arm was up, and Anya saluted, and it was now, and she thought only of how she knew it felt up there, trusted her skill, kept her hips square in two connected back walkovers. It's a field, dirt and grass, soft on either side. I will go up into the air. And then she did what was not allowed in a compulsory routine, flaunted the rules of uniformity in the worst kind of attention-getting way. She jumped and executed a perfect back tuck.

She heard gasps from the audience but did not waiver. The man was in her periphery.

She went on with the routine as if nothing was out of the ordinary. She held her arabesque high above her head. She stuck her dismount. The claps were loud and approving. The judge's face was not.

Anatoly still looked stunned when she walked to the sidelines, like he didn't know whether to lift her up or slap her. When the score came up, she was docked a full point, the same as if she had fallen off the beam twice. She was in fourteenth place. They sat side by side without saying a thing.

"You're moving to vault," he said finally. "I don't know. I don't know. Just do your vault."

Anya saw that she was walking but couldn't feel her feet on the floor. Shrinking, shrinking. A curdled feeling in her gut. But there was something else there too. She was right. She was right to do what she'd done. You don't get anywhere without taking a risk. Anatoly had taught her that.

It was just a handspring vault. Easy. She flew over the horse, barely touching it. And again. And she was done. Her score was good, and after the remaining girls went, it remained the best. But her all-around was compromised by the fourteenth place, and she didn't make it to the podium.

"No one wants a gymnast with her own ideas," Anatoly said.

But then there was the man next to them. He barely looked at her, but Anatoly stood quickly.

"You know how Latynina feels about tricks," he said. "Elegance. Femininity. Artistry. Like Tourischeva."

"Tourischeva is over," Anatoly said, surprising Anya with his boldness.

The man raised his eyebrows with a half smile.

"You're putting all your stock in this one." He nodded at Anya. "It was a gamble out there. Too bold, maybe. But you got my attention."

"We won't beat the Romanians with elegance," Anatoly said.

The man lowered his voice. "Tourischeva, she can barely do a back handspring on beam. Saadi, Dronova, they are women, they are old. Koval, inconsistent. Korbut, falling apart."

It was audacious talk, and Anatoly stayed quiet.

"They won't win under Latynina in '76."

"You have a plan." Anatoly was cautious. It was a minefield of a discussion. The man could do a quick switchback and end Anatoly's career right there.

"Shaposhnikova, Davydova. They are the future. Latynina refuses to accept it."

"You are the best candidate for the job, of course."

The man smiled. "Of course."

"Three years, if she keeps going like this." He nodded his head at Anya. "Junior national team. I have my eye on a few others. The new wave. Have them train at Round Lake."

Anatoly pursed his lips to hide an emerging smile.

"Get her to the Druzhba Tournament next year. It's in Baia Mare. International competition. Experience the Romanians. Learn from them. I'll be there."

"The Romanian girl dominated last year."

"Only eleven. Comaneci. She will win in Montreal. That's what we're up against. We need to play the same game."

And the man was gone. Anatoly turned and patted Anya's back in a gruff hug. She was used to him poking, stretching, swatting her in the gym. But this was the first real affection he'd ever shown. Their futures were knotted together, tight as lace.

* * *

After ice cream—vanilla, the hotel did not have strawberry—Anatoly took Anya on the bus out to the City Park of Culture and Recreation. It was snowy, empty, the late afternoon light already thin. They were the last on the bus, and they disembarked at the edge of the woods, a small sign pointing to the park. They took a path that cut through straight, tall pines. A squirrel ran across, reddish fur and billowing tail. Anya jumped back with a squeal; she'd never seen one before.

In the clearing, there was a giant blue wheel against the sky, ringed with caged baskets, "Сургут" in script through its center.

"What is it?" Anya asked, staring up.

"A Ferris wheel. You sit in one of the little cars and it spins around."

The structure was still, the cars swaying slightly in the wind.

"I want to ride it."

Anatoly looked around. They had reached the asphalt play area, lined with brightly painted game stalls, closed for the season, their shutters padlocked.

"Must run only in the summer," he said.

But just then they heard hammering at the far side of the playground, a metal-on-metal clang ricocheting through the quiet.

It was a caretaker in dark green coveralls, an older man, his legs bowed. He glanced at them as they approached, and then went back to his slow, methodical work.

Anatoly took off his hat and scratched his head, sighing heavily.

"Excuse me," he said. "Can you run the ride for her? We've come all the way from Norilsk."

"Closed," the man said. "Until May."

"*Tovarishch*," Anya said.

The man stopped and looked at her, smiling a little.

"Yes, comrade," he said.

"I'm a gymnast."

"Is that so?"

"How about I show you a trick and then I can ride?"

The man folded his arms across his chest. "Okay."

Anya took off running and flipped into a pile of snow.

* * *

She rode alone. Twice she swooped down and up and around, and then the third time the wheel stopped while she was at the very top. Time stretched out and slowed in the wind and quiet and cold. She thought maybe she was a little closer to her mother up here in the sky. She saw the Ob in the distance and the infinite snowy taiga in every direction, and she thought if she looked far enough, she could see Norilsk to the north. Her father and Irina at the kitchen table. Vera with her *schyoty* and her icon and her memories. Sveta starry-eyed from fumes and laughing with the street boys. Ledorsky bandaging the wing of a gull.

I am happy, she thought, aren't I? I have no reason to be sad. I'm doing it, Mama, she thought. Maybe you watched me today. Maybe you are lost. Maybe you'll see me at the Olympics one day and you will come back. Her hope spun and spun. I will be good. She held it out, an offering. But she was not so little anymore, she knew, and she felt heavy with effort.

Her little cage lurched before beginning its slow descent. Anatoly waved and she waved back even though she knew he couldn't see her.

Katerina stepped lightly, in a quick balancé, *as she moved away from the District Office and across Ulitsa Moskovskaya. Was the man behind her? She sensed he was there, but she wouldn't turn to look. She would continue to pretend that she didn't know she was being followed, and maybe that would grant her more distance from him. Her head hurt from the sulfuric gas in the air, but it was more than that. Secrets knocked around her skull. She pulled her coat tighter. The sun was weak, a slender warmth trying desperately to reach her.*

The girl Inna would be waiting outside the dance studio by now. She was the daughter of the director of the copper plant, Yuri's superior. Katerina would have to apologize, to make it right. Galina would be eyeing the clock, crumbs on her lips, her self-satisfied anger growing with each passing minute.

Katerina saw the bus approaching out of the corner of her eye. She kept walking on the other side of the street, passing the bus stop without slowing down. At the last moment, she sprinted back across the street and jumped aboard. The man lumbered toward the bus but was too slow. Do svidaniya, tovarishch, *she said to herself as the bus pulled away. At least for another day. It was a small victory she would pay for, but for now she felt the bubbly freedom of escape.*

She rode the bus through the city, and when she was far enough away, took another and then another. The heater lulled her; warmth had returned to her fingers.

She turned over a memory she had kept buried for years, the details of which she'd never told Yuri. She had been just fourteen, the slightest girl, when the Bolshoi went to Sochi to perform at the Winter Theater. Stalin had requested a special performance by the young up-and-comers, the future of the Soviet Union, an abbreviated version of his favorite ballet, Swan Lake. *A matinee performance. She would star as Odette and Odile, the white swan and black swan. Not the whole ballet, but some of its famous scenes. Zakharov was disgusted by the medley format, but they all knew it was an incomparable honor.*

Stalin was perched in a gilded loge box, his chin thrust forward, his wrinkled wedge of a face impassive. She found him in the audience, radiated everything to him. In her Act

III solo as Odile in her black tutu, she spotted him in each of her exhausting number of fouetté turns, breathtakingly precise, she knew, even at her young age.

Katerina had told Yuri only that she had performed in the company in Sochi, but never had told him she'd been a soloist for the performance, never told him that after she had come off the stage, as they milled about, waiting for the important men to clear out of their seats, a bespectacled man in a black livery uniform had come up to her.

"Our dear father Stalin would like to meet you," he said. "He has gone on ahead."

She was whisked away, still in her white tutu and feathered headband from the final bow, her face a mask of powder and painted lips.

"We are forbidden from wearing our pointe *shoes outside," she said.*

"It doesn't matter, child," he said.

He drove her in an open-roofed, dove-gray Phaeton, like she'd only seen in Red Square parades, swiftly along the impeccable Stalinsky Prospekt, which was cleaned three times a day. In the early August evening, the light was rich with gold and orange, wind in her face. They turned off the road, up high on a hill, to a moss green dacha, palm trees in front. She could see the Greater Caucasus mountains in the distance.

The man dutifully showed her through the beechwood-paneled rooms, her pointe *shoes tapping the parquet floors. Here, a billiards table, which she'd never seen. Here, a small oval pool filled with seawater from the Black Sea, lined with mosaics of peacocks on pine boughs. She had never seen anything as sumptuous. At the cinema hall, the man backed out of the room and closed the door behind her.*

Stalin was an old man by then, his hair, still thick and low on his forehead, was all gray, as was his mustache. He was imposing, but he leaned to the side in the front row of theater seats. He couldn't turn his head without turning his body. His clay-colored pallor had a dull sheen in the light.

"Ah," he said. "Come." He slurred some when he talked.

Katerina could barely breathe. She held her hands demurely in front and walked down the aisle to stand before him.

"Such a little thing. Twirl for me. Go on." His dentures whistled.

She executed a perfect triple pirouette en pointe. *In that moment, she felt fully alive and right in purpose.*

"Look at that," he said.

He did not ask her to sit.

"I wanted my daughter to dance. But she was clumsy. Now she's grown, still clumsy. Not like you." He sighed. "Oleg!" he barked.

The man who had driven her appeared at once. He leaned down as Stalin whispered something, and then he was gone.

"You will be a treasure of the great Soviet Union, the way you dance," he said. "I know everything."

Oleg quietly reappeared and dropped something into Stalin's palm, then exited without a word.

"Come," *Stalin said to her.*

Katerina took a step toward him.

"Hold your arm out to me. Your wrist is so delicate. Easy to snap."

He fumbled with the tiny clasp of the bracelet, his fingers stiff. She held her breath as he grumbled and then finally somehow got the small ring in the silver claw, and the bracelet settled on her wrist, its beads of amber glowing in the low light.

"It was my Lana's, but now it is yours. I don't see my daughter much anymore."

"Thank you, gospodin." *She could barely make sound come out. What else should she say? She curtsied low before him.*

His gaze drifted. She feared he was falling asleep.

"They are all blind like kittens," *he sputtered.*

The lamps dimmed, and a beam of light shot forward from the projector high on the back wall.

"You know Charlie Chaplin?" *he asked.*

She shook her head no.

"Ah. He's funny. He makes a fool of Hitler. Too bad you can't stay to watch."

He waved his shaky hand to shoo her away.

When he died two years later, she had wept. For him, yes, but also for her.

For years she held the memory like a jewel. Why had she never told Yuri? At first it was because she felt special; the experience was hers alone. She had been chosen by the greatest supreme leader. A Soviet treasure. The bracelet a reminder. And then too much time had passed. And then it would seem like she valued her own glory. And then she was embarrassed. And then the shame of holding it dear after what she'd learned from Vera.

Add it to the list of things she kept hidden.

Katerina was the only rider left on the bus. She was let off at the end of the line, at a garbage dump at the base of the hills. She climbed up and up the ridge, her breathing hard and sharp. Past the rusted-out cars and slag heaps, past the dead trees that once had been a boreal forest. She crunched on the top layer of snow, which had melted in the sun and was beginning to freeze again in the afternoon.

Despite it all she had kept the amber bracelet, wore it still. She had once valued it for who had given it to her, but now she saw it as an emblem of her endurance. Keep going and going, like those fouetté turns. Except now she did not have it on. She had left it with the surly man who fixed watches and clocks near the ballet school. ("It will be ready Wednesday. Do not be late to pick it up or I don't know what will happen to it.") To make it smaller to fit Anya. It was time to pass it on to her. To remind her girl of what they could not take away.

She looked behind her just once. A city in a snowy desert. Haunted by Vera and all the thousands like her. She didn't want to see Norilsk just now, or its smokestacks, or the ugly grid of its dirty pastel buildings.

Winded, eyes watering, Katerina exhaled in the wide-open Arctic tundra, under a pale, watercolor sky. She held her arms out and spun among the hummocks of permafrost—soil, ice, prehistoric plants, bits of frozen mammoths, musk ox, woolly rhinoceroses, wolves. Out here in the wilderness, away from all the disappointments.

Part II

Ozero Krugloye, 1977

CHAPTER 12

Anya fumbled with her laces in the predawn darkness. It was Moscow cold not Norilsk cold, so breathing the air didn't bother her like it did the other girls. They lined up outside the dormitory and waited for Sasha, the trainer. No one dared be late. No one spoke to each other. They all felt the need to prove that they belonged here. Anya felt the insecurity like a drumbeat: You are replaceable, don't blow it, work harder. The USSR may have won Olympic team gold in Montreal the year before, but it was no longer untouchable. Tourischeva's bronze in the all-round signaled the end of Latynina's dynasty. Olga Korbut looked drawn and tired, hobbled by injuries, her little-girl pigtails a mess. Nellie Kim won gold on beam and vault, even received a ten for her Tsukahara with a full twist. And yet the world saw only the Romanian, Nadia Comaneci. Her youth, her grace, her skills, her perfect tens. Anya knew her job: beat Romania, restore Soviet dominance.

Tourischeva retired. Latynina was forced out soon after, and Aman Shaniyazov was in. "Modern gymnastics requires greater complexity than ever before," he said again and again. Gone were body curves and balletic classicism. The scout who had seen Anya in Surgut three years before was no longer there, but he had been right: the new ideal was young, small, athletic, daring. Anya, now twelve, had ridden the wave to the junior national team at Round Lake.

At six a.m., Sasha jogged up, did a quick count, then blew his whistle.

The girls took off running, crunching through snow, toward the path that wound around the perimeter of the vast grounds, past where the fencers and swimmers trained, and then on to the gym for an hour of ropes and conditioning before breakfast. Round Lake was only twenty miles from Moscow, but it was surrounded by thick woods, completely contained—gym, clinic, dormitory, dining hall, massage center, library, classrooms—an isolated, insular universe. Anya picked up her pace, passing Yulia, a twelve-year-old from Vladivostok, whom she could hear crying on the other side of the dorm wall at night. They'd both competed in the 1976 Friendship Tournament in Győr, Hungary. Anya had gotten third all around, besting Yulia's fourth. *Vyshe, silnee, bystree,* Anya chanted to herself, getting ahead of the girl. Higher, stronger, faster.

The air was sharp with pine and snow. Anya did not miss the chemical sweetness she was used to from copper smelting. It was the birdsong she found most surprising. After a lifetime of hearing only clangs and booms and the occasional gull cry, a universe of birds awaited her in the early morning, their sounds reassuring, optimistic even, about the day upon her. Chirping, twittering, cawing, chittering, calling-and-answering, lamenting. Anya heard the birds in a conversation somehow meant for her. The natural world, so stark and lacking in Norilsk, was alive to her now. She understood why her mother had craved it so living in the Arctic. "Your mother wondered how different she might have been if she lived among flowers and trees and animals and birds," Vera had told Anya. "She didn't believe in God, but she believed in nature. Its power, its effect on her. I think she needed more sunshine." Even after just a few days here, Anya held the kernel of a secret: she never wanted to live in Norilsk again.

She fell in step behind a girl from Moscow whose small face reminded her of Sveta's, whom she'd last seen at the old playground a month before she left. Sveta had a boyfriend, one of the street kids, a fifteen-year-old who'd once gone to their school but had long since dropped out. "He's funny," Sveta said. "You'd like him. He might chase away your gloom." She pulled down the corners of her mouth in an exaggerated frown.

Sveta had grown past Anya in so many ways; Anya hadn't even spoken to a boy since she had left school four years before. Within the confines of gymnastics, growing up was feared, and socializing was a distraction. Anya wondered what Sveta did with her boyfriend. She was too embarrassed to ask.

"Do your parents know?"

Sveta snorted. "I still go to school," she said. "They don't care beyond that."

Her father's mind had eroded, and he never left the apartment. Her mother hated him and threw plates at him when they argued.

"I go home every few days," she said. "To make sure they're not dead."

Sveta swiped at her nose with the back of her hand. She skipped into a *chassé* and then threw a perfect aerial, just like she used to, her spindly legs a windmill through the air. They didn't pretend anymore that there could be hope for Sveta in the state system, that someday they would be gymnasts together.

"You are really going to Round Lake," Sveta said. "In my head it looks like a castle."

"I'm sorry I'm leaving you behind," Anya said.

"You left me behind a long time ago," Sveta said. She smiled and stuck out her tongue to soften the sting. "At least I have you beat in one way." She pulled her shirt tight across her chest.

Anya felt a small flicker of panic at the sight of Sveta's developing breasts.

"I don't want them," Anya said. "I never want them. There are shots to keep it from happening."

"Boys don't like a pancake, Anya Yurievna."

But judges do, she had thought.

Anya tried to imagine Sveta jogging next to her now, her hair tied tightly back, the only one who could keep up with her. It was early spring, but a thick layer of snow clung to the ring road as the group of them plodded on through the thin light of the morning. Her ankle hurt, her back, her shoulder, but it was just the way it was. Injuries were shameful to her, and she knew not to complain; they all did. "You know what you should think?" Anatoly had said. "You think, 'My grandfather fought in the Great Patriotic War. And I'm competing for my homeland. Compared to what people endured then, gymnastics is easy.' Yes? So what if your ankle is hurting?" She ignored the pain as her muscles warmed up. It was always worst in the morning. Besides, she was excited, a live wire. Her energy sparked and crackled. She had made it to Ozero Krugloye and the junior national team.

Anya had arrived four days ago with Anatoly. Yuri had wanted to come, of course, but he did not have the money or the clearance to fly to Moscow. Yuri and Irina had risen early with her, packed her sardines and bread, and chattered about how much warmer it would be at Round Lake, how she might see the swirling domes of Saint Basil's from the air. Anya had wanted her father to tell her something, something she could hold close to remind her of him. But his eyes grew shiny, and he hugged her instead. She had watched him and Irina recede as the taxi drove away, swaddled in coats, shrouded by their fog of breath. They seemed rooted to the ground like thick, strange trees. She was twelve years old, and her life kept moving forward. Better and better at gymnastics, better and better at needing no one but herself.

The sun inched up from the horizon as the girls reached the gym with their wind-burned faces, chugging air, hands on their knees. The lights were on, the seniors already at work. Anya was still starstruck. Nellie Kim was on beam, sulking, her mouth set straight, as she listened to her coach. She was beautiful and intense—half Korean, half Tatar, from Tajikistan—the first to do a double back salto—two full flips—at the Olympics. She was as mean as vinegar. No one talked to her.

"She's twenty," Anatoly had said. "She's done anyway. Like your Korbut."

The senior girls, training for the World Cup, never looked their way as they walked along the wall to the workout room. New girls were a reminder of how short their careers would be, how they could never get comfortable at the top. The young ones were quiet, eyes darting up to their idols. And then there she was right in front of Anya—Olga Korbut. She was the same girl from the Olympics, from the television, the one who had electrified Anya, made her want to be a gymnast, but now she was a hardened version of herself. Her hair was ratty, stuffed into a rubber band, her face worn, angry. Korbut was twenty-two, but she'd aged well beyond that. Her body was pared to sinews. She smoked and gesticulated to her coach, who had a sinister air about him with his helmet of black hair, his sneering set mouth. He reached out and gave her a cruel pinch above her hip, and she hit his hand away.

Anya felt something wilt inside her, a fern after a frost. The image of Olga Korbut she saw here could not find a place to settle in her brain. Her Korbut was a myth, a glittering idea. The Korbut flip, standing on the top bar and flipping backward to catch it! The Korbut back dive layout, landing with a chest roll on the floor! Here was a woman posing as the little girl. Anatoly was right; she was over. Anya could tell by the pallor of her skin, the ugly way she held her mouth.

Anya closed her eyes and took herself to the coldest Norilsk morning, eyelashes crusted in ice, breath like a knife. When she opened them Korbut was exhaling the last smoke of her cigarette. They met eyes. Anya opened and closed her mouth like a fish. Korbut smirked and then hurled her body against the door to the locker room, and she was gone.

"Anya Yurievna!" Sasha yelled. She scurried to catch up to her group.

They were the chosen six, these eleven- and twelve-year-olds from all corners of the Soviet Union, with their short, little-girl bodies, muscled and lean, as bendable as wire. They were comrades but not friends. Competition was too fierce. Not all of them would make it to the seniors, and their families depended on the stipend they received from the state. They trained eight hours a day, six days a week, with two hours of tutoring wedged in where it could fit. Meals were monitored for small portions; Anya was never full. They did not talk on the telephone to their parents. The training camp lasted for six weeks, and then they went home, not knowing if they would be invited back for another session. Each had an individual coach in addition to coaches for conditioning, tumbling, ballet, choreography, and specialists in each apparatus.

It was disciplined, difficult, serious, dangerous, unrelenting. Anya loved it. She was getting better every day, and she could do skills she hadn't known existed a year ago. She was among the best gymnasts in the Soviet Union. She didn't have any room left to miss home. Gymnastics was an extension of her body and mind. Her power and purpose. The pain was a thing she could endure, could shove aside when she needed to.

The girls Latynina had not favored were now center stage. Maria Filatova, Natalia Shaposhnikova, Stella Zakharova, Yelena Davydova. They were all trying new elements, never-been-done skills. Release moves on the bars like the men did, front salto mounts onto the beam.

They taped disks of foam to their heels to save them from the hard landings on wood.

Anya felt an air of wildness, of possibility. Look at them, she thought, making up new moves! She wanted to be one of them, and she watched those girls with a hunger akin to lust. For her country, yes, but Anya didn't have Russia on her mind when she threw a double twist. It was only the moment and how it felt to do it right, to land, to conquer a skill.

The girl Yulia pulled Anya's arm.

"There she is," Yulia said.

"Who?"

"Ludmilla." Anya looked back at her blankly. "Tourischeva!" the girl hissed, gesticulating with her hands.

Tourischeva had cut her hair, now shorter with bangs, and she wore a drab sweater and pants. It seemed in less than a year she had transformed from a champion, a Soviet hero, into a regular adult, thicker around the waist, a hard edge to her eyes. She assisted her old coach with the rising star Shaposhnikova.

"Imagine if she was your coach," Yulia said.

Anya could imagine no coach but Anatoly. It was his approval she still sought, his methods that seemed the only way forward.

"She's still pretty I guess," Anya said.

"She's getting married."

"Married?"

"Valeriy Borzov," Yulia said. "The Olympic sprinter."

Anya never thought about life after training. Gymnastics would go on and on, and if it didn't, the picture faded, blanched white.

The two girls were starting on ropes. The pads of Anya's hands were scabbed from rope burn. If they used their legs at any point to get up, they got five more climbs. Sasha reset his stopwatch.

"*Raz, dva, tri!*" he shouted.

And they were off. It wasn't a race, but of course it was, and Anya knew that she would give what it took to win.

You are hollow, she told herself. You are weightless. There was no place for that cold black pebble of loneliness, as heavy as lead, lodged behind her ribs.

* * *

Anya sat alone in her little room, on the top bunk, the bed below empty, the mattress bare. She'd been at Round Lake almost a week, and her roommate hadn't appeared. She wasn't used to the quiet of having her own room, the space of it, so she closed her eyes and imagined she was home—the lamp, the dresser, her father's bed an arm's reach away, the wind biting at the window frame. She taped up a photograph of herself with Yuri taken last year at the Friendship Tournament. He looked old, his beard graying. Now that Irina cooked for him all the time, he had a bulging middle. In the photo Anya looked like someone else, her dark eyes looking squarely at the camera, her hair behind her ears like little black curtains tied back. She'd grown a little taller, still as lean as a whip. She sometimes wondered if her mother would recognize her, or if she would recognize her mother if she passed her on the street.

At the bottom of her suitcase was the packet of Tsvetaeva poems she'd found in her father's things and had taken without telling him. He was with Irina now, and he was soused every night anyway. He would never notice.

Anya's roommate, who had yet to arrive, was a senior who was returning to Round Lake. Anya assumed that like the other seniors, she would be brusque and want nothing to do with her. She rolled over onto her back and picked at a callus at the base of her pinkie, then bit it with her teeth and tore it off, leaving a bloody hole. When she wasn't in the gym, she feared she might float away, untethered. She could hear stifled sobs on the other side of the wall. Yulia again. You're not allowed to feel lonely, Anya told herself. Think of Sveta. But thinking of Sveta, who felt lost to her, made her feel more alone.

A small girl pushed open the door. Reddish light-brown bangs, hair in a ponytail, big hazel eyes. She looked as vulnerable as a baby bird, but old, somehow, knowing. Anya felt her chest warm and expand, a rush of relief, and she couldn't help smiling, liking the girl already.

"Hi," the girl said. She smiled, just barely. "Here." She held a tea cake up to Anya, powdered sugar whitening her fingertips. "My *babushka* made them. I won't tell the evil Albina. Have you met her yet?"

Anya nodded. Albina was the pointy-faced matron who monitored their meals so they wouldn't gain weight.

"We better eat them all tonight." She set her small satchel on the bed below and brushed the crumbs from her hands. "I'm Elena."

"I've been waiting for you," Anya said.

CHAPTER 13

Elena Grishina was seventeen and trained at Central Red Army Moscow.

"She was nothing special," Anatoly told Anya, as she paused between vaults. "But then Kapanov took her on." He nodded at the man on the edge of the bars. He had been a men's coach and had taken what he knew to train Elena.

"She got second at the USSR Championships this year. Eyes will be on her at the World Cup."

Kapanov was working with Elena on a release move on bars like Aleksandr Tkatchev did on the high bar, a giant swing forward, then letting go of the bar and blindly catching it again in flight in a straddle. She kept missing her hands, landing hard on her front. Elements kept getting more and more difficult. What once was impossible was now expected. Anya wondered where it would end.

"Watch that one," Anatoly said. "Be more like her. Look how serious her face is. Okay, stop stalling. Your run is weak. How are you going to pull that Tsuk around? Go. Sprints."

Anya didn't need Anatoly's encouragement. She already wanted to be more like Elena, was warmed by the thought of her. She hadn't had a real friend since Sveta.

"Have you seen polar bears in Norilsk?" Elena had asked.

"Only once, in a cage inside an apartment!"

"Norilsk sounds like a magical place."

"It's not. It's cold and polluted," Anya had said.

"Maybe it made you tougher though."

"What about you? You have steel nerves in the gym."

"Oh, I just pretend. Don't tell anybody."

Elena was older, but it didn't matter. They had an ease with each other. Anya wanted the gym day to be over so she would have Elena to herself in their little room.

In two weeks, the seniors were headed to Oviedo, Spain, for the World Cup in preparation for the European Championships. The mood in the gym was dark, tense. Coaches berated girls for their incompetence. Kapanov didn't let up on Elena.

"What was that, huh? What kind of try? A quitter's try. Do it again," he spat.

Anya took it all in, feeling both protective and proud of her new friend, who showed nothing on her face—no fear, no weakness, no hurt—no matter how cutting the insult or cruel the remark or impossible the expectation.

Inscrutable Elena, powerful Elena, graceful Elena. Anya watched her whenever she could sneak a glance. A desire had sprung loose in her from their first meeting. She wanted to be like her, yes, but it was more than that. Elena gave her a feeling like the first spring sun.

* * *

Anya was on her bunk, Elena below her. They had made it through the day but were too tired to get up and brush their teeth.

"What's Moscow like?" Anya hung her head down over the side.

"It's a place. Lots of people. The May Day parade in Red Square is a good show. I like Gorky Park in springtime. There are ducks. But you know what it's like. Doesn't matter if it's Moscow or Siberia. For us it's the gym and the apartment. I live with my *babushka*."

Elena had a preternatural calmness to her, but her eyes gave away the churning underneath.

"What about your parents?" Anya asked. The blood had filled her face upside down, veins pounding, so she lifted her head and went back to looking at the ceiling. She closed her eyes and imagined Elena's face.

"I never knew my father. He was in the army. My mother died in a fire when I was five," she said.

"I don't have a mother either," Anya said, her voice so quiet she wasn't sure she had said it out loud. It felt like a revelation, something she could have never said to anyone else.

"What happened to yours?" Elena asked.

"I don't know. She disappeared when I was five too."

"What do you think happened to her?"

"Sometimes I think she went for a walk and lost her way out on the plains when it got dark, or maybe she fell into the river. You can't last long in that water even in the spring." Who was she, Anya thought, telling her secrets, turning herself inside out for someone else to see?

"Do you remember her?"

"I have some memories. But sometimes I don't know if I really remember her or if I have imagined the pictures in my head." Anya felt guilt and relief.

"It's the same for me," Elena said. "Do you want to come down here so we can see each other?"

Anya bit her lip to stifle her smile. She wanted to spring out of her bunk, but she didn't want to seem too eager.

"Sure. Okay," she said. She shimmied down the bed frame and lay in the warm space Elena had created by scooting over to the wall. She smelled like wheat and honey.

"When I do gymnastics, I don't think about my mother though," Elena said. "I don't think about anything except what I have to do."

"I know what you mean. It's like I step into another world. And then I'm spit out of it when I leave the gym."

"My *babushka* says it's like I'm possessed by a spirit. She's superstitious like that."

"Are you ever scared?" Anya asked. It was dangerous to talk about fear. They all pretended they were immune. "When your coach makes you do something? I saw him yelling today."

"Mikhail says taking risks is as important as talent, as strength. If you can do something, you should do it; you should show it to the world."

"Even if you fall."

"It's not about playing a game of points or deductions. It's about showing the best gymnastics that you can in a pure sense. At least that's what he says. I don't know."

"Do you love it like you did when you started?" Anya asked. She wanted Elena to talk on and on.

"It's not a question of love, is it. It's part of me, for better or for worse. I *have* to do it. You know what I mean, don't you? I saw you today," she said. "You're good on beam."

Elena had noticed her too.

* * *

At the World Cup in Spain, Filatova got the gold, East Germany's Kraker got silver, Shaposhnikova and her one-armed handstand on beam got bronze. Comaneci was not there. The Americans were never a threat. Elena came in a disappointing fifth after putting her hand down landing a vault. But in the event finals she roared back with gold on beam and bars. There was something about her, and everyone knew it. The Olympics in Moscow were three years away. No one needed reminding. Glory for the Motherland and proof that the Soviet system worked better than Western decadence.

Anya would be fifteen by then, old enough.

"You will be there," Anatoly had said after yesterday's practice, out of earshot of everyone else. "Because of what you dare to do." It was unheard-of bravado to assume she would join the ranks of those top senior girls. But it was what Anatoly had planned on all along. Anya believed it because he said it, but she knew her chance at the Olympics was as tenuous as a filament, the slightest wisp of a spider's web.

She hopped back up on the beam, having fallen again on a back handspring, back layout step out, her ankle wobbly. She was due for another shot, another round of numbing. Landings sent a stab of pain up the side of her leg.

"Stupid," Anatoly said, slapping his thigh. "This is your job, do you hear me? It's harder to get each detail perfect than to throw something new. But just as important. You fall off beam again in this rotation, you don't have to bother showing up this afternoon."

Anya stood facing the end of the beam and closed her eyes, imagining being surrounded by whiteness, out on the windy steppe. Arms up by her ears. Go. Her hips were squared in the back handspring, and she spotted the beam in the layout. She checked her balance but didn't fall.

"Again," Anatoly said.

She thought of Elena, willing her quick return from Spain. She wanted to be back in their world, to tell her things, to have her asleep below her, to dance around the room to Radio Mayak, the songs of Alla Pugacheva and Valery Leontiev, to brush her hair, to hold her small hand in her own, rough and dry from bars and chalk, as they lay next to each other, whispering.

* * *

Anya and Elena lay side by side on the bottom bunk, pushing up the mattress above them with their feet.

"What was Spain like?" Anya asked.

"Wondrous. Warm. I only saw it from the bus window. People get to live there! I bet it never snows. There are a lot of churches. And squares with strange trees. Medieval buildings."

"What's medieval?" Anya's education was so spotty, her knowledge of the world, of history, a narrow, lopsided lens.

"Old. It looks like a fairy tale."

"And the competition?"

Anya knew the results, but she wanted to know what Elena would say.

"I didn't do that well. I disappointed Mikhail. I let the pressure rattle my head. I got scared."

She had taken home two golds, but Anya knew her fifth in the all-around meant failure.

"Everyone gets scared. They just don't admit it."

Elena turned to her and laughed. "Except you! You're a daredevil. My coach wishes I were more like you."

Anya felt a glow, radiant from the compliment. It was true; she was not held back by fear. She knew how important it was to hide her emotions, to tuck away nerves as deeply as pins in a cushion.

"The three *T*s," Elena said. "*Talant, terpeniye, i trudolyubiye.* That's what they say makes a good gymnast. For me, I think I have some talent, a little patience, and a lot of diligence. But risk-taking has to be part of it. There's no greatness with fear. I have fear all the time."

Anya looked sidelong at Elena as a tear spilled over and slid down her temple to the pillow.

"But you do everything, Lenushka," Anya said.

"I do what I'm told."

"It's important to do what they say. Anatoly says it's more than talent. Like that girl on my team, Sofia. She's a hothead. Talks back to her coach."

"She won't make it doing that."

"If I ever disobeyed Anatoly I would be done. I feel like I would shrivel and die."

"Sometimes I think they don't care about us at all." Elena started to cry again and shook her head. She took Anya's hand and smoothed it with her rough palm. "All the girls in my school loved figure skating. Do you remember Irina Rodnina? They would cut her picture out of the newspaper. Then she fell out of a lift during training the day before Worlds and hit her head on the ice and was in the hospital. She competed anyway, dizzy and faint, and won, and everyone praised her courage. Why was it good she went back out on the ice when she couldn't think straight?"

Anya didn't know how to respond. She had never questioned the importance of sport, that it was a noble endeavor. Honor for the team, for the country.

"The system is not thinking about us." Elena shrugged and sighed. "There's no stopping a steamroller. You know what Mikhail told me once? 'Until you break, no one will let you go.'"

A chill crept down Anya's back.

"Don't say that, Lenushka. It makes me scared."

"I'm sorry. I forget you're still young. *Myshka.*"

Elena lifted her arm so Anya could snuggle into its crook.

"Stay away from the men," Elena said. "Arkayev, the men's coach. *Pristayot.* Don't be alone with him."

Anya flashed back to Dr. Bazhanov in Norilsk, his hands all over her. Shame curled around her limbs. She couldn't speak of it.

"He goes in the steam room and wants to give full body massages."

"Ew," Anya said. In a deep wooden voice she said, "How are your thighs doing today, Elena? Are they tight? Let me rub them for you."

Elena giggled and Anya did too, and the bunk beds creaked as they shook.

A knock on the door quieted them down.

"Lights out, girls," the monitor said through the door.

Elena jumped up and turned out the lights and then hopped right back onto the bed next to Anya. Anya held her breath, afraid Elena might move away. The feel of her skin, arm against arm, a current between them.

"Anya," she said, her voice low and quiet.

Anya turned to her in the dark.

"We are motherless. It makes us different, you know."

Anya had read the Tsvetaeva poems of her mother's so many times the words had slipped into her memory:

> *Your name is a—bird in my hand,*
> *a piece of ice on my tongue.*
> *The lips' quick opening.*
> *Your name—four letters.*
> *A ball caught in flight,*
> *a silver bell in my mouth.*

She blushed, the words too cryptic, too intimate to say out loud. But she took Elena's hand and brought it to her lips, a kiss as quick as fire.

* * *

The Druzhba, the Friendship Tournament, was the most important junior competition. The top four girls who'd proven themselves in training camp took a four-hour flight to Warsaw and a three-hour bus ride to Zabrze in Silesia in southern Poland. Anya, Yulia, Nadezhda, and Sofia, mighty mites in matching white warm-up jackets, CCCP in blue across the front. They weren't friends, but they were civil to each other. Outside the gym, their coaches, middle-aged men whose former athletic frames had gone bulky and soft, acted like awkward fathers, patting the girls' shoulders, unsure of how to act when they weren't barking orders.

"You must be the gymnasts," the hotel manager said as they got off the bus. A family by the door pointed at them and smiled. The other girls waved, but Anya did not. She pulled herself in, an imagined carapace around her. Nadia Comaneci had won the tournament in 1973 at age eleven. Anya had gotten third last year. Now she was twelve, and she planned to win. She could see only forward. There would be no distractions until competition.

At dinner, Anya pushed the *golubtsy* and boiled potatoes around her plate. She wasn't hungry, which was strange since she was always starving. Her head ached from the travel, and she just wanted to lie down. Her hand shook when she picked up her water glass. A little girl approached the table and asked for their autographs, a request the others happily obliged. But by the time the paper got to Anya she knew something was wrong. Scribbling her name left her exhausted.

A fever rose through the night. In a dream a woman carrying empty water buckets came toward her. It was a bad omen, and Anya wanted to run but couldn't move. As the woman came closer, she could see that it was Elena. She started to wave, but when Elena came near she turned into her mother. Katerina smiled and handed Anya one of the empty buckets.

Anya awoke having sweat through her nightgown, shivering under the thin blanket of the hotel. Yulia was next to her, teetering on the edge of the bed. The cinnabar sun was sliding up from behind the pillared Kino Roma across the street, and Anya remembered that she was in Poland. Competition. She rolled over and her brain knocked against her skull. Two lumps were in the other bed, Nadezhda and Sofia.

"You look bad," Nadezhda said, looking over. She gave Sofia a conspiratorial look. No one envied Anya having to tell her coach. "What are you going to do?"

Yulia looked stricken that she had shared a bed with a sick girl. She walked a wide circle to get to the bathroom.

"Don't cry about it," Sofia called after her. Nadezhda laughed. They bounded up and rummaged for their leotards in their bags.

Anya watched the sun inching up into the sky. Pretend you are fine, she told herself. She closed her eyes and visualized her floor routine, vault, bars, beam. She saw herself performing with straight legs, pointed toes, stuck landings. Full extension, strong hollow, big punch.

"Are you coming?" Nadezhda asked.

Anya rolled over, having lost minutes in her head, the three girls dressed by the door.

"Not hungry," she said.

It took all she had to get out of bed, her legs rubbery and weak.

She was late for call time in the lobby. She shivered in her leotard and warm-up suit, her hair in an off-kilter ponytail. Anatoly stood looking at her, his hands on his hips.

"What?"

"I'm ill."

"What do you want me to do about it?" he spat.

Anya felt battered and cold. But she knew she did not have a choice.

"I won't make the Tsuk. I'm so tired. And my head. I won't make it around."

"You will," he said. "You better. You will not ruin this chance."

At the competition she noticed nothing, not the other gymnasts or the large, appreciative crowd. She waited at each apparatus until Anatoly pushed her forward.

Her tumbling was lethargic. She made it around on her vault, but she landed low with her chest down. She didn't fall on beam, and she hit her skills on bars well enough. Her body remembered, running on reserves. In between rotations, she sat alone, Anatoly three seats away, seething.

She took the all-around silver.

After the raising of the flags, a medal around her neck, she stepped off the podium and collapsed in delirium. The crowd gasped and then came to its feet when Anatoly scooped her up and carried her out. They cheered for her determination, for her bravery.

At the hotel, Anatoly put her to bed in her leotard and pulled up the covers. He sat on the edge of the bed and ran his hands through his hair. She drifted, and then he spoke.

"I want to coach an Olympian," he said. He sounded tired, his voice raw edged and quiet. "I don't want to coach mediocre, but I know you know that."

She tried to open her eyes and pull herself up from the spinning world, but the light hurt; her bones felt as heavy and cold as metal.

"I knew you could do it, Anya Yurievna," he said.

She wasn't sure she'd heard him; the tenderness was a shock.

"I didn't win," she said.

"You did good."

* * *

The training camp session was coming to an end, and Anya was soon going home to Norilsk. The senior team had gone to Prague for the 1977 European Championships.

At the end of the day, after the ballet instructor had belittled Anya's turns and scoffed at her leaps, Anatoly found her as she was heading to the dormitory.

"Do you want to come to my apartment? I have a television. To watch Europeans. I can cook for you."

It was rare casualness in her coach. She was still fatigued from Poland, but hungry, always hungry, and curious. Anatoly reappeared each morning, but what was he like when he wasn't coaching? And she would get to watch Elena like she had never seen her.

"What can you cook?" she asked.

"I have some *soya* patties. I can fry potatoes too."

"You'll tell the matron?"

"I will call her. Anything else?"

"Let's go!"

They arrived at one of the drab buildings Anya had never noticed, tucked behind the main gym. The apartment was small, one narrow main room with a sink and a stove at one end, the walls white but yellowed, the sofa a stained beige velour. The walls were bare except for a framed reproduction of an oil painting of the Kremlin, hung unevenly and too high above the sofa. There were no photographs, no evidence of Anatoly other than a pack of Laika cigarettes and a glass ashtray on the kitchen counter. He lit a cigarette and busied himself cutting potatoes.

"Turn on the television. To the Sixth Programme," he said. "I'll be in in a minute. Oh, I have a surprise for you."

From the small refrigerator he pulled out a bottle of Orange Fanta.

Anya hesitated, as if it were some kind of trap.

"Go on," he said. "I won't tell Albina."

She had never had soda, let alone a Western brand. The glass clinked her teeth, and a flood of syrupy sugar hit her tongue, the bubbles sharp in her throat. The sweetness made her jaw ache. It was the best thing she'd tasted in her whole life.

The food was greasy and too salty, and Anya ate two platefuls without letting up. She ate the potatoes and onions so fast they got lodged in her gullet and she had to wash them down, afraid Anatoly might suddenly pull the plug on her binge. He ate a little and drank plenty.

Suddenly there was Elena on television in a navy-blue leotard dotted with little white flowers, a white yarn bow in her ponytail, the number eight pinned to her back. She looked fragile, mysterious. I know you, Anya thought. Elena looked bigger on television, impassive, intimidating in her reserve. She never smiled.

The first rotation was under way. Anya knew Elena's fear of the bars, but her friend hid it well, without a furtive glance or hesitation. Clean, clean, clean, and then there she was balanced on the top bar with her feet, for a moment standing before flipping back blindly in a Korbut loop, while twisting her body a full 360 degrees. Anya gasped. Anatoly grunted his approval.

The others followed: tiny Maria Filatova with huge white bows in her pigtails. She had high difficulty but form breaks. Nellie Kim, quick, quick power, but lacking in grace. And then the one to catch, Nadia Comaneci. Elegant, perfect lines.

"It's going to be a dogfight," he said. He swilled his drink and sat forward on the sofa, his shirt raised up and his sweatpants too low, exposing, to Anya's horror, the hairy top crease of his backside.

On beam, Kim was as confident as ever, never wobbling, landing a gainer full twist dismount. Filatova had sprightly power, a wolf turn into middle splits, a double back handspring into a double-pike dismount.

Come on, Lenushka, Anya thought. Elena was breathtaking up there. An effortless front tuck and back tuck, with the poise of a dancer. As fluid as a river.

Comaneci was lean and unhurried, her routine without pause. She scored a ten, to the delight of the audience. Anatoly scoffed and slapped his thighs.

"Unfair!" he shouted. "That was not perfect. Where are the judges looking? They're looking with their assumptions. It's only popularity. Bah."

Vault, Elena's weakest event, went fine, without a hand down like in the last tournament. And then onto floor, the showcase, the star-making stage. The scores were close after three rotations, and added with compulsory scores, Comaneci, Filatova, Kim, and Elena were all bunched up at the top.

Kim attacked her floor routine with a soaring double back salto, but even her smile looked hard-edged, forced.

"Where's the artistry? Where's the lightness?" Anatoly said.

Elena opened with astonishing difficulty, a full-twisting double back.

"Ah," Anatoly said. He whistled. "They will name it after her."

"The Elena?"

"The Grishina."

Elena moved effortlessly between masterful tumbling and the ethereal precision of her dance.

"Even Latynina would have been happy," he said. "Elena is old and new at once."

My Lenushka, Anya thought.

"We will get a move named after you one day. Maybe a triple twist. You will get it. Maybe first. If you do what you're told. Work harder."

Anya smiled. It seemed impossible but not. She could already do a double with ease. In gymnastics she felt unstoppable, always moving forward. It was what she was meant to do. Fear, sadness, her mother—she would tumble her way ahead of it all.

When Elena had finished her routine, she waved to the crowd.

"She smiled!" Anya shouted.

"Ha. It was so quick I missed it," Anatoly said.

"She's so happy it's over," she said.

Comaneci followed, wowing the crowd with her youthful routine and flawless tumbling.

"Elena should win," Anatoly said. "But Comaneci will. This time."

He was right. Nadia won gold in the all-around, but Elena was right behind her with the silver. They both looked so sad on the podium.

Elena and Nadia tied for gold on bars, Elena took gold on beam and floor.

"Eleven medals USSR, three Romania, one GDR," Anatoly said. He clapped his satisfaction. "You see, Anya Yurievna? This is why we do it."

It wasn't just the medals for her. It was a bone-deep need to be better and better, a wolf at her heels. She could never let up.

He downed the rest of his drink, wheezing with the burn of alcohol. He set down his empty glass too hard onto the small metal table, wobbling the lamp.

"It will be Elena Grishina at Worlds," Anatoly said. "You watch."

All hopes were riding on Elena. It was a crushing weight, Anya knew.

"And then it's our turn," he said.

Anya blew the hair from her face. She tried to imagine the feeling of the darkened arena, the equipment on raised spotlighted platforms, television cameras, all those faces in the audience.

"When we go back home, we need to eliminate all the pauses in your routines, replace them with transfers. And your face is always dark and moody. Lighten up, lift your eyes. You're so serious and glum. No one likes to see that."

He rose from his chair, uneven on his feet, and swooped her up and spun her around before dropping her heavily back onto the sofa. She was so startled she didn't say anything, her heart jumpy and loud in her ears.

"I don't like Shaniyazov," he said, "but we have to mind what he says. Complicated routines. Original elements in all the exercises. So that's what we'll do. Newer, more difficult. Always pushing forward."

Anya always pushed forward. She spun her foot to gauge the pain in her ankle. She hoped a day out of the gym to travel home would ease the knots in her back.

"And you need to smile. Is that so hard?" He reached over and smashed up the sides of her mouth with his thick fingers that smelled of onions. "You and your China-doll face," he said.

* * *

Anya had taken down her father's photograph and packed away her mother's poems. She and Elena had stripped the beds. There were no ballet or strength training or flexibility sessions. There was no gymnastics on their last day. Anya felt a strange mix of freedom and restlessness.

The girls ran to the woods with giddy abandon, their hair down and blowing every which way in the wind. The air was fresh with spruce and silver fir, and earthy with moss and lichen. Snow still clung in the shadows of broad-leaf birch and larch trees. Little villages of mushrooms huddled near new ferns.

"Have you ever ridden a horse?" Elena asked.

"Norilsk doesn't have horses," Anya said.

"They are so graceful," she said. "I would like to ride horses after gymnastics is over."

"I would like to drink Fanta," Anya said. "Sit around all day and drink bottle after bottle until my teeth turn orange."

"But first you come back to Round Lake. You are going to be the best in the world someday, *Myshka*. I think so."

"After you," Anya said.

Elena smiled wide and linked her arm through Anya's.

"I wish I could get rid of my doubts," Elena said. "If I had a wish."

Anya would wish for her mother back, but she didn't want to make it hurt more by saying it out loud.

"What was Nadia like?"

"I had only seen her before on television. But when I watched her in warm-up I realized she's just a regular girl. She fell and made mistakes too. So in the competition I didn't see her as the Olympian, just an opponent I could beat." Elena laughed. "Well, I didn't. But I felt like it was possible."

"You were beautiful," Anya said. She ran ahead behind a tree, cheeks burning. She scooped up a handful of icy snow and crumbled it in her hands. She had loved Sveta, but this was different.

"I was hoping you were watching," Elena said, catching up.

They held hands and walked the pine-needle-strewn path.

Elena stopped and froze. "Look, a *lis*," she whispered.

Just ahead a silver fox trotted out into the open, its fur a glossy bluish gray, its thick white-tipped tail floating behind it. It slowed and grew still, and then jumped, its long body in a graceful arc. It pounced on its prey, a mouse, which the fox crushed in its jaws before trotting off into the woods.

"He's always sly and mischievous in stories," Anya said. "But he doesn't seem like that at all."

"He is what he is," Elena said. "Trying to survive like everything else."

"I will miss you, Lenushka," Anya said.

"We will be together again soon," she said. "My little *Myshka*. Back here at Round Lake."

Elena pulled her into a hug.

It was time to go home, but Anya didn't want to go. Norilsk was a dark, blurry memory. Here with Elena she felt she had become more fully herself. Anya squeezed back tight. Her tears came hot and ragged.

Never let me go, she thought.

CHAPTER 14

Vera craved *borshch*, which she hadn't had since she was pregnant, more than fifty years ago, when it was the only thing she could stomach, so she trudged across town to State Store 42, navigating the spring ice and buckled sidewalks and polar wind off the steppe and even the dirty bus, to get the ingredients. Beets, parsnips, cabbage, garlic, *smetana*—always sour cream—bones for the broth. She remembered the recipe from when the cook would make it for them on Sunday afternoons when she was a girl. She and her sisters would rub the beet peels on their cheeks and lips.

The travel and the waiting in lines filled almost an entire day. Vera pushed herself forward with her heavy bag, afraid if she sat down to rest, she would never get up, her body going rigid until it turned to stone. A body was not meant to live this long, she thought. She dropped the bag inside the door of her apartment and fell heavily onto the sofa, her head back, eyes closed with relief and exhaustion. She wondered if she had stayed alive so long because of her memories or in spite of them. The burden of them, the responsibility they exacted. The good ones, the ones of Pyotr and Ilya, left her feeling bereft, a wave that washed in and then pulled everything back with it as it receded; the bad ones, the horrible ones, had taken on a dull flatness. What is a life worth? Two lives? Millions of them? Vera opened her eyes and reached for her *schyoty*.

Click, a life, click, another life, click, her son, click, her husband, click, click, click.

Katerina had been gone for seven years. Click, Katerina.

Just days before she disappeared, Katerina had stayed home from her job at the dance institute with a fever, Anya at kindergarten. She was restless, her eyes darting about, her face aglow with heat. Vera tried to calm her, afraid that in her agitation, Katerina would do something rash.

"When you destroy beauty, Vera Vasilievna, what does that say of your humanity?"

"Humanity is a mystery," Vera said. "How the capacity for good and its opposite can coexist in the same person."

"Norilsk is cold and ugly and full of death. It's built on *skelety*," she spat. "How can you stand it?"

"Because those bones are my bones," Vera said. "I have lived a long life, Katerina Vladimirovna. You imagine that everything is always like this, and everything will always be like that. In fact, everything changes all the time."

But the present contains the past, she knew.

"I wish Anya could play on grass and climb trees. I wish I could sit with my face to the sun and get so hot I shiver. I wish we could read what the poets write without secrecy. I wish we could travel to Paris. I wish I could eat bananas. I wish Yuri would admit we are not free, that this socialism is authoritarianism," she said. She paused and took a breath. "I received a letter, from the District Office."

Vera held Katerina's small hands in her own and shushed her like she had Pyotr as an infant.

"I am dangerous to them, I guess," she said. "The way I think."

"What does Yuri say?"

"I haven't told him," she said. "They will accuse me of things. What if they take away my job? Then what?" A frightened, aberrant laugh escaped from Katerina. Her forehead glazed in a sheen of sweat. She had spun loose, and Vera worried there was no pulling her back. "Maybe then I will have to go. To run."

"We all adjust," Vera said quietly. "In the camp, in spite of everything, those of us who made it shared the desire to create some sort of life. To find beauty somehow. To sew a scrap of ribbon onto a coat. When our hair grew out, to braid it. Trading tobacco for wildflower seeds to plant behind the barracks in the spring. Relishing a sip of water when our insides felt desiccated."

Katerina began to cry, big, silent tears spilling onto her cheeks.

"We were fools," she said. "I was a fool."

"You have Anya," Vera said. "Even if every pleasure is taken away, you have her."

Katerina had nodded over and over, her small shoulders hunched, her hands clenched. "What if I took Anya with me? I have thought about how we might do it. Oh, Vera Vasilievna. There is something else," she had said. "Something I haven't told anyone yet."

Time lurched forward and Vera opened her eyes. Darkness had seeped in all around her. She rose and went to the kitchen. She filled a pot in the sink and set the bones to boil with bay leaves and an onion. She wished she were in the kitchen of her childhood home in Novgorod, the smells of woodsmoke and baking bread, *povar* cleaning out a chicken at the sink. "Shoo, child," she would say, "or you'll get the smallest dish of cherry *vareniki*." The older Vera got, the more she wanted to go home, to her girlhood, to a time when she knew nothing at all.

Another memory came to her, four years into her sentence, winter. It was dangerous to stay still during head count because the cold could take hold the moment she stopped moving, but also dangerous to expend energy she didn't have. She bent her knees, curled her toes in her too-big boots. They marched off toward their work duty, through the fog of their breath that hung and froze in the air. The brigade's job was to clear snow from the road leading to the mine, a Sisyphean task that made Vera's back spasm a mere hour in.

"Accuracy begets speed, and speed means happy and easy work," the guard shouted. The propaganda was a joke to him, to this *nadziratel*, but he said it anyway to needle them. He was not mean, more indifferent, vaguely irritated by his charges. Some guards were cruel. Stealing from *zeki*'s meager belongings, systematically beating them, raping them, forcing others to stand in the snow without shoes until they froze to death. Some shot prisoners they pretended they'd caught trying to escape so they could get rewarded in rubles. Vera had learned to sniff out the sadistic ones and stay as invisible as possible to them. But this one, Boris, didn't seem to see the prisoners as enemies.

A *zek* in her brigade touched a metal shovel through the hole in his glove and cried out as it tore the skin from his hand. Blood ran and froze, and Boris exhaled in annoyance. But he let the man go to the infirmary, where it was warm and you got to lie down, which made Vera think the man had maimed himself on purpose, which then made her mad because there was one fewer worker contributing to a production norm already set impossibly high. That would then mean a smaller piece of bread ration, always raw in the middle to weigh more than it would have otherwise, to cheat them at every turn.

A *buran* swept in that day, swirling snow and screaming wind, and blotted out the stingy sun, everything disappearing into whiteness. Vera couldn't see anyone or anything. It sounded like the descent of angry ghosts. She stumbled and opened her arms wide, hoping to make contact with something or someone, or she knew she would die in the storm. She felt as if she'd fallen into a frozen lake, unsure which way was up, her senses useless. She had lost her husband and son, was cold and hungry, was alive but not living, survival the goal day after day. But for what? Vera fell down into the snow. She allowed herself to think about giving up. She could stop. It could end. She could feel herself slide toward oblivion. Sad relief. She pictured the Madonna from the cathedral of her youth, the Mother of God of the Sign with her sad eyes, knowing she would lose her son. Vera asked God to lead her.

And then a big-gloved hand shot through the white, grabbing her arm, lifting her up. Shaking her until she could stand without collapsing. Vera was so unused to kindness she thought she might already be dead.

"Hold on!" he yelled.

It was a voice without a body, and then she could see enough to know that it was a guard. It was Boris. He took her hand and half dragged her though the blinding storm to a lean-to toolshed where others were huddled. And he set off again into the whiteout.

Vera stood at the stove and skimmed the foam from the bone broth. She chopped an onion, the parsnips, garlic. How could she be the same person as the one ready to die in the blinding snow? She had kept living,

on and on. That day had been a turning point. Boris. She stopped herself, as she always did, from thinking more about him.

She peeled and grated the beets, as *povar* had done. Her hands hurt,
her joints stiff and reluctant. With Katerina gone, and now Anya, Vera
had no one left with whom to share her memories. She felt a flutter of
panic cinch her breath. It would all cease to be, and history would die
with her. Live through the next day, stay alive, don't get sick, work less,
eat more. She thought of Ledorsky living with his crippled animals.
Ledorsky, who had been a camp informer, a fixer. They had let him be
a *dneval'niy*, cleaning and keeping watch over the barracks. They had let
him keep mice in a cage.

The *borshch* was half done, but Vera was no longer hungry. Her hands
looked bloodstained from the beets. Four years into hard labor, she had
stopped caring about the right thing to do. Frozen corpses had been
stacked by the fence until the thaw, when they could dig a giant grave
and dump them. She hadn't wanted to become one of them. The day
after the snowstorm, she'd gone to see Ledorsky.

Vera tried to rub the red stains from her fingers, but it was futile. She
turned off the stove and sat heavily into a kitchen chair. So many had
vanished. Her fellow prisoners who went out to work in the morning
and never returned to the barracks in the evening. All those rounded up
and sent to Gulag camps never to be heard from again. Katerina. What
had happened to her? Her father, who left only blood in the snow. At
least she knew Ilya and Pyotr had died; she didn't have to wonder.

Get up, Vera, she said to herself. You are not dead yet. She rose slowly,
straightening her back as best she could, her muscles brittle, her bones
knocking. Was there meaning in survival? Or was it just an instinct all
animals had? Here she was, alive another day. She filled a saucepan with
water to boil for tea. Cold stole its way in through a crack in the window,
despite the coming of spring. Had all these long years of being alone
been worth it? Ledorsky was the only one she could ask, the one person
who might know. She'd never had the nerve to go to him.

Vera, she said to herself finally. It is time.

CHAPTER 15

Yuri waited in line at the administrative building downtown, his third queue of the day, with a pile of forms in his hand, some stamped, some not. He counted the people in front of him and then wrote the number on his palm with a ballpoint pen. It was early spring, the hard cold not yet broken, but the light was back, an orange late-afternoon glow. He closed his eyes and faced the sun, hoping for a little of its energy and brightness. He felt neither. He could use a drink.

"Happiness in Rus means drinking; we can't live without it," Vladimir, the prince of Kievan Rus, supposedly said in 988 when he chose Orthodox Christianity over Islam. But was Yuri an *alkash*? He drank, needed to drink. But didn't everyone else?

He was standing behind thirty people waiting for official stamps on marriage certificates, residency permits, and pension authorizations, in order to have his wife declared dead. It was necessary if he and Irina were to marry, but he felt queasy nonetheless. Because there was no body, there were interviews and processes and fees and waiting before a judgment would be made. He had not told Anya. He thought he might ask her permission in a letter, but his attempt sounded oddly formal, and in the end, he was a coward and could not send it. He would tell her in person when she returned from Round Lake.

"Be her father," Irina had said. "Don't make her part of it. You take the burden."

He didn't want the burden either, but okay.

The man in back of him, middle-aged, his nose red and bulbous, tapped Yuri on the shoulder.

"The five-hour window is closing," he said. "We will not make it."

Queue waiting was almost a national sport.

"Is that so," Yuri said, not falling for the bait. He laughed and didn't drop from the line.

"A laugh without reason is the sign of a fool," the man said. He sniffed and looked away.

Yuri could barely believe that he had been, not ten years ago, part of the Party bureaucracy. He had not been a member of the *nomenklatura* by any means, the privileged echelon who lived well above the average Soviet, but there had been perks: celebratory meals out with Party leaders, complete with caviar and champagne. There weren't *beryozki* in Norilsk, those special shops open to foreigners and *nomenklatura*, but he had access to goods, like the silk scarf imported from Germany he bought Katerina for her twenty-fifth birthday.

She had grown to disdain the disparity between the better-offs and the rest.

"Everyone has a job, has cradle-to-grave security!" he would proclaim.

"Let the bigwigs go to an ordinary store and stand in line like everyone else. And then maybe those lines that we're all sick and tired of will be eliminated."

She all but called him a hypocrite.

It wouldn't have taken much for someone to overhear her as she grew less worried about what others might think. She thought artists and writers had a sacred mission to tell the truth and carry it to the people. She stopped wearing her scarf.

Yuri thought it might be good for her to take a holiday to a sanitorium, that a few days of health treatments might help. Salt therapy, mineral baths, massages. He could watch Anya.

"I'm not an achy old woman," she said. "This is bigger than that."

He had inquired about it anyway, from his Party patron, a man he'd known since arriving in Norilsk. Hadn't his wife gone to a sanitorium to do magnetic therapy to help her back? Yuri received a notice a week later that his services were no longer needed at the City Committee.

Katerina had been right. The Soviet Union was not classless. Some had more money, some had more privileges, some got better apartments. Even now, he received two hundred rubles a month because of Anya. A worker was still just a worker. Lines for bread, lines for boots that did not fit, lines for what was left of the meat after the higher-ups took what they wanted, lines to declare your wife dead.

He plodded forward in line. Katerina had been right about so many things. He looked down at the papers in his hands. I'm sorry, he thought. He had felt something once, when they set out together, when Communism seemed the answer to an unjust world. But now? Maybe he had been wrong all along.

In 1950, his class had written a letter to the youth of 1975 to be included in a time capsule buried under a small pedestal in a square near school: "We bequeath to you the ardent love for the great leader of the working class, Vladimir Lenin," it began. Had the capsule, a metal box, been dug up and read? "We believe that in 1975 people will be safe from war and hunger. The world will be more just than it is today, and there will be no capitalists left." He had been the classroom scribe, had written the letter over and over again until his letters were neat and even.

Hope was not something Yuri had reserves of these days, but there were bright spots. Anya, of course. She had done so well at the Druzhba Tournament, even though she'd told him on the phone that she had not been feeling her best. "She competed bravely for her country," the letter from the Party office had said, notifying him that he would receive an additional twenty-five rubles per month. "She must continue to work hard." As if she would do anything less. There were those quiet moments when he thought maybe he had let Anya down. But he wasn't immune to pride. She had a great talent. And though he could only admit this to himself, it reflected well on him, to have a daughter whose accomplishments put her in such good standing with the Party.

Up ahead in line a fight broke out between women in flowered kerchiefs.

"I was here. My niece held my spot."

"I don't see a niece. I see a line cutter."

"*Teeshe, teeshe,*" an old man said. They didn't quiet down.

Yuri had had enough for the day. Anya was soon to arrive. He would head home while it was still light out, stop for a quick drink at the *traktir*. Katerina would be officially alive for one more day. He stepped out of line. The man behind him moved up with a self-satisfied lift of his chin, and Yuri walked away.

* * *

After her flight from Moscow, Anya held her father's hand all the way home from the airstrip, the taxi bouncing in and out of potholes, windows open to combat the stench of the driver, who smelled like he hadn't bathed all winter long. Norilsk looked smaller and more run-down to her, the chimneys churning foul-smelling smoke into the air, the sweet taste of copper gas on her tongue. As they drove through town, she followed the dips and rises of the dirty snow line that rimmed the first floors of buildings.

"Papa!"

She pointed through the window at the charred remains of the giant scarecrow burned for Maslenitsa. She'd always loved the festival that celebrated the passing of winter into spring. They would gather in town for sweets and watch the *stenka na stenku*, the choreographed sparring of men in traditional folk clothing. It looked more like dancing than fighting. They went every year, even when she was just a baby and they got caught in a late snowstorm, her father told her, Katerina insistent on getting up close to the fire.

"You didn't miss much this year," Yuri said. He eyed the driver to see if he was listening. "They allowed the scarecrow but not the rest of it. I don't know what was different this year. There's been some crackdown on anything seen as religious."

The driver looked back in the rearview mirror and returned his eyes to the road.

"No pancake week then?" she asked.

"Irina's got a surprise for you at home," Yuri said.

Anya was struck by the dinginess of their apartment—the worn-out linoleum floor, the yellow-tinged light, the soot-dirtied windows. Plants now covered the windowsills, grow lights jury-rigged from the ceiling.

"Irina says plants are good for health," he said.

He shrugged and smiled, and Anya was happy to see it. She felt her shoulders drop in the comfort of being home. She didn't have to worry about being yelled at or shamed or about hurting herself or failing. She didn't have to be back at her old Norilsk gym until tomorrow.

"We're making *bliny!*" Irina said, emerging from the kitchen. She hugged Anya into her scratchy sweater. "You're so skinny. Don't they let you eat?"

"Not a lot," she said. "A mean witch smacks your hand if you reach for pudding meant for the coaches. No one wants a bad weigh-in."

Irina scoffed. "That sounds miserable. Come."

Anya followed her into the kitchen. It smelled of melted butter.

"Are you ready? I put two glasses of flour in the bowl there. Now you start mixing and gradually pour in three glasses of milk. But don't stop stirring; it's very important."

Anya could tell that Irina knew where everything was in the kitchen. She wondered if, when she'd left, Irina had moved in. There was a rough edge to the realization, but she tried to let it be. Her mother was gone. Her father didn't have to be alone.

"Add half a teaspoon of salt and three tablespoons of sugar," Irina said. Anya measured out the ingredients and added them to the bowl. "Excellent. Now crack four eggs into that small bowl and beat them." Anya worked her fork with speed. "Good. When they're foamy pour them into everything else."

Anya tilted the bowl toward her.

"Yes! Now mix it all again and we are ready."

Irina poured the thin batter into a hot buttered pan. The *bliny* cooked in seconds, brown and curling up at the edges. The kitchen was warm and smelled good. Anya was home.

Irina peered at her through her glasses, her eyes large, blinking.

"Now you can make these whenever you want," she said. "You can make them for all the hungry gymnasts."

Anya lived in two separate worlds. No one from this world could really understand gymnastics, and gymnastics didn't care about the world on the outside. She missed Elena.

Yuri took a *blin* and bounced it in his fingers, too hot to hold. Irina playfully elbowed him out of the way.

"Let's smother them in *smetana*," she said.

Anya took a spoon and dropped a heaping dollop of sour cream onto her plate. She licked the spoon and closed her eyes. She was cheating, she knew, but couldn't resist. She couldn't gain weight in a day, could she?

"Is Ledorksy keeping any new creatures?" Anya asked.

"I haven't heard any roars or squawks coming from his door," Irina said. "But I'm sure he's got some kind of menagerie in there."

It was strange to be home again, where life had gone on without her. Her body felt as though it had gone soft in the day she'd been out of the gym. She rolled her ankle to feel the cracking and pain.

Yuri's face looked deflated, despite his bloated middle. His cheekbones were ledges, and his beard was leached of its red. Irina's hair had gone wilder, wiry strands going every which way. They kept looking at each other with slight head shakes and widened eyes. They had secrets between them, and Anya felt a barb of annoyance.

"What?" Anya asked.

"Hmm?" Irina said.

Anya felt her peevishness like an itch she couldn't reach. "What is it?" she asked, surprising herself with the shortness of her tone.

"Nothing," Yuri said, taking a long sip of vodka. "Just happy to have you home."

Anya sighed, trying to act more grown-up than she felt; it was more of an adjustment to be with her father and Irina than she had anticipated. Maybe she no longer belonged here. But she had missed Vera. Her soft and spotted hands, her *schyoty*. The haven of her affection. Being close to Vera was keeping a tether to memories of her mother.

* * *

It took Vera a moment to register the knock on the door.

It was the girl. Her arrival was a kind of answer to Vera; maybe she lived on to feel this spark of joy. Anya with her raven hair and inscrutable eyes. There was nothing frivolous about her. How she wished Katerina could see her daughter now.

"I haven't done one speck of math since I went away," Anya announced. She was small for twelve but getting taller, and Vera could feel the sinews of her back in her hug.

"Come in, come in. Tea in the kitchen."

Anya bounded away, and Vera followed slowly, her back curved over. Her head felt too heavy to hold up without great effort. She rested her hands on the counter, winded, and set a *podstakannik* in front of Anya at the table. She wiped the dust from the glass and set it in its holder, her old hand quivering.

"Sit. I'll do the rest," Anya said, hopping up.

Vera fell into the chair with a rattled breath, too tired to pretend.

Anya prepared the teapot and another glass. She eyed the bowl of chocolates as she sat at the table.

"Go on," Vera said. "I'll pretend you came to see *me*."

After she'd eaten three chocolates and sipped her tea, Anya sat back in her chair with a contented smile.

"Sometimes I dream about rooms full of fruit and cakes," she said.

"When I was in the camp, I would imagine peeling an orange, the oil misting, the rind in my thumbnail. The ritual sectioning. The silky membrane. The tiny sacs of sweet juice."

"What was the first thing you ate when you got out?"

"I wish I could say I ate five oranges. Or a big dish of ice cream. But it wasn't like that. One day they read out my prisoner number and said I had fulfilled my sentence. I walked away from the *lagpunkt*, out the front gate, and had nowhere to go. So I ended up in town. I had been officially rehabilitated, so I was given a residency permit in Norilsk, a stipend. This apartment. I went to the store, but it was all too much. I bought only an onion."

Anya laughed. "An onion?"

"Can you believe it? After all those years. I baked it and ate the whole thing."

"Did it taste good?"

"It was no bowl of ice cream."

"When I'm too old for gymnastics I'm going to eat ice cream every day."

"You could do that now."

Anya shook her head. "There are Nationals, Europeans, Worlds, the Olympics even. If I work hard enough."

"In the camp we had work norms, the amount of work we were required to do in a single shift. If you did more, you were deemed an excellent worker. An *otlichnik*. That's you."

Anya considered this as she sipped her tea.

"A new trick," she said after a moment. "A skill you couldn't do before, and then all of a sudden you can, and then you work on it until you know it in your body and it's yours. It feels like warm sun that shines only for you. It's the best feeling there is."

"But it's a sacrifice too. Not to be a normal schoolgirl."

"Oh, but I made a friend at Ozero Krugloye!" The girl's face grew wide, her eyes lifted. "I feel like I have known her forever. I miss her now. I can tell her anything."

"I felt that way about your mother," Vera said.

Katerina had been the one person who had ever asked her about what it had been like, the one true friend. Telling Katerina had eased some of her burden. The camp was not something to be forgotten. Forgetting didn't work anyway.

"When I die, you can have anything of mine that you wish. It will all go to you."

"Even the chocolates?"

"Especially the chocolates."

"Vera Vasilievna?"

"Yes, *dorogaya*."

Anya looked away from her toward the window.

"I don't remember her really. A moment here and there, a feeling. But I can't even see what she looks like in my mind sometimes."

"You remember her in your gymnastics. How you move. You make beauty like she did. It's your inheritance."

"You'll be able to watch me on the television one day."

"I better stay alive then."

Vera went into her bedroom and retrieved her icon, carrying it back out with both hands.

"This will be yours when I'm gone."

"It's beautiful. But what will I do with it?" Anya asked.

"You can't take it with you to the gym. It's for when you are grown and have a place of your own. But make sure to hang it upside down for three days."

"Upside down?"

Anya leaned over and craned her head around to see what it would look like.

"It's good luck! No matter where you are, you will always come home."

Vera wondered where that would be for Anya. Somewhere far away from Norilsk.

"Did you hang it upside down when you moved in here?" Anya asked.

"No," she laughed. After Ilya died, after Pyotr, home had lost its meaning. Besides, Vera had stopped hoping for luck long ago. But Anya was different. She might still find it. "But it's a nice idea, isn't it?"

After Anya went home, Vera spent a minute with her icon, taking herself back to church at Saint Sofia when she was a girl, the cold stone through the soles of her shoes, the swish of skirts, the lingering sooty sweetness of rose and frankincense. Kissing the icons—Jesus on the feet, saints on the hands. They stood in a row, her parents between her and her sisters to prevent any tittering or whispering between them, shifting from foot to foot through the whole service. It was easy to believe in God when a skinned knee or a mean sister was as bad as it got.

And now, after everything? She had to believe. Without God, Pyotr would just be bones in the dirt. She rose to her crooked height and went into her bedroom. She raised her chin and appraised herself in the silver hand mirror she'd been given on her fourth birthday—her mother had hidden it inside the old clock in the crate she had sent before she died—propped against the wall on her dresser. She rebraided her long white hair and twisted it into a bun. She smoothed her eyebrows. Her hazel eyes were greener now, sagging pouches of skin below. What an old woman I am, she said to herself. There was only one person to face who had known her in camp. It was time; there was little time left.

She walked slowly down the hall to the stairwell, grasping the handrail, two feet up to a step then again up to another. It was late, but light fanned out from beneath Ledorsky's door into the darkened hallway. Vera caught her breath and knocked.

* * *

Anya sat on her bed and Yuri sat on his, just out of the circle of light from the lamp. He had changed so since he'd trained her in the apartment, frog-jumping with her, counting out leg lifts, clapping his encouragement. He didn't look like he could do a push-up. He coughed, wet and deep.

"I have missed you, *Dochka*," he said. "I'm proud of you. They will make you a Master of Sport. You are a hero for our country."

"I don't think about that. Only what to work on to get better."

He scratched his chin through his beard.

"I need to tell you something. You like Irina all right, don't you?"

"Yes, Papa."

"We are going to get married."

It was not unexpected, and not unwelcome. She knew her mother had been gone for so many years, and her father was not good by himself. But it was barbed news to swallow nonetheless.

"I'm happy for you," she said, sounding wooden, formal.

"But to do that"—his eyes filled, and he began coughing again. "Your mother wanted to leave Norilsk. She said she needed trees and flowers. She wanted sunshine. She wanted poetry. But she would never have left you."

Anya nodded.

"She will be declared dead," he said. "Officially."

Her mother was dead. As much as she knew it was true, that it made the most sense, to hear it took something from her. The energy that was holding her up receded. She fell back onto her bed and turned away from Yuri. She wished she were back in the dorm room with Elena. The two of them, motherless girls.

"All the never-answered questions," he said. "Maybe we can let them rest."

She imagined herself on the bars, hands tight but loose enough, straddle to handstand, shoulders open, and the half moment of shifting her weight into a fall before she had to harness the downward momentum to rise again.

"What do you think happened to her?" she said. "How did she die?"

She turned back to look at her father, who sat with his back hunched. Sadness seemed to tug the corners of his eyes downward as he looked at the night dark through the window. He sighed and closed his eyes, bracing himself before opening them. Anya thought that maybe this time he would reveal something that would give her a story she could latch onto. Yuri cleared his throat then leaned forward with his elbows on his knees.

"It was a day like today," he said finally. He met her gaze and then looked away again. "Early spring but the light was holding for longer. The dripping of melting snow made a steady tap tap everywhere you went. I remember she had been in a good mood that morning, and it stood out to me because in those days, her spirits had grown darker. I thought maybe she was coming back to her old self again. She sang the *zaichik* song to you to get you to finish your porridge." He smiled. "She said we needed toothpaste. She said she would wait at the butcher so she could make a stew. I have gone over the day so many times. Was there something? I hit on all the same details again and again. It was a normal day. When it was time to go teach ballet, she kissed us good-bye and left."

Anya rolled onto her back. Tears she rarely allowed herself leaked from the corners of her eyes.

"Sometimes I follow her when she left the dance school that day," her father said. "The sun is on her face and she feels newly hopeful and she walks and walks toward the edge of town, past it, up onto the snowy hill toward the wild open, and she runs and leaps until she can't go another step. And then she just goes blurry, and she is gone."

* * *

It was the middle of the night but Anya could not sleep. She was alone in the bedroom—her father had gone to Irina's to sleep. She had been home for only a day, but her body was restless from being out of the gym. She couldn't keep her legs still. Her ankle ached, her wrists hurt, her calf muscle was sore from an earlier pull, but she wanted to be back at gymnastics. When she was away from it, she felt purposeless, floating, a balloon cut loose from its string.

She rose and went over to the small window, the glass cold against her palms.

In the sky, a rare late appearance of the northern lights swirled above the building across the courtyard. Spectral, moving, like water.

"Mama," Anya said.

The undulating aurora was a green glow in the darkness.

"I have a new friend. Her name is Elena. She is the best gymnast in the world. I want to be just like her."

The lights shimmered, faded, and then there were just the stars pinned to the night sky.

"Maybe you sent Elena to me," she said quietly. "I know you are never coming home."

She didn't care about the work and the pain, the long hours she faced, the swift punishment by Anatoly. All she wanted was to be back in the little room with Elena at Round Lake. It was more home than home. She would do anything to get back there again.

CHAPTER 16

"Who is it?" the naturalist asked.

"It is I. Vera Vasilievna Kuznetsova," she said, fighting the tremor in her voice. Thirty years collapsed in this moment. She was afraid, still, of facing the one person who knew, who understood.

Ledorsky opened the door. The top of his smooth head reflected the light. He was small and stooped, and he pushed his glasses up on his nose to see her better. Despite the hour and his isolation, he wore a too-large black suit, white animal fur sticking to the sleeves.

"I was hoping you might one day come," he said.

Vera felt nervous, but the sight of him calmed her some. They were witnesses to human beings at their worst. They were perpetrators of their own moral failings. He knew the choice she had made. But today, nearer to death, she felt it had less power over her.

"Anya would like to know if you are keeping any animals," she said.

"Come in and meet Narkiss the cat. He has no teeth, so I feed him a paste of herring. I also have a one-winged gull who doesn't seem to want to leave."

"Did you really have a polar bear in here?"

"Ah, Aika. I miss her. She was a feisty one."

He held out his arm, and Vera took it. He looked fragile, but his arm was strong and steady.

Inside his apartment all the lights were on. Stacks of old newspapers teetered about. A dirty gull hopped around a large cage, its one good wing extended. A row of plants at varying stages of growth lined the counter under a lamp. The fusty air was covered by the smell of baking bread.

"*Chyornyi khleb,*" she said.

"I always have black bread. I make it with dark molasses and a bit of chocolate," he said. "Sit. Introduce yourself to Narkiss."

The cat was huge, orange, old, draped across a ripped upholstered chair spilling matted stuffing. Narkiss eyed Vera as she sat down opposite; he swished his tail but didn't move.

"He must keep you from being lonely," she said.

"Yes. I understand animals. Better than people I suppose."

This time she would not shy away from their shared past. "I remember the mice."

In the camp he had traded information for a rusty little cage. The mice he had caught on his own.

He nodded. "They helped keep my mind glued together. Having something to take care of, to talk to. You know what the judge said to me when he sent me to prison? 'The iron broom of Soviet justice sweeps only rubbish into its camps.'" Ledorsky pulled the loaf from the oven, the crust a luxurious deep brown. "I didn't believe it—he was sending me!—but I did believe it too. Some tiny voice said he was right."

"For a long time, I held on to a magical notion that it was a mistake that would be corrected," Vera said. "'We are so sorry, comrade. You are free to go home.'"

"Who turned you in?"

"A colleague informed on my husband. We had been friendly with this man. We'd had him and his wife to dinner. His son played with my son when they were little," Vera said. "But he had always been envious of Ilya. The man had lost a promotion to him. There were moments when I was in prison that I blamed Ilya, somehow, for provoking his colleague. It is painful to admit that."

Ledorsky glanced at her and then tapped the top of the bread, a perfect hollow sound.

"Let's let it cool," he said. He brought over a tray with a teapot and small china teacups. "These were my mother's. She bought them in Paris in a shop on the rue du Bac, where she'd gone to be fitted for her wedding dress."

"And you?" she asked. "Who turned you in?"

"My wife," he said. "She was having an affair with an NKVD officer."

The gull's cry made Vera jump.

"Oh, come now," he said, tapping the cage. "Everyone thinks he will be the moral one. But no one knows the extent of his courage or cowardice until tested. I knew going in though. We are animals too. Survival requires putting kindness aside. I had to learn to live without pity."

"Did you have children?" she asked.

"No. I was at least grateful for that."

"I had a son," she said.

"I know," he said.

"I have never gone back to the *zona*, what's left of it," Vera said. "I suppose I am afraid. To feel those things. To be on the same ground. But I couldn't leave Norilsk either."

Ledorsky nodded and laced his fingers together between his knees.

"Do you remember when that inmate escaped?" he asked. "It was right after the end of the War. He wandered for seven days and ended up only eight miles from camp. He turned himself in. 'Freedom isn't for us,' he told me. 'We can escape, but in the end we'll come back.' He wasn't even punished because he was doing such good propaganda work."

"I suppose he was right," she said. "Look at us here."

Vera tried to imagine what her life might have looked like if she had gone back to Novgorod. Walking along the Volkhov, the papery shimmer of birch leaves, the glint of the golden dome of Saint Sofia. But she would have still been the same woman, with the same losses and pain and memories; there was no distance that would have been a salve, that would have been far enough away.

"I went out there in 1958, after they had dismantled the camp," he said. "No barbed wire, no guard tower. The barracks were turned into storage sheds for snowplows. Like it had never existed."

"When I was released and first went to town, there were shops, theaters, parks," she said. "Like an apparition. How could it be?"

Ledorsky sipped his tea.

"I thought that I would skip out of the camp, elated with freedom," he said. "But when I walked past the last guard, I didn't even feel happy. It was summer, hot. Clouds of mosquitos. I started walking. There was a mother with her children, three of them, two girls and a boy, laughing, chasing each other through the wildflowers. The mother stood there in her pretty dress, smiling after them. How could you? I thought. How could you be happy as if everything is normal? As if there weren't such misery and depravity down the road."

"I thought people might ask about it," Vera said. "Congratulate me for making it through. Offer me solace in some way, or apology. Something. But no, no one talked about it. Norilsk was full of those who had been in prison and those who had kept us there. Norillag was still going, but everyone shrugged and ignored it. *Vsyo tak, kak ono yest'*. Just the way it is. To acknowledge the horror of it would mean questioning the Soviet Union itself."

"It was too frightening, too dangerous," he said. "To question. No one wants to acknowledge complicity."

"Even us. The camp went on for ten more years after we got out," Vera said.

"What could we do?" Ledorsky asked. "What could anyone have done?"

Vera shook her head. She picked up her teacup but set it back down again.

"I took a job as a cashier in the produce market, computing change on the abacus," she said. "Once my former brigade leader came in and handed me a bunch of carrots. He looked at me, and I could tell he was about to smile because I looked familiar, and then his expression melted into fear. Fear of me. Can you imagine? What did he think I would do, reach over and bash him with the carrots? I said, 'Hello, *tovarishch*.' And he looked at me dumbly, his mouth open. 'You're looking well,' he said. That was it. I handed him his change."

The degree of suffering wasn't the same for everyone; there wasn't a scale of fairness. She sensed that she and Ledorsky had both accepted this early on. She wished she could have talked openly to him long ago.

Narkiss sauntered over and jumped onto Ledorsky's lap. He scratched between his ears. Vera felt warm and drowsy, drained of nerves. This little man nursing his animals.

"I always wondered if they believed in what they were doing," he said. "If any of them, all the way up, if they believed in the danger of us to socialism, to the Motherland. Did they really think we were more dangerous than the thieves and murderers, or did they just need the people to believe it? All the questions we will never have answers to."

In the ten years inside, Vera had only been fortunate enough to be granted one blissful night in the camp hospital. It was during the War, when things were even worse, starvation rations, impossible work norms, an influx of foreign prisoners, bodies piled up along the fence and covered with snow. She'd passed out, consumed with fever, and she awoke in a bright room on a bunk with a white sheet. No bedbugs dropped from the bunk above. The room smelled of bleach, free of the rancid odor of human decay and the dirge of sorrow that infected the barracks at night.

The doctor, a prisoner himself, round faced and big bellied, came in the next morning and asked how she was feeling. It was as if they were in a play, this polite exchange. She swallowed and moved around a bit and found herself feeling better, the fever broken. "I see you still have a high temperature," he said. The lie was a gift he was giving her. "A day in the recovery barracks is ordered." She wanted to tell the doctor how grateful she was, but of course she could not, so she reached out and squeezed his hand instead. She was moved next door. In the bed next to her, a young Polish woman who'd shoved a nail into her uterus was recovering from the self-inflicted abortion. In the other bed raved a man with pellagra, his skin loose and dry like he would shed his skin, his eyes gleaming in hallucinatory fervor. For Vera, it was a day free of the daily *rezhim*, the most delicious feeling of rest. A nurse gave her a sip of fresh cool water, and the pleasure of it nearly made her weep.

Every once in a while, there was something that carried her to the next day, and to the next. A kindness. A glimpse of beauty. A smooth bit of black stone that had taken millions of years to form, which she kept in a pocket she'd sewn into her jacket.

But she needed to know now why Ledorsky had taken the devil's bargain.

"Was it a difficult decision for you? To choose your own life?" she asked.

He looked at her through his thick glasses, eyes large and seeking, to judge the venom of her question. But he didn't get defensive, didn't protest.

"I was invited to speak to the Operative Commander early on," Ledorsky said. "He ushered me into a cozy room with real chairs and classical music playing on the record player. It was disorienting, entering into a different world. 'Are you Soviet?' he asked me. 'Yes,' I said. He offered me a biscuit, and I took it. And he pulled out this sheet of paper with a pledge written on it, a promise to report news on prisoners planning to escape or information on any other anti-Soviet activity. I could have said no. Others did. I knew what I was doing. I knew what it would mean to be an informer."

Vera sipped her tea. How much hatred she had harbored for Ledorsky and those like him. She'd had to walk past the escapee who'd been caught and strung up on the guard post, his swollen tongue protruding obscenely from his mouth. His frozen body was kept there for weeks. Someone had turned him in. Not Ledorsky, maybe, but someone like him.

"I didn't relish in it. And I fed them useless morsels of information," Ledorsky said. His hands fluttered up in agitation. "I knew I would be a pariah. But it was the only way I was going to make it. Dostoyevsky said that man is a creature that can get used to anything. But I would have died on a work brigade. To make it we each had to find our threshold. For pain. For hunger."

They had all paid for their survival with shame.

"Like it or not, we are survivors, you and me," he said.

He knew the bargain she had made too. But he did not sit in judgment of her. All those years of avoiding him felt wasteful to her now. He had not been waiting to castigate her. He did not see her as a bad woman. And he was not a bad man.

"Once I had decided I needed to live through it," Vera said, "I never questioned it. I didn't have anything to live for. And yet it was my obsession to make it out alive. It was some kind of victory over that place, over injustice. But now, I don't know. Why did we make it through? You and me over two other people? Was there purpose in it? That's what I wanted to ask you. I am an old old woman, and I still don't know what to make of it."

"What, of suffering, of surviving?" He smiled and sipped his tea.

"We're Russian, that's what we do. Maybe we become better and stronger by suffering and overcoming."

Vera almost laughed. "We must be strong enough to lift a house by now."

"I suppose one feels an obligation to live," he said. "Despite its burdens. It felt like a choice when we had no choices. A false one, perhaps. And I would never suggest your husband and son or any of the dead chose not to live. But I had to feel like it was my choice to survive."

"Yes," she said. "I felt it was my choice too."

"Let me slice you a piece of bread, Vera Vasilievna."

She knew there could be no grand realization; life was too messy for that. But she felt something sitting here with Ledorsky, something new and solid, like a warm little creature she could hold in her hand. She opened her fingers and let it go.

* * *

The old gym looked smaller and more dilapidated, the smell of mildew stronger, the other girls mere background. Sergei and a new coach ran the program, while Anatoly worked only with Anya. Masha was doing punishment half-ups from the bar. She had told Anya there were three new girls, one who could do double backs even though she was only eleven. Masha told her the older girl Karolina had disappeared from the gym, and the rumor was that Sergei had made her pregnant.

Anya stood on beam after a series of leaps, as Anatoly barked at her.

"Why do you move like the beam is on fire? You have thirty seconds. Show off your transitions. The show is where you are lacking. Think about it." He shook his head and lit a cigarette. "The winner will be the one that works the hardest. If you fail, it means you weren't trying hard enough."

Anya walked back to the end of the beam and began again with her leap pass, trying to slow it down, extend through her fingers.

"You've got to fight yourself every day. Make your body listen to you. Your willpower determines everything."

She gathered herself for a moment, took a long pause before her cartwheel layout step out. She landed it but wobbled; her leg shot out to check her balance.

"Well," Anatoly said. His eyes lowered to reptilian slits. He spoke quietly, his voice a facetious slither. "What do you think? Is that the landing of a national champion?"

"It's not there yet," she said.

"Oh no? What might be the problem? Not enough repetitions perhaps?"

"Yes."

"Yes. Then why have you not done them? I'll tell you. Weak character. You were all bent and square with that last one. Soar in the air like a rainbow."

Again, again, again. I'm coming back to you, Elena, she thought.

* * *

When Anya left the gym, Sveta was there waiting for her. Anya felt something rise and then fall in her at the sight of her oldest friend. The once tiny Sveta had grown past her, taller, thin but with a curve to her hips. At thirteen she looked older than even Elena. Her hair, in the late sun of spring, was greasy but still hauntingly light, her face more angular, a streak of dirt across her forehead.

They fell into their rhythm, despite how long it had been.

"Were the girls nice? At the training camp?"

"Not really. Except one." Guilt made Anya's tongue feel thick in her mouth. Elena felt like a betrayal.

"Did you meet Olga Korbut?"

"I saw her. But I didn't talk to her. She smokes cigarettes. She's going to marry Leonid Bortkevich."

"The singer?"

"*I can now confess, I then fell in love,*" Anya sang with mock seriousness.

Sveta laughed. "Do you think he sings to her instead of talking?"

"Do you think she does a flip before setting out his tea?"

Anya fished two chocolates from her pocket and handed one to Sveta, whose nails were bitten short and edged with dirt.

"Tourischeva was there too. As a coach. Anatoly said they let her help with the team because she's good for the cameras."

"Oh, remember Viktor from grade school?" Sveta asked.

"The fencer. The nose picker."

"He's dead. Jumped in the river on a dare and got stuck under the ice."
Anya rubbed her arms as if to warm them.

"That must have been a scary way to die," she said.

"I guess," Sveta said. "It was stupid, that's for sure."

"It makes me sad."

"You can't be sad. You have everything," she said.

Anya took the barb, felt it sink into her like a thorn.

"Let's see your aerial," she said. Anya wanted to make Sveta feel
included.

"I don't do silly stuff anymore," Sveta said. "Don't pity me, Anya
Yurievna."

"I don't," Anya said, even though she did. Sveta was drifting, batted
about, rough. "Did you watch the European Championships?"

"Who has a television?" Sveta looked around one shoulder and then
the other.

"Are you waiting for someone?"

"My mother has to check in with the KGB. Soon they will be on my
tail."

Anya didn't want to ask about her father.

"I'm going to go to America," Sveta said. "Someday. There's nothing
for me here." She stomped in a pile of slush, spraying it onto Anya's
feet.

"Sveta Nikolaevna!" Anya whispered. She pulled her friend's sleeve,
leading her closer to the street. "Be careful what you say."

"What? It has to be better than this dump. You should ask Olga Korbut about it. She got to go and even met their president. If we can get
on a truck going to Dudinka, we can sneak on a boat going north on the
Yenisei to the sea. It'll stop in Murmansk, and we can walk to Finland.
That's what Nikita says."

As they crossed the street, Anya could see a boy slouched in the doorway of a building, his hands in the pockets of his coat. He was twitchy,
tall but folded in on himself, eyes a cold blue.

"Nikita," Sveta said, shoving her shoulder toward the boy.

Nikita pulled Sveta into him, and they started kissing, angry, like they
didn't even like each other. Anya stood in front of them for a moment
before putting her hand up in a wave and walking toward the bus stop.

"I don't hate you," Sveta called out after her. "I should but I don't."

Anya bit down on the inside of her cheek. I'm sorry I was chosen, she thought, but she wasn't sorry. I love you, Sveta, but she knew it meant nothing.

* * *

Anatoly was agitated this morning, a trail of old cigarettes as he paced about. Anya was working on triple twists into the foam pit but only making it around two and a half times.

"Are you going to do it like that at nationals?" he taunted. "Again. Shaposhnikova is working on it too. You must get it first."

Anya held her side as she sucked air trying to catch her breath.

"You're twisting right off the floor. You have to wait until the height of your jump to twist. That's the difference." He pointed to his temple. "Use your mind. Don't rush the skill."

She walked back and sighed, trying to find some reserve of energy. Fatigue heavied her limbs. Her father and Irina had kept her up the night before, drunk and singing in the next room. When she'd finally risen and asked them to be a little quieter, her father had slurred, "Don't be so serious all the time, *Dochka*. No one needs your rain cloud."

She remembered her anger and ran hard into her round-off back handspring but fell short again on the twists.

"*Vot blin*," Anatoly cursed. He crouched down on his haunches then slapped his knees and rose to his feet. "It is game to you? This?" He circled his hands in the air. "You think you can flip around for a couple years and go back to normal life?"

He left her there and disappeared into Marta's office before returning with a folded section of the newspaper. He swatted her ear with it and then handed it to her.

Moscow News Competition Results

The combined women's title was won by 17-year-old Elena Grishina, from Moscow, a first-year student at the Institute of Physical Culture, after a grueling and tense battle against Maria Filatova. We talked to Elena right after her appearance on the dais to collect her award, and she was still excited, caught up in the competition:

Q: Did you think you would win?

A: I really can't give you a definite answer. These competitions are brief, and no mistake, even a tiny one, is pardonable. Only when I was standing on the dais did I feel that I had the title wrapped up.

Q: What are your impressions of the competition?

A: This competition has always been a very exciting one, and the proof is this year's new names and technical innovations. I liked the American girls. Their routines were not very complicated, but by 1980 they will be. I am getting ready for the Moscow Olympics. I have to iron out all the technical difficulties but still keep my program fresh and vibrant.

It was strange to see Elena in this way, public, confident. It didn't sound like her at all. So grown-up and poised. Anya worried for a quivering second that Elena had moved on from her, that she had left her behind.

"You know who's a good gymnast?" Anatoly asked, swiping the paper from her. "Your friend Elena. You know who's a lazy *porosyonok*? You. Oink, oink." He reached out and pinched her thigh, squeezing her skin until she yelped and jumped back. "No lunch for you today. Look at little Olesya over here."

Olesya was new to the sports school, small and lithe, working back handsprings on the floor. Anya flinched: You are replaceable.

"Nice, Olesya Ivanovna," he called. The girl beamed and lifted her chin.

"You know how old she is?" he asked Anya. "She's only six. Soon she will pass you by. You're a *babushka*."

"I will work harder," Anya said. "I promise."

"Every pupil ends up spitting on your soul," he said. He leaned in again, and she stiffened, looking down at her feet, waiting for what he might land on her. He spoke in a calm, quiet voice. "Do you not understand, Anya Yurievna? Without gymnastics, without me, you are nothing."

She blushed, heat traveling from her face to her neck to her chest.

"If you can't look at me, you can just train on your own."

"I can't do it on my own," she said.

"Exactly," he said. "Go walk around for five minutes. When you come back, be ready to work."

On the way to the bathroom, Anya saw Karolina, the one Masha said was pregnant, slip out the door of the massage room. It was always surprising to see a gymnast in regular clothes. Karolina wore a red skirt and white blouse, her hair down, tucked behind her ears. She was twenty-one by now but still looked like a child.

"You're back," Karolina said, spotting her. She bit a piece of dry skin on her lip. Her eyes were ringed red. "The little flipper." She touched the top of Anya's head. "I have kept up with your competitions. I wonder what it must be like for you."

"It feels the same as always," Anya said.

"It seems exciting to me."

"Do you still do gymnastics?"

"No."

"What's that like? Do you sleep in in the morning? Eat a big breakfast?"

"I can barely walk in a straight line. Six concussions will do that to you. I didn't make it to regionals again last year, so that was it for me," she said. She adjusted her skirt and smoothed it down in front. "Do you know what they say about being a gymnast?"

Anya shook her head.

"First you just love it. It's hard to remember back that far, isn't it? Second you need it; you can't live without it."

"And then?"

"Third is when you realize you don't belong to yourself anymore. That's probably where you are now. I remember those days. A little scary, but freeing too. But then there is the fourth. The fourth is when you still want it, but nobody wants you anymore."

Karolina stared ahead, blank, until her eyes turned glassy and she looked down. She ran her hand over her stomach.

"I have to go. Anatoly is waiting," Anya said. "You know what he's like." She pushed open the bathroom door.

"You're lucky, though," Karolina said. "To be special."

Yes, Anya thought. But she wasn't sure she believed it.

* * *

The other girls had gone home. Sergei was stacking mats. Anya was finishing the last of the day's conditioning, five rope climbs, legs to the side in a pike. She had made it through another day.

"You do it now on the floor," Anatoly said.

"Do what?" she asked.

"The triple. Go on."

She had never tried it on the floor, never even made it around in the pit. Even she knew that one bad landing could take out a knee for good. Her anger pushed tears to the surface. He was showing off to Sergei.

"I'm too tired," she said. Her body was done, all shaky arms and cumbrous legs.

"Excuse me? You're too tired or too scared? You do as I say."

Sergei widened his eyes in surprise. "I can spot," he offered.

"You, shut up," Anatoly said. "Anya. I mean it. Do it. Or you will regret it."

Fear entwined her body. She closed her eyes and visualized herself jumping straight up, as high as the ceiling, bursting through into the sky. Up, up, up, straight, whip your head, tight twist, lightning fast, go, go, go. Spin me, Mama.

She opened her eyes and took off in a run, hurdle, round-off back handspring and she was off the ground, two seconds in motion, her body spinning through the air. Her feet hit the floor. Her knees didn't buckle. She got her bearings. She was looking back in the direction she had come from. She had landed it, made it three times around.

The gym was silent. She felt the elation gather in her chest and threaten to burst.

"Woooo!" Sergei said finally, clapping his hands.

Anatoly didn't pump his fist. He didn't smile. He stood with his arms crossed, a satisfied, gloating line to his mouth. But for the first time Anya didn't care. She stood, right where she had landed, and felt her own power. This is mine, and you will never know what this feels like, she thought.

"Marta wants to see you," Anatoly said. "I'll see you in the morning."

Anya couldn't quite rid herself of her smile. She knocked and entered the old office with its teetering stacks of ledgers that never seemed to change. Marta was scribbling something and looked up over her glasses.

"You look like the cat who ate the canary."

Anya cleared her throat to look serious.

"Gymnastics demonstrates the aesthetic, spiritual, and physical superiority of Soviet athletes. Don't you agree?"

"Yes."

"It is your duty. To give everything."

"Yes."

"Congratulations, Anya Yurievna. You're going back to Round Lake."

CHAPTER 17

It was 1978, and Anya counted the days to her return to training camp at Round Lake. She had a dream about her mother as a wrinkled old woman, a *krest'yanka* with her hair held back in a red kerchief, sitting by the edge of a lake, but before she could call to her, Anya was awakened by the nee-naw of a *militsiya* siren speeding past their building. The dream left her with a residue of sadness, a dusting of guilt. It felt accusatory in some way, like her mother felt forgotten. She didn't tell her father about it—he and Irina had gotten married—but she told Vera when she went to say good-bye.

"That's just your brain worrying," Vera said. "You don't need to think of her to remember her. Your body remembers her. Even how you are sitting there, leaning forward a little, with your ankles crossed like that. She sat exactly the same way."

"Vera Vasilievna. When you die do you think you will see them again? Your husband and son. My mother."

It was the first time she had heard Anya say it out loud, that her mother was dead. Vera looked at her alabaster face with those serious brown eyes to calculate what it had cost her to say it. Giving words to something made it real, imprinted it. She herself had been reluctant to ever say what she felt was true. That Katerina was dead. But Anya had come to the end of her fantastical thinking. Necessary, she knew, but it yanked one down to earth with painful finality. Vera slid a black bead down the wire of the abacus.

"I will tell her all about you," Vera said.

Vera guessed it would be her final winter, and there was some relief in that. Never to feel that slicing frigid wind in her face. The clumpy feel of frosty eyelashes. The itching of her hands if she left them exposed for too long. Never again to wake to full days of heavy darkness. Never to have the fear that spring might never come. She had struggled and endured, lived and kept living, and now here she was at eighty-one years old. Old enough.

Anya bounced on the sofa as she sat, unable to be still.

"Ledorsky is now keeping a rabbit," Vera said. "I didn't think there were any in Norilsk, but I have seen it for myself. A big floppy thing with ears that have a hard time staying up."

"I would love to have a bunny," Anya said. "Maybe I can take care of it next time I'm home."

"I will put in a good word for you."

Anya yawned and stretched, the ropey muscles of her arms shifting just beneath the surface. There was nothing extra, no fat, no softness, her body defined as if she'd been whittled from a piece of birch. The loss of her mother a tender sore buried deep somewhere in the middle.

"I have to go pack," Anya said. She kicked up into a handstand and walked on her hands to the door.

"Good-bye, *dorogaya*," Vera said. She felt tears hit her eyes at the thought that she would soon leave the girl too.

What would Anya be like if Katerina had lived? It was impossible to pull out all the threads of cause and effect, the nods of fate. She would be a different girl. Probably not one of the best gymnasts in the Soviet Union. Perhaps it was true that there was no beauty without suffering. Or maybe that was an excuse for all the bad things.

After Anya left, Vera went to visit Ledorsky. Talking to him worked her memories out like splinters. Their shared experience no longer divided them. It turned out they liked each other's company.

"People think suffering gives them meaning," he said. "But sorrow and pain aren't ennobling. They exist to be endured. Do you think a polar bear thinks better of itself if its paw is cut?"

Vera set down her teacup. The maimed gull was out of its cage and hopped around the living room.

"Do you remember the *monashki*?" she asked.

The old women were steadfastly devout and refused on principle to work for the Soviet cause. They were housed in special punishment barracks of the *lagpunkt*, and a guard took them to the latrine twice a day.

"I remember the sound of them singing hymns. Those tremulous old voices," he said. "It was haunting."

"I remember the shrieks of pain when the commandant went in there with his whip," she said. "No words begging for mercy. Just involuntary crying out."

"They were never dissuaded from praying, from fasting. Even with all the abuse. I can imagine the rage of the bosses. It was humiliating."

"And then one day they were gone."

Vera and Ledorsky sat looking at each other.

"Are you trying to make me feel bad about the things I did?" Ledorsky asked. He was impatient. "Or make yourself feel bad? For our weaknesses. Even now?"

"Maybe I am a little. No, no. I'm just marveling at those women. I haven't thought about them all these years. They could not be broken. It was as if they had separated their spirits from their bodies."

"They were shot, Vera Vasilievna. I'm not sure they bested the system."

"I only saw them once, when the guard was marching them to the latrine. They walked with their chins up. Their eyes were so huge in their sunken faces. Each kept one hand on the shoulder of the woman in front of her, and their eyes never left the sky, as dull and heavy as it was. It was like they knew something. They almost looked like they were happy."

Ledorsky picked up Narkiss and ran his hand from the cat's head to its tail.

"Aristotle said that what constitutes a person's happiness is relative. When he falls sick, he thinks health is happiness; when he is poor, wealth. Maybe those twice-a-day glimpses of the sky were the nuns' happiness."

Vera thought about happiness, about the moments in camp when even she felt the horror lift.

"There was one night I fell asleep right where I was working," she said. "After I moved to the job inside. I had finished cleaning the kitchen and stopped to rest. The bakery was empty. I sat on the flour-dusted floor, it was supposed to be only a minute, but I woke up hours later, toasty warm as the ovens heated up, the smell of fresh bread luring me from sleep. The bakers had seen me, but they didn't turn me in. The pleasure of that moment."

"Did you steal some bread?"

"Alas, no. But I swept some flour from the floor into my hand and filled the pocket of my jacket."

Ledorsky took off his glasses and rubbed his eyes. Without them on he looked younger, his eyes vulnerable.

"*Chelovek cheloveky volk,*" he said.

"We are wolves to each other," she said. "But not always."

Vera closed her eyes and relished the warm tea in her belly, the yeasty smell of bread in the oven, and how, at the low-lit end of her life, she had found a friend in Ledorsky.

* * *

Anya returned to Round Lake with her head up and her mouth set. She was thirteen, ready, stronger than she'd ever been.

Elena had won the all-around gold at the World Championships in Strasbourg, beating Nellie Kim and Natalia Shaposhnikova, even beating Nadia Comaneci.

"Mikhail said, 'Don't fool yourself into thinking you can relax now.' As if that were ever an option," Elena said.

Anya walked up and down on Elena's back and legs, reading a newspaper article:

Several thousand spectators gathered that evening in the stands of the Penieu Hall and enthusiastically welcomed the new world champion. She performed complex compositions with the bravery of Olga Korbut, the grace of Elvira Saadi, and the concentration of Ludmilla

Tourischeva. And with all this, the style of this Muscovite is vividly individual. She can't be confused with anyone.

Anya read on. "It says you want to become a full-time trainer. You do?"

"What else is there? I don't know. I want to work with horses, but I couldn't say that."

"'She should be good at that job because she listens closely to people, looks carefully at the world around her, and therefore notices the small and accidental things, which are so important,'" Anya read.

The girls started laughing, and Anya stepped off and switched places so Elena could walk on her.

"What about you? What do you want to do after?" Elena asked.

"I don't want to live in Norilsk."

"Ah! I haven't told you about the United States, *Myshka*. When I went to New York City."

Elena had been allowed to travel as part of a promotional exhibition of USSR gymnasts.

Anya thought of Sveta, how she wanted to go to America but had no possible way of getting there. A jagged chunk of slag lodged in her gut.

"I can hardly believe you went there. What did you see?"

"We saw the tall buildings only from the bus. They let us have a taste of pizza after the demonstration." She stepped off Anya and fell onto her bed.

"Lucky! Was it delicious?" Anya jumped next to her.

"It was weird but good. I liked seeing the people on the sidewalks. Families and women in fancy clothes. Just walking around. People there look busy. Kids at the playground look the same as kids at our playgrounds. I saw McDonald's where they serve only hamburgers."

"Did they look happy? The capitalist people? My father always says that there's no way they could be happy when there are people all around without enough food to eat."

Elena smiled at her. "I missed you, Anya."

"I missed you too. I thought you might forget me."

"You are special to me, *Myshka*. You know that."

Anya felt herself grow warm and melty, and she had to look away she was so pleased.

"Who went with you to New York City?"

"The girls from Moscow. Lidia Gorbik. Olga Koval. That creepy coach Arkayev went, I don't know why. He sat next to me on the bus from the airport. I crossed my legs and faced the window as best I could."

"And Mikhail?"

"They didn't bring our coaches. Just Shaniyazov. 'You do politics with your performance. You do more than diplomats,' he said. 'Give all you have to strengthen socialism.' It made the pressure feel so much, squeezing me into a tiny little ball. I had to put it out of my mind."

"Did you miss Mikhail?"

Elena cocked her head and looked at her. "Are you joking? I rejoiced to be away from him. Imagine doing routines without Anatoly there, without him watching and you wondering what he found wrong. It felt like cheating. Like I was getting away with something."

"I hear Anatoly in my head even when he isn't there."

Anya couldn't say these things to anyone else. She buzzed with relief and pleasure to be with Elena again. She was here for gymnastics, but it was her friend who made her feel not alone in the world.

"I know," Elena said. "I felt that way a little when I was back in the hotel room. But you should have seen me. They cheered so loud. All those nice people. I waved! Me! I felt like a film actress."

"I wish I could have seen you like that," Anya said. "You are the best in the world, Lenushka. Does it feel different now?"

"No. Not really. We never make it. There is no destination."

"The Olympics?" Anya asked.

She shrugged. "They'll just want something else."

It was true. Gymnastics owned her, almost all of her. But this part, Elena, was hers.

* * *

Anya was summoned to the clinic for a health evaluation. The first time she'd arrived at Round Lake, she'd seen a jovial old doctor who had given her a peppermint. He was not here now. This doctor was dour with wet lips and close-set eyes, sparse black hair on his arms. He didn't introduce himself. He looked at a chart and then back at her.

"How are you feeling?" he asked.

"Fine." She would never admit to injuries, and pain she could deal with.

"You need a shot in the ankle?"

"Yes."

"Any changes we should know about?"

"No."

"Get undressed to your underpants."

The clinic was cold: the vinyl of the table, the silver instruments, the draft from the window. She crossed her arms and held them tight.

His hands were colder still. He put one on her back, the other on her chest, one side and the other, moving his palm in a slow circle. She felt that sick ooze in her gut.

"No *grudi* yet. That's good!" he said. "Congratulations."

She dug her fingernails into the padded table and sat rigid, her spine curved in a hunch, as if that could offer protection. In a swift motion the doctor pinched her nipple and let out a small giggle, his eyes wide like a clown.

"Come now. Why so glum?"

Anya looked at her lap, her thighs white and blue with veins, marred with bruises and scars.

"They have high hopes for you," he said.

She felt the world recede. It is Elena and I on the Arctic ice, she thought, and no one can reach us. A small wooden house with a stone fireplace and bread in the oven.

"I will do my best for my country," she said quietly.

"I'll keep my eye on you," he said. "Come to me if you need anything. I have all sorts of magic potions." He wiggled his fingers and laughed again in that vile way. She didn't dare put her shirt on until he told her she could.

"*Nikomu*," he said. "Speak about it to no one."

But she had Elena now. You cannot get to me, she thought. To us.

"I will give you a passing report," he said. "Don't forget to thank me.

When you're up there on the podium." He filled the syringe and took her ankle roughly in his grip.

*   *   *

Anya was granted a spot on the senior national team. At the USSR Championships, Elena came in first, Anya came in seventh. She was rising, rising.

"We're gaining on them," Anatoly said.

*   *   *

Yuri couldn't sleep. He had thought declaring Katerina dead would quiet the questions in his head, but it had done no such thing. He rose from the bed, leaving Irina to her snoring, and went to the kitchen. He poured himself some vodka and sat at the table in the dark.

"I have been in denial," Katerina had said. "But I am not confused."

Yuri had wanted to cover her small body in a soft blanket and lie with her until she felt soothed, until the anger went away, and they could go back to how they'd been. Her growing dissatisfaction had coalesced into outrage, the quietly seething kind that takes a while to bubble to the surface and doesn't disperse easily. Her lips were chapped, her eyes dark wells. It was as if she didn't see him at all.

"It is not the greater good," she said. "I know it. I can't go on pretending I don't. I can't pull the curtain back over my eyes. The Gulag, Yurka. What is the answer to that?"

He didn't have an answer then; he still didn't. He took a sip and then another.

In rejecting Soviet purpose, she was, Yuri admitted to himself now, rejecting him too. Maybe she stumbled out into the street that afternoon to get away from him and all he represented, to plunge herself into the wilderness, to the safety of isolation. Fell into a crevasse, ate poisonous tundra berries, was eaten by a polar bear, had a heart attack from an unknown defect she'd had her whole life, lay down on the cold hard ground and watched the sky go dark for one night and then another until her body became part of the earth.

The day Katerina disappeared, a KGB officer came to the door instead of the local *militsiya*. He wore his uniform, khaki army coat with its leather belt and cross-strap, a gun at his waist. He took off his blue-and-red hat in the doorway and strode into the apartment. He sat on the sofa and looked around the room.

"Had she talked to anyone?" He pulled a small notebook from his front pocket, but he didn't write anything down.

"I don't know what you mean."

"Anyone suspicious. She had expressed some unsavory ideas, hadn't she?"

"I don't know."

"Comrade. Wouldn't you say you knew her better than anyone?"

Would he? Probably not anymore. He had not wanted to hear any of it. She had talked to Vera instead.

"She had been overheard expressing anti-Soviet views," the officer said. He tapped the notebook against his thigh.

Yuri was a battered hull. His breath burned his chest. He said nothing.

"Surely you were aware?" The man smiled. He leaned forward, elbows on his knees. "Had she wanted to leave?"

"No."

But had Yuri hesitated just a little? He had felt such fear then. Where had she gone? he wanted to ask this man, as if he knew.

"Sometimes she went for walks," Yuri said. "To clear her head."

"What was troubling her?" The officer put the notebook back in his pocket, as if to signal to Yuri that he was his confidant.

Don't you remember how it was, *moya lyubov*? Yuri wanted to ask Katerina. When we were young, when we were believers, when we came to make a home in the great north? To live with meaning!

"Marital difficulties, comrade? Was there another man? It's hard to imagine a mother leaving a child." The officer tented his fingers and glanced at the closed bedroom door.

She might have left him, but she never would have left Anya. She will come back, Yuri thought, of course she will.

"We will let you know if we find anything," he said abruptly.

They didn't care about finding her. They only wanted to make sure she hadn't gotten away. Someone with a file like hers.

"One more thing, *tovarishch*," the officer said. He pulled something from another pocket. "Does this look familiar?" He held up Katerina's amber bracelet before letting it drop with a loud clack onto the table.

Yuri started. He reached his hand for it but then stopped, as if he might be stung.

"I can see you recognize it then."

"Where did you find it?" Yuri could barely croak out the words, afraid of an answer.

"Evidently she'd taken it to be fixed. But the repairman alerted us to a curious thing when we spoke to him."

The man waited, his mouth a sealed trap.

"Who is Lana?" he asked.

Yuri blinked, confused.

"Not your wife. Not your daughter. 'Lana' is engraved in tiny letters on the back of the bracelet. You want to see?"

Yuri didn't pick it up to see. That fucking bracelet, he thought. Probably from the choreographer Zakharov, though she never admitted it. Who was Lana? Secrets and more secrets.

"Who is she?" the man asked, his eyes locked on Yuri.

"I don't know."

"Who gave your wife the bracelet?"

"I don't know. She had it before we met."

When the agent had gone, Yuri jammed the bracelet into the trashcan in his anger. But later he fished it out and left it in the junk tin of stray kopeks and rubber bands and aspirin tablets. When Katerina came home, she would want it. He would ask her what it all meant.

Outside the window, the middle night was dead quiet. Yuri knocked the bottom of his glass against the table.

"Yuri Alexeievich, come to bed," Irina called.

He rubbed his face with his palms, wet with tears he didn't know he'd cried. The mystery would never end. Since Katerina went missing, he had been scared to know the truth, to admit that maybe she was not the wife he knew. He had thought they were happy enough, that she would come around, and he had not had the courage to learn otherwise. But where had it gotten him? He might never know what happened to her, but there was a question that could be answered. What did Vera know?

* * *

The Olympics were the sounds of hooves galloping toward them. The girls were berated, belittled, ridden hard, driven to exhaustion.

"Are you crying, Lena?" Mikhail sneered at Elena. Anya, on beam, looked over to see Elena stepping gingerly on one leg, her face scrunched.

"Focus on what you're doing!" Anatoly yelled at her. "You've been working on the layout for a year, and it looks like garbage."

Back in their little room, the girls lay together like spoons, Elena's arm wrapped around Anya. They spoke in a hush. Anya pressed her body against Elena's. Closer, as close as she could get.

"Would you trade a gold medal for yourself for a gold medal for the team?"

"I should but I wouldn't. Don't tell," Elena said.

"Would you trade five silvers for one gold all-around?"

"No."

"How about one gold on vault for a silver all-around?"

"That's a hard one. I don't care one *pyatnyshko* about vault."

"Me neither," Anya said.

"Your whole life lives inside you. That's what my *babushka* says. She tries to say that gymnastics is just one small part of it. But it's hard for me to believe that."

"A girl at my gym is going to marry her coach."

Elena made a face of disgust. "I am only a gymnast to Mikhail," she said. "Not a person. I don't even think he likes me."

Anya thought of Anatoly, and how the black hair of his chest curled over the low neck of his shirt, his cigarette breath. Did he like *her*? He wasn't as mean as some of them. She made him angry a lot, but he didn't smack her.

"He needs you," Anya said. "They need us."

"The coaches at CSKA used to call me a coward. But Mikhail saw something different. I'm grateful to him. He says in dirty hands flowers will die."

"You are the most beautiful gymnast in the world." Anya was glad she was facing away. "It hurts to watch you sometimes."

"Tell me some of your Tsvetaeva."

Anya recited:

Your name—impossible—
kiss on my eyes,
the chill of closed eyelids.
Your name—a kiss of snow.
Blue gulp of icy spring water.
With your name—sleep deepens.

"We can live together in Moscow," Elena said. "When this is all over."

"We'll eat figs and oranges and cheese and sweet buns."

"We'll sleep late."

"We'll go see the Bolshoi."

"We'll wear dresses and high heels."

"We'll stroll along the Volga."

"We'll run and dance, and nothing will hurt."

"We'll never do another pull-up."

"We'll never yell at each other."

"We'll never hurt each other."

They fell asleep, their fingers intertwined.

* * *

Elena was on floor with the tumbling coach, one full-twisting double back after another, with only a month before World Championships. It was dark out, and the other girls had gone to dinner, but Mikhail and Anatoly had not let their girls go. Anya hadn't eaten anything since breakfast, a cup of coffee and a piece of cheese.

"What is that, Lena?" the coach yelled. "Set higher. You're rotating too early. Again."

Anya glanced at her friend panting, hands on her knees, but could not catch her eyes. She refocused on the beam and blew out a breath, visualizing a Korbut back handspring landing in a straddle instead of on her feet. Her hands didn't take enough of the impact, and she landed hard on her already bruised vulva, crushing it against her pelvic bone.

She tried to control the wince on her face. Anatoly whistled a little and shook his head.

"That did not feel good," he said. "Get it higher. Land on your hands. Spare your—" He waved his hand in the air.

She got to her feet, unsure how she would land again on the throbbing soreness between her legs. She looked up just as Elena came down too short in the last rotation of her double. The crack of bone was so loud, Anya could hear it from the other side of the gym.

Anya watched the slow-motion horror of the coaches running to the mat, circling the great Soviet hope. Elena, my Elena. She could not hear her scream. Anya stood dumbly on the beam, biting her finger like a lost child. Life had taken a sharp swerve; how easily they could break. Do not leave me, she thought. Mikhail carried Elena out of the gym, and the others followed.

By the time sound returned to her, Anya was alone on the beam in the empty gym, as cold as she'd ever been in Norilsk.

CHAPTER 18

I f there had been no February Revolution, no October Revolution, Stalin would have become a priest in Tbilisi, her father wouldn't have been killed, there would have been no purges of politicals, or false trials, or hundreds of Gulag camps. Vera and Ilya would have moved to the small stone house near the university, and Pyotr would have played among the trees, and they would have had Christmas dinner with her parents, goose with apples and sweet *kissel*.

Now she might be an old woman sunning herself on the porch in the countryside outside Novgorod, at the family dacha, on land gifted to her grandparents by the czar. She would feel fall was coming, despite the velvet air and green leaves shimmering all around her. Ilya, long since retired from his academic post, would come out with a blanket for her lap.

Vera allowed herself these what-if scenarios now, kept them going for long stretches. She had spent half a life thinking about what she had lost, and imagining what could have been was a bittersweet indulgence.

* * *

After Vera had been rescued by the guard Boris in the snowstorm, she decided she would do whatever she had to do to get a job indoors— the kitchen, the infirmary, the sewing shop, the *banya*, all those coveted positions taken by informers and criminals and anyone who had curried favor with the *lagpunkt* administration. Something in her center had ossified that day. There was nothing left for her to lose.

Boris was not a bad man, Vera kept repeating as she walked to find Ledorsky. He was a guard, but he was not a bad man. He had saved her when he didn't have to. He called her by her name sometimes. He didn't smell like rot. It was her choice; she could pretend it was her job to be his. What was shame when she'd already been deprived of her humanity? What was disgust when she had already lost her family?

Ledorsky was an informer, and he was allowed to stay at the barracks all day, keeping them clean. He was also the arranger. He had some power, but, in return, he was hated by his fellow prisoners. When your hunger and fatigue overpowered your moral compass, you went to see Ledorsky.

Vera skipped her bath allotment and found him sweeping the snow from the pathway. She knew he had been a scientist of some sort, but someone who only studied animals, and, like Ilya, wasn't useful enough to the authorities to work on special projects. He could have been her husband's colleague back at the university. He was small and unassuming, bespectacled, one lens cracked. It was a wretched feeling to arrive in front of him. She didn't have information to trade or special skills to offer. All she had was her body.

She balled her hands into fists in her gloves to keep them warm, bouncing on her toes.

"Boris" was all she said.

"He likes you," Ledorksy said. "He's okay as they go."

Was she a whore if she didn't get paid? If she was with Boris, even the *vory* wouldn't try to touch her. Boris was younger than she was, his hair dark and receding, with a large paunch his coat couldn't hide. She had heard of other arrangements with guards that involved ropes or beatings or humiliation. Boris had a wife in town. He whistled.

"I want a job inside," she said.

"The *banya*," Ledorsky said. "Or if it works out, if you're lucky, maybe the kitchen."

She wouldn't have called herself lucky. But the kitchen. She would do almost anything to bake the bread, to sneak the scraps, not to be hungry. She hated that her mouth began to water.

"He will come to you," Ledorsky said.

He met her eyes in what light there was from the moon, with a look so bare and hopeful she had to look away. No one talked to Ledorsky other than to facilitate transactions. Vera saw how needy he was, how much he longed for some connection. She would not acquiesce.

"I can get you seeds," he said. "I have dried some from purple saxifrage. Delicate little blossoms."

"I'm not your friend," she said.

Ledorsky held up his hand in apology and then turned away.

No, Boris was not a bad man. Most of the time he was not too rough with her. The first time he asked if he could kiss her. She pretended it was mutual, and, of course, the thought of bread, always the thought of bread.

"Pretty, pretty," Boris said, and she wondered what he saw when he looked at her with her patchy hair and protruding ribs. He once brought her a piece of candy—licorice—which she sucked with her eyes closed until it melted away to nothing, her tongue darting about afterwards seeking any trace between her teeth.

After a few weeks, Vera was moved from general work to the cafeteria as a dishwasher. The *zeki* all licked their plates. But the guards, the administrators, left heels of bread, dregs of soup, chicken bones not sucked clean. Her arrangement with Boris lasted for years. He never hit her. She was well into her forties and didn't get pregnant. They met in the *banya*, mostly, but once he took her to the guard tower, and she saw the far view, out past the *zona* to the mines, to the growing town of Norilsk, beyond to the great curve of the frozen Yenisei River, as he worked on her from behind, her head bumping the window. He would caress her face sometimes, and other times he would grunt and walk out, leaving her to wipe herself and get back to work. It was no secret, and she was protected because of it.

One day Boris was gone. When she was released, Vera wondered if she might see him in Norilsk. A face through a car window. His name in some small newspaper story. But she never did.

* * *

Vera stood, slowly, creakily. She wrapped herself in her old scratchy scarf, tied another around her ears, pulled on her overcoat. The windows were frosted over, but the temperature had been strangely mild for winter over the past few days. She took her abacus and forced herself forward, out the door, down the steps, stopping just outside the door of the building. The sky was low and gray, a cement ceiling, one of the few hours of daylight. She stood still and closed her eyes as an unexpected streak of winter sun carved a path through the clouds. She felt the warmth on her face and, for just a moment, felt a quiet stillness settle, before the cold rushed in, stiffening her joints, stinging her face.

She started walking. She took a bus to Dolgoye Lake. In what little light of the day was left, she watched the channel of water near the heating pipes churn through the frozen edges. She was done with counting. She dropped her *schyoty* in the water where it bobbed for just a moment before sinking down to join the bones at the bottom.

CHAPTER 19

Elena had broken her tibia clean across. The coaches were furious at her. Her leg was put in a cast, and she was sent home to her grandmother's to recuperate. She would not be able to compete for six months.

Anya was as lonely as a star, a galaxy of cold space between her and Elena. She sat alone in their little room and cried herself to sleep.

* * *

Much to Anatoly's outrage, Anya was not one of the six chosen for the USSR team headed to Fort Worth, Texas, for the 1979 World Championships. "She's only fourteen. Her time will come," he was told. He knew not to argue, but he sputtered to Anya about it.

"There is some other reason they put Naimushina there. She's barely older than you are. She is a not-so-good version of Grishina."

"She's good on beam. Her dismount series," Anya said.

"She wobbles. You never wobble."

Anya was disappointed not to go to the United States—"Texas is where they have cowboys," one of the girls had told her—but Elena was supposed to return for conditioning soon, and she couldn't wait to see her, a bright light that showed her the way forward.

She watched Worlds on the small television in Anatoly's apartment. Maxi Gnauck from East Germany landed a triple twist on the floor. Anya would not be the first to perform one in competition.

"She looks like a little boy," Anatoly scoffed.

He set down his glass of vodka and bit at a hangnail on his thumb, bobbing his foot up and down, unable to hide his nerves. Without Elena, the Soviet team was beatable.

Nadia was back, fifteen pounds lighter. She looked emaciated and wore garish pink blush and green eye shadow.

"*Blyad*," Anatoly said.

Anya didn't dare look at him. Was he calling Nadia a whore, or did he somehow mean her?

And then the standings were posted on the screen. Romania won team gold. For the first time ever, the USSR had lost. Anatoly let out a long, low whistle.

Nellie Kim went on to win the gold all-around, but it meant little. A team silver was a disgrace. The only other Soviet medal was a silver on vault for Stella Zakharova. She didn't smile on the podium. Anya's breath caught; she knew there would be punishment to come in the gym. They all knew what losing meant.

Anatoly leaned over and plopped his head into her lap, taking her aback.

"Don't you ever get lonely, Anya Yurievna?"

It was such a strange turn for her coach. She was lonely for Elena, but she wouldn't dare answer truthfully.

"Do you?" she asked. Her boldness surprised her, but he wasn't acting like his normal self.

"Sometimes," he said.

"Doesn't your wife come to visit?"

"Wife?"

"The lady at the airstrip. When we went to Surgut."

"Pfft. She's not my wife." He rolled over onto his back, his hairy belly lolling from under his t-shirt. "I can see up your nose," he said. He reached up and pinched it shut, and Anya felt panic like she couldn't breathe before he flopped his hand down and sighed. His head was a boulder on her legs. She couldn't get up.

"It is going to be bad. At the gym," he said. "For all of us."

He rolled over again, onto his side, his face to her stomach. She could hear him breathing. He cleared his throat a little. She stilled every muscle.

His hand came up to her cheek. What was happening? she thought. She welcomed his hand though, warm and gentle, despite her wariness. Maybe he did care about her after all.

"You're a pretty little fox, even if you are as prickly as a porcupine. My little *dikobraz*."

Soon he was asleep, gurgling snores that stopped for one second, two, before he snuffled and started again. She squirmed from under him, until his head dropped onto the sofa.

She sat in the bathroom, perched on the edge of the cold toilet in her clothes. The beige tiles were framed by mildew-darkened grout. On the sink, his toothbrush bristle-side down. She knew nothing about this man whom she feared and loved and hated. She sat until she knew the tears would hold.

On her way out the door, Anatoly rolled over.

"Don't let me down, Anya Yurievna," he said.

It is not a choice I make, she thought. She dug her fingernails into her palms, letting the door close behind her. She skittered away, fast down the empty hallway, in case something was lurking in the shadows.

* * *

The months following Worlds, the mood was icy and dark at the training center. Elena returned, much to Anya's relief, but with less than a year before the Olympics, pressure was on her to get ready to compete, despite the cast on her leg. Elena looked softer, her muscles less chiseled.

"You've gotten fat, Elena Vyacheslavovna. Sitting around on your *yagoditsy* while your *babushka* pours food down your gullet." The tumbling coach stubbed out his cigarette.

They had her on a rigorous conditioning regimen, strict food control to lose the weight, stretching, bar work. She looked wan, ashen under her eyes. A penitent.

Anya was the youngest on the senior team, but it was becoming clear that she was a force, that eyes were now on her to help them beat the Romanians. She stuck triple twists on floor more often than Shaposhnikova. Her degree of difficulty rose above nearing-the-end-of-her-career Nellie Kim. Filatova had faltered at Worlds. Zakharova was good but lacked sizzle. There was Davydova, sidelined by the flu at Worlds, who was strong and exciting, with her front tuck beam mount, and airplane propeller tumbling speed. And then Elena, of course, if she could return to where she'd been. Anya could feel her own status rise, and even Anatoly had new energy. They rode a current, and she knew it. Her time, her time. Yuri Titov, Chief, Gymnastics Administration, USSR State Committee for Physical Culture and Sport, appeared in the gym in his dark brown suit with his slicked-back hair. He stood and chatted quietly with head coach Shaniyazov. They called Anatoly over, and the three men stood with their arms crossed, watching her on bars.

Anya felt the charge in their gaze, felt herself warm in the glow of it. But since Elena's injury, there was something new with her now: a cold drop of fear, insidious and shape shifting, she could not shake. No, she thought, you will not get me.

The men watched her as she skipped up to the bar. There is no one here, she told herself. I am a part of the bars, my hands are connected even when they are not touching, grip, regrip, hollow body, swing to full height.

Her dismount was an underswing to a front tuck salto with a full twist. But she was going to show them; she was going to go for more. She spun her body hard, spotting for an instant the bars as her feet came down. Her heart jerked in her chest. She'd made the extra half twist.

She glanced over at the men. Titov raised his eyebrows, the corners of his mouth downward, impressed. Anatoly gave her a slight nod. She rubbed her calloused hands against her thighs and chalked up again.

At night, bodies sore and spent, Anya and Elena clung to each other in their room, away from the glare of gym lights, the punishing repetitions, the pressure of expectation. Anya felt her fear trickle through in rivulets she couldn't stanch.

"If I think about it, stop and think about what I am doing, I can't breathe. If I stop for an instant, go blank in the air, what happens then?" Anya buried her face in the pillow.

"Don't," Elena said. "You can't think about what could happen. You could break your neck."

"Anatoly says people like me don't break their necks."

"It's easy for him to say that. It's not *his* neck."

"I hear the sound of your leg breaking at odd times in the gym. That crack. And my heart turns to ice," Anya said.

"I had a dream where I picked up my leg from the floor and cradled it in my arms."

"Oh, Lenushka," Anya said. "Does it hurt?"

"In the dream?"

Anya knocked her with her shoulder and smiled. "In real life."

She gave Anya a look—of course it hurt.

"I'm not healed," Elena said. "I know my leg isn't ready. But they are going to take the cast off anyway."

The doctors at Central Institute of Traumatology and Orthopedics worked for the national team first.

"It makes me scared for you." It made Anya scared for herself too. Fear, a sharp, cool draft, left her in goose bumps.

"I don't have a choice," Elena said. "You know how it is. What's one person in comparison to the victory of a nation? Isn't that what we've been taught since we were little?"

Anya took Elena's cold hands in her own and rubbed them. If only they could stay like this, Anya thought, safe, with each other.

"I'm sorry to frighten you, *Myshka*. Let's think about something good. Like being on horses, galloping across a wide-open plain, holding on to the manes, our hair flying back behind us in the wind."

Elena ran her hand through Anya's hair. Anya did imagine it. On the run from it all, together. She reached out and touched Elena's hair, tucked it behind her ear.

"My father told me about this place," Anya said. "An island in Ozero Seliger, not far Moscow. Have you heard of it?"

Elena shook her head.

"He said there used to be a monastery there, where monks went for solitude a long time ago. It was a hospital during the War. A long footbridge connects it to land. I imagine it sometimes when I'm going to sleep. Trees and sun and water. We are there, and no one can get to us."

"Let's go," Elena said. "The two of us."

"They'll never allow it."

"We'll tell them we are going to visit my *babushka* in Moscow. On a Sunday."

Anya swallowed the rising thrill. She would go anywhere with Elena. "I'll be Sister Alenushka and you'll be brother Ivanushka."

"I'm not the brother!"

Elena laughed. "Okay, I'll be Ivanushka. But that means you have to rescue me when I turn into a deer."

"We don't have a wicked stepmother."

"No. At least there's that."

"Really, we will go?"

"I'll figure it out," Elena said. "After they take the cast off. It will be a great adventure."

I am happy, Anya thought. I know I'm happy when I'm with Elena.

* * *

"The Americans are boycotting the Olympics," Anatoly said. "They've convinced Canada, Japan, China, and West Germany to do the same."

"Why? Why would they miss the Olympics?" Anya asked.

"Because they are cowards. They want the Soviet state to fail. They think Afghanistan should be given to the rebel Islamic forces they supply."

Anya knew nothing about Afghanistan, only that Soviet soldiers, young heroes of the people, were dying there.

"It won't affect the competition," another coach sniffed. "The Americans don't matter in gymnastics."

But they all knew it was bad news. Somehow it meant winning—a display of Soviet skill, grace, and courage—mattered even more.

* * *

Round Lake was quiet on Sundays. It was the athletes' one day of rest. Elena's cast had been removed, and her leg was withered. She walked with a slight limp, unsure whether the leg would hold her up. The doctors had proclaimed her ready to train, but Anya could see Elena's fragility; her face twitched when she tried to walk normally. She didn't complain, but she carried worry in her stooped shoulders. She attempted a few punch jumps in their room and winced. But they knew without saying it that this was their last chance to steal away. Tomorrow the relentless push toward Olympic victory would begin.

The girls sneaked some bread and cheese when Albina turned away, and they slipped two bright green Simirenko apples into their pockets.

Spring was upon them, the trees leaved and full, the air still fresh before the summer humidity pressed in. Outside, the calls of nuthatches sounded like laughter in the trees. They shared a green *marshrutka* taxi van with three other Round Lake employees heading to Moscow. It was extravagant: ten kopeks just for getting in and another five per kilometer. But Elena had five rubles her grandmother had given her for emergencies, and this, she joked, was definitely an emergency. They rolled down the windows and let the wind blow through their fingers. Anya was slack-jawed as the city grew nearer, the apartment buildings taller, the Skodas and Ladas and Trabants clogging the city center, dull colored and honking their tinny horns. She glanced at Elena, but her eyes were closed in the sun, a Muscovite, almost nineteen years old, who knew so much more than Anya did.

They were the last to be let out, in east Moscow, at Yaroslavsky railway station. "It's where the Trans-Siberian Railway begins," Elena said. "You can catch a train here and take it all the way to Vladivostok. Ten thousand kilometers."

The station was huge to Anya, with its Russian Revival flourishes and princess tower and fairy-tale roof. Inside the hall was a giant golden rooster, a large clock with signs of the zodiac, and, above, a chandelier that looked like planets orbiting the sun. The ceiling was bright blue, brighter than the sky, swirls of gold filigree around frescoes championing socialist construction projects, economic development in the new Soviet republics, and worker marches. Anya felt a wave of vertigo and looked down.

"Stay close, *Myshka*," Elena said.

Anya held tightly to Elena's hand as she led her through the bustling station, through the cumin odor of bodies and food, to the departure board, which clacked its changes every few seconds. Elena looked up and found their track. They had fifteen minutes until their train to Kalinin. They dropped a kopek into the water machine and sipped from the communal drinking glass chained to the dispenser.

Their train arrived, and they boarded behind a group of old women in black dresses, hair in black kerchiefs, crinkled, crepey skin, watery eyes. The girls walked along the corridor until they found an empty bench, the vinyl torn, the window smeared with handprints. The car smelled of urine and dill. Anya and Elena sat with linked arms and watched the city recede from the window.

"We will remember this forever," Elena said.

Anya smiled and tried to swallow the happiness that threatened to spring loose. Here with Elena. The ever-present fear receded to a small marble, cold and smooth. She pulled the apples from her pocket, shined one on her shirt, and handed it to Elena.

"My leg doesn't feel right," Elena admitted.

"It will get stronger." Anya hoped.

"I will be glad when the Olympics are over."

They held eyes; it was an admission she could not make to anyone else.

"Will you quit after?" Anya asked. She could not imagine gymnastics without her.

"It's not for me to decide," she said.

"Maybe you will meet a handsome prince who will sweep you away to—"

"Kiev?"

They laughed.

Anya had been allowed her weekly telephone call to her father the night before, sitting in the office near Mila, the large-limbed secretary who wore the same skirt every day. Anya hadn't told him where they were going today—too many ears—but he had sensed something in her voice.

"You sound excited, *Dochka*. Is training going well?"

"Yes, Papa," she said. But what could she tell him really? "I'm landing the triple."

He whistled. "Extraordinary," he said. "Irina says not to forget to eat."

"How is Vera? Have you seen her?"

"She is old, I'm afraid."

"Tell her I miss her."

Anya had moments of longing for her old life, though more moments when she didn't.

"Irina has been approved to teach in a friendship exchange with an American university."

"America?"

Mila looked up from the desk, her heavy brows cinched together.

"Will she go?" And for Mila's benefit she added, "On this state-approved visit?"

"I think she will go." His voice dropped, heavy. But then it rebounded. "After the Olympics, of course."

"I haven't been chosen," she said.

"I have been told there is a chance," he said.

"Who told you that?"

"Your coach."

She felt a wringing in her stomach, to know that her father and Anatoly had discussed her, some object they shared.

"They are pleased with you, Anya."

No one was ever pleased for long, she knew.

* * *

An hour into the train trip, a blond, high-cheekboned man wandered up the aisle and sat across from them. Elena glanced over and nudged Anya with her elbow. The man was refined, Scandinavian-looking, his shirt an un-Soviet light blue.

"Mishka Kosolapyi?" he asked, holding out four Clumsy Bear candies in his palm. Anya had never tasted the confection—they were expensive, four rubles a kilo—but they all knew the dark-chocolate-covered praline candies by their wrappers, aqua blue with an image of three bears, a fragment of Shishkin's *Morning in a Pine Forest*.

Elena took one and Anya followed. The man kept his hand out until they had each taken two.

"Thank you," Elena said.

"You're welcome," he said. "I always have candy on hand when I travel. I find it sweetens the view."

"Where are you going?" Anya asked.

"Up north," he said. "To visit my aunt. And you girls?"

"Gethsemane Hermitage," Elena said. "Do you know it?"

"Ah yes. Where the monks used to farm potatoes. A long time ago."
The man unwrapped a piece of candy for himself and lodged it in the
corner of his cheek. "I was wondering. Do you want to see some pictures I have?"

Anya felt a peculiar fluttering in her stomach. Elena shrugged.

He pulled out a stack of playing-card-sized photographs. On the first,
a plump woman on an iron bed, lace pillows. She was naked and smiling,
her breasts spilling to the sides, her legs spread wide. Elena shrieked and
laughed and covered her eyes. Anya felt a strange, uncomfortable heat
looking at the pornographic picture. Thrill and disgust one-upped each
other. Her cheeks prickled. Why was the woman smiling like that? Who
took the picture? Why did it make her feel flushed? She thought of Elena,
her eyes, of touching her skin; she couldn't help it.

"Three rubles for a set of five," the man said, a small smile curling at
the corners of his mouth.

Anya glanced at the woman again and saw a painting behind her on
the wall, Shishkin's bears!

"No?" the man asked.

Elena shook her head.

The man laughed a little and closed his valise, then rose to look for
customers.

The girls giggled nervously and settled back into their seats. There
was so much outside the gym that Anya didn't understand. But she knew
Elena stirred something in her that was both soothing and searing, question and answer.

The station at Kalinin was a squat beige building lined with news,
tobacco, and fruit kiosks. The girls checked for bananas just for fun—
Anya had never had one—but there were only figs, plums, and a few
lemons. Once they were outside, the sun was high and bright, glittering
off water in every direction from the Volga, the Tvertsa, and the Tmaka
rivers. The day had grown warm, and the air was heavy with humidity,
under clouds like gauze pulled thin.

Anya spun around and breathed in the smell of green with the slight
dankness of water. They were so far away from gymnastics. They waited,
along with the wrinkled, black-clad women, for a local bus to take them

to Ostashkov, and then another bus to the small village of Svetlitsa on Lake Seliger, near the headwaters of the Volga. The wind rippled the water and carried the crisp smell of fir and cedar.

How could she have lived in Norilsk, Anya wondered, when the world could look like this? She thought of her mother, imagined her losing color, fading in the cold, white Arctic.

Across a wooden footbridge was Stolobny Island, and the Baroque golden domes of Nilo-Stolobenskaya Pustyn'. But up close the buildings were shabby, windows patched, vandalized with spray paint.

"It was used to house juvenile criminals, then it was a military hospital during the Great Patriotic War," Elena said, reading a plaque. "Then a holding center for prisoners of war."

An old Orthodox woman watched them through heavy, sagging eyes.

"All killed," she said in a Polish accent. "God sees." She trundled away to join the other pilgrims.

The girls looked at each other. Anya thought of Vera and the camps. How little she knew of anything.

They walked through soaring upright pine trees, clusters of mushrooms, and thickets of wild blueberries.

"Maybe we'll get lost," Anya said.

"And they'll never find us."

"It will be okay," she said, "when gymnastics is over." She wasn't convinced, but maybe it could be true if she had Elena.

"Over?" Elena put her hands on the trunk of a tree and stretched the back of her bad leg. "There are years to go."

Anya pulled one of the Clumsy Bear candies from her pocket and let the chocolate melt on her tongue. She was soon to be fifteen. The very oldest gymnast was twenty-one. Six more years. She thought about how Vera was still alive, and she was in her eighties. There would be a lifetime after gymnastics, wouldn't there be?

"I'm scared we will never be free of it," Elena said.

"Olga Korbut married a singer and had a baby. That could be us someday," Anya said. Her voice sounded high, false. It was a fantasy, but she held on to it. She took Elena's hand. The wind stirred the trees, and they walked, wandered, neither wanting to remind the other about getting back to the bus.

Through a clearing in the trees, they reached the rocky shore, and in front of them, perched on an exposed branch out over the water, was a large white-tailed eagle. Krick krick krick it called through its open yellow beak. The lake was vast, dotted with green islands.

The eagle dived then, its enormous wingspan out full, grasping a flailing fish in its talons before lifting off again up and up, wings working hard, off across the lake to the forest on the other shore.

Elena grabbed Anya in a fierce and tender hug.

"I am yours," Anya murmured.

"I am yours," Elena said.

She held Anya's face in her hands and kissed her forehead, her lips chapped but still soft. At once Anya wanted lips against her lips. She tilted her face up and pressed her mouth against Elena's, a warm force through the center of her.

"I love you, Lenushka," Anya said.

She no longer felt the ground beneath her.

Chapter 20

With a month to go before the Olympics, the training center was a hive of activity and anxiety.

"Again!" coaches barked. "Again!"

The crash of the springboard, the thuds on landing mats, the slap of feet on the beam, the muted piano music from the dance studio. The girls didn't say anything; they followed orders.

"You're rotating too soon out of the back handspring," Anatoly yelled. "Where's your set? You're throwing your head back. Why do I need to tell you these things? Again."

Anya went again. She had turned fifteen just in time. There was a chance she would be chosen for the final roster for Moscow. She did whatever Anatoly asked of her.

Elena had rushed to compete at the Europeans, the first time back after her injury. She'd won bars but struggled on other events with lingering weakness in her leg. Comaneci had come away with all-around gold yet again.

Word came down from the Kremlin that less than gold in Moscow was not an option. What would happen if they failed? Anya didn't know. Go to jail? Get beaten? Disappear? Rumor had it that if his health allowed, Brezhnev would be in attendance.

There were daily visits to the gym from bureaucrats and administrators, groups of men in suits who watched the girls from the sidelines.

They squinted and pointed and exchanged sotto voce comments. Sometimes they clapped with avaricious grins. Ludmilla Tourischeva, in pink lipstick and a new fashionably short haircut, showed the men around.

Anatoly was in a particularly black mood. Anya was working on a new beam dismount, a double back, like Shaposhnikova's. She landed it but cowboyed her legs to pull her rotation.

"That is so ugly," he said.

"It's not a deduction," she said.

"*Zamolchi*," he said. "Don't question me. It looks nasty. Again. No, wait." He sighed. "Come down here."

He motioned her to follow him out of the gym, out the back door. She blinked against the sunshine. Despite the warm day, her bare feet were cold against the asphalt. He lit a cigarette and blew the smoke out fast and hard.

"The reserve. The alternate," Anatoly said. "That's what Titov says, as of now. Naimushina came in seventeenth at Europeans. And you're the alternate." He threw his hands up. "'Aim for 1984 when she's nineteen,' he said. Like four years is nothing."

She would go to the Olympics, but she would not compete. She wouldn't get a team medal. The news was a lead sinker in her gut. She had not wanted to admit her own ambition, her hope. Four years stretched out in front of her. She was at once so tired. Her head spun in disappointment.

Elena had been training at CSKA Moscow for the space and concentration, but she was back at Round Lake for the week. She was worn down from grueling weight-loss workouts. The fullness to her cheeks was gone, but they wanted her smaller, flatter, tighter. She still favored her left leg when she landed. She'd taken out her signature floor pass, replacing her full-twisting double back with a series of twists. Her double back was too low. She was not back to where she'd been. Her coach and the higher-ups were pushing for something new and flashy to elevate her floor routine—the Thomas Salto, named after the American gymnast Kurt Thomas, an element thus far performed only by men. She'd begun work on it before she broke her leg, but since then had only attempted the move into the foam pit.

A round-off back handspring into a one-and-a-half back salto with one and a half twists, landing in a forward roll. She would be the first woman to perform it in competition. It depended on being able to get enough height and speed to make all the flips and twists, and it took near-perfect timing to avoid either under-rotation and landing on her chin, or over-rotation and landing on the back of her head.

"I'm scared," she told Anya. "I don't have it. I don't feel mastery."

"Tell them you can't do it."

"You tell them," she said, laughing. "Mikhail says I'm falling back into my old cowardly ways."

Elena looked older to Anya. Dark circles haunted her eyes. She had washed her hair and it hung lank, dripping from the ends.

"You're still the best gymnast in the world," Anya said. But she knew Elena wasn't ready. She wanted to protect her, to hold her to her chest like a baby.

Elena shook her head. "It doesn't matter what happened yesterday. The past is past. Besides, you will surpass me. You are younger, stronger. You want it more than I ever did."

"I don't." But she did; Anya knew it was true.

"You do," Elena said.

"It doesn't matter what I want anyway. I'm only the alternate."

"I'm jealous. I wish you could go in my place. They are sending me to Klin tomorrow, outside of Moscow, a gym all to myself. To try and fix me. All I want to do is stay here with you and sleep," Elena said.

Anya closed her eyes and felt the chill of Norilsk wind off the steppe.

"I will miss you," Anya said. "Hurry back to me."

A kiss on the forehead—erases misery.
I kiss your forehead.

A kiss on the eyes—lifts sleeplessness.
I kiss your eyes.

A kiss on the lips—is a drink of water.
I kiss your lips.

A kiss on the forehead—erases memory.

* * *

With only twenty days to go until the Olympics, Elena had not returned to Round Lake. Each day Anya would come back to their room at night, hopeful, only to find it empty.

"Where is she?" she asked Anatoly.

"She injured herself again," he said. "Fell on her beam dismount or something." He waved his hand, dismissive.

"What? What did she hurt? Is it her leg?"

"They are saying she'll recover quickly. Hopefully in time for Moscow."

"Where is she now?"

"Still in Klin. Stop talking. You're piking on your second layout. Go again."

Anya heard the crack of bone again. She knew they would make Elena compete, no matter how much it hurt, how much it might damage her body. Injections, pills, tape, threats.

Anya continued to practice morning until night, but it was as if she was watching herself from behind a hoar-frosted window. There she was, a blur on the floor; there, on bars, going by body memory, her mind not with her. The days went by, and new rumors sprouted about Elena. It was her fault. Reckless or cowardly? She fell on beam, or was it vault? She hadn't worked hard enough on getting back into shape. If Anatoly knew anything more about it, he wasn't telling Anya.

With only two weeks until the Olympics, Anya arrived at the gym after the morning run, and Anatoly met her outside. He led her around the building, away from the others. It was still dark, but the air held the warm and humid promise of a scorching summer day ahead.

"I have news," he said.

"About Elena?"

"It has been decided. You are taking her place."

"No." No, not this way.

Anatoly slapped her across the face. She was stunned, eyes watering, cheek on fire.

"We are going to Moscow," he said, his voice low, measured. "This is everything. You will do the best performance of your life. For your country. For me."

She knew enough not to protest.

Anatoly sighed and dropped to his haunches, his thumbs pressed into the hollows above his eyes.

"It was the Thomas," he said quietly.

Anya let out a small whimper. She leaned over with her hands on her knees.

"She landed short," he said.

The image was sickening to her. Elena not making it all the way around and smashing her chin into the floor. No, no. A vertiginous wave toppled her over onto the asphalt. She sat panting, saliva filling her mouth.

"What happened to her?"

He shook his head. "I don't know the details."

Elena, Elena, Elena.

"She has the best doctors in the country. She will be fine, Anya Yurievna. You must put it out of your mind. You must move forward. We have fourteen days to be ready for the world."

"I have to see her. I have to go to her."

Anatoly slapped her again. Anya felt hot needles where his hand hit her face.

He put up his hands. "Stop," he shouted. "She is in Klin."

Darkness swirled at the edge of her vision like ink in water.

"When is she coming back?"

"She cannot be moved right now. They are being cautious," he said.

Anatoly sighed and then lit a cigarette.

"You know my father was a *kulak*? He gave over his land to collectivization but was still exiled to the north, to settle Norilsk," he said. "He always said that being a farmer is being used to every last thing going wrong. Only a farmer understands fairness. There isn't any."

* * *

At the clinic the same awful doctor she'd seen before filled a syringe for Anya's ankle.

"It is a great honor. To represent the USSR. How are you feeling?"

He had made her take off her shirt again, and she sat with her arms in an iron lock across her chest.

"Fine," she said.

"Fine," he said. He jammed the needle into her ankle, and after the pain of it a cool numbness took hold. "Are you nervous?"

"A little."

"I can give you something. To help you focus. Stay calm. I'm told to give you whatever you want."

"I don't want anything."

"Put your arms down for me."

Anya bit her cheek and lowered her arms.

"Tsk, tsk," he said, looking at her small breast buds. "It's too bad. How old are you now?"

"Fifteen," she said.

"I will ask about what they want me to do for you. For now, eat less to keep them from growing." He looked at his clipboard. "Go get massaged." He turned away and then back again. "Good luck."

* * *

Anya felt like she had been taken apart and put back together the wrong way, and here she was on the way to the Olympics. She had heard nothing more about Elena. She punched her thighs to try to regain control of her thoughts, bit and bloodied the inside of her cheeks to think only of what she needed to do next.

The Palace of Sports of the Central Lenin Stadium in Moscow was a massive, sharp-cornered gray stone building, circled with gold panels glinting in the July sun. New plantings ringed the building, and Olympic banners billowed at the entrance. Anya hadn't watched the opening ceremonies the night before—the Misha bears or the torch or the thousands of synchronized dancers in the arena, or Brezhnev clapping from a loge. She'd slept fitfully and dreamt about being late, about saluting to the judge in shorts and no shirt, about shouting to Elena, who couldn't hear her, as she swung on bars, loose and wobbling.

Inside, thirteen thousand spectators filled every seat from the arena floor to the rafters. When the Soviet team marched in, in their red

CCCP warm-ups, the applause swelled. Anya glanced up, but with all the lights she could see only smudges for faces, white teeth. Her leotard was so tight her arms felt like sausages. She marched with the girls of her team around the arena until they stopped to pose for the photographers. The Romanians passed by, already down to their leotards, and there she was, Nadia Comaneci. She was older, still pretty, mythic. Anya couldn't help staring at her breasts, the biggest of any gymnast there. She is just another girl, Elena had said. But Anya was awed.

The competition space was vast. All the mats were blue. Somehow she had imagined that it would feel like Round Lake, sunlit through the windows. But it was a spectacle: hot lights and cold air pumped down from the ceiling, girls from different countries paraded before the fans. When the warm-up began, the Soviet girls stripped to their leotards, red with white stripes down the sides, a white panel in the front like armor. The girls with longer hair, like Anya, tightened their ponytails and adjusted their ribbons. They didn't talk to each other, didn't encourage one another. Only Yelena Davydova smiled at her, and Natalia Shaposh-nikova wished her luck. Nellie Kim looked right through her.

Individual coaches were not allowed on the floor, so Anatoly had to sit in the seats and not talk to Anya. She sat alone on a bench apart from her teammates and closed her eyes, trying to reach the cold of Norilsk, that singular feeling when she could no longer sense her body, and she focused all her energy into a dot the size of a pin. Anya felt a fierce ache for Elena but tried to blot it out, because otherwise she feared she would fall apart. Do not think; your body knows what to do.

* * *

After compulsories, Anya was holding steady at fifth. But in the all-around contest, on her first vault—a full-in full-out like Olga Korbut had done—Anya stumbled and fell back when she landed. She never missed this vault. She scrambled to her feet and saluted, refusing to look at Anatoly. Her second vault, a layout Tsukahara, was clean. But this was the first Olympics in which the two vaults were averaged instead of taking the better of the two. One of the team coaches patted her on the shoulder. Anatoly sat red-faced in the stands, trying to contain his fury. She sat down with her back to him. She felt herself recede, smaller and smaller. I will do better, she said to herself. I will do better. I can do better. It is all there inside you, Elena had told her.

On the beam, she held her back handspring layout step out, but had a major balance check on her front aerial, side aerial combination. She tuned out the clack of cameras, the whir of video recorders, the applause for other performers. She stood on the end of the beam preparing for her dismount, took a breath—*it is a meadow, your feet know where to go*—and spotted the end of the beam. Round-off double back. Stuck. 9.85.

*   *   *

"She is a wonder," Vera said.

Irina was delayed by a department meeting—she was too nervous to watch Anya anyway—and Vera sat on the sofa next to Yuri with a blanket on her lap despite the season. The summer evening sun was still bright, the air cool through the window. She had allowed him to carry her to his apartment since she could no longer navigate the stairs by herself. It was the last thing she needed to do, to see her girl.

"She looks so much like her," Vera said. On the television, Anya chalked her hands, next in line for bars. She rubbed her cheek with the back of her wrist and left a line of white. Her face was stony in concentration as she waited.

"She is different from Katerina though. More realistic. Serious," he said. "Self-contained," he said.

"How could she not be?" Vera asked.

On the screen Anya mounted with a run and jump half turn on the springboard to catch the top bar from behind, and she was off, kip up to handstand, wrapping her body on the bottom bar to beat back up to handstand.

Vera wondered what it felt like to move like that. Now she could barely move her legs to walk. On the low bar Anya did a cast to a free hip to handstand with enough flight to grab the top bar behind her. Vera gasped. Anya moved with ease and command around and through the bars. Soon it was the dismount. Vera couldn't make out the number of twists. Anya landed without a step.

Yuri whistled. "I wish her mother could have seen her like this."

"I wish for a lot of things," Vera said.

Anya received a 9.8. Yuri smacked his thigh. "She deserved higher." He could not sit still. He finished the vodka in his glass. "Vera Vasilievna, Anya might just win an Olympic medal for the Soviet Union. The honor of it." His eyes were glazed in tears.

Vera could see that despite everything, Yuri was still a believer. Even in the camps there had been those who were devastated not to be allowed pictures of Stalin, not to look upon their leader, not to be called comrade. But now she could see their belief was what kept them alive. And Yuri needed it too. Their belief wasn't so different from her belief in God.

"I have never asked you," Yuri said. He looked quickly at Vera and then back at the television, a break in the action between rotations. "I have been afraid. But I know if I don't ask, I will always wonder. You knew her better, I think. At the end."

He went to the kitchen and refilled his glass. Vera waited for him to gather his nerve. Through the open window she could hear the faint cry of a baby, the sputtering of a far-off car. Yuri returned and sat back down. His hand shook some as he raised his glass to his lips.

"My great fear is that she was so unhappy here," he said. "Here with me."

"Katerina was unhappy with unfairness. Disillusioned, I suppose." Vera smoothed the blanket on her lap with her palm, the back of her hand spotted, her fingers no longer straight. "I wonder now if I should not have told her things about the camp. If she was too sensitive."

Vera thought about what else she knew, what Katerina had told her the last time she saw her. Would it change anything for Yuri to know?

He got up and stood at the window, pressed his palms together to his lips for a moment, and sat back again next to her.

"Could she have killed herself?" Yuri asked. His voice cracked. He rubbed his face with his hands to get back in control.

"She would have never left Anya, you know that," Vera said. "No matter how lost she felt."

Yuri nodded.

Vera glanced at Yuri, his eyes reflecting the television. She knew the feeling of helplessness, the refrain: Could I have done something more? It will hurt him to know, she thought, but maybe he will no longer wonder what he could have done. Tell him the truth, she told herself.

"She did not commit suicide, Yuri Alexeievich," she said. "I know she didn't."

"How do you know?"

"Because the last day she came to see me she told me something."

Yuri turned from the television, a sheen on his forehead, his eyes pink rimmed, expectant.

"She was pregnant."

His chin fell to his chest, and he let out a breath like he'd been punched.

"She hadn't been to the clinic," Vera said. "But she knew she was. She was going to tell you. She was happy about it. She knew you would be happy too. It didn't take away her restlessness, maybe, but it reminded her of joy. Reminded her of her family."

* * *

They had tried for years. She'd had an early miscarriage the year after Anya was born and then nothing. She had blamed it on the poisoned air of Norilsk. A boy? A girl? How different life might have looked as four. Might we have been happy again? Yuri pulled himself inside, retracted into the tangled center of himself. Sadness rushed at him, a *burya* of pummeling wind. He would not deflect it this time. He let it come. But he felt buffered—so much time had passed, and he felt old and tired. Katerina had last seen Anya when she was five, and now there she was on the television, almost grown. They had made it through well enough.

"Thank you," he said to Vera. "It is better to know, I think."

She patted his arm with her gnarled hand.

"But not easy," she said.

Yuri took a drink. There was no reasonable scenario for how Katerina died, no good reason for why she was gone. And there never would be. But knowing she didn't choose to leave them was something small and good.

* * *

Anya was headed to the floor, her final rotation in the all-around competition. She didn't calculate scores, but she knew she was in the race for a medal. Maxi Gnauck from East Germany was in the lead, on vault for her last event. But her hands hit too early on her layout Tsuk and though she made it around, she landed too close to the vault. She received only a 9.70. There was room for any of them. Davydova then scored 9.95 on beam, and was followed by Comaneci, who was not who she had been. She had her lines, her unique style, but her face was drawn, her movements effortful. She took a small step back on the landing. The Romanian head judge argued about the scores from the other judges for twenty-eight minutes before her complaint was disallowed. She refused to punch the final score into the computer, so a Soviet official stepped in and entered it while she continued her tirade. Comaneci finally received a 9.85. She would not win.

* * *

Vera had told Yuri about Katerina being pregnant and had not told him other things. Not about the letters from the choreographer, or that Katerina had thought about leaving, or that she had been ordered to report to the District Office. Vera had decided in the moment that it might be too much for Yuri, might crush his lingering faith, might drive him to despair anew. Anya still needed him, and she was Vera's last love.

"She's come a long way from her first pull-up in the door frame," Yuri said.

"Yes. We have come a long way," Vera said. "I think I'm ready to go home now."

"After the break there is only one rotation to go! Don't you want to see what happens? Anya could get a medal!"

"I don't care much about ceremony. I have seen her," Vera said. "Tell her I got to see her, and she was glorious."

* * *

Anya was up next on floor. Anatoly pressed his hands into his skull, his lips moving fast, talking to himself. Unlike the modern, slightly disco beats of Kim's and Comaneci's music, Anatoly had changed Anya's floor music only a few months before to something classically Russian, the lively strings from Act III of Tchaikovsky's *Swan Lake*. She opened with her triple twist and landed it without a step, adrenaline sending her higher than she'd ever gone. She hit every pass, leaped with height and confidence, didn't fall out of her double turn, closed with a double pike stronger than what any of the others had opened with. It was the best floor routine she had ever done. But Anya was an unknown, and she didn't smile or play to the crowd, which tempered her score. She received a 9.9.

Davydova won the gold, Maxi Gnauck the silver, and Anya tied with Nadia Comaneci for the all-around bronze medal.

On the podium, as the red flag with yellow hammer and sickle was hoisted to the soaring national anthem of the USSR, Anya felt numb. It had all led to this, and yet what was it in the end? A bronze disk hanging from a striped ribbon. Anatoly held his chin up, his eyes shiny. He nodded at her. She had done well and fulfilled her duty. She realized then that her father was watching her on the television, and to that she gave a little smile. When the anthem was over, Anya ventured a small wave to the crowd.

In the team competition, the Soviet Union won its eighth straight Olympic gold in women's gymnastics. The men from the Kremlin and the other *nomenklatura* in their suits stood together and clapped, nodding with knowing rightness. Anya stood at the end next to Davydova for the official photo. She wondered if she would appear in the photograph or if she would be merely a blur, a figure in motion without a distinct face. She looked out into the crowd, searching for Elena. She knew she was not there—there was no realistic way Elena could even be in Moscow— and yet Anya's logic was no match for her hope. If Elena could see her, somehow she would be able to feel her body here in this moment.

When the applause quieted some, she saw Anatoly in the first row, one side of his mouth curled in a small smile. It was never a question that she would go back to the gym; it wasn't up to her anyway. But she had done what she had trained to do. She reached up to feel the cold medals heavy on her chest.

A swish of a ponytail, reddish hair. Anya blinked hard as the girl up in the stands turned back around. She was too young, the bangs too long in her face. It could almost have been Elena, but it was not. The others from the team were walking offstage, and Anya jogged to catch up. She could no longer hold off the realization that flooded her now: Elena might never come back.

* * *

MOSCOW NEWS, AUGUST 1980:

World Champion gymnast Elena Grishina broke three vertebrae in an accident during training leading up to the Olympic games. Neurosurgeons from Moscow fought to save the girl's life.

Some Western newspapers that supported the shameful introduction of the boycott of the Moscow Olympics shouted that without Grishina the team of Soviet gymnasts was depressed and that the gold could be taken from them. Yes, the team grieved. It was such a misfortune! But they weren't afraid to compete. They felt sorry for their Lena. How could they help her? They knew her character, the character of a true athlete. And they had to show that same character on the Olympic platform and pour into themselves Lena's moral forces for a new victory for Soviet sport. And that's what they did. Gold in the individual competition was won by Yelena Davydova, and the USSR team won first place. It was excellent medicine from friends.

"The restorative period," says Arkady Vladimirovich Livshits, "is designed for the long term. I'm optimistic about her future. I'm confident that Grishina will return to socially useful activities. Look at her: she's cheerful, happy, and energetic. We believe that the time will come when she will return to the gym."

Anya's two medals hung from a nail in the wall next to her bed. She grabbed them and then hurled them across the room. She felt a dark, hot circle at her center. Three vertebrae. Crack, crack, crack. Elena lying in the hospital while Anya performed at the Olympics. She had smiled to the crowd and even waved—the memory of it brought bile to her throat.

Anya lay down on the floor beside Elena's empty bed. She closed her eyes and imagined her tears freezing into pearls as they rolled from her eyes. Come back, Lenushka, she willed. I will wait for you.

CHAPTER 21

E lena did not return to Round Lake. Anya pressed Anatoly, but he claimed he didn't know anything. She asked her father, even, on the phone, if he could find out how she was, knowing it was useless. A few weeks after the Olympics, the national team coach, Shaniyazov, came in to talk to another coach about an issue with one of the beams. Anya saw her chance. She hopped down from the bars and walked toward him, determined.

"Anya!" Anatoly hissed through gritted teeth.

She stood near Shaniyazov until he stopped talking and noticed her.

"Ah, Anya Yurievna. I'm surprised you're not wearing your medals."

"When is she coming back?"

"Who?"

"Elena Grishina. *Gospodin.*"

He cleared his throat and looked around, as if he might find someone to help. Anatoly put his head down and pretended to adjust the bars.

"Elena has much recuperating to do," he said.

"But she will be okay?"

"Of course she is okay," Shaniyazov said. He was both placating and short with her, unused to being questioned. But Anya pushed on.

"Has she returned from Klin?"

"She's with her grandmother. At home in Moscow." Shaniyazov nodded once to end the matter and turned to go.

"She's here?" Anya started, her heart careening in her chest. "I want to go see her! Can you tell me her address? I will take a taxi."

"I can't do that." He had lost patience, and he motioned to Anatoly to come. "She doesn't want to see anyone right now. She's not taking visitors."

"She would want to see me," Anya said.

"Why don't you write her a letter, and I will see that it gets to her."

Anya nodded, defeated.

"Back to bars," Anatoly said.

"You did good for your country, Anya Yurievna," Shaniyazov said. He put his hand on her back and nudged her forward. "Go work on that new release move. I want to see it at Nationals."

She believed what he told her because she had no alternative. She would write a letter. It was a start. She felt her pulse hitch at the prospect of seeing Elena again soon.

*   *   *

Dear Lenushka,

How are you? They say you are coming back. When can you visit? I think about you all the time. No one will tell me anything. Mikhail has not been back to Round Lake, and Shaniyazov walks around like a preening cat, as if he had done anything to earn the team gold. Did you watch the Olympics? I thought it would feel bigger than it did. You were right about Nadia. She is pretty but just a girl like us. In the end it was another competition, and when I was doing gymnastics I didn't think about anything else. Anatoly is still *choknutyi*, but now that the games are over he is a little calmer maybe. The other girls have gone home to train, but he has convinced them to let us stay. I think he just doesn't want to go back to Norilsk.

Irina is going to teach in America for six weeks as part of a cultural exchange program. She is going to a place called Brooklyn, which she says is part of New York City, so that is exciting to me.

Please write to me here and tell me when I can visit you. Or better yet, come back. I miss you all the time.

A kiss on the forehead—erases memory.

Lyubov'

Anya (*Myshka*)

* * *

After a month, Anya stopped asking Mila, the secretary, if she'd received a letter. She felt sore inside, pulpy. Did Elena really not want to see her? Or did they not want her to see Elena? Anya continued training. Her ankle wobbled, numbed by an injection a trainer gave her each week. Her back hurt so much she had to roll over onto her side and push herself up from bed. Her shoulder made a scraping noise when she moved her arm. She had tendonitis in her Achilles tendon and wrist. But she would not go to the clinic. She would never go there again.

Even though she knew Elena had gotten hurt on the floor, Anya imagined her flying off the bars and never coming down. She saw the image when she closed her eyes, a loop of Elena swinging a giant before a dismount, her hands slipping from the bar, her body launched into a dark abyss.

Anya stood next to the bars and rubbed chalk into her palms.

"Let's go," Anatoly barked at her. "You're not arching enough on the Tkatchev. Don't embarrass me at Nationals."

She felt so tired. She kipped up to a squat on the low bar, jumped to high bar, kipped up to the high bar, and stopped.

"What is it?" Anatoly yelled. "Go!"

Anya did a cast handstand, but as she descended into a giant she couldn't get the image of Elena out of her head. She rose and arched, letting go in the Tkatchev as she came over the top of the bar, but missed her hands and fell flat and hard on the thin mat, knocking the wind out of her.

Anatoly walked away, disgusted. Anya got to her knees and gulped air until she could breathe again. The sounds of the gym around her seemed tinny and far away. She was receding, each day a little further from the gymnast she had been.

On beam she fell on her layouts, again and again.

"You're not centered! Square your hips!" Anatoly screamed at her. "What are you doing? You are messing up everything we have worked for. Gold, Anya. 1984. California. Don't you want to win? Huh? It is yours to lose."

He looked old in that moment, weathered, pouches under his eyes. And for the first time, she thought he looked sad.

"I'm trying," she said. But the words were sticky in her mouth.

Anatoly exhaled loudly and lit a cigarette.

"If she wanted to reach you, she would," he said, so low she could barely hear him. "Stop acting like a child."

At the USSR Championships, she placed eighth.

Without Elena, she floated, unable to find her bearings. Her body had lost its way. She didn't even feel disappointed in her lackluster performance because deep down she knew she didn't have more to give.

* * *

Anya didn't know where Elena's grandmother lived, but one Sunday she went to Moscow anyway. She wandered in the city center, walked to Red Square, passed the line at Lenin's Mausoleum, looked up at the candy-painted Saint Basil's. She was overwhelmed by the heroic size of it all.

She took a taxi to the famous Arbat Street, where her father had met her mother all those years ago. Summer had waned, but the sun cut through clouds in short slices of warmth. The wide old brick street was lively with pedestrians, and Anya looked at faces, watching for any girl who looked like Elena. She took in the booksellers and portrait painters and mouth-organ players and children in red knee socks and cafés with colorful awnings and *matryoshka* doll souvenir kiosks and bobbing pigeons and the light blue house of Alexander Pushkin. It felt pretend to Anya, like a scene cut from paper.

At a gray-box payphone she dialed 09.

"What name, please?"

"Elena Grishina."

"What city?"

"Moscow."

"We have no listing for Elena Grishina in Moscow."

Anya hung up. She knew Elena wouldn't be listed, and she didn't know her grandmother's name.

She also knew Elena wouldn't be back at her old gym, but Anya set off for CSKA Moscow anyway. She took the wrong metro and ended up at the Prospekt Mira station, north of the city in the shadow of hulking block apartment buildings, soot-stained against low gathering rain clouds. She looked around for someone she could ask for directions, and saw two young women in short dresses sitting on a bench on the platform with their legs stretched out. A man passed by, and one of the women, her Tajik eyes half closed, her dark hair in a sharp line of bangs across her forehead, lifted her foot with tired insouciance before crossing it over her other leg. Prostitution didn't exist in the Soviet Union, but of course it did. Elena had told her about these women, who had their price—three or five rubles—written on the bottoms of their shoes.

Anya was so tired she thought if she sat down here, she would never move again. Her hope for finding Elena had dried into a mess of dry brambles, brittle and thorny.

"*Chto ty khochesh?*" the other woman asked. Her face was divoted with pock scars. She had sweat rings around her armpits.

Something about her made Anya think of Sveta with her ragged edges and flaxen hair, hoping to find some way out of Norilsk.

"Nothing," Anya said. "I'm looking for someone. I got lost. I'm tired."

"Yeah, well I'm tired too," she said. "*Eedee!*" She flicked her hand to shoo her.

Anya got back on the metro going toward the place she'd come from.

* * *

Ilya had once told Vera that the painter Ryabushkin had gone to Novgorod at the end of the nineteenth century, choosing to tour the oldest towns in Russia instead of Italy or Paris. He worked on frescoes for the redecoration of Saint Sofia. His father and brother had been icon painters, and you could see that influence in the flattening of figures, the rich hues, the solemn expressions.

But the one painting of his that Ilya had loved had no people in it at all. Ryabushkin had done *Novgorod Church* in 1903, before he died of tuberculosis. Ilya had been an atheist long before it was required, but he admired the restraint and directness of the painting.

"I find its spiritual simplicity remarkable," he said.

He'd seen it as a boy in what was then the Russian Museum of His Imperial Majesty Alexander III, on Arts Square in Saint Petersburg.

"We'll take the train to Leningrad for the day," he said, one lazy Saturday morning. "So you can see it."

A week later came the knock at the door in the middle of the night.

Vera could not move. She had fallen to the floor while making tea. She could see the legs of the kitchen table and chairs but could not call out, could feel nothing.

She closed her eyes and saw the place Ryabushkin had painted, just as Ilya had described, a small white orthodox church with a pale green roof, on a treeless hill, under a cloudless sky of the lightest gray blue. There was no one to be seen, a stillness to the autumnal day, a clarity. She walked toward the church. Nothing hurt; her body was strong and young. She took hold of the cold metal ring of the front door and started to pull. She could smell the cool air from inside, earthen and ancient, and somehow she knew Ilya and Pyotr would be inside waiting for her. The door creaked on iron hinges, opening one centimeter at a time. She felt herself grow lighter and lighter, light enough to spin through the air like Anya, light enough to be free of age and memory and body. She heard singing, faint and then stronger, a woman, her mother, singing "Beryozka." Her mother rocking her when she was just a baby, before she knew suffering, before she knew the burden of humanity.

Standing in the field, little birch tree
Waving in the breeze, little birch tree
Loo-lay-loo, little birch tree
Loo-lay-loo, little birch tree

"I'm coming," Vera said. The door was open far enough. She stepped inside.

CHAPTER 22

In the months that followed Elena's vanishing, and then the death of her beloved Vera, Anya could not see herself clear of the heaviness that greeted her with each day. She rose from bed with the dull ache of sorrow wrapped around her shoulders. She could barely brush her teeth. She and Anatoly had been allowed to stay at Round Lake, and she dutifully showed up at the gym each day and followed his orders, but she couldn't make her body do what it had done. She no longer felt gymnastics as an extension of herself; it was work with no reward. Anatoly was the only one who didn't accept that she had lost the fire, and without the fire, the slow downward slide had begun.

A year after the Olympics, Anya barely qualified for the European Championships in Madrid. Shaposhnikova had retired, so had Kim. There were young newcomers on the team who'd risen from the juniors. Anya was, at sixteen, one of the veterans. She felt as old as Vera had been, her movements clunky and stiff. Elena had never answered her letter, and she'd never come back. Nothing more had ever been printed about her recovery.

Anya watched Madrid bustle from her hotel window, remembering how Elena had traveled to Spain once too. For the briefest moment she imagined them running outside hand in hand, ducking into shops, eating *rosquillas listas*, those donuts with the lemon glaze she'd heard about. But, no, she would not think of Elena anymore today.

The Soviet team was not allowed to venture from the hotel, but Anya didn't much care. She nibbled on a piece of toast from the tray that had been left outside her room. Today's competition felt distant. She was not nervous. The best gymnasts in Europe would be there, and she knew she was no longer one of them.

* * *

Anya began on bars. Midway through her routine, just before a piked Tkatchev on the high bar, her mind strayed—Elena—and in that momentary lapse of focus she released too early. Her hands caught the bar off-center and too far on top. She tried to kip back up, but her hands gave out, and she fell to the floor. She did not cry. She sat on the mat and looked at her hands. Her left one hurt, but she could move her fingers. The right was swelling and turning purple as she watched. Anatoly rushed over and carried her off the competition floor.

She had spiral fractures in four metacarpals. The Soviet trainer gave her shots of novocaine and packed the hand in ice. When the swelling had gone down some, they took her to a Spanish hospital for a cast. The room was white with blue tiles on the floor. All she wanted to do was stay, to lie down on the white sheets that smelled of bleach and listen to the rustle of the nurse's skirt, in and out of the room, and sleep. But she was not allowed. They would not risk a defection, as the figure skater Ludmila Belousova had done the year before.

Weeks later, when the bones had grown back together and the cast came off, Anya's hand was not right. She held it up but couldn't hold it straight. On the X-ray some of the bones had healed twisted, but it was too late to reset them. Like Elena's leg, she thought, glued back together, the seams rough and uneven. Anya couldn't quit, but she knew she had given up.

She trained on painkillers. Her tumbling was low and labored, her dance heavy. She could do only rudimentary bars. She didn't make the cut for Worlds, the all-around won by Olga Bicherova, who they all knew was secretly only thirteen and too young to compete.

Anya, always tired now, began to cheat on conditioning, skipping stations, not finishing circuits. In the cafeteria, she stuffed biscuits in her pockets when Albina wasn't looking, trying to quiet her ever-present hunger. The pills she took dulled the pain in her hands, and dulled everything else too—she was lethargic, muted, slow. She watched first with horror and then resignation as her body started to change: small breasts emerged, her thighs lost definition, her leotards grew tighter. She could feel the effort in everything; her center of gravity had shifted; her strength was not what it had been. Gaining weight would have once left her panicked, but now she viewed her new fullness with remove, as if she were looking at someone else's body. It felt irreversible, inevitable. Losing control of her body was confirmation that there would be no turning back. She saw the end even if Anatoly couldn't.

It was late afternoon, the sun waning, the lights in the gym turned on for the training push toward evening. Anya was attempting another full-in double back—the Grishina, Elena's eponymous skill—into the pit. She hadn't done it well for months, unable to get her body rotating fast enough to pull around the second tuck. Girls worked tirelessly around her, but Anya had no stamina, sucking air after each pass.

Anatoly raged at her, spit flying from his mouth. "Work harder! Focus! Longer back handspring into it!"

She climbed out of the pit on her hands and knees, panting. Anatoly walked over and crouched down next to her. Without a word he shoved her back in.

"I didn't coach you to be fat and lazy," he seethed. "You are losing it!"

She lay still for a moment, suspended in the chunks of soft foam, and watched the ceiling lights and listened to the punch of a springboard, the squeak of bars, the thwack of feet on the beam, and wondered if she would miss those sounds. She sat up and clawed her way to the edge of the pit, hoisting herself up to the floor.

Anatoly stood and pressed his fingers to his temples.

They both knew she wouldn't make it to 1984.

"Again," he said. But it came out flat, without energy or conviction.

For the first time, Anya looked at him and shook her head no.

"You ungrateful *suka*. I have given you my life," he said.

"And I have given you mine," she said quietly.

His hand came up as if to slap her, but then it slowly sank down, hanging defeated at his side. Without her desire, he no longer had the power to make her do anything.

"Just go," he said.

It was the end of her gymnastics career.

Anatoly had no purpose at Round Lake other than as Anya's coach, so he was sent back to the sports school in Norilsk. He came to her room on his last day and stood in the doorway in his old suit, his belly pushing against his shirt.

"There's a new girl at the gym at home. She's nine. Looks like Filatova. Strong like you."

Anya nodded and bit the inside of her cheek. It was hard to imagine that this was it, that she no longer had a coach, that Anatoly was leaving.

He sighed, and dropped his chin to his chest. She wondered if he felt tired too, but she couldn't ask him. She wanted to both hug him and kick him. She wanted him to stay, and she wanted never to see him again.

"I don't forgive you," he said. "But I wish you good things."

He turned and left. And for the first time in her life, Anya was truly alone.

* * *

Anya had Olympic medals, and she had served her country, so she was allowed to stay on at Round Lake as an assistant coach for the juniors. There was a kind of freedom to it, this new lack of expectation. No one cared about her anymore. I am no longer a gymnast, she thought. She laughed at how absurd it was. If only Elena could share it with her, she might have felt optimism for what was next now that she was retired. If she lived as long as Vera, she had almost seventy years in front of her, and no one to make her do another leg lift.

Anya thought about the dome of Arctic stars at home, those shards of light that made her dizzy if she looked at them for too long. That dark and glittering sky that made her feel safe from the vastness of space beyond. She'd been lonesome long before Elena, all the way back to when her mother didn't come home. She could keep it at bay, but she would never be rid of it. Vera had understood perhaps best of all.

Anya walked outside into the brisk night along the path she no longer had to run each morning, to her new room in the coaches' quarters; she had left the room she'd shared with Elena to two new girls who would surely go beyond what she had ever done. The bright whole moon and the lights of Moscow to the west kept the stars in check.

She couldn't help herself; she started to run.

* * *

Yuri peeled off his coveralls. True Communism was to be a classless society that contained limitless possibilities for human achievement. Wasn't that the promise? What had happened? He lingered on the floor after the announcement: Leonid Brezhnev, general secretary of the Communist Party of the Soviet Union, chairman of the Politburo, was dead. He'd been the leader most of Yuri's adult life. His old face like a block of granite. But the Soviet Union had become a country of toadying yes-men. Avoid conflict, repress personal opinions, show obedience. Had his been a misplaced faith all along?

Yuri sighed, and pulled his coat from his locker. He felt restless, befuddled. Sometimes he felt like an old man already, as if time had sped up for him. He had developed a "copper cough" from the sulfate, and his vision was deteriorating at an alarming rate. Irina said he was having a crisis. It didn't mean the years had been wasted. Beliefs change. But there was a loneliness that came along with it. You live for something and then you don't. He missed Anya. He had missed years of her life. What now for all of them? He had finally reached the place everyone around him had reached long ago. Resignation. Communism would not save the world. It couldn't even save him.

Irina admitted, in whispers, that she had liked many things about America, even while feeling guilty for it. The toilet paper. The bananas. "Three a day, Yuri Alexeievich, the browner and sweeter the better." No lines. She'd developed a taste for hamburgers at McDonald's, and she'd gained four kilos. But mostly it was that her students there were interested in what she taught, in what she had to say about her Soviet life. It scared him, her zeal. The great Soviet secret of wanting and not getting was laid bare in America. He couldn't imagine fending for himself in the United States. No one cared about anyone else. If you didn't have a job, too bad! Sleep on the sidewalk. But. To be out of Norilsk. Sunlight and seasons. Maybe it didn't mean moral weakness to want life to be easier. He could barely say this, even to himself. Maybe he didn't owe his life to a cause that no longer existed.

*   *   *

Anya walked in the woods and took day trips to Moscow and tried to forget about the ones who were lost to her. She coached the younger girls and was chastised for being too morose, for being too easy on them. Her body had gone soft. Her hips were rounded, her breasts had grown seemingly all at once. She began to menstruate; she was officially no longer a child. Rock music and jeans were now legal, and she dabbled in both. She started wearing blue eyeliner. Anya was, from the outside, a regular teenager; it was still a novelty to her. She woke up each morning with pressure in her chest about the gym before she was alert enough to remember she wasn't a gymnast anymore. She sometimes stood on her hands in her room where no one could see her. She waited, knowing that some plan was being made for her, that she couldn't stay at Round Lake forever, but she told herself it would be an adventure to move to a new city and make a life.

The summer of 1983, she received an official correspondence. A coaching position in Norilsk. She was eighteen years old. She could not stay at Round Lake or even move to Moscow without a salary, without a residence permit. She could not say no, or she would lose her gymnastics pension. She had never considered Norilsk, and now the track of her life curved in on itself—a circle she could not escape. She cried in bed; there was no use fighting it.

Norilsk loomed a cold nickel prison. But she could barely muster anger at Anatoly for requesting her placement; they were both part of the same system after all. *Ne mi takie—zhizn' takaya.* It's not our fault—that's just the way life is. She would move into Irina's apartment. There was no mystery to what came next. She had grown up.

*   *   *

She took a train from Leningradsky station headed north to Murmansk to the White Sea, where she would board a steamship that would take her to Norilsk. She found a window seat and watched Moscow slide away, the suburbs sparser, the trees bigger, the *kolkhoz* fields, endless rows of the leafy green tops of potato plants. The train rattled through towns and countryside, hour after hour. The car smelled of cabbage. She closed her eyes and slept, the years of exhaustion crashing down. When she awoke, the train had mostly cleared out; her car was empty save for an old man who was missing most of his teeth and carried a rooster in a cage. She traveled back in time as she moved north, away from cities and technology and modern life. Wooden *izby* dotted the edge of the forest. Young peasant women sat on hills of potatoes, smiling and waving to the passing train.

Good-bye, Lenushka, she thought. I leave you in Moscow and in memory. Anya had come to accept that she would never see her friend again. Remembering her brought a fierce ache, and she wondered how she might have been different if she had had Elena by her side. Good-bye, Elena, and good-bye to that version of me too.

The thought of Norilsk closed in on her, and at once she couldn't catch her breath. Anya rose and pulled her small suitcase from the rack above her seat. She had no plan, but she could not go further, not yet. The train stopped at a town called Kirillov, and she stepped off onto the empty platform. There was no station, no taxis. The air was rich with green and soil. After the train pulled away with its screech and hiss, quiet took hold once again, and she could hear birds, and beneath that, a faint rush of water. She patted the medals through the side of the suitcase. She was in the middle of nowhere, and it was a delicious feeling to know that no one knew where she was.

Anya walked down the dusty path from where the train had stopped. The sun was high, starting to fall, a wash of pink behind it. She came upon a peasant woman in a blue kerchief, her mud-colored dress frayed and patched. The woman carried a bucket of forest berries. She smiled and bowed a little, her eyes glacial blue in her angular, sun-darkened face.

"Is there a river?" Anya asked.

"The Sheksna," the woman said. She held the bucket up toward Anya, who took a handful of the smooth black-purple fruit; the berries tasted like mulled wine and raspberries. "Walk through those trees. You'll come to it. The gypsies are there. They gather snowdrops in the woods to sell in town."

They had set up faded blue-and-yellow tents on the bank of the river, next to their covered wagon. There were filthy children running around the camp in bare feet. Near the wagon, a bear, its belly fur matted and muddy, was huffing and howling, pulling on its chain. A large pot of stew bubbled over an open fire. One man played a guitar, another a balalaika. Anya smiled, and the musicians motioned for her to come closer, to sit. They passed her a jug of some sour, burning *samogon*, and she drank it deep, drank it again when it came around. She would not allow herself to think of all the cold, dark days ahead in Norilsk. A man handed her a piece of charred meat from his dirty hand, and she ate it, wiping the grease on her jeans. The river beyond was still and wide, reflecting the sky, the last of the tangerine sun.

A woman emerged from one of the tents in a flowing polka-dotted skirt and bangles that sounded like the clinking of little bells. She saw Anya and danced up to her, spun her skirt wide, and snaked her hips toward a young man in a suede hat. He rose and took her hand. Another commanded the bear to rise. When it didn't, he hit its hide with a switch until the animal got on its hind legs with a raspy roar.

For the most fleeting of moments, Anya thought she would tell Vera about the dancers—the bear danced, too, Vera Vasilievna!—before she remembered that Vera was dead. Anya took another drink. Her vision blurred; she was mesmerized by the fire.

The Ruska Roma spoke a dialect mixed with Russian, German, Polish. They didn't ask her why she was there or where she had come from. A young man with a black mustache held out his hand to her to dance. She demurred with a shake of her head, and he shrugged and danced on.

She laid her head on her suitcase, the heat of the flames on her face. She was so very tired. The men sang.

> They were riding in a troika with bells,
> And in the distance there were glimmering lights.
> I'd rather go with you, my dears,
> I'd rather distract my soul from the yearning.

The music played on, and Anya fell asleep.

In her dream her mother walked along a street in Norilsk, her hair in a bun, a fur-collared red coat belted tightly around her waist. Her small feet turned out as she walked. She had somewhere to be. She looked one way and then the other, but the streets were quiet. She boarded an empty bus.

Wait for me, Anya thought, but she couldn't make sound come out.

When the bus came to a final stop, her mother slipped out of her coat and was now in a white dress with a tulle skirt and *pointe* shoes, and she had been transported to the Putorana Plateau, the volcanic massif covered with forests and lakes, around bottomless canyons, where the rivers broke from the rocks into tumbling waterfalls, where the Evenki once roamed with their deer herds. The tundra was red and yellow, and her mother in white danced across it. Floating, turning, leaping in the sun. The sky was a glowing cerulean blue.

All at once her mother stopped, in *attitude en pointe* on the edge of a water-cut gorge, above the thundering Talnikovy Waterfall. A still pose in all that wild nature.

Anya awoke sweating, out of breath. She felt as though something had been revealed to her. The dream was as good of a story as any as to what had happened to her mother. Anya decided she would accept this sad and beautiful end as memory; she would not wonder about it again. The warm glow of embers burned on. Brighter and darker, and then a breeze would raise the ashes brighter again. The others had gone into their tents, and she was alone.

The stars were so close, the sky seemed to wrap around her. She thought she could see the curve of the earth from where she lay. She dug her hands into the sand and let the world spin beneath her. She felt something settle in her body, a body that had been returned to her.

I am here, she thought.

Katerina listened to the quiet of the snow-covered plain. She was feeling better, the air cleaner, her head clearer, her heart more sure of itself. She could face those small-minded men at the District Office tomorrow. She would not be afraid.

"I'm sorry," she would say with deference. "I was confused. I see now the rightness of things."

If she could just fuse the various parts of herself, then maybe everything would be all right. Life was not a pas seul. She would love Yuri again; she would tell him about the baby. She could imagine a better world for them. She thought of little Anya and all that burning life—My love, will you dance or flip? Paint or write? Read all day? Solve great mathematical equations? Take all that you can, even if they don't give you permission. I will not let you be stifled.

Maybe Anya would have a chance to get out of Norilsk, to walk among trees, to see the ocean. It buoyed her to think of it.

Your name—impossible—
kiss on my eyes,
the chill of closed eyelids.
Your name—a kiss of snow.

Fog as thick as a blizzard had moved in and now shrouded the steppe, and Katerina realized she had lost her bearings. She kept walking, hoping she was moving back toward Norilsk. What time was it? She needed to pick up the bracelet before the man closed his shop. ("Will you remove three links to make it smaller, tovarishch? And buff out the name etched there on the back?") The bracelet would remind Anya, always, of what was hers alone.

Katerina's feet were numb, her boots damp through, and her ears burned in the wind. There was a sound. She stopped and listened. A dog barking? Someone out walking? She choked on relief, barely getting the words out.

"I'm here!" she yelled.

Yes, I am here, she thought. She wanted, just then, only to be with Anya and Yuri again in their dreary apartment, to drink tea with Vera, to live an ordinary life. She stumbled forward. I will never write to Zakharov again, she thought.

There on a rocky outcropping in the windswept snow was a snowy owl, almost all white. It turned its head, bright yellow eyes meeting hers.

Krooh krooh, krooh krooh. Almost like the bark of a dog. The owl hopped away and took off in a swoosh of white wings.

But then she saw a small blue glow ahead in the murky light. She moved toward it, running now, as the lights of the smokestacks blinked on in the valley. How happy she was to see the beacons of her terrible city.

It is enough to be alive, she thought. Vera had taught her that. What a wondrous thing it is to be alive. She touched her belly. She felt it would be another girl. Long-lashed and dark-eyed like Anya. Maybe she could forget that she had wanted to leave.

When I get home, I will tell Yuri everything, she thought. I will take Anya in my arms and never let her go. Katerina imagined herself from above, her coat a splash of red in all that white. It felt as if she had lived for a thousand years. She burrowed her chin in the soft fur of her collar, her steps quick and light over the frozen ground. She would be okay. She would find her way home.

PART III

BROOKLYN, 1998

CHAPTER 23

Anya was thirty-three. She lived in Brooklyn, in an apartment above Reliable & Franks Naval Uniforms on Flushing Avenue at Adelphi Street, near the row of abandoned admirals' houses decaying behind a high chain-link fence; one's roof was caved in, another had a tree growing right through it, the remains of peeling wallpaper visible through broken-out windows. These houses must have been so elegant, she always thought when she passed by, as they were grand still in their tumbledown state. Ten Soviet families would have happily crammed into one of them. But here they were left to decay. She lived down the street from the old harborside prison called the Brig, or what remained of it. Behind rusted barbed wire, the cells were lit up to keep squatters away. It took up an entire square city block. But the brutalist hulk and drabness of the prison and Building 77 across from it—especially when the cold winter wind swept down Flushing—felt familiar, and in this neighborhood, she could afford to live by herself.

She'd gone up to the bodega on Myrtle for coffee and forgotten her keys, so she had to walk through the navy uniform shop to reach the back stairs to her apartment. The Navy Yard had stopped building ships twenty years before, so it was a mystery who came to the store.

"Hey, Ruski, what're you doing tonight?" Pablo asked.

"*Neechevo*, Pablo, *neechevo*," she said.

He was young and muscled, his black hair smoothed back with

something shiny. He sat behind the counter, entering numbers into the computer.

"Are you in the Navy?" she had once asked him.

"Why, do you have sailor fantasies?"

"I don't have fantasies," she'd said.

"You kill me, Ruski. Really you do."

Pablo was harmless. He was better than the *mafiya* posers who came into the Rusalka, bad tippers who put their hands wherever they felt like. He looked out for her. The neighborhood was home to storage warehouses, auto shops, the Sweet'N Low packing plant, and the United Talmudical bus depot for the Orthodox community to the north. It was an industrial wasteland, empty of people, trash blowing down the sidewalk.

"Why do you look like you lost your puppy? How 'bout you give me a smile," Pablo said.

"No," she said.

He laughed, and she waved over her shoulder.

Her father and Irina had moved to the United States first, a year after the collapse of the Soviet Union, and she had stayed with them in their cramped apartment when she arrived a few years later. They had scorned Brighton Beach at the beginning—"It's vulgar. All the tracksuits and samovar shops. Where Russians who fail to move forward get stuck."— but they had stayed, despite themselves, because of the language and the comfort. On her way to teach at the community center, Irina would stop by the Georgian bakery on Neptune Avenue for a cheesy *khachapuri.* Yuri played chess at the Arbat Diner. He had been sick with copper toxicosis since before they'd left the Soviet Union. His skin had gradually turned yellow; one day a copper band appeared around the irises of his eyes. Once in Brooklyn his moods began to swing, and he had trouble remembering things, once putting his shoes in the refrigerator, once calling Irina from a pay phone down the boardwalk to tell her that he was going home to Norilsk.

No one was surprised that he had been poisoned by a life in the copper plant, but Anya knew his heart was sick because of the faith he had lost.

"We were Communists, *Dochka.* We lived well and lived fairly. But now? It's rubble."

Anya let herself into her tiny studio. She had a kitchenette and a bathroom so small you couldn't stand up in it unless you were in the shower. Vera's icon hung on the wall above the Salvation Army pullout couch. When Anya had first moved in, she'd hung the icon upside down for three days, as Vera had instructed all those years before. Anya didn't believe in luck, but she liked to think that it would have made Vera happy. The gold had flaked off the Virgin's halo, but the icon was still radiant; it was one of the few things Anya had brought with her to the United States. Her Olympic medals were in a drawer of the small side table that doubled as her nightstand when she pulled her bed out. She didn't talk about gymnastics; Americans didn't believe the Moscow Olympics counted anyway.

In that first year, learning English and waiting tables at the Rusalka, she'd dated a Russian man, ten years her senior, who worked at his uncle's fish warehouse, and then a woman from Belarus, a preschool assistant she met on the subway, a compact little thing with the sides of her head shaved, who had left after Chernobyl. But after the initial ease of communication, Anya felt herself recede each time, having little in common with either of them other than the Soviet Union. She preferred to be alone. She didn't follow gymnastics, didn't need more reminding. She saw in the newspaper that Russia had won the silver in 1996, but she didn't recognize any of the names, girls all born after her time. She took English classes, and Irina helped her get her GED. She tried to make up for her lack of education by reading as much as she could.

Now she was dating an American, whom she had met on the boardwalk in Coney Island. He was taking photographs, and she was sitting on a bench eating an ice cream cone as she did as often as possible, regardless of the season.

"Can I take your picture?"

"No."

He smiled. "Tough customer," he said.

Josh lived in Manhattan, in the West Village, and worked as a copywriter at an advertising agency. Dark floppy hair and warm brown eyes, lean, a head taller than she was. From a small town in Minnesota.

"You can't imagine how cold it gets in the winter," he said.

"I cannot imagine," she said.

"Is that a Russian accent?"

"*Da.*"

"I like Dostoyevsky."

"What do you like about him?"

"It's like there's this feeling of something horrible nearby."

"The bitter end that awaits us," she said.

He laughed. "Exactly."

They didn't see each other all the time, but they met up regularly. She liked his American guilelessness, his unabashed love of literature, the way he would go up to people and ask, without apology, to take their picture, and they would usually say yes. He laughed easily and brought her donuts and held her hand when they walked. She told him that she had been a gymnast when she was young, but few of the details. She held those stories close in a fortress in her memory. Gymnastics was still her raw, red center.

When Josh had first seen her neighborhood he said, "This is some serious *Last Exit to Brooklyn* shit." The next time, he brought her a copy of the book, which she read, painstakingly, her first full novel in English. She hated it and yet couldn't stop reading it. There was something in the unforgiving cruelty that she could understand. Something about Tralala that reminded her of Sveta. They stayed up all night talking about it. It was shocking to her, the ease with which they exchanged thoughts. The softness of his hands.

She had been dating Josh for three months. She had never had a longer relationship. For the first time it felt like it could be something more, and she didn't have an exit strategy. She found herself looking forward to seeing him, wondering what he was doing, hoping he was thinking about her too.

"I will wait for you to talk to me," he said one night over sushi. "I'm in no rush."

She laughed. "I talk to you."

"You don't. Not yet. But I hope you will. Eventually."

His eyes were like burnished cedar. Anya blinked hard; her heart stuttered. How much loving Elena had cost her. But she was no longer a child, hadn't been one for many years.

"Okay," she said. "It is a deal."

"I like you, Anya. Like, a lot. There's nothing you could say that would change that."

She exhaled long and slow.

"I'll start," he said. "Here's something embarrassing about me. I wet the bed until I was ten. Okay, now you say something."

"I won a bronze medal in the 1980 Olympics."

Josh stared at her. The piece of sushi dropped from his chopsticks.

"Actually, I tied. With Nadia Comaneci. For the all-around bronze."

He laughed and shook his head.

"Well. That is not what I expected," he said.

"I can show it to you next time you come over."

"I would like that. I've never seen an Olympic medal."

"It is heavy. I have a gold one too, for the Soviet team."

"You are something else."

"Ah," she said. She waved him away. "I am not. It was a different time. A different life."

* * *

During the last years in Norilsk, Anya had seen her old friend Sveta only once. Gorbachev had resigned, the USSR ceased to exist, the chaos had begun. Her father was already ill but was still showing up each day for work, so close to retirement age, refusing to accept that the state pension system had gone bust. Sometimes after Anya was finished coaching for the day, she would go and meet him to see that he got home. It was winter, that bone-aching cold and mirthless darkness, and Anya had walked fast from the bus stop with her head down against the wind. She turned to the foggy, orange-lit window of Vzaboy, people smashed wall-to-wall in the bar. There was Sveta in a short skirt. From afar she looked the same, young and twiggy, her hair still blond. She was gesticulating with her hands, talking to a fat man in worker coveralls. But closer up, Sveta laughed, and Anya could see she was missing a tooth on the side, her eyes lined in thick black, her bleached hair held back by a lopsided gold plastic clip.

Sveta saw her through the window, and a look of surprise brightened her face. She stumbled closer and beckoned Anya inside where the air was thick with steam heat, alcohol, and bodies.

"Anya Yurievna! Look, everyone, it's the famous gymnast!"

Two men raised their glasses toward her, and then the bar went back to its loud business.

Sveta hugged her close, redolent of cheap fragrance, stale smoke, and body odor. Anya felt her old guilt swell. She had lost track of Sveta years before, had heard rumors about her hanging around the truck stop, the bars, but she wasn't listed, her mother having died and her father having been institutionalized in the intervening years. The truth of it was that Anya hadn't looked that hard to find her. She didn't want to face the reality of how Sveta had turned out.

But here was her friend, her oldest friend, and Anya melted at the sight of her.

"Sveta Nikolaevna! It has been so long. I didn't know what happened to you."

"I go by Svetlana now," she said. "I dance sometimes, you know at the Tzarevna. Make a little money. I do some gymnastics even. The men love it. I do the splits. A back walkover." She laughed. "And what about you?"

Anya shrugged and shook her head.

"I can't do anything anymore. I think I would break in half. I have arthritis like an old *babushka*."

"I know that's not true. I bet you could do a back flip right now. You are working here in beautiful Norilsk?"

"I coach. Back at the sports school."

"Ah! Of course. Set up for life."

"Who knows, now that the state is over." It was true, but Anya found herself still trying to underplay her circumstances to Sveta.

"You should go to America. Work at a gym there. As you can see, I never could get out. Still looking for someone to take me away," she said. She picked up her glass from the bar and downed what vodka remained.

"Sveta. Svetlana Nikolaevna. I have to go get my father. I will write down my phone number," Anya said.

"Yes, yes. We will reminisce about the old times. I don't have a phone, but I will use the phone box near Dima's." She nodded her head at the big man at the bar. "I stay there sometimes."

Sveta never called, and Anya never saw her again. Now that she lived in the United States, Anya tried to imagine Sveta here, what she would have liked about it—the beach, brightly colored clothes, unlimited Coca-Cola, up-all-night clubs, the possibility of being someone else. She would not have looked back.

She would not have been nostalgic about today either. It was Victory Day in Russia and in Brighton Beach—and Anya took the F train all the way to its end in Coney Island to take her father out to the parade. As each year passed, the tribute seemed more and more like a sad performance. But her father would never miss it; he came alive, smiled and cried on the sidelines.

Irina had died of a stroke a year before, and since then Yuri had lived at the Shore View Nursing and Rehabilitation home. Anya visited him once a week. Most of the residents were from the former Soviet Union, and they sat in the common room playing cards and dominos and chess, and bickering. There was a lost air about them. They had more stories than listeners. Some mourned for Soviet life, for a homeland that no longer existed.

Anya only knew post-Soviet Russia from what she read in the *New York Times* or the *Russian Bazaar*. Its economy had collapsed, the university system had imploded, inflation had soared, there had been a war in Chechnya and then another, Yeltsin had been deposed and then took power back, the oligarchs had gotten rich and the poor had gotten poorer. The stores now had everything but no one could afford it. But she understood the old folks and their loss of the known world.

The common room smelled of pine cleaner, a TV was on in the corner without sound, the couch was brown vinyl. A woman with a wispy cloud of white hair sat across from a shrunken man with an oxygen tube under his nose. Anya recognized Mr. Sokolov. He'd moved in when her father had, and he was the gadfly of the floor.

"Americans complain about everything. They will never understand Russians," the woman said.

"All Russians do is complain," he said.

"We have good reason," she said.

Anya looked around for her father but didn't see him. She smiled at the two in debate. They kept going.

"In my village if you had two cows and two horses, that was enough to make you a *kulak*," Mr. Sokolov said. "Get shipped off to Siberia to clear the taiga with a handmade knife."

"You know what? I liked it there," the woman said. "I liked living in a great country. Okay, then that makes me a *sovok*."

"Good morning!" Anya said, approaching them, her voice loud and cheerful; everyone here was hard of hearing except her father. The two turned to her.

"It's the gymnast," he said.

"Hi, Mr. Sokolov. Have you seen Yuri this morning?" Anya asked.

"Young lady, do you know why we didn't put Stalin on trial? Because to condemn Stalin is to condemn everyone. Your friends. Your neighbors. Your family," he said.

"I have heard that," Anya said.

"Stalin won the War. Do you want to live under Nazis? Without Stalin we would be licking the Germans' asses."

"I've heard that too," Anya said.

The woman turned and sized her up through her thick-lensed glasses. "You're the gymnast? Did you ever get to meet Brezhnev?"

"I never had the honor," she said. Mr. Sokolov guffawed. "Are you going to the parade?" she asked.

"Yuri understands what I'm talking about," the woman said. "Only a Soviet can understand another Soviet."

"Psht. You don't understand me at all," Mr. Sokolov said. He slumped his way over to the window.

A nurse pushed Yuri down the hall toward the room in a wheelchair. He was sixty-two years old but looked eighty, his chest sunken, his skin sallow. Anya had never gotten used to how his once-green eyes had turned eerily golden, or how, in the home, his face was shaven clean of his beard. His white hair was too long and yellowing; she needed to take him to get it cut.

His memory was full of holes. He always knew Anya, but it was as if she were some fixed idea of herself. He had moments of lucidity when he would recall recent interactions, but at other times he wouldn't know what year it was. She was comforted by the presence of him though. It was the two of them once again, a familiar configuration.

"*Dochka.* I have missed you." He rose some out of the wheelchair and kissed both of her cheeks.

"Hi, Papa. I brought you bananas," Anya said.

"Bananas!" the woman shouted. "You see that? That's what brought down the Soviet Empire."

"Would you like one?" Anya asked.

"Yes, I would," she said.

The old people took their places near the window to see what they could of the parade.

"My father was a carpenter," the woman went on, patting Mr. Sokolov's arm. "He could recognize the type of wood by its smell, from a single shaving. He said pine smelled like strong tea and maple was sweet."

"Lydya Sergeievna," Yuri called to her. "Put your soul away."

Anya was pleased to see that her father was having a good day, his mind firing in the present. He was gruffer than he had been as a younger man, but never with her. She was antsy to get out of the home and away from the moth-eaten nostalgia that held them all captive and pressed in on her. She wanted to shout at them: We are not in Russia anymore, and there is no going back! But then she summoned her empathy for *toska*, their feeling of homesickness that would never leave.

Outside, the day was not warm, but the sun made up for it. Anya wheeled her father to the edge of Brighton Beach Boulevard. The crowd was a mix of families and older people, chins held high. The men had donned their best suits and attached their military medals to their lapels. Victory Day commemorated the surrender of Nazi Germany in 1945. The old men were shrunken and frail, the Great Patriotic War more than fifty years past, and they shuffled along basking in the honor. Little girls and boys held up framed photos of grandfathers, great-grandfathers. The military march music, the same piped through Soviet radios for decades, came through a loudspeaker mounted on a pickup truck.

World capital, our capital
Like the Kremlin's stars you glow
You're the pride of the whole cosmos
Granite beauty, our Moscow. . . .

Her father got teary and nodded at the men passing by.

"It's dangerous to live too long," he said. "I think one should die with one's era. We'd be happier. When can we go home?"

Anya didn't know what home meant to him. Her mother? Irina? The Soviet Union? Norilsk? Or maybe back to Shore View and its institutionalized predictability. He never complained about it, and she thought he didn't mind being taken care of.

"Just a while longer, Papa," she said. "We have to get your vitamin D. Make up for all those long, dark winters."

After the small parade had passed, Anya wheeled him to the boardwalk to see the ocean. She pushed him up the ramp; sand crunched under the wheels. The seagulls cried out at them, greedy, used to being tossed food by passersby. Anya shooed them away.

"Do something," her father said. "A flip. One of your tricks."

Anya laughed and shook her head. "You're crazy."

He grunted a laugh. "I know, I know. I'm out of my head sometimes. I know you're grown up. But I bet you can still do things."

Anya dreamed about gymnastics every night. She thought about what it would be like to run across the sand into a round-off back handspring. Her body still knew exactly what to do.

"I didn't see it turning out like this," Yuri said.

"No," Anya said. "Neither did I."

"The beach is nice. I'll take the sunshine. I don't know how we lived in that cold for so long. Your mother was right, I think. We were not meant to live without fresh air, without life around us."

Yes, Anya thought. But she knew that growing up in the Arctic had left its dark imprint on her; it was inextricable from who she was. We can adapt to almost anything, she thought. She took her shoes off and jumped into the sand. It was sun-warmed on top, and her toes dug into the cool underneath.

"Next time I'll bring you *bliny*," she said.

"Sour cream here is, eh. Not as good as *smetana*."

"No. But now we have strawberries."

"Do you have a companion, *Dochka*? Someone to take you out?"

"I have been seeing someone. Remember? The one who takes photographs?"

Yuri nodded, but she could tell he didn't remember.

"Does he have passion?" he asked. "You need passion, Anya." Her father looked up at her. "What is life without passion?"

Anya blew air out of puffed cheeks and then smiled at him. Passion was something she had kept safely hidden away for so long. Where had it gotten her mother? Sveta? The wind blew sand against her ankles. A shirtless man with giant biceps jogged past.

"Do you ever imagine going back?" she asked.

"There's nothing to go back to," he said, looking out at the waves. "The back that I want to get to is no longer there."

Anya did not think back on her gymnastics years with sentimentality, not yet anyway. She did not long to be special like that again. She hadn't forgotten all that had come with it. Maybe when she got to be her father's age, Vera's, she might forget what being chosen had exacted.

* * *

After she dropped her father back at the home, Anya went to the internet café and sat down with her usual Coke, no ice. There was one computer with a Cyrillic keyboard, but she tried to stick to the English one to challenge herself. She had once typed Elena Grishina into Yahoo, hoping, feeling sick in the seconds it took, but the results brought back only the roster for the 1978 World Championships.

For eight years Anya had worked beside Anatoly at the sports school in Norilsk.

She had found some satisfaction in coaching the girls, especially the young ones who didn't understand anything yet, who just loved to do gymnastics. Anatoly had softened. He once suggested they go to dinner together, like a date, but her look of horror made him never mention it again. He emigrated to Canada in 1992, where he worked for a gym before heading to Tucson, Arizona, to coach. He wrote her emails, often with rants about life in America.

Americans have no discipline. The kids do whatever they want. They don't listen to coaches, and we are forbidden from yelling at them. Also everyone is fat. The girls are fat. The parents are fatter. They want their children to feel good all the time. No one wants to do

what it takes to be good. They want to be told they are special. Who cares if they can't do a
press handstand? They smile! Why are they all so cheerful?

Sometimes I wonder what it was all for. But then I remember you, Anya Yurievna.
You were the very best.

Anatoly gossiped about all the old gymnasts: Yelena Davydova coached in Ontario; Maria Filatova joined a circus and now coached in Ohio; Natalia Shaposhnikova coached in New Jersey. Nellie Kim had coached the South Korean, Italian, and Belarus national teams, and was now an international judge, living in Minnesota.

I hear she is trying to have every move renamed "the Kim." Next thing you know she will
take credit for the handstand.

Nadia Comaneci defected from Romania in 1989 and married the American gymnast Bart Conner. They ran a gym in Oklahoma.

She never speaks badly of Karolyi, that asshole, but I bet she hates him. He's the king of
America now.

And you, Anya Yurievna. What are you doing? Why aren't you a coach? Come to
Arizona. We could save our money and open our own gym.

All of them had left. The world spun differently now. Time had flattened out. She remembered the seriousness, the worry, the pain, the all-consuming life she had lived, even if the particulars were fading. She felt the shadow of gymnastics in her body. The grinding in her ankle, the stiffness in her back, the arthritis in her knees, her hands that hurt when she made fists. After a night on her feet carrying trays at the Rusalka, she had to hold her breath just to get out of bed in the morning.

Anya was hoping to cut her restaurant shifts, so she checked the job board for anyone in need of a Russian tutor. She had an email about her English class schedule, and one from Josh from this morning: "You didn't tell me it was May Day! I'm coming with my camera. Meet me later?"

"May Day was a week ago," she wrote. "May ninth is something different. Did you make it in time for the parade? I was there with my father." She typed, "Next year you can come with us," and then erased it. "We should ride the Wonder Wheel sometime. I would like to see Brooklyn from forty-six meters."

Finally, there was the usual email from Anatoly. She sighed and clicked it open.

Type her name into the search thing on the computer.

She knew who he meant.

CHAPTER 24

Moscow was a giant flea market. Old women begging. Old women, their meager possessions laid out on blankets, everything for sale. Old women selling single cigarettes under splashy billboards for perfume. Tables lined the streets around Saint Basil's offering flasks, playing cards, clocks, key chains, lighters, mugs, t-shirts, commemorative plates. Stalin or Lenin, take your pick. There were Gorbachev *matryoshki* and Yeltsin *matryoshki*. Soviet military uniforms, red flags, pennants, hats, medals, peaked caps with red stars. Komsomol membership cards. On cardboard on the ground: salami in tattered cellophane, knitted socks, nails.

Anya was exhausted from the trip but whirring with nerves. Her eyes were grainy, and she could smell herself, but on the train she could smell everyone else too. The vaulted halls and ornate decoration of the metro stations were both more stunning than she remembered, and wrenching; trash bunched in corners, and what looked like lumps of rags were people sleeping on marble benches. She felt pulled back in time. Near the exit a blind man sat on a piece of cardboard and sang:

> *United forever in friendship and labor,*
> *Our mighty republics will ever endure.*
> *The Great Soviet Union will live through the ages.*
> *The dream of a people their fortress secure!*

Anya dropped some rubles into his copper cup.

"*Long live our Soviet Motherland,*" he sang in her direction.

"*Built by the people's mighty hand,*" she sang quietly back.

She took a taxi to Petrovsko-Razumovsky Alley northwest of the city, in a quiet, nondescript neighborhood of low apartment buildings. She made her way around a curve in the street to a labyrinth of courtyards until she found number sixteen and knocked. The door opened, and there was an old woman, shorter than she was, her hazel eyes lively.

"The famous Anya Yurievna Petrova," she said. "Come in, child. We've been waiting for you."

* * *

There was Elena. Her face was fuller, softer. The same clear eyes. The same sweep of bangs. It was as if she'd been insulated from age. She was a quadriplegic and sat in the sun coming through the front window, her hands resting on the arms of a wheelchair. She wore a baby-blue cardigan. Anya tried to breathe as tears pricked her eyes. Here was the girl she had loved and lost. Her Lenushka. She walked to her friend and dropped to her knees. She laid her head in Elena's lap. It had been eighteen years since she had last seen her.

"Hello, *Myshka,*" Elena said, her voice as soft as petals. "I have missed you for so long."

* * *

Her grandmother took care of her in the same two-bedroom apartment Elena had grown up in. Faded yellow-flowered wallpaper covered the reinforced concrete wall of the living room, and hanging there was a large black-and-white photograph of Elena at the 1978 World Championships, a leap on the beam, caught in flight, in the navy-blue flower-dotted leotard she had worn so often. Behind her thousands of people sat rapt in the stands.

"They took that photograph for *The USSR and Soviet Life,*" Elena said, as she saw Anya looking up at the wall. "I never saw the magazine, but they sent it to me a few years ago."

"They told me you would come back to the gym," Anya said. "That you would recover."

"They told me the same thing. But I knew. Think about bending a ruler until it snaps. It was inevitable that I wouldn't make it all the way around. I wasn't ready. You know when you fear something so much and then it happens? So, in some ways, it wasn't a shock. My first thought, when my chin hit, was Thank God I don't have to go to the Olympics. I didn't feel any pain. I felt relief. And then I passed out."

The brutal image left Anya with a wave of vertigo. She closed her eyes to steady herself. To think of the vulnerability of their bodies made her scared even now.

"I never knew what really happened," Anya said. "They fed us lies and then silence. I waited and waited for you. And then Anatoly told me it was that element you fell on. I wrote you a letter that Shaniyazov said he would get to you."

Elena laughed a little. "I never got it, of course. I was not good for morale, an unflattering representation of the state. They didn't want me to infect you."

"They wouldn't tell me your address. Sometimes I would come into Moscow and wander around looking for you," Anya said. "They said you didn't want to see me."

"You didn't believe that."

Anya shrugged. "I didn't. But sometimes I did."

"*Myshka*. I would have done anything to see you. But they did their best to strike me from the official history."

"You were the World Champion."

Elena squinted, the sun in her eyes. Anya rose and pulled the curtain.

"You know how it was. I watched you on television from my hospital bed. I was so proud seeing you out there. After the accident I hoped I would die in surgery, but seeing you changed my mind. You did the triple twist! At the Olympics! I sank into a dark place after that. I cried all the time. My *babushka* forbade any news about gymnastics."

"I started to fall apart after you didn't come back," Anya said. If only they had had each other then. She covered Elena's quiet hand with her own. "Look at us. We were girls and now we are women."

"I'm not going to pretend to you, *Myshka*. I hate this body. Hate it. It took so long to accept that I can do nothing to change it. My body is ruined, but my mind continues like a darting bird." She smiled a little.

"Lenushka."

"You know I was so used to doing what I was supposed to, being where they wanted me to be. But in those first years after the injury, all I could do was lie around. It was so strange and scary. I felt like I wasn't part of the world anymore."

"After you disappeared, I did what I was told, but I wasn't in it anymore. I started to go downhill. And then there was no way up."

"How is your life now, *Myshka*? Are you married? Do you have children? Do you coach in America?"

"It is okay. But it is none of those things," Anya said.

"I'm learning English. But I'm too embarrassed to say anything in front of you. Miss America."

"Anatoly coaches at a gym in Arizona."

"Where is that?"

"In the western United States. It's really hot there. A desert. He sends me emails."

"No!"

"He asked me out on a date once."

"No!"

"He thinks we should open a gym together."

"Would you?"

"No!"

"Mikhail coaches in Italy. I never saw him again," Elena said.

"He must have felt too guilty."

"I don't blame Mikhail. I feel sorry for him. He was just a small part of the whole machine. Doing his job. There was Shaniyazov breathing down his neck. And the other coaches who knew I couldn't do it and kept silent. And the men above them who demanded Olympic medals."

"Is there still a Round Lake?" Anya asked.

"There is no state-supported system anymore. In Russia or Romania or any of the others. Some good gymnasts, but the dominance is gone. I hear Round Lake is in a bad state. The ceiling leaks; the equipment is in need of repair. No one to pay for training."

"Our greatness required cruelty though, didn't it? I'm not sorry it's over."

"I should have said no to the Thomas Salto, but I didn't," Elena said.

"We couldn't say no like that."

"I suppose not. A Chinese girl did it at the '92 Olympics. That was the last time."

"I don't watch gymnastics," Anya said. She shook her head.

"Why not?"

Anya sighed and met Elena's gaze.

"Because of you."

"Anya Yurievna."

"Yes."

"It's okay to love gymnastics. In spite of everything."

Anya nodded a little. It was a radical notion to her, and it made her feel a simmering heat. After Elena had disappeared, she had shut off what she had loved about gymnastics. Flying, spinning, landing, conquering.

"Do you?" Anya asked. "Do you love it still?"

"I have dreams where I am back in the gym," Elena said. "That feeling of control and mastery. That feeling of having a secret power. Defying the rules of the natural order. You know just what I mean. How could I not love that?"

* * *

"How do you spend your days?" Anya asked.

"They still give me a gymnastics pension, which supports us. I have exercises I need to do each day. My *babushka* moves my arms and legs. Just getting out of bed is a long process. I'm working on an essay about Soviet sport for a magazine. My *babushka* transcribes for me. And I read a lot. And you, *Myshka*? What do you do?"

"I wait tables at a Russian restaurant. Take classes to improve my English. And I read a lot too. I'm trying to read books in English, but it's slow going."

"I've come to believe that all stories are about time. Time passing. How life changes. What something once was. Even our own stories."

"I wish you could have met my friend Vera."

"Your old neighbor."

"She said time could accordion or go flat and turn back in on itself."

"Yes. I understand that."

"I finally read *Anna Karenina*," Anya said. "Because I don't have a television. The last Russian person on earth to read it."

"You can get books in Russian?"

"There's a Russian bookstore in Brighton Beach, in Brooklyn. My father is there. The restaurant where I work is there. It's more Russian than Russia."

"Do American women paint their fingernails?" Elena asked.

"There are nail salons where you sit and someone massages your hands and cleans up your nails and paints them. And then you hold your hands under a dryer. I've never done it, but I watch through the window sometimes. The Ukrainian girlfriends of the *Vory v Zakone* have long, fake nails."

"Fake fingernails?"

"They click on the table when they try to pick something up."

"I would like to have my nails painted red."

"Next time I come I'll paint them for you."

"Oh, I have something for you," Elena said. She nodded her head toward the desk near the window. Anya stood and picked up the book. *Selected Poems, Marina Tsvetaeva.*

"She's not illegal anymore," Elena said.

"I still have the ragged *samizdat* of my mother's," Anya said. She ran her palm over the cover of the book, the black-and-white photo of the poet with a serious, almost defiant set to her mouth. "'Your name—impossible—kiss on my eyes.'"

"'The chill of closed eyelids. Your name—a kiss of snow.'"

"I will keep this forever," Anya said.

* * *

"You are beautiful, Anya. How come you are not married?"

"I have a boyfriend. I think you could call him that."

"Oh! Tell me about him. Is he nice? Is he American?"

"Both. He helped with a plane ticket here because he knows something of what you mean to me."

"Ah, he cares about you, that's good."

"He said maybe next time we'll come together." Anya pursed her smile and blushed.

"I want you to have that. Love."

"It's not love. Not yet anyway."

"It's something, though, no?"

It is something, Anya thought. Shutting yourself tight didn't protect you from losing the ones you love. Wanting more was hard for her. But it was time.

* * *

"Have you read Ernest Hemingway?" Elena asked. "He said there are two things necessary for a country to become fascinated with bullfighting. First, the bulls have to be bred in that country, and second, its people have to be interested in death. And it made me think about us."

"We were the bulls."

"We were the bulls."

* * *

For four days they talked and drank tea and ate *pryaniki* Elena's grand-mother made for them. Elena had a high tray and drank through a straw. Anya held cookies to her friend's mouth to bite. They went outside into the sun-dappled courtyard. The clouds passed swiftly across the square of blue above.

"Can you still do your splits?" Elena asked.

"What do you think?"

"All three?"

"Yes."

"Show me."

Anya slid down into middle splits and laid her body flat on the cob-bled ground in front of her, the stretch almost as easy as it had been all those years ago. She sat up and rolled her ankles out of habit.

"Where are your medals?" Elena asked.

"In a drawer."

"Anya Yurievna!"

"What am I supposed to do with them? Wear them to get coffee?"

"You are ashamed of them."

"Because I took them from you."

"I'm giving them back. They are yours."

* * *

Josh liked for Anya to tell him Russian words that didn't have English counterparts. His favorite was *bytiye*, which meant "being, existence," but something elemental, beyond consciousness.

"With this piece of apple pie I have reached *bytiye!*" he proclaimed.

"That's not how you use it," she said, laughing.

Then he put his thumbs to his middle fingers in a mudra and closed his eyes.

"Like this then?"

She shook her head and took a bite of his pie.

Her favorite was *kapel'*, which meant a sunny day when water starts dripping from icicles. When the sky is as blue as blue. The very start of spring that puts you in a good mood. That was how she felt now, a new upturn. She marveled at how quickly life could change. Elena was no longer lost. Life offered up these moments despite everything.

It was her day to visit Yuri. She was going to take him to lunch at the Arbat Diner, his old favorite. When she arrived at Shore View, the community room was empty, the residents all at lunch. She sat on the old sofa and clicked off the muted soap opera on TV. A young nurse's aide named Maria wheeled Yuri out, her nails bright purple, matching her scrubs. He was disheveled, his copper eyes roaming.

"We're having a day today," Maria said. She sighed. "We've been trying to clean out his room. Organize it a little." She shook her head. "He was dead set on finding something."

Yuri was agitated. He didn't rise to greet her.

"What were you looking for, Papa?"

"Have a nice lunch, Mr. Yuri," Maria said as she retreated. "Bring me back some of that bird's milk cake."

He watched the nurse go.

"I couldn't find my Party membership card," he said, his voice low. "I found Irina's. But I couldn't find mine. And then I panicked that we'd left without it."

"Papa." Anya reached for his hand. "It's okay if you can't find it. You don't need it anymore."

"I found it, I found it. Eventually. There was a box of old little things. Irina must have packed it before we left home. She was good like that."

"I know," Anya said, "she was."

He leaned to the side of his wheelchair to get something out of his pocket. A small yellow envelope.

"I found this too."

His hand shook as he held it out to her.

Anya took it and poured the contents into her hand. The silver was tarnished green and gold, but the amber was rich and clear, the color of cognac, translucent. She closed her hand around the bracelet, to feel the small weight of it. Her breath fell away. It felt otherworldly, a talisman. Years dissolved, and she felt herself, for a moment, the child she had been, the comfort of her mother near. *It brought me you, my love.*

"I know it was your mother's. I can't remember where she got it." Yuri looked up at the sky through the window. He squinted at the brightness and then turned to look at her again. "But she was wearing it when we met."

"She always wore it," Anya said.

"Maybe you will want it. To have something of hers."

She nodded.

"You were the one she loved most in the world," Yuri said.

Anya breathed in and breathed out: yes. It was, finally, enough to know that. The deep and heavy longing she'd always carried with her shifted and grew a little lighter. She draped the bracelet over her wrist. What a wonder, she thought.

"This couldn't have fit her," she said. "Look how small it is." *It will be yours. It will be ours.*

"I don't know, *Dochka*. I gave up trying to figure out the mysteries a long time ago."

Anya sat for a long time rubbing her thumb on the smooth amber stones, still, always, warm.

* * *

After lunch, after Anya returned her father to Shore View for a nap, she went to the Wonder Wheel by herself. It was a chilly Tuesday, and there was no line. She hadn't ridden a Ferris wheel since her first competition in Surgut. She picked one of the swinging cars that rolled on a serpentine track. When the ride ascended, the car zoomed forward, and it felt like she was going to slide right off the edge into nothing. It was thrilling. Her hair whipped around her face. Higher and higher she climbed. At the top, the wheel stopped, and it was quiet, only the far-away pings and clangs of carnival games below. To the south, beyond the rides, the beach stretched empty to the ocean. The wind rocked her car; she didn't mind the cold. No matter how far her eyes could see, she would not reach where she was from unless she rounded the top of the earth.

She imagined her mother and father, just kids, really, with their burning hearts on a rough-and-tumble train heading as far north as they could go. Vera walking out of the camp gate after ten years. A motherless girl from Norilsk becoming one of the best gymnasts in the world. How ordinary lives became extraordinary and back again. She thought of all the things she would write in her next letter to Elena, which books she might send, along with a jar of peanut butter, packs of chewing gum, red nail polish. She felt her mother's bracelet in her pocket.

The wheel swept her around again.

Anya was, she realized, the same age her mother had been when she walked out of the dance institute in 1970 and was never seen again. Katerina Vladimirovna Petrova: principal dancer with the Bolshoi, member of the Komsomol, settlement pioneer, wife, mother. But what did Anya really know of her? She smelled like lavender, she moved with stunning grace, she hungered for poetry, she loved with the power of the sun. Anya was shaped by her and by the loss of her, an ever-shifting equation. She had missed her forever.

Spin me, Mama.

Hold tight, Anushka. Don't let go.

Anya descended now, a fast swoop, her stomach dropping, her car shooting back to the center behind her. The wheel slowed as it neared the ground.

When it was over, she climbed out of the ride and walked to the boardwalk, the wind salty from the sea. Two little girls ran past her, ahead of their mother, ditching their sneakers as they reached the beach. They laughed, kicking up sand as they cartwheeled all the way to the water's edge. They fell over, dizzy, as their mother reached them, snapping a photo with her camera.

Anya rolled her old bad ankle and felt the familiar ache and snap of her scar-healed ligaments. Above her the sky was a vast pale blue that faded to white at the horizon. She worked her stiff wrists and stretched one elbow behind her head, and then the other. The beach unspooled before her toward a froth of choppy waves that curved and buckled along the shore. She hopped in place a few times before she pulled off her socks and boots, placing her folded jacket on top. *Vsegda gotova.* Always ready.

She stepped off the boardwalk and onto the sand. Go.

ACKNOWLEDGMENTS

This novel grew from my great admiration for the Soviet gymnasts of the era: Ludmilla Tourischeva, Olga Korbut, Nellie Kim, Natalia Shaposhnikova, Yelena Davydova, Maria Filatova, Stella Zakharova, and above all, as gymnastics aficionados will no doubt recognize, Elena Mukhina (1960–2006), on whom the character of Elena is based. The newspaper excerpts that appear in the novel are modified from articles that ran in *Moscow News* and *Pravda* about Elena Mukhina.

I am indebted to Anne Applebaum's *Gulag* and Svetlana Alexievich's *Secondhand Time: The Last of the Soviets*, both of which inspired and informed this book.

Thank you to Ilya Kaminsky and Jean Valentine for their translations of Marina Tsvetaeva's poetry, and to Alice James Books for permission to include excerpts. And thanks to Julia Tapkharova for the Russian proofreading.

A tremendous, heartfelt thank-you to: my high school Russian teacher Kariana Boettcher (1916–1995); my steadfast and ever-encouraging agent Elisabeth Weed; my fantastic (I still can't quite believe how lucky I am) editor Amy Einhorn; my eagle-eyed and generous copyeditor Maggie Carr—I know this one was a doozy!; the wonderful team at Henry Holt, who shepherded this book with so much care; my friend and master connector Pamela Klinger-Horn; my life-cheerleader and gymnastics-mom other half Chriscelyn Tussey; my gymnastics partner (and my idol), the indomitable artist Steffani Jemison; believer, supporter, and all-around awesome Ryan Hawke; my dear family: Jane and Ron Meadows, Ronny Meadows, Susannah Meadows and Darin Strauss, Kathy and Peter Darrow, Jessica Darrow and Mike Koehler, Mónica Folch and James Darrow; and finally, my big loves: Alex, Indigo, and Olive.

ABOUT THE AUTHOR

Rae Meadows is the award-winning author of four previous novels: *I Will Send Rain, Mercy Train* (in hardcover as *Mothers & Daughters*), *No One Tells Everything,* and *Calling Out.* She received the 2019 Goldenberg Prize for Fiction for her story "The Kings of Gowanus," which was published in the *Bellevue Literary Review.* Her work has appeared in many publications including *Under Purple Skies: The Minneapolis Anthology* and *Contexts,* and online at NPR, Lit Hub, and PEN Center USA. She lives with her family in Brooklyn, New York.